About the Authors

Carol Marinelli recently filled in a form asking for her job title. Thrilled to be able to put down her answer, she put writer. Then it asked what Carol did for relaxation and she put down the truth – writing. The third question asked for her hobbies. Well, not wanting to look obsessed she crossed the fingers on her hand and answered swimming but, given that the chlorine in the pool does terrible things to her highlights – I'm sure you can guess the real answer.

Award-winning author **Louisa George** has been an avid reader her whole life. In between chapters she managed to train as a nurse, marry her doctor hero and have two sons. Now she writes chapters of her own in the medical romance, contemporary romance and women's fiction genres. Louisa's books have variously been nominated for the coveted RITA™ Award, and the NZ Koru Award and have been translated into twelve languages. She lives in Auckland, New Zealand.

Born and raised just outside of Toronto, Ontario, **Amy Ruttan** fled the big city to settle down with the country boy of her dreams. After the birth of her second child, Amy was lucky enough to realise her lifelong dream of becoming a romance author. When she's not furiously typing away at her computer, she's a mum to three wonderful children who use her as a personal taxi and chef.

Her Christmas List

CAROL MARINELLI

LOUISA GEORGE

AMY RUTTAN

MILLS & BOON

First Published in Great Britain 2020
By Mills & Boon, an imprint of HarperCollins*Publishers*
1 London Bridge Street, London, SE1 9GF

HER CHRISTMAS LIST © 2020 Harlequin Books S.A.

Playboy on Her Christmas List © 2016 Carol Marinelli
A Baby on Her Christmas List © 2014 Louisa George
Navy Doc on Her Christmas List © 2017 Harlequin Books S.A.

Special thanks and acknowledgement are given to Amy Ruttan for her contribution to the *Christmas in Manhattan* series.

ISBN: 978-0-263-29826-0

MIX
Paper from
responsible sources
FSC® C007454

This book is produced from independently certified FSC™ paper to ensure responsible forest management.

For more information visit: www.harpercollins.co.uk/green

Printed and bound in Spain
by CPI, Barcelona

PLAYBOY ON HER CHRISTMAS LIST

CAROL MARINELLI

PLAYBOY ON HER CHRISTMAS LIST

CAROL MARINELLI

CHAPTER ONE

'HOLLY, PUT THE decorations back. I've already told you that there are quite enough already. This is the emergency department, *not* the children's ward.'

Holly, dressed in baggy scrubs and weighted down with tinsel and glittery silver snowmen, jumped when she heard Kay's strong Irish accent and realised that the nurse unit manager was sitting at the nurses' station.

Caught!

Holly had also thought that locum registrar Daniel Chandler was on his supper break but, no, he was drinking a coffee at the desk. Holly's blush spread like spilled red wine across her chest as she stood, dripping glitter, and was scolded in front of the very suave Daniel.

'I thought that you'd gone home,' Holly admitted to Kay.

'I know that you did,' Kay tartly responded, but then she let out a long sigh. 'I'm staying back to try and sort out the Christmas roster.'

'But it's already done.' Holly frowned. The last thing she wanted were any alterations to the roster—her plans to be with her family over the festive break had been made weeks ago. But Kay had other ideas and proceeded to tell Holly the reasons that things might have to change.

'Yes, but since then I've had two members of staff go

on extended sick leave. Thank goodness for Nora, she's offered to work Christmas night but things are *very* tight. Now, put the tinsel back where it belongs, please and, when you've done that, tie up your hair.'

'It's already tied up.'

'No, Holly, it's not.'

Holly's long, curly brown hair always started the shift in a neat ponytail and then proceeded to work its way out of its confines, curl by wild curl.

As Holly slunk back to the storeroom Daniel found himself smiling.

He'd only been doing locum shifts at The Primary for a couple of months but it was enough to know that Holly Jacobs took her Christmas decorations very seriously. She had been waiting all afternoon for Kay, who was supposed to have finished at four, to go home so that Holly could, as she put it, 'Christmas the place up'.

The Primary Hospital was a modern, busy, North London teaching hospital. It was very different in character from the prestigious Royal, where Daniel had started as a medical student and worked his way up to Accident and Emergency Registrar.

Working at The Primary was a step down, his father, an esteemed professor of surgery, would say. Certainly, renowned Professor Marcus Chandler could never fathom why his son was doing locum shifts at various hospitals around London when he could have any hours he chose at the Royal.

For Daniel, though, working at The Primary felt, if not a step up, then a step in the right direction. When he had commenced his first shift here Kay had rolled her eyes at the prospect of giving a tour to yet another tem-

porary doctor but had soon realised Daniel was very good at his job.

More importantly, Daniel was really enjoying his work. Here there was no reputation to uphold; instead, he was slowly making his own.

And it had been noticed.

'You know there's a consultant's position coming up,' Kay said. She stared at the computer as she spoke.

'I do,' Daniel responded, and confirmed that he had been approached. 'I've already told Mr Edwards that I'm not interested.'

'Are we not good enough for you, Daniel?'

'There was a consultant's position at the Royal when I left,' Daniel pointed out. 'I wasn't interested then either.'

'You're a mystery,' Kay said, and gave a soft laugh then brushed from the desk some glitter dust that Holly had left in her wake. 'Holly would have glitter everywhere,' she tutted. 'It's an emergency department, not Santa's Grotto. People don't need festivities waved in their face when they come here. This time of year is often hard enough for our patients. I'm already over Christmas and it's only the second of December.'

'You're preaching to the converted,' Daniel agreed.

'Are you not a fan of Christmas?' Kay asked.

'Nope.'

'Nor me,' Kay agreed. 'It brings out the worst in everyone. You should see this place on Christmas night.' She got back to the staring at the computer screen, though she carried on chatting with Daniel. 'Are you going to the emergency department Christmas party tonight?'

'Nope.'

Kay laughed at his truculent response but then she frowned. 'How come you're still here? I thought you were

just doing a few locums until your friend got married. The wedding was last week, wasn't it?'

'It was.' Daniel nodded and carried on writing.

He had finished up his role at the Royal at the end of September and had just been killing time until his best friend Rupert's wedding had taken place. Soon he would be taking a year off. First he would hit the ski slopes in Switzerland and then…well, he'd see what happened when it happened.

'Why didn't you just start your travels and fly back for the wedding?' Kay asked.

'Oh, no…' Daniel shook his head. 'Once I'm gone, I'm gone for good.'

'That sounds profound!' Holly was back, minus tinsel and snowmen. Her hair had been scraped back into an even tighter ponytail but was now dotted with glitter. She had a worried expression aimed at Kay because she really *needed* Christmas off this year.

Holly knew that, if the roster had to be changed, she didn't really have a leg to stand on—around this time last year her mother had been diagnosed with breast cancer. Then, despite Holly being rostered to work Christmas and New Year, Kay had been wonderful, giving Holly ten days off so that she could have some family time.

The trouble was, a cancer diagnosis didn't follow a specified timeline with a neat conclusion to signal the end.

The last year had been a fraught one, with Holly taking her little red car up and down the motorway every chance she could and wrestling the off duty around her mother's treatment. Esther had recently had to have a second round of chemotherapy, and while the news was a whole lot better Esther really wanted her family home for Christmas.

And lately, what Esther wanted, Esther got!

Holly blew out a tense breath. She loved her family dearly but things had been a bit difficult lately, to say the least.

While she hoped that Kay would understand when she came to make the necessary changes Holly needed to be sure. 'Kay, could I have a word?'

'If it's about the Christmas roster, the answer is no. Your request has been noted. And, yes,' she added. 'I do know it's also your birthday.'

'Were you a Christmas baby, Holly?' Daniel asked.

'Why do you think I'm called Holly?'

'Because you're so prickly.'

It was a small joke—Holly was the *least* prickly person. She was happy and sunny and that they could tease each other about such things without having to explain they were joking, well, it was sort of where they were at.

'So,' Daniel asked, 'do you miss out on your birthday?'

'No.' Holly shook her head. 'My parents always make sure that both are celebrated.'

'Of course they do, Polly.'

She got the Pollyanna insinuation and gave him a sweet smile. 'Better than cynical. So,' she asked, returning to the conversation she had walked in on the tail end of, 'why didn't you just fly home for the wedding?'

'There was the stag night to organise,' Daniel explained. 'Actually, there were two of them.'

'You could have just flown back for a couple of weeks.' Holly repeated Kay's assumption but Daniel shook his head.

'Rupert had a highly strung bride-to-be who was worried that I'd be a no-show if I left the country. She was actually right to be concerned—as I said, when I'm gone, I'm gone.'

Holly didn't like that.

Daniel had worked quite a few shifts now and she was getting used to having him around.

Or rather she was starting to get used to the feeling that an egg beater had been set at full whisk in the middle of her chest.

Daniel was, for want of a better word, gorgeous.

Yes, yes, he was tall and had thick black hair and a scent that had her toes curl, he had *all* of that but it was his eyes that had first sent Holly's world spinning.

Absolute navy.

It was as if the artist had meant to get back and add silvery flecks and little dots of aqua but had forgotten to. Yet he was no unfinished masterpiece. Those eyes were just this delicious navy rimmed with a halo of black and, at first look, Holly had been unable to stop staring. She had wanted to apologise, to explain she was looking for said silver specks and dots of aqua, but instead she had stared.

And so had he.

At green eyes that had appeared startled.

'Is everything okay?' he had checked.

'I have an abdo pain…' Holly had attempted to explain that she had a patient she would like him to see in Cubicle Four but she had been so flustered that it had come out all wrong. 'And vomiting.'

'Then go and lie down and let me take a look at you.'

His voice was snobby, his humour *hers,* and she had been tempted, almost, to call his bluff and do just that. Instead she had smiled. 'I'll see you in Cubicle Four.'

Holly's abdo pain had turned out to be a twenty-year-old with query appendicitis. Daniel had walked in to where Holly had been holding a bowl for the patient and he had given her a tiny smile to insinuate he had rather hoped she had been lying in wait for him.

'Pity,' he'd said.

Yet a little flirt, though huge to Holly, was just a walk in the park for him. He was suave and from what she gathered he dated a lot, and, in truth, neither was the other's type.

Except...

'What was the wedding like?' Holly asked. She was curious to know more about the reason for delaying his trip.

'Like all weddings are,' Daniel said, as Holly jumped up and sat on the bench beside where he was trying to write his notes. 'Long.'

'What did the bride wear?' she asked.

'From memory, a dress,' Daniel said. 'Possibly it was white.'

'I love winter weddings,' Holly sighed. 'Especially if it's snowing.'

'The church was freezing,' Daniel told her, and from his voice it was clear that he had a rather less dreamy take on things. 'And then it poured with rain for the photos.'

'Who was your plus one?' Kay asked, without turning her head from the computer screen.

'I never take a plus one to a wedding.' Daniel shook his head. 'Well, I haven't for a long time. I learnt the hard way that if you bring a date she assumes that it must mean you're serious. Anyway, I was the best man for this one so all that was expected from me in that department was to get off with the chief bridesmaid.'

'And did you?' Kay asked.

'That would be telling,' Daniel said. 'And I never do.'

He looked at Holly then—just an itsy-bitsy look that told her she'd be in very discreet hands.

God, he was forward!

Yet she smiled at the tiny flirt behind Kay's back.

'Anyway,' Daniel continued, 'I wanted to do the right thing by Rupert. He was very good to me when…' He didn't finish, or rather he just didn't continue with what he had started to say. 'He's a very good friend.'

'So how come you weren't out on the first flight after the wedding?' Kay pushed.

'Just…' He gave a small shrug and it was there that the conversation ended.

Daniel simply didn't answer—he did that a lot.

He might be forward with his flirting but when a conversation veered too close to personal he simply halted it.

Daniel got back to his notes and, interlude over, Kay carried on staring at the off duty, but finally she gave in.

'I'm going home,' Kay said, and closed up the screen. 'Daniel, shall we see you again?'

'I don't think so,' he answered.

Locums came and locums went but Kay gave him a smile that told Daniel he would be missed. 'Well, safe travels,' she said, and then turned to Holly. 'I'll see you tonight at the pub. The night staff should be coming in a little bit early so that the late staff can get to the party at a reasonable time. How are you getting there?'

'Taxi,' Holly said. 'Anna, Laura and I are sharing. Do you want to come with us, Daniel? There's room for one more.'

'I'm not going.'

He offered no reason and thankfully he didn't look up as he spoke because, despite her best efforts, Holly knew her shoulders had briefly slumped, but quickly she righted herself.

Actually, it was good news that he wasn't coming tonight.

The way Holly felt she was at high risk of doing something very stupid where Daniel Chandler was concerned.

Stupid as well as pointless, given that this was his last shift and that very soon he'd be heading off overseas.

Daniel, she had heard, was very into casual one-night stands. Whereas she was the complete opposite.

With one possible exception.

Him.

Oh, it would be bliss to be bad.

Sometimes, all joking and flirting aside, she felt him looking at her and there was a tension between them that Holly was almost convinced wasn't one-sided. Of course, Daniel was a natural-born flirt, but it wasn't just that, there was something in his eyes that could flip her stomach like a pancake...

Egg analogy again, Holly thought to herself, and decided that she must be hungry.

'I'm going to go for my supper break while it's quiet. I'll see you later, Kay.'

'You shall,' Kay said. 'Oh, wait. I got you a present.' She smiled at Daniel. 'I got you one too.'

Kay was big on presents.

Silly things, happy things, she passed on what had made her smile. Her charity wasn't just for the staff, though—there were regular fundraisers held throughout the year on behalf of the homeless.

Kay took the displaced seriously.

She took an overfull bag from beneath the bench and handed them both a slim card from a choice of many.

'An Advent calendar!' Holly beamed.

'I got them at the discount store,' Kay said, clearly delighted with her purchase. 'There's one for everyone.'

'There's chocolate in here,' Daniel said, opening up one of the little windows.

'Of course there is. Have you never had an Advent calendar?' Kay checked.

'Actually, no.'

'It's December the second so you get to eat two,' she told him, 'but after that it's just one a day.'

Daniel gave Holly a sideways smile that told her all twenty-five would be eaten the very moment Kay had gone and Holly smiled back as she shook her head. 'One a day,' she warned him.

'I'm lousy at self-restraint.'

Ouch.

Sometimes, in fact a little too often, he threw out those lines and usually Holly could shrug them off, but it had been getting harder and harder to of late.

'Well, I've got excellent self-control,' Holly replied, and watched the slight questioning rise of one eyebrow.

They were talking about chocolate, Holly told herself.

At least where chocolate was concerned she had self-control.

Where Daniel was concerned it was melting just as fast. It was a good job that he was leaving, Holly decided.

She had a king-size crush on him and she wasn't used to them, well, not for a very long time. At twenty-eight, Holly had rather thought that the days of wild dreams and fixating on someone's every word were long since gone.

They weren't.

Kay was just about to go when Laura, the nurse in charge this evening, came in swiftly.

'Holly—Resus,' she said. 'We've got a cardiac arrest coming in. Fifty-five-year-old male collapsed at home.'

Holly nodded and, supper forgotten, she jumped down from the bench and Daniel got down from his stool to go and prepare for the incoming patient.

'I'll just stay and see if I'm needed...' Kay offered. And Holly was expecting Laura to, as she usually did,

point out that they'd be fine and could more than cope but instead Laura gave Kay a worried look.

'Can I have a quick word, Kay?' she asked.

As Laura pulled Kay aside Holly put out an arrest call to alert the medical team to come to Emergency and then started to set up for the incoming patient. Until the team arrived Daniel would be in charge but from working with him she knew that he could more than cope with anything that presented.

'What's going on?' Daniel asked, as he taped some syringes to the vial of medication he'd just pulled up in anticipation of the patient's arrival. He nodded in the direction of Laura and Kay, who were still huddled together and talking.

'I'm not sure.' Holly frowned. 'But something is.'

The alert meant that they had everything ready for the patient, going on the information they had, but just as a blue light flashed in the high windows above, Kay came over and offered more.

'Holly,' Kay said, and her voice was serious as she pulled on a plastic apron to indicate she would be participating in the resuscitation. 'The patient is Nora's husband.'

Holly swallowed. Nora Hewitt was second in charge to Kay and everyone adored her. More importantly, Paul, Nora's husband, was the good man behind a great woman. He was often at the department, picking up Nora or bringing in the lunch she had forgotten and had left sitting in the fridge at home. He always had a friendly word for everyone and should have been at the emergency department Christmas party tonight with his wife.

Instead, he was being raced into Resus on the very edge of death.

There were the sounds of sobs and tears coming from outside, though Holly could tell that it wasn't Nora.

'The daughter is *very* upset,' the paramedic informed them.

'Anna—' Kay called for assistance '—can you stay with the family?'

'Where's the team?' Holly asked in an urgent tone, desperate for them to appear so that Paul could be given the very best chance.

'We'll be fine,' Daniel said in his composed deep voice and Holly glanced over at him.

He was at the head of the resuscitation bed that the paramedics were moving Paul onto and Daniel was his usual mixture of aloof and calm.

It was everything that was needed now.

CHAPTER TWO

'ON MY COUNT,' Daniel said, and Paul was transferred from the ambulance stretcher onto the solid resuscitation bed.

Everyone was a touch flustered. All the staff knew Nora, including the paramedics, and so this was incredibly personal.

But not to Daniel.

He checked the placement of the breathing tube and looked at the monitor once Paul had been transferred to the emergency department equipment. He asked Kay to recommence massage and called for the necessary drugs and did all this as he listened to the handover.

Apparently things had been rather chaotic back at the house. Paul's daughter and her boyfriend had become agitated and distressed and had got somewhat in the way.

'He was in the bathroom when he collapsed.'

'Was someone with him?'

'It was hard to get a clear history.'

Daniel nodded as Holly handed him the drug he had asked for but, aware that everyone was tense and there was the potential for mistakes to be made, he checked and double-checked everything.

Paul was still in an arrhythmia and not responding to drugs, and though he had been shocked several times

both at home and en route they had been unable to revert him to a normal rhythm. Daniel delivered more of the same and then called for the defibrillator to be charged and asked for fresh pads to be placed on Paul's chest.

Holly could see that her hands were shaking as she did as asked.

'Is anybody getting a fuller history from the family?' Daniel checked.

'I've sent Anna in to speak with Nora,' Kay said. 'I don't think he has any previous history, though.'

'I want to hear what Nora says.' Daniel was firm. This was no time for hearsay and Kay nodded as for now they worked on.

The emergency team started to arrive and gradually took over. Daniel had it all under control so that they were able to get a full handover as he worked on. Kay was massaging Paul's chest and her face was red and sweating.

'Can you take over, Holly?' she asked.

Holly did so. She was slight and really had to put in an effort to deliver effective massage. She glanced up at the clock and then back to Paul. There had been absolutely no response since he had collapsed back at home.

'Step back,' Mr Dawson, the cardiologist, ordered, and Holly climbed from the bed and once she was safely standing back another shock was delivered.

'So he collapsed at five?' Mr Dawson checked the timeline of events.

It was now five forty-five…

Holly could smell burning from the repeated shocks to his body and she looked over at Kay, who looked up at the clock.

'Was he found collapsed?' Mr Dawson checked.

'We're just waiting to have that verified,' Daniel said. The paramedics had been very thorough in their treat-

ment and had done well but there were still some gaps in the history.

Anna came in then. 'There's no previous history and he's on no medication. Paul was standing in the bathroom, chatting to Nora, when he developed chest pain. Nora sat him on the floor and called for an ambulance. She gave him some aspirin and stayed with him, and a couple of moments later he arrested and she commenced resuscitation straight away.'

It had been a witnessed arrest, which was incredibly relevant, especially given Nora's skills. It was now evident that he'd had effective cardiac massage delivered from the very start.

Not that it seemed to be counting for much.

'Resume massage,' Mr Dawson ordered, and Holly was about to climb back on the bed when Daniel halted her.

'Hold on a moment.' He had his fingers in Paul's groin to feel for a femoral pulse. 'He's got a pulse.'

And then, better than any music, better than any other sound in the world really, the monitor started to deliver bleeps.

Two at first, followed by a long pause, then a run of three and then sinus rhythm kicked in and there was the beep-beep-beep of a rapid heart rate and suddenly there was hope.

It was tainted, though.

Paul had been down for some considerable time. The cardiologists were going through his ECG tracings and deciding whether to take him straight up to ICU or directly to the catheter lab to see exactly what had occurred. The hope was that they could dissolve the blockage and open up the blocked vessels in Paul's heart and minimise damage to the heart muscle.

'I'll go up with him,' Kay said, as she gathered up the necessary equipment for the urgent transfer. 'Daniel, can you go and speak with Nora and explain that Mr Dawson is busy with Paul but he'll be in to get the consent…' Her voice trailed off. 'You know the drill.'

'I do.'

'I forget how experienced you are.'

'That's fine,' Daniel responded with ease, but then he asserted himself—not just with Kay but also with the cardiologist who would like Paul up in the lab, preferably ten minutes ago. 'First of all, though, we need to bring in his wife.'

'Time is of the essence,' Mr Dawson said.

'I'm sure she'll understand that.'

Nora must have been getting ready for the party and chatting to Paul as she did so, with no idea as to what was about to come. One of her eyes was made up with glittery eye shadow and the other was not.

Seeing someone so visibly shaken who was always so together and strong, but doing her best to hold it together, had Holly on the edge of tears.

'He's going to go up very soon,' Holly told Nora quietly, once Mr Dawson had obtained her consent and explained that they'd be moving him to the catheter lab. Holly watched as Nora took one of Paul's hands and held it in both of hers as if trying to warm it.

'He was telling me he'd just hidden my Christmas present.' Nora looked at Paul as she spoke. 'Please, don't leave me,' she asked him, and then, looking at Holly, said, 'I knew the day I met him that he was the one. He took a couple of weeks to get used to the idea…'

Holly didn't know what to say.

What was there to say to add to a love that had lasted for more than thirty years?

And so instead of saying the right thing, Holly found herself wearing her nervous smile.

Thankfully, Nora knew her well enough not to take offence.

'I just need a minute alone with him,' Nora said.

Holly nodded as Anna popped her head around the curtain. 'Nora, your daughter wants to come in.'

'No.' Nora was firm. 'She's too upset and she'd just distress him.'

Kay nodded her head and called for Holly to come the other side of the curtain, leaving Nora with Paul and the anaesthetist. Holly had turned up the volume on the monitors so that the staff could move in quickly if there was any change.

And they listened as Nora told her husband she loved him and to stay strong and that she'd be waiting for him once the procedure was done, and she did it all in a voice that did not waver, just in case Paul could hear.

Holly knew that voice only too well.

She could remember her mother going in for surgery and, because Holly was the only remotely medical person in the family, all questions had been aimed at her. All decisions had been run by Holly too and it had felt overwhelming. Her father had asked her to come with them up to Theatre. When he had started to break down it had been Holly who had stepped in. Holly had concentrated on keeping her smile in place while trying to ignore the fact that her mother was so very weak and frail from the chemotherapy and doing her best not to reveal that she wasn't terrified for her.

'What do you think?' Kay asked Daniel, and Holly looked at his grim face.

'They're giving him every chance.' His response was noncommittal but for Holly it said enough—he didn't think things looked good.

The quiet start had turned into a very busy shift and it didn't relent.

Holly felt all shaken but there was no time to sit down and reflect on what had happened. There was no pause button in Emergency, especially when you needed one.

Just as Paul left, another critically ill patient came in.

Kay handed Paul over to the care of the catheter lab staff but, given she was officially off duty, remained with Nora in the waiting room there. Holly was so busy that she had forgotten completely she was going out tonight and frowned when she saw that it was eight and that the night staff were starting to arrive.

'What are you doing here?' Holly asked.

'So you can leave early for the Christmas party.' Gloria grinned and then saw Holly's serious face. 'What is it?'

And there was no point in not telling the arriving staff—one look at the admissions board and they would see the truth for themselves.

'Nora's husband was brought in…'

As she brought the night staff up to speed Holly admitted that she had changed her mind about going to the party tonight, but Kay had other ideas. She had popped down to Emergency for that very reason, in fact, and called Holly round to her office.

'I need you to give the landlord the cash we've been collecting,' Kay said. They'd all been putting into the collection for a few weeks. 'Holly, I know the last thing

you feel like is partying but word is already getting out about Paul. Nora's daughter has put it up on social media and honestly…' Kay let out a long sigh. 'Nora wants the party to go ahead. She thinks if it's called off now it means that we've given up on Paul.'

Holly nodded. 'How is he doing?'

'He's over on Intensive Care. He's in an induced coma and really we shan't know for a few days. Oh, I don't know, Holly, I don't have a very good feeling about it. He was down for a long time.'

'Less than an hour,' Holly pointed out.

'I know but…'

Kay looked as if she was about to cry and Holly had no idea what to say so she offered the only thing she knew might help. 'Do you want a cup of tea?'

Kay laughed the simplicity of Holly's solution and then she let out a little sob. 'I do,' she admitted. 'A quick one and then I'll head back up there. Have one with me?'

Holly brought in a tray as Kay got the envelope from the safe.

'I'd better not lose it,' Holly said, peering inside.

'You'd better not!' Kay barked, and then closed her eyes and leant back in her chair. 'It's nice to relax for five minutes.'

'Did you call Eamon and let him know?' Holly asked, referring to Kay's husband.

'I did. He's going to come and get me when I'm ready but I think I should stay awhile. Poor Nora. Honestly, that family of hers…' Kay rolled her eyes. 'Do you know? Her daughter asked what was going to happen for dinner! Does she not know how a bloody vending machine works? Fancy bothering her mother with that?'

'And fancy bothering you with this,' Daniel said, as he knocked on the half-open door.

'What do you want?' Kay asked. But as Daniel came in, though he gave Kay a smile, he then looked at Holly as he spoke.

'All the night staff are here but Laura is having no luck getting a taxi. The wait is an hour at best. I said that I could drop you all off at the end of my shift, which is right about now.'

'Then you'd better get ready,' Kay said, moving to stand. 'And I'd better get back up to Nora.'

'Finish your tea,' Holly suggested, and thought of the times she had sat with her own family, waiting for news, and how utterly exhausting it was. 'Have a few moments to yourself.'

'I might just do that,' Kay agreed. 'You're not on to-morrow, are you?'

'No, I'm off now till Monday, but I'll call in the morn-ing and see how Paul's doing and—' Her voice halted abruptly as Holly stopped herself from saying what she had been about to—fancy bothering Kay with a stupid thing like the off duty while Paul was so sick, but Nora had been the one practically keeping the off duty run-ning over the Christmas break.

It could wait, Holly knew that, and felt guilty for even considering raising it now.

So instead of worrying about tomorrow, or the next, or the next, she went into the changing room and had the quickest shower ever. There was just time for a dart under the jets and a quick soap and rinse then she dried herself and pulled on her little black dress.

'That's nice,' Anna said as Holly came out. Anna was hogging the one tiny mirror and applying eyeliner, while looking stunning in a very slinky, very red dress. 'You *always* look good in that.'

It was such a backhanded compliment that Holly ac-

tually stopped in her tracks for a second, before sitting down on the bench and pulling out her make-up bag.

'Thanks.' Holly smiled, pretending she had missed the rather bitchy comment. Oh, she was in no mood for make-up but it was certainly needed! As well as that the steam, even from a very brief shower, had made her curly hair even more so.

'Daniel's waiting,' Anna said rather pointedly as she turned from the mirror, all ready, just as Holly got her mascara out. 'We don't really have much time.'

'Daniel can wait for five minutes,' Holly answered. She hadn't asked him to play taxi driver and, more to the point, she wouldn't have minded the long wait for a taxi just to be able to get ready and allow for some time to jolt herself out of her morose mood. 'Or you guys can go on without me and I'll see you there.'

'No need for that. I'll go and wait with Daniel,' Anna said.

'Sure.'

'I'll see if I can persuade him to stay for a drink. After all, it is effectively his leaving do.'

'It's been Daniel's leaving do since October,' Holly said. There was a knot of disquiet in her stomach, though, at the thought she might not see him again but Anna merely shrugged.

'Then I might just have to kiss him goodbye!'

Holly, whether she liked Anna or not, was genuinely curious. 'Doesn't it bother you that he'll be gone soon?'

'Any one of us could be gone soon.' Anna shrugged. 'If working here doesn't prove that, then I don't know what will. I intend to enjoy every moment.'

And Anna was off. Teetering out on skinny legs and high heels and leaving that thought hanging in the air as heavily as her perfume.

Finally Holly had a moment alone.

She leant her head against the wall and closed her eyes and thought not just of Nora and Paul but of her own parents.

This time last year had been fraught, with Holly accompanying her mother to appointments and dashing to be there on her days off to offer support.

Tomorrow, after she'd done some shopping, Holly would be back on the motorway and again headed for home.

One year on it felt as if not much had changed. And in a year where there had been a rather marked absence of fun, in the latter months Daniel had somehow brightened her days.

She was, very possibly, never going to see him again, and that *wasn't* the reason for the sudden threat of tears, Holly told herself. No, it had been an emotional shift and it was coming to the end of a difficult year.

That was why she was suddenly teary.

It had nothing to do with lost opportunities.

Had there even been any? Holly pondered as she sat there and thought back over their time. Yes, there had certainly been a few occasions where a little flirt could have maybe spilled into more.

But to what end?

Maybe she needed a more generous dose of Anna's thinking instead of her usual caution where men were concerned.

Or maybe, Holly conceded as she put on her coat and walked out of the changing room, she was just looking for an excuse to misbehave.

She made her way through the department.

There was Daniel looking all sexy in black jeans and

a really thin jumper that almost looked silky and the fabric was so thin that she could see his nipples.

Talk about *Think Like a Man*.

'Are you coming after all?' Holly asked, seeing that he looked dressed for, well, anything.

'No. Why?'

'Because you've changed.'

'I've changed because I'm a locum,' Daniel pointed out. 'If I didn't throw my scrubs in the linen skip at the end of my shift I'd have quite a collection at my flat by now from the various hospitals I've worked at.'

As they walked past the nurses' station he retrieved his Advent calendar. 'Do you want yours?' he said.

'Yes.' Holly said, and smiled at Gloria. 'I don't trust the night staff a bit.'

She added it to her bag, which she would lock up with her coat at the pub.

Really, she would far prefer to be on her way home than heading off to a party, especially one that Daniel wasn't attending.

They walked out of the hospital and towards his car. It was one of those cold, damp nights and Holly was glad she hadn't made any attempt to tame her hair.

So was Daniel.

He was used to seeing it tied back and wrestling its way out of confinement, but now it fell in a dark cloud past her shoulders and some curls fell forward as she stopped for a moment and checked inside her bag.

He had seen her out of uniform before—arriving at work in jeans—but he had never seen Holly dressed up before and he found himself wanting to know what she wore under that coat.

They fell into step as they walked towards the car

and it was Anna who asked the question that was on Holly's mind.

'When do you fly?'

'I haven't booked it yet,' Daniel answered. 'Probably next week.'

'Where are you going first?'

'Switzerland.'

He aimed his keys at a black car, which lit up, and then everyone loaded their bags into the boot and then piled in, Laura and Holly in the back, Anna in the front, and suddenly Daniel knew that one of the reasons he wasn't indulging in a little *après ski* right about now was Holly.

Several hospitals had called, asking him to work, and the answer had been no. It was only when a shift had come up in the emergency department at The Primary that he had accepted a shift.

And now, as everyone climbed into his car and Anna got in the front, it felt wrong—as if Holly should be the one in his front passenger seat.

Holly felt the same.

It was odd and it was with absolutely no reason, yet Holly found that she resented the way Anna had jumped in the front. Holly sat behind Anna and when Daniel turned his head to reverse out, for a moment their eyes met. Holly was tempted to wind down the window because it had suddenly become very warm in the car and the heater had barely gone on.

Daniel moved the car out of the parking spot and then drove to the barrier and swiped his ID card. There he glanced in the rear-view mirror, not to check for traffic, more to see if her eyes were waiting.

They were.

All too often she averted her gaze, failing to complete what they started.

Not tonight.

Holly hoped it was dark enough that he couldn't see she was blushing and then a car tooted behind them.

'Daniel,' Anna prompted, because although the barrier was up the car hadn't moved.

'Sorry,' Daniel said. 'I was miles away.'

In bed with Holly!

'Everyone's asking about Paul,' Laura said, going through the messages on her phone. 'What do we say?'

'As little as possible,' Daniel suggested.

They were on the main road now and he glanced back into the mirror but Holly was now looking out of the window, watching the world go by and lost in thoughts of her own,

She liked Daniel far, far too much, Holly knew.

There was nothing wrong with liking someone except she wasn't wired like Anna. For Holly it would be foolish at best to get involved with a man who was days away from leaving the country.

Except she already was.

In her head Holly was already involved and yet she had not a single memory to draw from.

Was it time to change that?

'We're here.' Laura nudged her and Holly wiped the steamed-up window and looked out at the pub—a regular venue for Emergency dos. They often hired a room at the back and a lot of good times had been had there.

'Come in for one,' Anna said to Daniel, and Holly felt her skin prickle because Anna could flirt for England and she was seriously flirting now.

'I'm driving.'

Holly's eyes went to the mirror and again met his. Both of them knew that she would usually have looked away or been halfway out of the car by now.

'Come on,' Anna pushed, oblivious to the current coming from behind. 'You might enjoy yourself.'

'You know, I think I might,' Daniel said.

And so, instead of them climbing out, Daniel drove to the car park at the rear. It was packed but he found a space and soon they were all walking to the pub.

All except Holly, who was still by the car and going through her bag.

'What are you doing?' Daniel asked her because since they'd left Emergency he had seen her go through her bag many times.

'Compulsively checking that I've still got the envelope that Kay gave me.' Holly said. 'I have to pay the landlord…'

They went in the main entrance and there was the lovely pub scent but mixed with the woody smell of a fire in the entrance, and Holly felt her cheeks go pink for no other reason than it was lovely and warm.

The women all handed over their coats and their hands were all stamped so that they could get in and out of the function room. As Laura and Anna went through Holly asked where she should put the bar money.

'You'll need to see Desmond,' she was told, and was pointed in the right direction. 'He's in the lounge bar.'

'Thanks.'

'I'll come with you,' Daniel offered, and Holly nodded.

It had been well worth coming in, Daniel decided, for under Holly's coat she was wearing a black velvet dress, or rather it was raven. As he walked behind her Daniel noted the deep blue hue shimmering on the curves of her hips. Holly's legs were dressed in very sheer stockings and her heels were high, and as he moved forward to hold open the door, Daniel resisted placing his hand on the small of her back to guide her in.

Holly already felt as if he had, for her spine felt warm and her bottom too big, just from the burn of his gaze.

Desmond wasn't there, but they waited at the bar while one of the staff tracked him down.

It was a lovely old pub and there was a pine Christmas tree that was beautifully decorated and its scent filled the room.

'Christmassy enough for you?' Daniel asked.

'It's lovely.' Holly smiled but it was a bit of a forced one.

'Are you not in the mood for a party?' Daniel said, toying with the idea of suggesting they skip it when Holly nodded.

'I feel awful.'

'He might be okay.'

'No, I feel awful because…' She shook her head.

And then, for Daniel, something rather untoward happened—instead of wondering how quickly they could dispense with the small talk and get in the car and back to his, he actually wanted to hear what Holly had to say and *then* get back to the essentials.

'Tell me.'

'No,' Holly said, but then her guilty conscience demanded full disclosure. 'You know Kay was saying how, when they were waiting outside the catheter lab, Nora's daughter asked her what was for dinner…'

Daniel laughed a black laugh, it was nothing he hadn't seen with relatives.

'I'm as bad,' Holly said.

'Why, did you demand that Nora feed you?'

'No.' Holly smiled but then it changed. 'I almost asked Kay what would happen to the off duty for Christmas.' It had worried at her all evening. 'I mean, Paul's lying there half-dead, and I'm stressing over the off duty.'

'I'm quite sure Kay is.'

'I doubt it,' Holly sighed. 'Nora and she are best friends.'

'Off the record?' Daniel said, and Holly nodded.

'Kay's words to me just before she headed off to the catheter lab, and I quote, "How the feck am I going to sort out the roster now?"'

'Really?' Holly laughed.

'Really.' Daniel nodded. 'And I bet Nora, if Paul is now stable, is worrying about the million and one things that you women seem to worry about at this time of year.'

'That's very sexist.'

'Just an observation.'

'A wrong one.'

'I can only go by what I've seen. My father never did a thing for Christmas, I aim to be far away from it…' He thought for a moment. 'My uncle leaves it all to my aunt…'

Desmond came along then and he took the money and wrote out a receipt, which Holly put in her purse for Kay. 'What can I get you?' he offered. 'On the house, before you go in to that mad lot.'

Oh.

'I'll just have a soda water, thanks.' Daniel said.

'Well, he's a cheap date.' Desmond smiled at Holly. 'What can I get you?'

'I'd love a Scotch, please.'

She really, really would.

Holly wasn't a big drinker at the best of times but a lovely Scotch felt about right and Daniel motioned to a table near an open fire and the tree and they took a seat there.

'Maybe I am in the mood for Christmas after all.' Holly smiled, sitting back in the chair and relaxing to

the lovely crackle of the fire and inhaling the scent of her drink.

'I want one,' Daniel admitted.

'Tough.' Holly smiled and then took a sip, enjoying the burn of the liquor. 'I don't really like spirits but my dad loves Scotch so I always keep a bottle at home and every now and then I have one.'

'Well, that's good to know.'

'What?'

He smiled and she realised he was perhaps inviting himself to her home for a drink.

Or had she been inviting him?

Hmm.

Holly still didn't know where this might lead, but it was just so nice to be out in the real world with him and without buzzers and patients and others around. And it was definitely nice to squeeze in five minutes' pause after work before they headed into the party.

'Do you get on with your parents?' he asked.

'Very much so.'

'They live…?' Daniel frowned. He wasn't sure, though he knew that it was some distance that she often travelled to get home.

'Up north,' Holly said, and then told him the village where her family lived.

'So how come you're in London?'

'Because I get on so well with my family.' Holly smiled. 'I trained up there and it was all too easy to just live at home… I knew I needed a change.'

'Yet you're still home a lot?'

'My mum hasn't been very well.' Holly said, and decided the night had already been grim enough without

going further into it. 'What about you? Are your family in London?'

She didn't know him at all, Daniel realised.

Holly could have no idea just how refreshing that was. Even before he had started medicine there had been a constant stream of 'Marcus Chandler's son'. His father had been head boy at the boarding school Daniel had attended and his record was just as impressive at med school and beyond. Even Kay had made a few comments and had asked if he was any relation to the esteemed Professor Chandler.

Holly had no idea as to that side of his life.

'Yes.' Daniel answered the question as to whether his family was in London very simply.

'Do you get on?'

'Nope,' Daniel said.

'Why?'

'Because my father is an arrogant git,' he said, and then looked at her Scotch. 'Given that I'm on soda water tonight, I shan't be sharing.'

Holly laughed. 'What about your mother?'

'She's dead.'

Well, that wiped the smile from her face.

'He married again. I've got a sister...'

Daniel refused to call Maddie a half-sister.

'Do you get on with her?'

'I do when I see her. And that reminds me, I must get her a Christmas present before I head off.'

Holly's phone buzzed, indicating an incoming text, and she glanced down and saw that it was Anna, asking where they had disappeared to.

'Has our absence been noted?' Daniel asked.

'It has.'

The pleasant interlude was over but it had been nice,

Holly thought as she drained her drink and then stood. It had been a tiny but very welcome pause before she pushed out a smile and faced the masses.

He knew it was pointless suggesting that they didn't go through.

Holly took her Christmas party as seriously as her decorations.

'Time to be positive...' Holly said, though she didn't really feel it. 'It *is* Christmas and if ever there was a time for miracles...'

'Please,' Daniel scorned, pouring a bucket of iced water on that. 'There's no such thing as Christmas miracles.'

'Are you always so negative?' Holly asked as they headed towards the function room.

'Always.'

The doors swung open and there were a few shouts of 'Holly!' but there were a lot more shouts of Daniel's name! Clearly a lot of women were very glad to see him.

Anna, of course, leapt to his side and handed him an elaborate-looking cocktail.

'I'm driving,' he pointed out again.

'It a virgin.' Anna smiled. 'I had it prepared just for you.'

Oh, please. Holly thought she might spit at the suggestive tone, but she refused to be rattled by Anna. Instead, she put on her smile and chatted with friends.

It was a difficult night. Everyone wanted first-hand information and Holly knew that wasn't her place to give it. It was up to Nora what she wanted to share and for now Nora wanted upbeat and so that's what Holly did her best to be, but by ten she was done.

She looked over and Anna and Daniel were locked in conversation.

Or rather Anna was conversing and Daniel was locked, given the slight eye roll that he gave her.

Holly smiled but it was a regretful one because she simply didn't know how to run wild. How to go over there and be all sparkling and witty and flirt...

Except, as it turned out, she didn't have to go over there to flirt. Holly quickly realised that standing in the middle of the room and blatantly staring at the object of your desire seemed to work rather well too!

Yikes.

She hadn't meant that!

Holly watched as he said something to Anna and Holly realised he was excusing himself and about to make his way over.

It was time for a quick getaway.

'You're not going already?' Trevor, one of the male nurses, asked.

'I am.' Holly kept up that smile. 'I'm hitting the shops tomorrow and then...' She didn't finish. An absolute novice in the field of sexual adventure, she found her coat and headed outside.

'Leaving?'

She turned and there was Daniel.

'Yes.'

'Do you want a lift?'

'I've just called for a taxi,' Holly lied.

'It's no problem.'

'I live miles away.'

'I'll save you the fare, then.'

'No, thanks.'

Why? Holly asked herself. Why was she saying no? Because she *couldn't* say no to him.

'Come on.'

He jangled his keys and Holly nodded. Really, it was

just a colleague giving her a lift home and it would be bliss not to have to make small talk with a taxi driver or sit in the back as he chatted on his phone.

Liar, liar.

They got in his car, and this time she was in the front.

That's better, both thought but didn't say.

'Address?' he asked, and she gave it to him.

Daniel typed it into his phone and that took care of that, and then he started the engine.

'Head north,' his phone said.

'I hate that,' Daniel admitted. 'I have no idea which way north is. I need a compass in the middle of my steering wheel.'

'She means turn left,' Holly said.

'Thank you.'

'Are you all packed?' Holly made a feeble attempt at small talk and he nodded.

'Sort of. I'm trying to rent out my flat. Apparently December isn't an ideal time to find tenants.'

'So it that why your plans keep changing?'

'In part.'

'Well, you might just as well stick around for Christmas…'

'I doubt it. I might even fly out then, it's just another day.'

'You don't mean that.'

'I do,' Daniel said, and he gave her a smile. 'We're polar opposites.' And then he stared ahead at the road and it did not need stating—that opposites attracted.

Both already knew.

CHAPTER THREE

SHE SHOULD HAVE said goodbye to him back at the pub.

Then there might have been a hope that, should they meet up in the future, all they would be were ex-colleagues who had flirted a little on occasion.

Back at the pub she could have wished him well for his trip and, yes, of course she could do the same when he pulled up at her flat.

Holly didn't want to, though.

How did it even work? Holly thought. She was way too far out of her comfort zone. Did she offer him a drink, or did she leave it to him to suggest coming in?

And what about the morning?

Holly wished that she didn't overthink things, she wished she could be more like Anna and just worry about the day, or rather the night, at hand.

She wanted the traffic lights to turn red, for a pause, to turn and tell him that the flirty version of Holly he had met at times wasn't the real one. That the woman who had laughed at the suggestive tone in his voice when he'd told her she'd be in discreet hands, did not, prior to his arrival on her part of the planet, exist.

Yet the lights all stayed green and afforded swift passage.

And anyway, Daniel knew all that.

While he was driving he was trying to convince himself that this wasn't any different from what he was used to and that Holly could more than handle a hook-up. And he was also trying to convince himself that he didn't care in the way he actually did.

He couldn't afford to care. It wasn't an emotion he sought, and he was leaving after all.

His phone told him that the destination was on his left and he slid the car into a parking space outside her flat and his conscience won—Daniel didn't want to risk hurting her.

'You'd better go in,' Daniel said.

And so this was it.

'Thanks for the lift.'

'No problem.'

'It's been nice working with you,' Holly said. 'I'm going to miss your sulking face.'

'I'll miss your smiling one.'

And this really was it.

There was a charge in the air that should signal thunder but instead Daniel turned and looked ahead.

Holly reached to open the door and he did nothing to halt her so she got out.

They were both congratulating themselves on how adult and sensible they had been.

Now she could breathe, except, despite the cool and the drizzle, the night felt as humid as if it was summer.

Holly looked at the path to her door and she was six, maybe seven steps away from saving herself from a rather big mistake, except she wanted so badly to turn around and to follow desire rather than walk away.

Just once.

It was her choice as to what happened next, Holly knew.

Could she keep it light, without revealing how deeply she felt?

Daniel was just about to hit 'Home' as his destination when she tapped on the window.

'What?' he asked as it slid down. His voice was surly. He didn't want to do this a second time, especially as now that she was bending down there was the pearly white of her breasts at eye level.

And she looked at him and, no, she would not be so cheesy as to ask him in for a drink and then somehow, whoops, they'd up in bed.

She wanted a kiss, Daniel knew, but he was also rather certain she wanted a whole lot more than that. Not just sex, but the part of himself he refused to give.

'What?' he said again, and then his face broke into a smile, as, very unexpectedly, Holly, sweet Holly, showed another side of her.

'Are you going to *make* me invite you in?'

'Yes.'

'You're not even going to try and persuade me with a kiss?' Holly checked.

'You want me or you don't.' Daniel shrugged. 'There's no question that I want you. But, Holly, do you get that—?'

She knew what was coming and she didn't need the warning—he had made his position perfectly clear—so she interrupted him. 'I don't need the speech.'

She just needed this.

Holly had thought his hand was moving to open the door but instead it came out of the window and to her head and pulled her face down to his.

He kissed her hard, even though she was the one standing. The stubble of his unshaven jaw was rough on her face and his tongue was straight in.

He pulled her in tight so that her upper abdomen hurt from the pressure of the open window and it was a warning, she knew, of the passion to come.

Even now she could pull back and straighten, say goodnight and walk off, but Holly was through with being cautious.

In a second she would be falling through the open window for all the neighbours to see and sucked into the dark vacuum of his car.

Holly simply didn't care.

Her bag dropped to the pavement and he then released her.

Holly stared back at him, breathless, her lipstick smeared across her face, and all it made him want to do was to kiss her again.

But this was a street.

Holly bent and retrieved her bag and then walked off towards her flat. There was a roaring sound in her ears and her heart seemed to be leaping up near her throat.

Daniel closed up the car and was soon following her to the flats.

She turned the key in the main door to the flats and clipped up the concrete steps.

She could hear his heavy footsteps coming up the steps behind her as she turned and Holly almost broke into a run.

Daniel actually did!

He had thought her cute, sweet and gorgeous these past months and had done all he could not to think of her outright as sexy.

Except she was, and seriously so.

Those heavy footsteps chasing her were thrilling and caught up with her just as she was getting her key into the door of her own flat. Holly was breathless with ex-

citement and the rush and power of him grabbing for her almost toppled Holly as they burst in through the door.

The hall was in darkness; he could just make out some Christmas-tree lights in a room down the hall but there was no time to get to the lounge.

Daniel had no patience now.

Holly had never known anything like it. Never, in her almost twenty-nine years, had she had that simply-have-to-have-you feeling.

And Daniel *had* to have her.

Every obstacle he dealt with.

He hitched her lovely raven dress up.

Stockings?

No problem, he expertly removed them and then her knickers too.

And when he wanted a better view of her breasts he lowered her zipper at the back, just enough to free them.

Holly looked down at her exposed breasts, and then at her stockings and knickers lying on the hallway floor— she felt slutty and sexy. She liked it. So much so that she was pulling at his thin jumper just to reveal his stomach, and then running a hand up the heavy jeans-clad thighs, getting closer to the lovely bit in the middle. She dealt with the brass button deftly, though she broke a nail on the zipper, and then freed him. He was clearly as keen and eager as she, and Holly was so utterly ready for him she nearly forgot about condoms.

To Holly's mind there was nothing sexy about condoms, but he changed that in an instant, for he pulled out his wallet, found one, tossed the wallet to the floor and tore the foil with his teeth.

'Put it on,' Daniel told her, and he started to squeeze and play with her breasts as she did just that.

She rolled it down slowly, which was quite a feat,

given the way his fingers were exploring her, and she felt the jerk of impatience in her hand.

Then he said the two little words that tonight she was desperate to hear.

'Get on.'

Gladly she did.

He bent his knees just enough that he could thrust into her and Holly's shoulders hit the wall. She arched back at the consuming pleasure as he stabbed inside her.

Totally consumed and controlled by him, Holly was close to coming as Daniel lifted her legs even further; she wrapped them around his hips.

'I've been wanting you all night.' He told her as she wrapped her legs tighter, wiggling herself down further so he could push deeper. 'I wanted you on sight.'

They stared at each other as he banged her into wall, kissing her with raw passion and digging his fingers into her bottom, holding her firm. Heat flooded her centre and she moved her mouth away. 'I'm going to come…'

Her voice divulged her own surprise. Not just because she usually took for ever, more because of the intensity that hit.

Daniel felt her gather and pull tight around him as he plunged one last time before letting go deep inside her.

He lowered her down and she stood a moment on legs that felt she was getting over a bout of the flu they were so weak.

They followed the Christmas-tree lights to what he assumed was the lounge.

Maybe he'd get that Scotch after all, Daniel thought.

Instead, they collapsed onto her bed.

'Holly?'

The room had stopped spinning and they lay on their

backs on the bed when Daniel started to take in his surroundings. 'Why is there a Christmas tree in your bedroom?'

'My neighbours are a bit noisy,' Holly explained. 'And so I tend to spend more time in here.'

'Oh.'

'And it seemed a shame to have a Christmas tree in a room that I don't spend much time in.'

They were half-undressed already so it took only a moment to throw off the rest of their clothes and to get into bed.

They lay talking, about nothing much as well as a lot.

And it turned out their paths had almost crossed.

'I went for an interview at the Royal when I was looking at moving to London.' She thought back to that time and her nervousness as she'd entered the huge Victorian building.

It was funny to think now that he might have been inside.

'How long ago?'

'I was twenty-one,' Holly said. 'So eight, nearly nine years ago. Were you there then?'

He nodded. 'Did you get the job?'

'Yes,' Holly said. 'But I got offered the job at The Primary in the same week and I chose to go there. I didn't like how they rotated the staff at the Royal. Too many night shifts.'

'Don't you like nights?'

'Not really,' Holly said. 'I don't sleep very well during the day.'

'I could have had you when you were twenty-one.' Daniel mused, liking that idea.

'No, you couldn't have.' Holly smiled at his arro-

gant assumption. 'I was seeing someone then. I nearly got engaged.'

And he lay there, not liking that idea.

'We might have ended up having an affair,' Daniel said, determined to have had her at twenty-one in his head.

'No,' she said. 'We wouldn't have.'

And he lay there wondering why the hell he was sulking over an event that had never even taken place some eight or nine years ago!

'Why did you break up?'

'He got offered a job in America,' Holly said. 'I didn't want to go and he did. We were too young, I guess.'

They were heading into territory that Daniel generally avoided so they started chatting about work.

'I don't do well with grieving relatives,' Holly announced.

'Yes, you do.' He frowned because the few times he'd been with Holly while breaking bad news she'd always been fine.

If a little quiet.

'Oh, I'm better than I was,' Holly agreed. 'I have this nervous smile…'

And Daniel found that he was smiling as she spoke.

'I didn't know that I had it, well, I sort of did but then Kay had to take me to one side…'

'You smile at bad news?' Daniel checked.

'No, but I smile when I'm nervous. You should see me in my school photos and when I go for an interview and things…'

And there it was again.

This wanting to look at old photos.

To hear more.

To know more.

It was everything he was trying to resist.

* * *

Freezing.

Daniel woke to the cold air and warm bed and rolled into Holly.

God, she felt good.

Her soft bottom was against him and as his hand went over hers he kissed her bare shoulder and then his mouth moved up her neck.

Last night had been amazing.

Now he wanted more.

And so did Holly.

His hand lifted her hair and his kiss was heavy on her neck as light fingers circled her stomach.

But then he stopped.

Daniel actually stopped in mid-kiss because fast sexy sex was one thing, but the way he wanted her now could only serve to confuse Holly.

Arrogant assumption perhaps but he knew she liked him, seriously liked him, and he liked her enough not to want to give mixed messages.

And so how did you end things nicely?

Usually he didn't give it too much thought, for he generally played to a far tougher crowd.

Holly closed her eyes at the abrupt end to his kiss on her shoulder. They were both in that lovely turned-on morning feeling and she wanted to turn her face to his mouth, to kiss him slowly and make love.

Yes, that.

She wanted the hand that had been slowly stroking her stomach to resume its perusal and move lower yet it didn't.

Too intimate for you, Daniel? she wanted to say, though didn't, but she did get her own back a little because she slowly stretched and yawned, just so he could

feel what he was missing, and then rolled over to face him and smiled.

Yes, she was nice but, oh, she could be wicked.

'It's so nice to have a weekend off.' Holly smiled and chatted as if she hadn't even noticed his erection.

'I've got every weekend off now.' Daniel smiled back as she gave him a small kick to let him know how unfair that was.

She was back to looking into those amazing eyes but from her pillow this time. 'Are you registering to practise overseas?' Holly asked.

'It's an option, I guess.' He couldn't tell her his plans because the truth was he didn't really have any. 'I just want to take a year and work things out.'

'Fair enough,' Holly said, but her slight frown told him that she didn't really get it. They truly were opposites, not just that he had made so few plans but also that he could afford to take a year off. Shouldn't he have worked this all out some time ago?

'I'll make coffee…' Daniel offered.

'I'll go,' Holly said. 'The machine's tricky.'

'I'm sure I can work it out.'

She lay there and wondered how this would end. Awkwardness was creeping in and she didn't know how to put on a brave smile when he left.

And then she heard her front door open and then quietly close.

'Bastard,' Holly breathed.

But then a moment or so later she heard the door open again and lay back on the pillows, recanting her curse as she realised he must have left the door on the latch so he could get back in.

Holly knew she was way out of her comfort zone here, so much so that she had actually thought he might just

walk off without so much as a goodbye. Instead, though, he walked in with two mugs of coffee *and* two Advent calendars that he must have retrieved from the car. He put the drinks on the bedside tables and dropped the calendars on the bed.

'Holly, why don't you have any food in your fridge?'

'There are eggs.'

'But no bread,' he pointed out. 'I heard the neighbours, or rather I could hear breakfast television and her shouting for him to get up…'

'I told you,' Holly said. 'It's worse during the week. She must call to him about fifteen times before he surfaces. Sometimes I want to go round there and pull the duvet off him myself!'

And he would rather like to pull the duvet from her but instead he just climbed in.

She reached for the floor and handed out cushions so that they could sit up in comfort.

Her bedroom really was rather lovely. Even aside from the Christmas tree! There were books and a pile of DVDs lining shelves and a television on a chest of drawers. There was her computer and phone and, really, apart from the occasional trip to the bathroom or kitchen he could absolutely see why she might not want to leave. 'You could bring the coffee maker in here,' Daniel suggested.

'I did think of that…' Holly nodded '…but then I'd need a little fridge too…'

'And then you'd get bedsores,' Daniel said, and was about to make a little joke about having to roll her every couple of hours, but he knew where that would lead.

'I'd better go soon.'

'Good,' Holly said, 'because I've got a lot to do.'

She picked up her Advent calendar and started to peel off the Cellophane as Daniel tackled his.

'I can't believe you've never had one of these.'

'I might have when I was really little,' Daniel said. 'I honestly can't remember.'

For all his inexperience he found the number one before Holly did and was soon pulling out a small circle of dark chocolate from behind the little cardboard window.

'I doubt it's very good,' Holly warned as she too found hers. 'Given that Kay bought a job lot. Still, it's the thought…' Her voice trailed off as she popped it in her mouth. It was the darkest, sweetest and most melt-in-the-mouth chocolate she had ever tasted, and Daniel clearly felt the same since he was already opening door number two.

'Oh, my!' Holly said.

'Wait till you taste December the second,' Daniel warned. 'It's some orange liqueur…'

'I think I'm going to come!' Holly said as she rolled it around her tongue.

'Well, lucky for you, it's December the third now, so you can have another.'

The third was behind a little door with a gingerbread man on it and the chocolate was a coffee and cream.

'They get better and better,' Daniel said.

The chocolate was so seriously superb that Holly was very much considering breaking her own rule and just eating all twenty-five in one go.

'If that's the beginning of the month,' Daniel said, 'then what's behind those double doors…?' He turned the calendar over and read the fine print. 'It's from Belgium.'

'So what's it doing in the discount store?'

'We should go and buy up all that's left.' Daniel suggested.

'I'll have to find out which one she went to.'

Hot coffee soon washed down the chocolate but in-

stead of Daniel heading for home and Holly to the shops they were back on their sides and facing each other.

'I'm starving,' Daniel said.

'There's a baker's across the street, they do really nice pastries.'

'Go on, then,' he said, but she shook her head.

'You go.'

And for someone who had been about to leave, Daniel was considering not just heading to the bakers on his way home but returning to her bed with a box of pastries.

'We could just go and get breakfast.' Daniel suggested the name of a very nice department store and as she licked her lips at the suggestion he waited for that ping of regret for prolonging things to descend in his chest, but it wasn't there. His only regret was that he might be leading her on, and yet, he reasoned, it was just breakfast.

'Sounds good,' Holly said. 'It has to be a quick breakfast, though…' She glanced at the time. 'I want to do some Christmas shopping.'

'And me.'

Daniel did, as he hadn't got anything for Maddie. She was already terribly disappointed that he wouldn't be there for Christmas and he hoped that it might be tempered by a lovely gift.

But what to get a five-year-old who has everything?

And whatever it was he would have to have it delivered. There was no way he was rocking up for Christmas dinner after the disaster of last year.

As he borrowed Holly's shower, Daniel told himself that the expedition he'd suggested was a terrible idea.

From sex to shopping?

And Holly was thinking the same, though along different lines, because as Daniel showered his phone rang and she looked at the screen and saw the name 'Maddie'.

Whoever Maddie was she was impatient, because she rang three times in the space of five minutes.

Holly tried not to mind.

Yet she did.

When he came out of the shower it was to the sight of Holly sitting on the bed and pulling on boots.

'I wish I'd done this before I put on my jeans,' Holly said and to Daniel it seemed there was nothing more on her mind than breakfast.

He picked up the phone and gave a small eye roll when he saw that there were a few missed calls from Maddie.

There often were!

He had a listen to check there wasn't a problem.

There wasn't.

'Hello, I've got your ticket for the nativity play.'

Next message. 'I'm an angel.'

And so on.

What on earth should he get her for Christmas?

'Let's go,' Holly said, trying to keep the edge from her voice as he blatantly listened to his messages. 'I think the café opens at ten.'

They arrived at a quarter past, which, as it turned out, was perfect timing because everyone who had been queuing for the café to open were pretty much served.

'I'll have the full English breakfast…' Daniel didn't even need to look at the menu.

'Well, I'm going to have mince pies and cream and a strong coffee.'

The fruit mix in the pie was warm and spicy and the cream sweet and it was the perfect breakfast really, although it had little to do with the food.

Despite their brief misgivings about their breakfast date, conversation was surprisingly easy.

Usually for Daniel the conversation ran out at first

kiss, or certainly by the time his head had hit the pillow, but Holly's company was just as pleasant this morning as it had been last night.

'Who do you have to buy for?' Holly asked as Daniel slathered brown sauce on his mushrooms.

'My sister.'

'Who else?'

'No one else. You?'

'Everyone!' Holly sighed and then took out her phone. 'But first I'm going to call work.'

'About Paul or the Christmas roster?'

'Stop!' Holly blushed. 'Don't you dare repeat that to anyone.'

'I never repeat pillow talk.'

'It was said in your car.'

'Yes, but by then you'd already made up your mind that you'd be hauling me into your lair.'

'No,' Holly said as she made the call, and having asked the switchboard operator to put her through to Kay she smiled at him. 'That was a last-minute decision.'

'I'm glad you made it.'

So too was she, Holly thought as she returned to her phone call.

'Kay, it's Holly.'

'He's stable, no real change, but that's good.' Kay got straight to it. 'No arrhythmias overnight but they'll keep him intubated for a couple of days.'

'How's Nora?'

'Exhausted. She's just gone home for a sleep. How was the party?'

'It was good,' Holly said. 'Everyone was concerned about Paul, of course, but I think it went well.'

'I heard that you left early.'

'Well, I wasn't exactly in the mood...you know that.'

'I also heard Daniel didn't just drop you girls off but came in for a drink.'

'He did.'

'Hold on a moment.' Holly sat there and she heard Kay closing her office door and Holly sat holding her breath, wondering if their leaving together had been noted.

She didn't have to worry, Holly soon realised as Kay spoke on. 'Anna was all over him, apparently?'

'I didn't notice.'

'Get out of here,' Kay scoffed. She knew Holly was always up to date with goings-on, although Kay prided herself on being The One Who Knew. 'So, who did he leave with?'

Holly sat there, watching as Daniel mopped up the egg with a thick bit of buttery toast, and she should be relieved, really, that Kay didn't for a second think it might be with her.

'I don't think he was with anyone,' Holly said, and her voice came out a little too high.

Daniel looked up when he heard her strained voice and saw her very red cheeks and he could guess what was being asked so he mouthed a suggestion.

'Do you want me to speak to her?'

Holly laughed at the thought of Kay's shocked expression if she handed Daniel the phone but shook her head and looked away, hunching her shoulders so she could talk without seeing the object of her sins.

'Oh.' Kay sounded deflated at the lack of gossip but when Kay spoke on so too did Holly. 'I'm going to have to take a long hard look at the roster, Holly.'

'I know.'

'And you know that I'll try to accommodate everyone but I do have to be fair. There are mums with little ones

who need their mum to be there at Christmas, but you know that I'll try to do my best for all my staff.'

'I do appreciate it.'

Holly hung up and as she did so Daniel gave her a thin smile. 'Off duty?'

She nodded.

'See, I told you it wouldn't take long. The real world always surfaces.'

And it was surfacing now because as she glanced at the time Holly knew if she had wanted to do her shopping and get to her parents' by dinnertime, then she needed to get going.

They finished up their food and wandered out, but instead of parting ways they looked at the floor plan.

'What does your sister like?' Holly asked.

'Elephants.'

'Oh.'

He didn't explain that Maddie was five.

In truth, Daniel was very touchy about the fact his sister could very well be his daughter. In fact, when they were out together they were always mistaken as such.

They joined the swarms of people all looking for the perfect gift that would make another happy.

There was no such thing, Daniel knew.

Holly swallowed when he held up a necklace with an ugly-looking elephant hanging on the chain, Of course she assumed Daniel's sister was close to his age, and she found that she was wearing her nervous smile, which she quickly righted and then made a suggestion.

'Why don't you adopt an elephant for her?'

Daniel rolled his eyes.

'If I loved elephants,' Holly said, 'it would be the perfect gift.'

And then she found *her* perfect gift!

It was beach glass, all wired and knotted together into the most fantastic necklace and earrings.

'I should get this for Adam,' Holly said, 'though it's a bit pricey.'

'Adam?'

'My brother.'

'Right,' Daniel said, to show he had no problem with all of that. 'Right! It's very nice.'

'The necklace would be for me, Daniel.' Holly smiled at his attempt to be PC. 'After too many disasters we now buy what we really want for ourselves and wrap it, though it's from the other.'

'I see.'

He didn't.

Daniel knew very little of family traditions and the little things that others seemed to do so seamlessly to make Christmas Day special.

But then, in the middle of a department store and completely out of the blue, he remembered something. He had woken up and there was this lumpy sock at the end of his bed and there was some fruit in it but also a tiny miniature of a castle. A castle he knew because they had been on holiday there that summer.

The holiday wasn't really a memory, more that the castle he had held in his palm that morning was, for he had looked at it in the gift shop.

His mum must have done that, Daniel realised. She must have bought it then and saved it for Christmas. Certainly it wouldn't have been his father.

He just stood in the busy department store, remembering something from a long time ago.

Something precious.

'Why are they queuing?' Holly nudged him and pulled him from introspection.

She had put down the necklace and looked up to see a long line forming towards the back of the store.

'Because they've got nothing better to do.' Daniel shrugged. 'Maybe it's to see Santa.'

'But they're mainly adults,' Holly pointed out.

'Maybe it's an adult-rated Santa,' he suggested, but Holly didn't smile at his joke. 'You don't approve?'

'I refuse to buy into your constant downgrading of the magic of Christmas. I want to know what they're queuing for,' Holly said, and they made their way over to see what was going on.

No, it wasn't Santa and neither was it an adult Santa. It was really rather amazing. They clearly weren't the only ones who thought so because and if the queue was big, so too was the crowd gathered at the end of the line, watching what was being made.

A little elf, okay, a person dressed up as a little elf, was typing on a miniature keyboard. Further down the line a tiny stamp-sized letter was printed. There another elf was placing the tiny letters in equally small envelopes.

It took a moment to work out that the letters were being placed within hand-blown Christmas-tree decorations.

They both stood and watched the glassblower and time really did run away that morning because it was simply fascinating to watch.

Once made and cooled another group of elves then decorated the glass bauble and added a silver chain to hang it from the tree and then it was placed in a gorgeous box that was tied with a heavy silver bow.

'What a beautiful gift,' Holly said, although Daniel, though interested, was too practical to be convinced.

'I don't get it,' Daniel admitted. 'You'd have to break the glass to read the letter.'

'That's the whole point,' Holly said. 'You don't break the glass. Or maybe you do…'

They were debating this when someone called his name.

'Daniel!'

They both turned and walking towards them was a rather beautiful woman around Holly's age but light years ahead in style. She had long straight honey-brown hair that fell immaculately and she looked as if she had just stepped out of a make-up salon, though it was subtly done, of course. She wore neat grey trousers and boots and had on a thin coat and she was one of those people who couldn't spill something on themselves if they tried.

Her cheeks were pink, though, and starting to fire up like a sunset as Daniel said her name.

'Hi, Amelia.' He responded to her greeting with a rather terse nod. 'How are you?'

'Busy,' she admitted, and held up a couple of shopping bags. 'I'm just trying to get a few things…'

'I see.'

It was all rather tense and uncomfortable and when Amelia looked over at Holly, clearly expecting to be introduced, Daniel said nothing.

How did you? Daniel wondered. Did he turn to Holly and say, *Oh, Holly this is my stepmother.*

He hadn't seen her in almost a year.

Not since last Christmas Day, when Amelia had had rather too much drink and had told Daniel that, though the money was nice, the marriage wasn't great. He had woken from a doze on the sofa to be told by Amelia that she was tired of sleeping with an older man and wanted the younger version—his son, namely Daniel.

And no one would ever have to know.

Daniel had got up, got his jacket and gone home, and hadn't seen Mommy Dearest since.

'So what are you up to?' Amelia asked.

'Not much.'

Those two words crushed Holly.

He could have said Christmas shopping, Holly thought, or that they had just been and had breakfast. No, she didn't want him to go into detail but to stand beside her and tell this woman 'Not much' had Holly's confidence shrink as if salt had been poured over it.

She stood there, wearing that stupid, nervous smile as they carried on talking while she was, at best, ignored.

'So what are you doing over Christmas?' Amelia asked him.

Avoiding you and my father, Daniel was tempted to answer, but his voice was its usual mixture of boredom and disinterest.

'I'm not sure,' Daniel said. 'Working or skiing.'

'I could have guessed it would be one of the two.' She gave a tight smile. 'I'd better get on.'

'Sure,' Daniel said.

Amelia walked off and now it was Holly and Daniel who stood in strained silence but the fun of watching the glassblower do his work had now left them.

Daniel glanced over his shoulder to make sure Amelia had gone.

Holly saw that he did and misinterpreted it as Daniel craning his neck for one lingering look and suddenly she didn't want to be here any more. She just did not want to stand beside a man whose mind was elsewhere. A man who couldn't even be bothered to introduce her and described their morning as 'Not much'. A man who listened to his voice messages from another woman straight after getting out of her bed.

He had come with a warning and, a little late perhaps, Holly chose to heed it.

It was time to put her big girl's blouse on and remember just what it was that she had agreed to—a one-night stand and then they parted ways.

This wasn't a date, no matter how much Holly wanted to convince herself of that. Neither was it the start of something. She'd agreed to abide by Daniel Chandler's standards last night, which meant they should have been over with several hours ago.

She made it now.

'I'm going to head off,' Holly said. 'I've got a lot to get and then I'm heading off to my parents'.'

'Sure.'

'Thanks for breakfast.' Holly smiled.

'You're welcome.'

There was a very good chance that she'd never see him again, Holly knew that. *And so how did you end it?* she wondered. *Did you say, Have a nice life? Did you kiss the other on the cheek when you went your separate ways? Or did you just give a sort of half-wave and then walk off?*

Holly chose the latter.

CHAPTER FOUR

HOME.

Holly had rung ahead to say she'd be late and just before seven she exited the motorway and saw the lights of her village in the distance.

There was no sense of relief at being at her parents', though. In truth, it had been ages since she'd had a full weekend off and it would have been nice to catch up with some friends. Or rather, given the turn of events, it would have been nice to spend a night in alone and watch a movie and dwell on what had happened with Daniel. Still, her mum wanted some help getting things ready for Christmas and so instead of being morose Holly waved to her mum as she got out of the car and smiled brightly as she headed up the path.

Inside, the tree was up and the decorations were all out, so her father had clearly been busy. Her mother went back into the kitchen to finish off making dinner and Holly went in to give her a hand.

'We waited for you,' Esther said.

'I told you not to,' Holly replied, because she'd told them to go ahead and eat.

The sound of the electric knife filled the room for a moment but when it went silent Holly knew that she ought

to give her mother fair warning so she spoke. 'Mum, there might be a change to the off duty over Christmas.'

'I thought it had all been done.' Esther turned and then looked at the calendar on the fridge. 'You're off from the twenty-third till the twenty-eighth.'

'I was supposed to be but a couple of people have gone off sick and...' Holly didn't really want to tell her mum about Paul. Everything seemed to upset Esther these days and they all tended to tiptoe a little around her. 'Well, Kay's just not able to cover the department.'

'Your brother's going to be in Mongolia next year,' Esther said. 'I've got everyone coming...'

'I know all that,' Holly said. 'And I'll do all I can to be here but I had last Christmas and New Year off and we have to take turns. There are mums with little children and—'

'Holly, I'm a mother and I *want* my family together this Christmas. Surely, given the year we've all had, that's not too much to ask?'

'I don't do the off duty, Mum,' Holly pointed out, but she could see that her mother was upset. So too was Holly. It had been a difficult enough day, without having to justify that she was needed at work, but Esther wouldn't let it go.

'Holly, they can't just expect you to change your plans at the last minute...'

You do, Holly was tempted to point out, but she didn't want to row.

Actually, she did.

Once they had been able to bicker, once Holly had been able to have a proper conversation with her mum, and she missed those times. 'I'm going to take my bag upstairs.'

She did just that and back in her old bedroom Holly sat for a moment on her old bed and took in a deep breath.

Pollyanna indeed!

She wanted to go back down and speak her mind, which was that she was tired of walking on eggshells around her mother.

Holly was, in fact, tired.

Not just from a late night and long drive but from a very difficult year. Right now she had problems of her own. Okay, not major ones, but she was wrestling with last night and wondering if she might never even see Daniel again, but there just wasn't a place for that now. Her mother had no idea what was going on in Holly's life and lately never thought to ask.

She looked up as there was a knock on the door and saw that it was her father. 'Your mum said that you might not be able to get Christmas off.'

'It looks that way.'

'Holly, I know they were good to last year but you know what Christmas means to your mum. Is there any way—?'

'Dad, the charge nurse who was supposed to be working over Christmas had her husband go into cardiac arrest in front of her last night.'

'Oh.'

'Yes, "oh". I want to be with my family at Christmas but so too does everyone else and Mum sending you up here to talk to me doesn't change that. Everyone's Christmas is important.'

Apart from the rather jumpy start it was a nice weekend. Holly went shopping with her mum and actually got rather a lot done, including ordering the turkey, but as pleasant as it had been, Holly arrived back at work more tired for her days off than when she had left.

There was no word from Daniel.

She hadn't expected flowers or a phone call, or a follow-up date.

But she *had* hoped.

And those hopes had been dashed.

What part of 'one-night stand' don't you get, Holly? she asked herself.

The 'one night' part.

How could something that had been so good simply end?

CHAPTER FIVE

HOLLY KNEW SHE shouldn't take her coffee back to bed.

It was five-thirty and she started work at seven so really she should be hitting the shower, but instead she allowed herself one small luxury that was becoming a habit of late.

Not just for Holly.

The whole emergency department were *thrilled* with their Advent calendars.

It was the fifteenth of December, which meant that so far fourteen chocolaty delights had been eaten.

They had ranged from raspberry to mulled wine, from salted caramel to sticky toffee, and each was a master-piece.

Every morning the staff all compared their treat.

Holly found the window that said fifteen and peeled back the little door and there it was—a little ball of chocolate with red and green dotted through it and dusted in icing sugar, and with a flurry of relish she popped into her mouth.

It was awful!

So awful that despite three chews waiting for the taste sensation to hit she ended up spitting it out into a tissue. It was glacé cherries and this sickly-sweet chocolate. It was so bad that, had that been the first day's chocolate,

none of the rest would have been opened and the calendar would have found its way straight to the bin.

Grumbling, removing the taste with a mug of coffee, Holly headed for the shower and then took the underground to work.

She caught sight of her reflection in the window and saw just how drab she looked, especially given that it was so close to Christmas.

It wasn't just her.

The department was rather gloomy.

Paul had at first rallied and been moved from Intensive Care to the coronary care unit, but just two days ago he had thrown off another clot and collapsed again. Now he was back on ICU on a ventilator.

It wasn't just that, though.

Now that Daniel wasn't around the days seemed longer and the run-up to Christmas, which Holly usually loved, felt just a little less, well, Christmassy.

Even the very thorough Kay was falling behind in her plans.

'Holly, can you sort out the Secret Santa?' Kay said as Holly took off her coat.

The underground had been packed, her boots had let in the rain and Holly's mood was a touch frazzled, possibly down to the fact she had her period, but she'd kill anyone who suggested it might be that.

'Nora usually does it…' Kay sighed.

'Sure,' Holly agreed.

'I'm going to have a cup of tea before we start.'

That sounded like a good idea to Holly.

'Hey,' Trevor said as Kay and Holly walked in with large mugs of tea. 'Did you have your chocolate this morning?'

Holly pulled a face and nodded.

'I still feel a bit sick,' Anna moaned.

'I think,' Holly said, 'that for the fifteenth one, the master chocolatier went on his break and left the work-experience kid in charge.'

They all laughed and then she startled because she recognised Daniel's. Turning, she saw that he was sitting behind where she stood. He was eating toast and drinking tea and Holly's heart told her to be wary.

This had the potential to really hurt!

'I thought you'd left,' Kay said.

'So did I,' Daniel admitted. 'But try telling that to Admin. They called me this morning at six and asked me to come in. I'm only here till midday, though.'

Holly ignored him.

It had been twelve days since she had last seen him.

The Twelve Days of Absence, Holly now named them, and if he expected her to be smiling and peppy and, oh, so pleased to see him then he was mistaken. Instead, she drank her tea as she sorted out the Secret Santa.

'What are you doing?' he asked Holly, who had taken a seat and written out a list and was now tearing it up.

'Secret Santa.' Holly said, but didn't look up, when usually she'd answer with a smile.

She didn't know how to be around Daniel. They'd been friends who flirted before, now they were…what?

Ex-lovers.

Or was that too grand a word to describe them?

Not for Holly.

She had no idea as to his feelings, if any, for her, no idea where she stood in the scheme of things.

Probably nowhere.

But Holly wanted to find out.

The morning flew by and all were kept busy, especially as Kay took herself off to the office to wrestle with

the dreaded off duty. The Christmas roster was the most awaited one of the entire year. Kay had tried to put it off as Nora had assured her she'd be back, but with Paul's further deterioration it was now clear that wouldn't be the case.

To have to change it at the last minute was not a decision that Kay had taken lightly.

And to forge the Secret Santa was not something Holly took lightly either. She just had to know how Daniel felt.

She slipped into the changing room and wrote 'Holly Jacobs', 'Holly Jacobs', 'Holly Jacobs' out about twenty times and screwed them up into little balls.

The original names she took out and placed carefully in the pocket of her scrubs and then added the duplicate copies of her own name to the envelope. Then she went out and found him checking results on a computer as Kay held out a form for him to sign.

'Pick a name,' Holly said, and waved the envelope under his nose.

'I shan't be here for Christmas,' Daniel told her, 'so there's no point in taking one.'

'Everyone takes a name,' Holly said. 'It's all about getting into the Christmas spirit.'

Daniel rolled his navy eyes, which indicated what he thought of that, and got back to the computer screen.

'Take a name, Daniel,' Kay said. 'You can drop it off on your way to the airport if you don't work again. If you can't manage that then I always have extras given half the staff are off for Christmas. It's just a bit of fun.'

Daniel didn't do fun.

Well, he did, but it was a rather more sophisticated type of fun he indulged in.

Not stupid Christmas-present swaps where people sulked if they didn't get what they wanted or you forgot,

but for the sake of peace he put in his hand and pulled
out a name.

Holly Jacobs.

Of course it was.

He looked at her vivid green eyes and mop of dark
curls that were, as always, coming loose.

'You're not allowed to say who you got,' Holly told
him. 'Just stick within the price limit and put it under the
tree. Usually we check when the name we have is work-
ing. So, say you had…' she plucked a name out of thin
air '… Trevor, well, he finishes up on—'

'I get the drift,' Daniel interrupted.

'Good.'

Daniel got up from his stool and stalked off and Holly
gave a little satisfied smile.

Now she'd finally know—if he got her something truly
awful, or forgot completely, then she'd have to simply ac-
cept that he cared not a jot for her and it had just been a
one-night stand. Maybe then she could turn off the fairy
lights that were perpetually twinkling in her head when
he was around.

'I'll take a name,' Kay said, and reached out her hand.

Oh!

For all her plotting and scheming, Holly hadn't thought
of that. Kay was about to reach in and she had to come
up with something fast.

Very fast! Because walking towards her was Anna,
and she hadn't taken a name yet either.

Holly suddenly had visions of twenty gifts all with
her name under the tree and it would look a bit suspi-
cious, especially as she was the one organising the thing.

'Are you okay?' Kay checked, as Holly whipped the
envelope away.

'No!' Holly said, and did the only thing she could think of.

She fled!

And one lie led to another, it truly did, because she had no choice but to dash off to the staff loos and close the door behind her.

'Holly...' Kay followed her in and stood on the other side of the door. 'What's wrong?'

'I just feel a bit...sick.' Oh, she was the worst liar but at least Kay couldn't see her blush as she quickly changed the names over. 'A bit dizzy.'

She finally came out and Kay looked at her with narrowed eyes.

'Do you need to go home?'

'No.'

'Thank goodness for that. Go and get a cup of tea and sit down.'

Oh, please don't be nice, Holly thought, but she did as she was told and took a seat back in the staffroom.

Daniel appeared ten minutes later.

'Kay said that you weren't feeling very well.'

'I'm fine.'

He grinned.

'What?'

'She's decided that you're pregnant.'

'Oh, God!' Holly groaned.

'You're not, are you?'

Daniel's grin had, she noted, disappeared.

'No.'

'You're sure? I mean, I know we were careful...'

'Shh...' Holly looked around to be sure there was no one near. 'There's nothing to worry about.'

'Well, if there was something to worry about...'

'There isn't.'

There wasn't.

'I've got my period.'

'Is that why you're in such a filthy mood?' Daniel asked.

'Nope, that would be the company,' Holly said. 'Don't worry, Daniel, there are no repercussions for you to worry about!' Holly gave him a tight smile and got up from her chair. 'I'd better get back to work.'

Daniel stood as she brushed past him and he knew that Holly was wrong, there were repercussions from that night. Their friendship had changed. Gone was the easygoing banter and the little flirts and gone too was the lie that once they'd slept together he'd be over her, as was usually the case.

Oh, he could blame it on being half-asleep that he'd said yes when Admin had rung this morning to ask him to work, but it was more than that. And he could insist to himself that he was still in England because he had found out that neither his father nor Amelia could make Maddie's nativity play this afternoon and so had decided to stick around for that.

He took out the bunched-up piece of paper from his pocket and read her name.

Holly Jacobs.

Yes, there were repercussions.

CHAPTER SIX

INDEED, KAY HAD pegged Holly as pregnant!

Before Holly could even make it back to the department, Kay had called her into the office for a little talk.

'I've worked with a lot of young women in my time and generally when they're dizzy and throwing up...' She went into her pocket and pulled out a pregnancy test. 'It's better to face things.'

'Kay, please.'

'You can talk to me, Holly...'

'I know that I can,' Holly said. 'But I'm not pregnant.'

As Kay held out the test, Holly refused to take it.

'You're not yourself, Holly!'

'Kay, I've got my period...'

'Well, it's the mother of a period, then, because it's lasted for two weeks. You've been awful,' Kay said, and Holly gave a reluctant smile. 'You can talk to me.'

Holly looked at Kay and she was touched by Kay's forthrightness and concern and, yes, she could talk to her. In some ways it would be a relief to tell someone how jumbled up she was feeling. Once she had been able to talk to her mother but those days seemed a long way off right now.

And so she told Kay the truth, well, a small part of it. 'I didn't feel sick or faint. I just had to come up with

something. I didn't want you and Anna to take a name because I fudged the Secret Santa.'

'You what?' Kay frowned.

'It was only my name written down,' Holly explained.

'So that Daniel would choose you?' Kay said, smiling as realisation dawned. 'That's very ingenious. We'll have to see what he gets you.'

'Nothing, I expect.' Holly shrugged and Kay saw the sparkle of tears in her eyes.

'I don't think Daniel's very into Christmas.'

And Holly didn't think Daniel was very into her either.

'He's leaving, Holly,' Kay pointed out. 'He's made it very clear that he'll soon be off.'

Holly nodded. 'I wish he'd gone already.'

'No, you don't.'

Kay was right. This morning when she'd seen him, though cross and confused, she'd felt her heart simply leap at the sight of him. And now she had to start back at the beginning of getting over him when the last days had been hell.

She didn't just like Daniel, it felt like a whole lot more. More than she'd ever liked anyone in her entire life.

Oh, she was trying so hard not to use the love word, even to herself.

Surely it couldn't be that?

'Be careful,' Kay suggested, and Holly nodded, even if it was a bit late for that. 'Now,' Kay added, 'while I can be terribly indiscreet I don't break confidences, so you don't have to worry about that. Daniel's lovely to chat to but I know his type—all he wants is inside your knickers, not your mind.' She saw Holly's pinched face and while she was delivering gloomy verdicts she decided to just get it over with. 'I've finished the Christmas roster. I'd better put it up.'

Holly knew that her cheeks had turned pink.

'Do you want a sneak preview?' Kay asked, and when Holly nodded she turned the computer screen around and Holly took a look.

She had been given a half-day on Christmas Eve, which meant that she finished at midday and was due back for a night shift on Christmas night, though she was off for New Year's Eve.

'I did my best,' Kay said.

Kay really had done, because at least there was a chance for Holly to make it home and spend the best part of Christmas with her family. Certainly Kay hadn't been gentle on herself—she was working all of it, just as she had last year and the year before that.

'Don't you ever want Christmas off?' Holly asked.

'Not really. Eamon used to get weary of me working it every year,' Kay admitted, 'but he's got used to it now. Next year I'm taking it off, though.'

She smiled that gorgeous Irish smile and Holly smiled back.

Kay's daughter, Louise, was due to give birth in the new year and Kay would be a first-time grandmother.

'I'm not missing that baby's first Christmas for the world,' Kay said as they walked through to the department.

The off duty had been posted and Holly stood back, chatting with Kay, as all the staff clustered around the computers.

'Louise might have the baby on Christmas Day,' Holly commented.

'God, I hope not,' Kay said, 'for the baby's sake. They never get a real birthday…'

'Yes, they do,' Holly said, and would have argued more

strongly but she suddenly remembered the Christmas that everyone in her immediate family would rather forget.

Because they'd forgotten her birthday.

Why today did everything make her want to cry?

'Holly!'

She looked over and saw that a patient was being wheeled in by Karen, a cheery paramedic.

The lady looked to be in her seventies and was very well dressed in a lovely woollen coat and scarf but she was sitting in the wheelchair, holding her arm, which was wrapped in a sling.

'This is Iris Morrison...'

It was a familiar injury at this time of the year. People were busy and the streets were slippery and when Iris had fallen she had put out her hand to save herself and had, it appeared, broken her wrist.

She was taken into a cubicle and Holly had a look at the wrist. It was causing Iris a lot of pain and she was also very pale, which meant Holly didn't really want her sitting for ages in a chair, so she decided to put her on a trolley.

The handover was brief. Iris was fit and well and was more cross with herself than anything.

'I haven't got time for a broken wrist,' she sighed when the paramedics had left.

'I think you're going to have to make time.' Holly smiled. It was terribly warm in the department and Iris's coat would have to come off for the X-ray, but Holly decided to do that after Iris had been given something for pain.

She told Iris she would be back in a moment and saw Daniel looking at *another* wrist X-ray.

'I've got a seventy-two-year-old lady...'

'I saw,' Daniel said.

'Can she have something for pain before I undress her?'

He nodded and took the patient card from Holly and then followed her in.

'Good morning, Mrs Morrison, I'm Dr Chandler.'

'Chandler?' Iris frowned and then looked up at navy eyes. 'I used to work for a Marcus Chandler, I'm guessing from those eyes that you must be Daniel!'

'That's correct.' Daniel gave her a smile. 'I'm sorry, I don't…'

'You were about five years old,' Iris said, 'so I don't expect you to remember. We've never actually met. I was your father's secretary for a year. He was a very impressive surgeon.'

'And you're a very tactful woman,' Daniel said, because his father was a very difficult man and he doubted any secretary of his had many nice words to say about him.

Iris laughed but then winced as Daniel gently examined her wrist. 'You don't need me to tell you it's broken?'

'No.'

'I'll get you something for the pain and then we'll get that coat off and get you straight round—'

'Actually,' Holly said, 'there's rather a wait for X-Ray.'

'I'll see if I can get you squeezed in,' Daniel said to Iris, and she gave a delighted smile at the upgrade.

Soon the coat was off and because of the strong pain-killers she had been given, Holly went to X-Ray with her.

Of course he had managed to squeeze Iris in because, from the way the radiographer was batting her eyelashes, she was another fan of Daniel's.

The entire female population was, it would seem.

'Gorgeous-looking young man, isn't he?' Iris smiled as they waited.

'He knows it,' Holly said.

'Well, he seems nice with it, though, not like his father. Oh, that man!' She rolled her eyes to indicate just how difficult Daniel's father had been. 'Such a fantastic surgeon but he was the coldest man I have ever come across. I tried to be nice, given that his wife had died, I mean I guessed it must be hard to be left with a five-year-old...'

Holly swallowed.

The thought of losing her mother had rocked Holly's world for more than a year and she was twenty-eight. Holly just sat there for a moment and tried to imagine a world without her mother in it from the age of five.

She couldn't.

And neither could Daniel imagine a world with a happy family in it.

They sort of danced around each other for the best part of the morning. Iris got a plaster on her wrist and was picked up by her daughter. Holly got caught up with a patient who needed to be closely watched as they waited for him to be admitted to the psychiatric unit.

At midday Daniel came out of the changing room to head for home and saw Holly sitting by the patient's trolley. She was reading a magazine while the patient slept.

'Still no bed for him?' Daniel checked.

'Another hour.'

She barely glanced up and Daniel, who was always so certain where woman were concerned, was less so now.

He didn't know what he wanted, and even if he did, he wasn't sure that an offer to catch up would be welcomed by Holly.

She didn't look happy, when Holly always had, and Daniel was sure he had contributed to that.

'Daniel?' Kay was walking past. 'I've just been speak-

ing with Mr Edwards and he said to ask you if there's any chance you could stay on till five.'

'Sorry.' Daniel shook his head. 'I've already got plans.'

'What plans?' Kay busied herself with his business. 'A date?'

'You could say that,' Daniel answered without thinking, as Holly did all she could to stop her top lip from curling like the family Labrador's when someone reached for his bone.

'Have a nice Christmas, Holly,' Daniel said.

'I shall.'

She would!

Holly had spent way too long daydreaming about him.

When her shift ended and Holly raced to the department store where she'd been with Daniel a few weeks before, she found herself watching the glassblower for a little while.

Thanks to her own meddling, she had Daniel to buy a gift for.

Yes, while she would have loved to queue up and buy him a hand-blown Christmas decoration and have the elves write a letter, she had no idea what she'd have them write.

And it was far too expensive.

And it would be embarrassing to reveal just how much he meant to her.

Anyway, he probably wouldn't be back to claim his Secret Santa present, let alone deposit hers.

And so instead of pouring her heart out in a tiny letter that would never be read she headed to the men's floor and tried to decide on a more appropriate present for him.

Yes, she exceeded the strict Secret Santa budget, but not by a ridiculous amount. Holly bought him a lip balm

for when he went skiing. It was a very nice lip balm, in fact, and as close to his lips as she'd allow herself to get again.

It was a nice little gift—personal but not too personal, and useful as well.

It wasn't a gift from the heart—Daniel had made it very clear that her heart was something he didn't want.

CHAPTER SEVEN

DANIEL HEADED STRAIGHT from work to Maddie's school but his mind was on Holly.

She was nothing like his usual type yet he had liked her on sight and that feeling had not just remained, it had grown.

The more he knew her the more he wanted to know, and for someone who did his best not to get too involved it was the oddest feeling.

It was also a very new feeling and one he'd done his best not to properly examine.

He knew that she liked him. And that wasn't arrogance speaking, that was concern. After all, Daniel knew his own reputation.

Then he got out of the car and knew that it was time to focus on Maddie. He was cross with both his father and Amelia for not being here today.

His mother had always made the effort to be there for stuff like that, Daniel thought, and as he did so he suddenly halted.

All these years later memories seemed to be coming in and he felt floored anew by each and every one of them. As he took his seat in the audience he remembered standing on a stage with a towel on his head and

his father's tie, and looking out and seeing his mother nod and smile to him.

And so he did the same for Maddie as she came out.

She was dressed as an angel and had a silver tinsel halo and didn't stay in character at all because she smiled and waved to him when she was supposed to be being serious.

Daniel smiled and waved back.

It was actually rather good!

Joseph's front teeth were missing and there was a worrying moment when he nearly dropped baby Jesus and he and Maddie shared a little *yikes* look but apart from that it went well.

'Which one's yours?' a woman beside him asked and nodded towards the stage.

'The loud angel,' Daniel answered, so glad with his decision to delay his trip just so that Maddie could have a family member in the crowd.

Afterwards, in the playground, she ran to him.

'You were fantastic!' Daniel told her.

'I know.' Maddie beamed. 'Did you see when Thomas nearly dropped the baby?'

'I did.'

'Where are we going?' she asked with all the confidence of a sister who knew she would be getting an extra treat from her brother.

'I thought we might go to the movies.'

'Really?'

'Yes.' He told her what they would be seeing but instead of her eyes lighting up they were suddenly worried.

'I wanted to dress up when I saw that!'

'I thought that you might,' Daniel said, and handed her a bag he had brought with him. It was her princess

costume that he had picked up from Jessica, the nanny, on his way back from work.

He waited as Maddie dashed off to the facilities and came out a few minutes later in all her finery and wearing a tiara, with her friends all oohing and ahhing as she paraded about.

'I love it when you pick me up from school.' Maddie said as he took out the booster seat from the boot of his car.

'I enjoy it too.'

He did.

'Why don't you do it more often?' Maddie asked as she jumped onto the booster seat, which Jessica had also given him, and strapped herself in.

Daniel didn't answer.

It wasn't picking Maddie up from school that was the problem, it was dropping her off and avoiding being asked in.

Maddie didn't notice his silence. As they drove off she did the royal wave to her friends from the back of the car.

'If you marry a prince do you *definitely* become a princess?' Maddie asked.

'Not necessarily,' Daniel said. 'You might become a duchess or a countess...'

'What's the point, then?' Maddie sighed.

Oh, she was her mother's daughter, but, unlike Amelia, Maddie made him laugh.

She was so cute and had the same navy eyes as he had and, for a five-year-old, was very good company.

'How is school?' Daniel asked as he drove.

'I love it,' Maddie said. 'How is your work at the other hospital?'

'I love it too,' Daniel said.

He did.

He'd *liked* working at his old hospital. He had been through medical school there, had worked his way through the ranks and had a strong network of friends. Yet for some reason working at The Primary felt right.

It wasn't about Holly, he wasn't that shallow. It was maybe that at The Primary he wasn't Marcus Chandler's son. There were no expectations. If anything, given that he was a locum there was the expectation he'd need his hand held and then an element of surprise when he shone.

Back to focusing on Maddie!

Except, even as Daniel parked his car, he rather wished Holly was here, for he had no idea what to do. He knew this wasn't going to be a quiet evening at the movies but there was an endless stream of little girls all dressed the same as Maddie and the queue for tickets was incredibly long.

For a moment he considered taking out his phone and booking on line—the nice seats where you had food brought to you—but he knew that wasn't the treat his little sister needed. Instead, they chatted with several other families as they waited to buy their tickets.

'How old is she?' a woman asked.

'Five.'

'Are you giving her mum a rest?'

Daniel gave a noncommittal nod—it was clear that again the woman thought that Maddie was his child and he certainly wasn't about to enlighten a stranger, or tell her that giving Amelia a rest was far from being the reason he was here.

'Is it nice to be out with your dad?' The woman smiled at Maddie.

'I don't get to go out with my dad very often!' Maddie pouted and the woman gave Daniel a cool stare and then turned away, no doubt assuming it was an access visit.

'Maddie,' he warned.

'Well, it's true. Me and Daddy hardly ever go out, he's always working. And when we do...' She blew out a breath that sent her fringe flying into her tiara. 'I hate it when he takes me to his club, it's so boring.'

Daniel said nothing but he thought of the long afternoons he had spent at that bloody club, sitting with a colouring book and pencils as the adults carried on outside.

He had hated it too.

Still, they were a world away from a stuffy club this afternoon. Instead, it was all about a bucket of popcorn and two large icy drinks and just a couple of hours checking out of the world.

The place was bedlam.

Children were cheering and singing along to the film.

One little boy was so overexcited and overfed that he vomited.

'Should you say you're a doctor?' Maddie checked.

'I don't think his mum needs a doctor to work out what's wrong.'

Maddie smiled and got back to enjoying the movie.

It was fun, it was light-hearted and it was exactly what big brother and little sister needed. All too soon though it was over and they were headed for home.

After a few hours of easy conversation as they sat in a line of traffic making its slow way out of the car park, suddenly Maddie was quiet.

'Are you tired?' Daniel asked looking in the rear-view mirror, where she stared ahead.

'No,' Maddie answered. And then, as only five-year-olds could, she asked a question. 'Why aren't you going to be there at Christmas?'

Daniel took a moment to answer. 'I'm going away on a trip, it's been planned for a long time.'

'But it's only ten more sleeps until Christmas…'

'Maddie!' His tone told her to be quiet and he sounded like his father so he changed tack. 'I don't know exactly when I'm leaving.'

But it wasn't just Christmas that was troubling her. 'I don't want you to go.'

She broke into noisy sobs and Daniel stared ahead, not really knowing how he felt himself, let alone what to say. He could point out that it was just for a year. But a year was for ever when you were five years old.

He wasn't about to change his plans because his little sister kicked up. He was thirty-two, for God's sake, he was hardly going to stick around because his father had decided to attempt to parent…

Only it wasn't about his father.

'I hardly see you any more,' Maddie said.

'We've been out tonight,' Daniel pointed out.

'Only because you're saying goodbye. I don't see you so much any more.'

Daniel hadn't seen much of Maddie for the first couple of years of her life.

He and his father had barely been speaking when Maddie had been born. Daniel didn't really approve of his father taking such a very young bride. In turn his father was furious that Daniel had decided he didn't want to be a surgeon. When Maddison had been born, he had been pretty much told to stay back and that Amelia and Maddison were his father's family now.

At first it had suited him fine. Daniel wasn't exactly into babies and he'd just dropped off a birthday present or stood at the christening and things. But then Maddison the baby had become Maddie the two-year-old, with a smile and a cheeky personality that had soon endeared her to him.

And she was his family now.

Daniel didn't want to be some distant figure so he had started to factor her more into his life.

Till last Christmas when Amelia had come on to him.

Daniel's intention had been to be as far away as humanly possible this Christmas, to just stay out of his father's life, only it wasn't proving that easy.

'Look,' he said as the car pulled up at the picture-perfect house. 'I don't know what my plans are yet. I've got a lot of things going on now, Maddie. Grown-up stuff.'

'I hate grown-up stuff.'

'So do I.'

He really did.

'Please can I see you for Christmas?'

Daniel wanted to be able to just say no. To go home and hop on the internet and choose a flight and hotel. He looked over at what had once been his family home and though there were few happy memories of his time there, it didn't have to be that way for Maddie.

No, he would not stay for long but, yes, he could drop in and make a five-year-old happy on Christmas Day.

'I'll come around on Christmas Day to bring your present.'

Maddie gave a little squeal and smile and then climbed down from her seat, which Daniel collected, along with her school uniform.

Jessica came to the door and Daniel explained they'd had a good time, but that Maddie had just got a bit teary on the way home.

'She doesn't want you to leave.' Jessica nodded.

'Well, I'll be there for a little while on Christmas Day.'

Jessica opened her mouth to say something and then changed her mind and just gave him a smile. 'That's good,' she said.

Both knew that he was just delaying the inevitable—Maddie was going to be very upset when it really came time for him to leave.

His phone buzzed as he got back into the car and it was the agency he had signed up with, offering him various shifts. He was about to decline and point out that he had finished up.

Yet, given to what he'd agreed to for Maddie, he was here for at least another week.

'Are you available to work Christmas Eve, nine a.m. until till four p.m., in Outpatients at The Primary Hospital?'

'No,' Daniel said.

'Well, there's a night shift on New Year's Eve at the Royal.'

'No, thank you!' His response was a little sarcastic. There was no way that he'd work a night on New Year's Eve, and especially not at the Royal, he had seen in way too many there. He was about to explain that he was no longer available when she offered him one more shift.

'Well, you can't blame me for trying. What about Christmas Eve in Emergency at The Primary?'

And maybe this shift was the one he had been holding out for and perhaps the reason he hadn't taken himself completely off the books.

'What time?' Daniel asked.

'Seven a.m. until four.'

Holly would be on that morning, Daniel knew.

But even though she sprang to mind first, it wasn't just Holly that drew him back to The Primary. He liked the department and vibe there. He thought of Mr Edwards and Kay who had come to see him a valued part of the team, and he wanted to know how Nora's husband was going.

There were worse places to spend Christmas Eve, Daniel reasoned.

One more shift and he could find out all that had been going on and see how Holly was doing and hopefully he could manage a much better goodbye than the tense, stilted farewell they had achieved today.

'I'll take it,' Daniel agreed.

And so, if he was to be working on Christmas Eve, it meant that he needed to shop and so on the Saturday before Christmas, possibly the busiest shopping day of the year, he found himself back in the department store he had been to with Holly.

If he was going to stick to the Secret Santa budget then here really wasn't the place.

Except he knew what to get Holly, and so Daniel spent three very long hours thinking of what to put in a tiny letter.

But where to start?

Given he was standing here weeks after the event, yes, it had been more than a one-night stand.

And yet he was leaving.

It was getting harder and harder to do that.

There was family, namely Maddie, who needed him, a potential consultant's position at The Primary, which he was coming to love.

And there was Holly.

Yet there was so much more that he needed to sort out. His whole life had been spent failing to live up to his father's expectations, and falling off the chosen path.

Daniel knew he needed to sort out what it was that he wanted, and to do that he needed to get away.

'Your turn.'

Daniel looked down at a very harried and angry-looking lady dressed as an elf.

'What do you want written?'

'I haven't…' Daniel could feel the impatience in the people behind him. It had been more than a three-hour wait and he hadn't yet made up his mind.

And then he decided and took a little seat and told the lady what he wanted to be written.

She started typing on her mini-keyboard.

'That's it?' she checked.

'That's it,' Daniel agreed.

'Anything else?' she checked, clearly less than impressed with Daniel's attempt at expressing himself.

'No.'

'Well, I think you can do better than that.'

'I wasn't made aware that the letters got graded,' Daniel told her.

'The elves have all been trained—'

'Stop!' Daniel said. 'We both know you're not a real elf.'

She pursed her lips but after a brief standoff finally she hit 'send'.

'You can move down the line and watch your letter arrive.'

'Thank you.'

Daniel moved along the line and waited by the magic chute, scarcely able to believe he was doing this. He pressed cynical lips together as he thought of the computer and printer beneath the festive arrangement and then out it came—his letter to Holly.

He was asked to verify that it was indeed his letter and Daniel peered through a magnifying glass and read it.

Despite the fake elf's misgivings, Daniel worried that it actually said too much…but he nodded in agreement and then watched the glassblower work his magic.

It had cost a fortune.

It wasn't the money, or the time it took to make it, it was the fact that it was the closest he had come to sharing what was in his heart.

It was stay or go.

And staying felt harder.

CHAPTER EIGHT

CHRISTMAS EVE HAD always been special to Holly, whether or not she was working. The last-minute preparations, the excitement and anticipation and a certain sense of panic all seemed to combine to make it a truly magical day.

Last year, finding out that her mother was so unwell had had meant that it had been busy and fraught rather than exciting.

This year…

Holly looked around the bedroom and there was no sense of panic because everything was already done. Her presents were all wrapped and under the tree, last night she had gone and got petrol and now all she had to do was load up the car, drive to work, do her morning shift and wait for that once familiar, excited feeling to arrive.

Last night, for the first time, she had let herself cry properly over Daniel.

Determined to just let it all out so she didn't rot up everyone's Christmas, Holly had had a very good cry over a man who…

What?

She couldn't be angry because he had done nothing wrong. Daniel had been open and honest from the start. It was she who had taken it all too seriously and had kept

looking for deeper meanings to everything. And so she had cried because she was simply sad that he was leaving.

Possibly he had already gone.

Half-heartedly she opened up number twenty-four on her Advent calendar and tried not to remember the time she and Daniel had done the same in this very bed.

It was a very nice-looking truffle, and when she bit into it there was a decadent shot of chocolate mousse.

Holly smiled because it was true—chocolate *always* helped.

A bit.

And there could be a chance that she would still see Daniel. Maybe he'd stop by with her Secret Santa present today, Holly thought, because there had been nothing under the tree at work last night.

And then she stopped.

Holly just stopped with hoping and wishing that things could be different between herself and Daniel and decided that she was being greedy and asking for too much. Last year, despite a rather dire diagnosis, she had prayed for a Christmas miracle and that her mother would still be here next year.

Esther was.

And so Holly got out of bed and showered and pushed all dark thoughts aside and refused to give her favourite time of the year over to a man who refused to embrace it or even bother to celebrate it.

Holly pulled on black jeans and boots and a red jumper for the commute to work. Her hair was particularly wild this morning but she just ran her fingers through the curls and decided to tie it back once she got to work. Red lipstick might be a bit much for the emergency department

but it went with red earrings that flashed and she *refused* to be miserable today.

It was Christmas Eve after all!

Daniel wasn't in the least miserable.

He woke early and found that he was still looking forward to his shift at The Primary.

Breakfast was coffee, along with the most amazing chocolate truffle that he had ever tasted. Once showered and dressed he went and got Holly's present from the cupboard where it sat beside Maddie's and also presents for both his father and Amelia.

It was looking a little more like Christmas in his flat than it ever usually did.

But even if he was in a good mood Daniel spent the drive to work worrying that the present he had got for Holly was far too much and she might end up reading more into it than there was.

Still, he wanted her to have it, even if it just served as a nice memory of the wonderful night they had spent.

It had meant something.

She finished at midday, Daniel knew. That meant he could give it to her on her way out.

But even so...

He'd play it by ear, Daniel decided as he parked in the staff car park and got out. He had a small satchel that held his laptop and things and he placed the decoration carefully in there and went to make his way over to Emergency.

'Daniel!' The shout went up almost as soon as he'd got out of his car. He'd know that voice anywhere and he turned to see Kay frantically waving and standing next to Holly.

'We need a hand,' Kay called out to him in urgent tones.

'Okay.' He nodded.

'Hurry!' Kay called, and Daniel moved faster, wondering if someone had fainted or, from the way Kay was urging him, been run over, or...

'What?' he asked when he got there to find that nothing seemed amiss.

'I don't think Holly should leave all her family's presents in the car in case they're pinched, so if you could help us to carry them in...'

'I thought someone was hurt!' Daniel scolded.

'Why would you think that?' Kay asked as she handed him several Christmassy-looking bags that were all crammed to the brim with gifts. 'I just don't want to be late.'

He and Holly smiled and it was the first time that they had shared a proper smile since, well, since that night and the morning after.

Things had been awkward between them but felt a little less so today.

'How's Paul?' he asked as they started to walk.

'Don't ask.' Kay shook her head but Daniel wasn't going to be fobbed off.

'I just did!'

Holly answered for Kay. 'They're going to try and get him off the ventilator this morning. If not, he'll have to go to Theatre for a tracheostomy. He's been very up and down but mainly down.'

'It's been more than three weeks,' Kay sighed.

And both Holly and Daniel looked ahead because, yes, it had been a little more than three weeks since their night together also.

Hope was fading for all concerned.

'We'll put them in my office.' Kay suggested.

'Okay.' Holly nodded. 'I'll drop these off and then go back for the last lot.'

'There's more?' Daniel checked.

'Yep.'

'Give me those,' he said to Holly, unable to believe just how many presents she had. 'Go back and get the rest.'

Holly passed all her bags and parcels to him and Daniel staggered inside. Kay dropped the few she was carrying by her desk and then dashed off to grab a quick drink before handover, and Daniel realised that he suddenly had a chance to hide the decoration he had bought for the Secret Santa.

He went into his satchel and took out her gift.

It was too much, Daniel knew, and would cause loads of gossip if she opened it in front of everyone as she would surely know, straight away, that it was from him.

Yet he wanted her to have it and he wanted her to know how he felt.

But only once he had gone.

And now he could see the way to do just that, and so he slipped it into a bag that had a picture of a smiling snowman on it. So Holly! he thought as he headed for the staffroom.

'Did you bring your Secret Santa gift?' Kay checked, and Daniel pulled a face to indicate that he had forgotten.

'Oh, come on, Daniel,' Kay said. 'I'll see if I've got something you can put out.'

There was time for only a very quick drink but they all took it.

'Morning,' Trevor said, placing a beautifully wrapped present under the fake Christmas tree in the staffroom.

'And a delicious, delicate chocolate mousse truffle morning it is,' Kay said, and everyone laughed.

Daniel included.

They actually made him laugh, Daniel thought.

They found the happy in the smallest things and then watered it till it grew.

'That Advent calendar should be illegal.' Daniel joined in the conversation. 'I've been to three discount stores now but they've all sold out.' He looked up to see that Holly had come in.

'We're all worried,' she said.

'Worried? About what?'

'That the same work-experience student that made the ones on the fifteenth was let loose again and that the big day shall disappoint.'

'It never disappoints,' Kay said.

Holly, as she glanced under the Christmas tree and saw that Daniel hadn't added to the pile, rather thought that this year it might!

'So this is your last shift?' Kay asked Daniel as they all headed into the kitchen to drop off their mugs before their shift started. 'He's like that rock star...what's-his-name?'

'I have no idea,' Holly muttered as she rinsed her mug.

'The one who keeps doing his sell-out farewell tour and then a year later comes back and does it all over again.'

Kay allocated the staff and Holly was to work in the main section, which was where Daniel would mainly be, unless he had to go into Resus.

Holly was conflicted.

Though she had thought she wanted to see him, now that he was here it was proving hard.

Happy!

Holly kept reminding herself that it was Christmas Eve and that soon she'd be on the much-awaited and hard fought-for drive home!

Yay!

The patient who had just arrived, though, looked as grumpy as she felt.

'Leave me alone,' he told the paramedics as he was moved over onto the trolley. 'I don't want to be here!'

Holly had already gathered that.

Albert—he refused to give his surname or his date of birth—was homeless and had been found collapsed in a doorway. It was unclear how long he had been unconscious. The paramedics explained that the shopkeeper who had called for an ambulance had said he was used to him being there when he closed up at night.

He was usually awake by morning and told to move on.

They just hadn't been able to wake him this morning but he had sat up when the paramedics had arrived and insisted that he was fine. Albert had tried to get up and walk off but had been unable to do so and had finally agreed to come to hospital and be seen.

He was cantankerous, and very, very unkempt, with wild white hair and sore, cracked skin, and he refused to get undressed. More worrying than his appearance was a deep cough and a tinge of purple to his lips and tongue.

Holly checked his oxygen saturation, which was rather low so she slipped on some nasal prongs to deliver a low dose of oxygen as she took his temperature.

'You've got a fever.'

He nodded.

'Let me help get you into a gown so that the doctor can examine you.'

'I don't want you cutting my clothes.' He was coughing and wheezing but finally he allowed Holly to start removing layer upon layer of clothes.

First a coat, then a jumper, beneath that a jacket and then another shirt.

Kay came in and helped with his boots and bottom half.

It was always a bit of a feat to undress the homeless, especially in winter.

Soon, though, it was all bagged into two large plastic bags that Holly put under his trolley. Albert held onto a small leather bag and refused when Holly offered to lock it up in the hospital safe for him.

'You're not touching this!'

So Holly didn't.

And neither did she get very far with all the questions that needed to be asked and forms that needed to be filled in. He didn't want to reveal even his surname, let alone his next of kin.

'Is there anyone I can let know you are here?' Holly asked.

He gave a derisive laugh.

'Do you have any medical history that we need to know about?'

Albert didn't answer, and neither did he let Holly put in an IV or take bloods. All he wanted to do was to be left alone to sleep. Soon enough Daniel came into examine him.

Albert was more responsive to Daniel's questions than he had been to Holly's and he did let him listen to his chest.

'How long have you had this cough for?'

'It's been bad for a couple of days.'

'You've got quite a high temperature,' Daniel commented, and Albert nodded.

'I've had that since last night,' Albert said. 'I got the

shakes and I couldn't get warm but I think I was burning up.'

'Okay,' Daniel said, and he helped him lie back on the pillows and had a feel of his stomach, and though he tried to talk to him Albert didn't really communicate.

'I'm going to take some blood and then get an IV started,' Daniel said. 'We'll get a chest X-ray…' He went through it all but Albert just lay back. 'You can have some breakfast while you're waiting to go around, it's a bit of a wait.'

'I don't want breakfast.'

'Well, a cup of tea…'

'I don't want anything.'

Daniel could see that he was markedly dehydrated. The IV he was putting in would take care of that but he was more concerned with his lethargy.

'Is there anything else going on, Albert?'

'Everything's fine!' Albert's response was sarcastic and Holly watched as instead of leaving Daniel remained.

'How long have you been on the streets?'

'Long enough,' Albert said, but then he opened up a little. He had lived rough, on and off, for eighteen years. 'Sometimes I stay at a hostel and I was at a halfway house once for a few weeks but it didn't work out.'

He relied on several charities and soup kitchens for some meals and had to beg for help with the rest and he didn't want to see a social worker.

'I just want my chest sorted out and then I'll be gone.'

'How old are you, Albert?' Daniel asked, and though he had refused to answer Holly, now he did.

'Seventy-two.'

'And winter's barely got going,' Daniel said, and Holly saw Albert close his eyes at the thought of the prospect

of another winter living rough but then he rallied and gave a shrug.

'It's not so bad.'

'Really?' Daniel checked, but Albert didn't answer. He just lay on his back and stared up at the ceiling as Daniel took some bloods and an IV was commenced.

'Would you like some breakfast?' Holly offered again once Daniel had gone, but again Albert shook his head.

'Leave me alone.'

The wait for X-Ray was a long one but finally he was back in the unit and sure enough he had lower lobe pneumonia along with a few more chronic issues.

He was started on antibiotics and as Holly added them to his IV she tried to engage him.

Albert was having none of it.

'I'm going to call the kitchen and see if they can send you something hot to eat,' Holly said, removing the untouched sandwiches that she had put out for him. 'I'll be back soon to do your obs.'

Daniel came in just as Holly left.

'She's a chirpy little thing, isn't she?' Albert grumbled.

'You could say that,' Daniel agreed. 'The admitting doctors will be down to see you, though it may be a while, but you're going to need to stay in.'

Often patients like Albert declined admission or set a very strict timeline for treatment, such as a few hours, but Albert nodded.

If anything, he seemed relieved that he would be staying in.

'How are you doing?' Daniel asked.

'Still coughing.'

'You shall be for a while,' Daniel said. 'I meant, apart from your chest?'

'I'm just…' Daniel waited patiently and finally Albert elaborated. 'I'm tired.'

It was as if everything was summed up in that short statement and Daniel knew he was hearing the very truth.

Tired of being sick.

Tired of a hard life on the streets.

And now that he had admitted just how tired he was it was almost as if he had given up because he lay back defeated.

'Albert, while you're waiting to be seen, I'm going to call the duty social worker.'

'What's she going to do?'

'Perhaps she can get the ball rolling on some accommodation for when you're discharged.'

'I'm not going to another of those hostels. There are too many rules.'

'Albert, why won't you let us help you?'

'Because I don't want your help.'

Daniel wasn't so sure that was true.

'So do you want me to ring the social worker?' he checked.

'Call her if you want to.' Albert shrugged. 'I don't know what she's going to be able to do, though.'

Daniel called the duty social worker from the nurses' station, where the radio was playing Christmas carols and there was a plate of star-shaped gingerbread out. Most of the nurses were now wearing tinsel, but for Daniel it all felt a long way from Christmas.

Actually, it felt like every Christmas he had known.

'Nora!' Daniel looked up as a flushed-faced Nora came in.

'I'm looking for Kay,' she said, and then promptly burst into tears.

He paged Kay, who was dealing with a domestic violence incident, and led a teary Nora around to Kay's office.

'Nora…' Kay rushed in.

'He's talking!' Nora said through her tears. 'He knows where he is and everything.'

Daniel blinked.

He had been absolutely sure that Paul must have died and from Kay's gaping mouth she must have been thinking the same. But it would seem instead that Nora had been holding things in all these weeks and now that the news was good she could finally allow some of her emotions out.

'They're thrilled with him,' she sobbed.

Daniel left them to it.

Who would have thought?

Not he.

He walked past the cubicle and there was Albert, just lying there dozing, but he opened his eyes as Daniel approached.

'I spoke with the social worker. Now that she knows you're being admitted—'

'She'll see me on the ward.' Albert knew the drill and finished Daniel's sentence for him.

Daniel nodded. With public holidays and a very heavy workload at this time of the year, they both knew it might take a while for Albert to be seen.

'You'll be here over Christmas,' Daniel told him. 'Is there anyone you'd like us to inform?'

'I doubt they'd want to know.'

It was an opening and the first hint of the life that Albert had left behind.

'Have you ever been in touch with your family?'

'No.' Albert shook his head. 'Well, I used to send a card to Emily, my great-niece, she's also my god-daughter, but

I wasn't well one year and I didn't manage to post it, then it seemed too late by the next.'

Daniel could see how it had happened. Oh, their lives were different in many ways but he could easily see how a couple of years of no contact might then make it hard to get back in touch.

And to know if you would even be welcome if you did.

'How old is she?' Daniel asked.

'Emily?' Albert checked, and Daniel nodded. 'She was two the last time I saw her. She'd be twenty now, I doubt she'd even know my name.'

'What about her parents?'

'Dianne is her mother,' Albert explained. 'She was my late sister's daughter. She's a chirpy thing too, like your young nurse. Dianne was good to me. Everyone took sides during the divorce but she always stayed back from doing that. I wasn't well.' He tapped the side of his head to indicate mental-health issues. 'Dianne always invited me over for Christmas but I'd always mess it up and start a row.'

'Why?'

'So that I could leave,' Albert admitted. 'I was embarrassed. I used to be a geography teacher. I missed out on head of department…they said I wasn't up to the responsibility but instead of proving them wrong, I proved them right and walked out. My wife had had enough by then and, looking back, I can't blame her. I lost my marriage, my job, everything really…' He shook his head. 'It's history.'

'I thought you said you taught geography.'

The silly joke made Albert smile but then Daniel watched as a very independent but very lonely man gave in then and started to cry.

It was very sad to watch but Daniel did so, and pulled

out some paper hand cloths from the dispenser so that Albert could blow his nose.

Holly came in to the sound of his tears but saw that Daniel was in there and left.

'Have you ever spoken with your wife?' Daniel asked when Albert had finished.

'I was admitted to hospital once when the divorce wasn't yet through,' Albert said. 'They called her but she told them that she wanted nothing more to do with me. I can't blame her for that.'

Daniel knew that the social worker would go through it all with Albert but that could be a few days away and, Daniel guessed, by then Albert could well have taken up his things and gone.

'Have you thought of calling your niece?' Daniel asked.

'Every day,' Albert admitted, and he went into the small bag that he would not let go of and took out a clear plastic bag. On it was a piece of paper and in very neat handwriting there was a number and his niece's full name and address. 'I don't know what to say if I call.'

Neither did Daniel.

Nearly two decades on, what did you say?

'They might have moved...' Daniel said as he looked at the address, but Albert shook his head.

'They're still there,' Albert said.

'How do you know?'

'Sometimes I walk past. There's a "For Sale" sign up, though. They shan't be there for long.'

It was now or never.

'Do you want me to try and call for you?' Daniel offered.

He rather hoped that Albert would shake his head. Daniel really did, because he didn't want to walk back

into the cubicle and have to tell Albert that his family had terminated the call, as often happened in situations like these.

There was a lot of hurt on both sides, no doubt.

But instead Albert nodded. 'I'd like that,' he said. 'Please.'

Daniel took a few more details and as he walked out, Holly was walking toward him, carrying a tray. Her hair was piled up high and her smile was bright, if a bit forced, when she saw him. 'I got the canteen to send Albert up an early lunch.'

'Good,' Daniel said. 'I'm just about to call his niece, they haven't been in touch for eighteen years. I think Albert's hoping to resume contact.'

He watched as her smile faded. Holly would know only too well that the chances of this call ending well weren't great.

Daniel held the cubicle curtain open for Holly and she walked in with the tray. 'I've got a nice potato and leek soup for you, Albert, and it actually smells rather amazing.'

'You have it, then.'

Holly arranged the tray on a table and pushed it towards him but Albert wasn't interested. Instead, he lay back on the pillows and closed his eyes and wondered what the doctor would say when he returned.

Daniel wasn't hopeful.

He dialled the number that Albert had given him. It had been many years and given the little history Albert had told him Daniel wasn't sure that he'd be speaking to the right person, let alone that the call would be welcome, or that anyone would even pick up.

Someone did. 'Hi!'

'Hello,' Daniel responded to the cheery voice. 'I was wondering if I could speak with Dianne Eames.'

'She's not here at the moment.' The voice was that of a young woman and she sounded busy. 'Who's calling?'

'It's Dr Daniel Chandler from the accident and emergency department at The Primary Hospital.'

That tended to get a response!

'One moment…' She must have covered the phone but Daniel heard the young woman call for her mother and a few moments later another woman came to the phone.

'Dianne Eames speaking.'

She sounded brusque and impatient but, Daniel knew, that was often the way to cover fear.

'Is everything okay with Vince?' she asked.

'We had a patient admitted to us this morning. Albert Marlesford…'

There was a long stretch of silence.

'How is he?'

Daniel had to think for a moment before answering. 'He's been admitted with pneumonia. But, I'm not sure if you're aware, he's been living on the streets for some time.'

'Yes, I'm more than aware. That was his choice.'

'I understand that.'

'We tried to keep in touch with him, he used to send the odd card or letter and I'd go out looking for him…' There was a tense, inward breath that was followed by the sound of tears. 'He always managed to mess up Christmas every year, you could guarantee it!'

Given that it was Christmas Eve, Daniel thought for a moment that the message was clear—Albert wouldn't be messing up this one—but it would seem he had misinterpreted, Daniel realised, as Dianne continued to speak.

'Now he's managed another. I guess there won't be turkey at the table tomorrow.'

'Sorry?'

'I was just on my way to pick it up but that can wait... He's at The Primary, you say...'

It was then that Daniel realised that Dianne was saying that she was on her way in. That, even after eighteen years of no contact, Albert's niece would drop everything, even plans for tomorrow's dinner, to come and see him on Christmas Eve.

'Dianne,' Daniel said. 'To be honest, I think by the time you've got your turkey he might be a little more ready to receive visitors.' He decided it might be better for Albert if he explained things now. 'It might be nicer for him to be a bit more presentable when you meet.'

'He was always too proud for his own good,' Dianne said, and then thought for a moment. 'Can you tell him that I'll be in to see him this afternoon...? Hold on a moment.' Daniel waited and there was the sound of chatter in the background. 'Can you let him know that Emily will be in to see him too?'

She gave Daniel her mobile number and asked that she be called immediately if there was any change.

And that was it.

The phone call ended but instead of going immediately to tell Albert, Daniel sat for a long moment staring at the phone.

He had expected a cool reception, even to have the phone hung up on him, or at best to be bombarded with questions. Dianne hadn't required an immediate update on all the missing years, all she had needed to know was where Albert was, to be there for him.

Daniel walked over to his cubicle and saw that Holly was still in there, trying to persuade him to at least try

and have a little something to eat, but Albert ignored her and simply closed his eyes.

'I just spoke with Dianne,' Daniel said, and he saw that Albert's eyes remained closed, no doubt bracing himself for rejection. 'She's going to come in a bit later with Emily.'

Then Albert's eyes opened.

'She said that?' Albert checked, and Daniel nodded and he watched as Albert's face broke into a smile.

'She was just on her way to pick up the turkey but she offered to come straight in...'

It was then that Albert started fretting. 'I can't see her looking like this....' How he looked was one of the many reasons that Albert hadn't knocked on his niece's door. 'I smell...'

'We can sort all that, Albert.' Holly spoke then. 'In fact, you get an early Christmas present!'

There was always stash of clothes in Emergency and Kay kept them in the same cupboard that she kept Christmas gifts. The clothes came mainly in the form of donations from staff and fundraisers and they were very valued, especially in situations such as this.

As well as clothes for Christmas, Kay ensured there were always presents, for the children, for the overnight patients, for people such as Albert, and she shopped throughout the year just for situations such as this.

Holly went into the dark storeroom and turned on the light. First she went through the men's clothes and found some smart navy pyjamas that looked large enough for Albert. They weren't new, but they were very neat, and the colour wasn't faded and all the buttons were on. Then she went through the wrapped gifts—they were separate barrels for men, women and children, and the gifts were also labelled by age.

On the shelf was a stash of chocolate stockings, already wrapped for anyone who might have been forgotten, but there were more pressing things than that needed for Albert today.

His early present was soap, deodorant and a comb.

As well as a wash Holly gave him a tidy-up shave with eyebrows and ears thrown in!

'Well, look at you!' Kay said as Holly prepared to move Albert up to the ward. 'You're looking grand.'

'I'm feeling it,' Albert said.

Okay, he was still rather rough around the edges and Kay looked at his feet, which were peeking out from the blanket. They would be attended to by the podiatrist at a later stage but for now he got an extra present of fluffy socks and he was certainly ready to meet his niece and great-niece again.

Holly smiled as she walked into the acute medical unit. It was far more elaborately decorated than Emergency—in fact, they had won the competition for Best Decorations.

Emergency hadn't even placed.

'Good morning, Albert,' a cheerful male nurse said. 'Actually, it's almost afternoon. You're just in time for lunch.'

'Good,' Albert huffed. 'I'm starving.'

'Have they been keeping you hungry down there?' The nurse smiled at Holly, who rolled her eyes. Her whole morning had been spent trying to get Albert to eat. 'We've put you in a four-bedded ward...' He gave directions to Holly. 'Bay Six.'

Bay Six had three other gentleman in it. Two were asleep but one nodded and said hello to Albert, who gave a cheery wave back.

'Thank you,' Albert said, once she had him settled in bed. 'Are you working over Christmas?'

'I'm just about to finish,' Holly said. 'Though I'll be back tomorrow night.'

'Well, thank you again.'

It was the nicest note to end her shift on. It was just so lovely to see Albert tucked up in bed and knowing that he'd be taken care of over Christmas. Holly made her way down to Emergency rather quickly. It was already after midday and she still had to get all her parcels out of Kay's office.

She would not be saying goodbye to Daniel, Holly had already decided. She had said it too many times, and on each occasion it hurt a little more. Anyway, he was busy with a patient and that suited Holly just fine. She loaded up the gifts and chatted to Kay, who was taking a quick break in her office.

'Have a wonderful Christmas, Holly,' Kay said. 'Now, don't go breaking your neck to get here by nine tomorrow night. I can stay back for an hour or so.'

'I should be fine.' Holly smiled. She had her presents piled up on a wheelchair and was ready to make a quick exit.

There was just one more thing, Kay reminded her.

'Did you get your present from under the tree?'

There hadn't been one there for her on her coffee break and Holly had tried to pretend that it didn't matter.

'Oh!' Holly feigned surprise, as if it was the furthest thing from her mind. 'I'll go now.'

She left the wheelchair with Kay and headed round to the staffroom and tried not to get excited but, unlike on her coffee break when she'd last checked, there was now a present under the tree.

But it was in the shape of a Christmas stocking but, worse, it was the wrapped in the same paper as the ones in the storeroom.

Holly knew with a sinking feeling that, not wanting her to receive nothing, Kay had stepped in.

Deep down she had known full well that Daniel would forget.

Yet she had hoped he wouldn't.

And even now, as she opened the little attached card, she hoped for something that might indicate she was more than an afterthought.

That was all she was, Holly realised as she read the writing.

Holly Jacobs
Happy Christmas

Daniel could not have cared less if he'd tried to.

Don't cry here, Holly told herself, just make it out to the car. And so she came out of the staffroom and walked around to the department wearing a big smile and added her parcel to the pile on the wheel chair.

'What did you get?' Kay asked as Holly walked past her office.

'A chocolate stocking.'

'That's nice.' Kay smiled.

Had she not known that it was from Kay's secret stash then it might have been a perfectly nice gift.

But instead of nice it spoke volumes to Holly.

Holly said her goodbyes and headed off but as she came out of Emergency and to the main hospital entrance she was just in time to see Daniel walking back from wherever he had been.

'Have a great Christmas, Holly.'

'And you.'

And this was goodbye, Daniel knew.

He was staying just long enough to see Maddie for Christmas and sort out the tenants but then he would be gone.

And he was not coming back here again.

This was hurting him too.

'It's been great working with you,' Daniel said.

Seriously? Holly thought.

We had sex in my hall and that's the best you can do?

She pushed the wheelchair and kept on walking but then turned around and Daniel did too and they stared at each other. She could not believe he would just let her walk away so easily, that their final goodbye was a thank you for being a good colleague.

And so, when she should have left it at that, Holly revealed a little of what she held inside. 'A chocolate stocking?'

'Sorry?'

'You couldn't even be bothered to go to the gift shop. Instead, you had to get something from the store cupboard to give to me. I think I deserved a bit more than that!'

For a moment he stood there but then, remembering the rules she had told him about Secret Santa, Daniel frowned.

'How did you know it was from me?'

'Because...' Holly said, and then wished that she'd never started this.

Oh, she wished, how she wished that she'd never swapped around their names in the first place.

An incredulous smile spread over his face and he

pointed to her as realisation dawned. 'You rigged Secret Santa.'

'I did not! I was organising it so I had to know who got—'

'Liar,' Daniel broke in. 'You rigged it. Why would you do that?'

'Because...' Holly said for the second time, only this time she continued to speak. Actually, this time she made an already bad situation worse! 'I was hoping to find out how you felt.'

'Felt?'

'About us,' Holly said.

'Us?'

'Not *us*, in that sense,' she hurriedly amended. 'Just that it felt like more than a one-night stand.'

She should be shot on the spot for admitting it, Holly knew, she should take her heart right off her sleeve and pop it back in her chest.

Holly couldn't roll like that with him, though. Somehow with Daniel she was her honest worst.

'What do you mean by more?' Daniel asked.

Holly decided that silence really was her best defence now.

More meant more!

She had glimpsed *them*.

Oh, she would work on her New Year's resolutions and become all aloof and sophisticated next year, but there was still a few days until then.

'Holly,' he calmly stated. 'We had a great night. Can't you just enjoy it for what it was?'

There was a chill coming up the corridor as the automatic doors slid open and closed. The floor was wet as people trudged in with wet shoes and dripping umbrellas and romance was, for Holly, officially dead.

'Enjoy your gap year,' Holly said.

'Gap year?'

'Isn't that what it is?' Holly jeered. Well, she attempted a jeer, but she wasn't very good at being mean. 'Isn't that what teenagers do when they want to sort themselves out?'

Daniel, on the other hand, was very good at being mean and he thought of her love of winter weddings and the dreamy look that came over her at times. He was standing looking at a woman who would rig Secret Santa to find out how he *felt*. And, far from telling her that he was feeling far too much of late, instead Daniel's words tumbled out on a sneer. 'Say hi to him for me.'

'Who?'

'Mr Holly,' Daniel said, and basically accused her of being on husband watch. 'Clearly that's what you're looking for. It was supposed to be a bit of fun.'

Fun!

And with that word he did Holly a huge favour, for he snapped any lingering hope that remained, like an icy twig in the park.

'Well, have a *fun* Christmas,' Holly said, and did her best, with a rickety wheelchair piled high with gifts, to stalk off.

And he let her go.

Daniel watched her walk towards the car park and told himself that he was well shot of some stalker who would rig Secret Santa and a woman who looked for deeper meaning in everything…

Then as he walked back into the department and as the world carried on around him, he regretted how they had ended.

Yes, there was another gift for her that she would find

perhaps later tonight, but there would be no chance of them speaking by then.

He couldn't even drop by her flat after his shift to apologise as she was heading straight to her parents'.

Daniel was very aware that most of his thirty-two Christmases had been ruined somehow and now he'd just gone and ruined Holly's.

'Let it go,' he said under his breath, and picked up a patient file.

He couldn't let it go, though.

'Where are you going?' Kay asked as he put down the file and went to walk off.

'I'll be back in a few moments.'

Yes, he really should have let it go, Daniel thought as he strode through the car park. It was freezing outside and pouring with rain and he was just wearing scrubs and no doubt he'd already missed her.

But he hadn't.

There was Holly, sitting in the driver's seat of her car, and she was hunched over the steering wheel and in floods of tears.

'Holly…' He knocked on the window and she looked up and in horror saw who it was, and got back to clutching the steering wheel and started crying some more.

It felt to Holy like humiliation heaped on humiliation, especially when he chose to be nice and came around the other side and climbed into the passenger seat.

She heard his sigh, felt his awkwardness and smelt the delicious scent of him.

'I am not crying about you.' Holly told him the truth, or part of it—for she was not solely crying about him, more the utter disaster of her Christmas Eve. 'My car won't start…' She turned the key to show that this time she wasn't lying and it emitted a terrible sound.

'Don't flood the engine…' he warned, as it choked and gasped its last.

'There's a lot that needs fixing,' Holly said. 'I've been putting it off.'

She knew she couldn't complain about her car breaking down. It was terribly old and had been on its last legs for the last six months but it had always seen her safely home.

Till now.

'I have to get home, though…' She was seriously panicking—the trains were a disaster on Christmas Eve and she had no idea how she'd manage getting all the presents home. 'I can't miss it. I'll call a taxi…'

'Holly…' Daniel just didn't get it. Yes, he was aware that he had little family to speak of but Holly was at the other extreme. If she had five kids waiting for their mother he might understand more. 'These things happen. A taxi, if you can even get one to agree to take you, would cost a small fortune. As well as that you'd then have to get back for tomorrow night and there are no trains on Christmas Day.'

'I can borrow my mum's car to get back.'

'Can't you just miss it?'

'We're not all like you,' Holly said. It was far easier to carry on being mean. 'Some of us want to be with our family at Christmas.' And then she stopped gripping the steering wheel and leant back as the need to score points faded and the truth came in. 'My mum's not very well…'

She'd told him that, Daniel remembered. She just hadn't revealed how sick her mother was.

Now she did.

'Why didn't you tell Kay?'

'She knows,' Holly said. 'Last year I had both Christmas and New Year off. Mum's actually doing better

lately. This was supposed to be the real happy Christmas after the fake happy Christmas last year. To tell the truth, it's all a bit strained at home, Mum's become rather too used to getting her own way.' Holly took a breath. 'She's going to have to understand that these things happen…'

'Will she, though?'

'Probably not.' Holly actually smiled and then wiped all the tears away with the sleeve of her coat and looked over to where he sat and saw that he was wearing only thin scrubs and that his hair was all wet from the rain.

'Why did you come out?' Holly asked him. 'Did I forget to sign something?'

'No. I came out because I hated that we ended things on a row.'

'So do I.'

'I think we can both do better than that,' Daniel said. 'Why don't I drive you home? I don't finish till four but—'

'I can't ask you to do that.'

'You didn't ask,' he pointed out.

'It's Christmas Eve…' Holly flailed, yet he was calm.

'Hence the emergency.'

And it was an emergency, at least it was to Holly.

'How far away do you live?' Daniel asked.

'Three hours on a good day. Four if it's…' she looked out of the window and saw the sheets of rain and factored in the Christmas traffic. 'It might even be five.'

'That's okay, but I won't stay,' he warned.

'I know.'

'Just let's get you home.'

'Thank you.'

'Do we have to carry all the presents back into the department?' Daniel asked, and Holly laughed.

'No.'

It was decided that they would lock them up in his rather more secure car and Holly would take the underground home.

'I'll come and pick you up as soon as I finish.'

'Thanks.'

'Go and eat some chocolate,' Daniel said.

'Oh, I shall.' She held up the blasted chocolate stocking and they both shared a smile. 'I've got plenty after all.'

Holly, as she headed for home, was thrilled with the thought of a few more hours with him because Daniel was right...

They deserved better than to end it on a row.

CHAPTER NINE

DANIEL WORKED THROUGH the afternoon and at two he took a call from the acute medical unit.

'What time did Albert Marlesford's family say that they'd be here?'

'His niece had some shopping to do,' Daniel explained.

'I told him that she must be busy and to stop fretting.'

Daniel ended the call and told his cynical self to be quiet.

Of course Dianne would be in, he had spoken to her himself.

He was worried for the old boy, though.

'Shouldn't you be off?' Kay checked a while later, and Daniel glanced at the time.

'I should be and I am,' Daniel said. 'And this time it's for good. It's been an absolutely pleasure to work with you Kay.'

It really had been.

So much so that once he'd got his head sorted out, Daniel was wondering if, maybe a year or so from now, he'd be back—and not as a locum. But there was too much going on in his mind right now to voice very tentative thoughts.

And neither would it be fair to Holly to say he was considering returning someday.

'Don't forget your present,' Kay reminded him.

He went to the tree and there was a little parcel wrapped in silver with a curly bow. If Holly had rigged the Secret Santa so that he would get her name then presumably she had chosen a present for him.

He checked the attached card and saw her loopy handwriting.

'Open it,' Kay said.

'Later.'

He didn't go straight to the car; instead, he took his cynical self up to the acute medical unit and found that Albert's relatives still hadn't arrived.

Albert was comfortable, they said.

Sleeping.

And that was surely better than the streets but for a moment there Daniel had entered a world where families reunited.

After that he walked out to the car. It was already starting to get dark and he really should press on. Yet he sat for a moment in the driver's seat and wondered what she had bought and what had been written on the card but, rather than find out now, Daniel put it in his glove box. This journey had the potential to be awkward enough, without finding out that she'd bought him a little Holly & Daniel snow globe or...

Well, he didn't possess much imagination in the romantic Christmas present department. Still, he would guess that if she was *that* upset about the stocking, well, there was going to be something rather special for him in that silver parcel.

He'd open it tomorrow, Daniel decided. He'd open it when she was safely home.

Safely, because he liked her.

More than he cared to admit to himself and certainly more than he dared to admit to Holly.

Of course she was confused, because so too was he. For the best part of a year Daniel had been planning for this trip and desperate to get away.

Now, though, it felt as if there were more and more reasons to stay.

Daniel pulled up outside her flat and did his best not to recall chasing her up the concrete stairs, and as he knocked on the door he tried not to remember them falling through it.

'Come in.' Holly beamed.

'I'd better not,' Daniel said. He really, given what had taken place there, didn't want to stand in the hall! 'The traffic sounds pretty bad.'

'Of course…' She was a little flustered. 'I'll be one moment.'

He stood on the doorstep and then realised that Holly was on the telephone and so, rather than being like his father who would sit in the car, pressing on the horn until everyone came out, he stepped in and waved a hand as if to say to take her time.

Holly headed into her bedroom, which was really her living room. She had the television on, he could see, though the sound was turned down.

'We're just leaving now,' he heard Holly saying. 'No, don't worry about that. I'll see you shortly.' Then another pause. 'Mum, I really do have to go. Daniel's already doing me a huge favour.' She came to the bedroom door and rolled her eyes. Clearly her mother thought there was a lot that had to be discussed between now and three hours' time when Holly would be there.

'Yes, I've got the cheese,' Holly said.

So, rather than drumming his fingers and appearing impatient, Daniel went through to a small lounge room and took a seat and listened to the neighbours shouting.

'Sorry about that,' Holly said as she came through to the rather cold lounge. 'The logistics of Christmas in my family. Honestly…' She blew out a breath and picked up a coat from the chair. 'I'm ready.'

'I'm not,' Daniel admitted. 'I'd love a drink.'

'Sure.' Holly said. 'Coffee?'

'Please.'

He followed her into the kitchen.

'Do you want something to eat?'

And usually he would say no, but he hadn't had lunch and, given that he had no intention of stopping on the drive to her home, it would be a long time until he'd be eating again.

'Thanks.'

She made toasted sandwiches. Turkey, Brie and cranberry.

'It's Christmas after all.'

They smelt delicious.

'Now I can see the end of my movie.'

It wasn't a plan to get him into the bedroom, Daniel knew, given that she practically lived there.

And so she flicked the television back on and it was one of those stupid movies that ran every Christmas.

'Holly,' Daniel said, 'even I know the ending.'

She just smiled and sat on the edge of the bed to eat her own toasted sandwiches while Daniel took a seat on a small chair, though, rather disconcerting for him was this sudden wish to lie down and open a bottle of wine and watch the movie and…

…spend Christmas in bed.

'I love this bit.' She turned up the sound on the movie

as they ate and even Daniel laughed, because it was cheesy and funny and it was just very, very nice to be here.

'Did Albert's family come and visit him?'

'Albert?' Daniel checked, and then shook his head. 'How would I know?'

'I thought they might have popped into Emergency, or that you might have...' She gave him a smile. 'I bet they're having a good old catch-up right now.'

Daniel didn't return her smile; instead, he stood.

'Come on, we'd better go.'

The traffic was hell and the car inched its way through the streets but finally they hit the motorway.

Then the car stopped inching its way.

It just sat in gridlocked traffic as both pretended not to notice it was now after six.

'What are your plans for tomorrow?' asked Holly, just trying to be polite.

'No definite plans,' Daniel said.

'Will you see your family?'

'I'll pop in for ten minutes.'

He briefly turned and saw her rapid blink and saw the wrestle as she tried not to judge.

'Things are a bit complicated at home,' he said, when usually he offered no reason.

Thankfully the traffic eased a little and for the next hour they made if not good then reasonable time.

The phone rang out in the car, making her jump as it came over the speakers, and she glanced at the dash.

Dad.

Daniel didn't answer the call.

Then five minutes later it happened again and she could feel the tension in him.

There were signs for a service station and guessing

he might want to speak to his father without having it broadcast over the speakers for her to hear Holly asked if they could stop.

'Holly…' He glanced at the time on the dashboard. 'We need to push on.'

'And I need the loo.'

He gritted his teeth as they pulled into the service station and Holly got out. 'Do you want anything?' she offered.

'To get there this year. Just hurry.'

He watched her disappear into the building and then realising he could call his father Daniel did so. He kept an eye out for Holly as he was connected and they briefly spoke.

'Amelia's trying to sort out numbers for dinner…'

Daniel let out a silent mirthless laugh. From the way his father described it Amelia was counting out potatoes and fretting as to whether she had enough, when, in truth, she'd just give the number expected for dinner to the maid.

And as he sat there he could well recall coming home from boarding school where Christmas preparations had been in full swing to a house where there were none.

His father had often worked and no matter how nice the nanny was, she would far rather be on the phone to her own family on Christmas Day than entertaining him.

And he remembered with clarity the loneliness of Christmas and he was so over the pretence and the farce of it all.

'I shan't be there for dinner,' he told his father. 'I'll drop by with Maddie's present but I really can't stay for long.'

'We'll be going to the club in the afternoon…'

Daniel opened his mouth to say something, but wasn't

sure it was his place. At least his father made some effort now, at least, for Christmas he tried to be home.

'When do you fly?'

'I still haven't booked,' Daniel admitted.

He didn't know if he wanted to go.

Holly was right.

Thirty-two was pretty old to be taking a gap year.

He was running and a little like Albert he was suddenly tired. 'I'll see you tomorrow,' Daniel said.

'Maddie wants to speak to you.'

'Tell Maddie I'll see her tomorrow,' Daniel told his father, because he could see Holly making her way back to the car. 'I have to go.'

Despite his telling Holly to hurry, she had taken the time to stop for refreshments and he had to reach out and open the door as she was carrying two take-away cups.

'Christmas coffee!' Holly smiled, handing him one of the cups and then climbing in.

'You find the Christmas in everything.'

'I do.'

He took a sip and pulled a face. 'What the hell is this?'

'Coffee and cinnamon, I think,' Holly said. 'And maybe a bit of nutmeg?' Then she got to the real reason she had taken so long. 'Did you call him?'

And one of the reasons she irked him and one of the reasons he liked her more than she knew was because of moments like this—Holly had done the polite thing, Daniel now realised. Guessing that he might not want her around while he spoke with his father, she had made a polite excuse to leave.

Then she had ruined her tact by asking if he had called him!

'Yes,' Daniel said. 'He just wanted to check on numbers for dinner.'

'Are you going?'

'No,' Daniel said as they again hit the motorway.

'I'm sure he'd love it if you came along...'

Daniel said nothing and Holly could sense he'd prefer it if she didn't either.

'I'll leave it,' she offered.

'Please do.'

He stared at the car registration in front of him and then at the wall of traffic ahead and, of course, Holly simply could not leave it.

'But surely at Christmas...'

'Holly.' Daniel turned. 'I didn't offer you a lift home to indulge in a cosy chat about my family situation. I don't need your take on it.'

'Friends talk...' Holly started, and then gave in. Who had even said they were friends?

She didn't even have his phone number and he had never asked for hers.

'I wonder when it will stop raining,' Holly said, and Daniel rolled his eyes at her attempt at conversation. 'Is that banal enough for you? We can talk like strangers at a bus stop.'

'Holly...'

'I mean, it's not as if we're even friends. You couldn't even be bothered to introduce me to your ex.'

He knew she was referring to Amelia.

'She's not my ex.'

Holly rolled her eyes. 'An old one-night stand, then.'

'I've never slept with her.'

'I don't believe you.'

'You don't have to believe me, Holly.' God, she had a nerve. 'I don't have to explain myself to you.'

He wanted to, though.

It had been excruciating in the department store and

it had been that way for Holly too and no doubt why she had decided to walk off.

'I know it was awkward for you at the shop…'

'It was awkward long before that,' Holly sighed. 'Maddie called three times when you were in the shower. Was she your date the other day?' When he didn't answer she stared out of the passenger window. 'Honestly, Daniel, I don't know how you juggle them all.'

Then again, he hadn't attempted to juggle or hide, Holly thought, he'd just listened to his messages while she'd sat there, pulling on her boots.

'Amelia, the woman you met that day is my stepmum.'

To her credit, Holly said nothing, not even a little shocked gasp. She just turned back to look at him.

'That date I had last week was with my sister, Maddie.'

'Maddie's your sister?'

'Yes, and she's five.'

'Why didn't you just say?'

'Because I find it awkward. When we're out everyone assumes that she's mine.'

'Is that why you're still here?' Holly asked, and looked at him.

'Yes, she wanted me to see her in the nativity play and she's getting upset about me going away.'

'You'd be like a rock star to her.'

Daniel nodded. 'It's not all one-way, she's actually very good company. We go to the movies and things but I don't really go over to the house.'

'Because you don't get on with your dad?' Holly frowned. 'Surely you can get past that for her sake?'

And then his phone rang again and she glanced at the dash.

Maddie.

'What's she doing up this late?' Daniel asked, though more to himself.

'It's Christmas Eve.' Holly answered anyway! 'She's probably excited.'

When he answered the call, though, Maddie sounded a little strained.

'Is Father Christmas real?' she asked him. 'Thomas said it's all made up.'

'Thomas?' Daniel checked.

'He was Joseph in the nativity play.'

'The one with no teeth?' Daniel checked, and Maddie started to laugh. 'The one who nearly dropped the baby? I wouldn't be paying too much attention to him.'

'So there is a Father Christmas?'

'Yes.' He could say that because for all Amelia's faults she would make sure there were presents under the tree for her daughter. 'So you can stop worrying and go to bed and I'll see you tomorrow.'

'For dinner?'

'Not for dinner, I'm…' He could feel Holly's ears on elastic as she pretended not to listen and he couldn't even come up with an excuse. 'I'll see you tomorrow.'

'Why can't you just go for dinner?' Holly said once the call had ended. 'I mean, how hard could it be?'

'Holly, my father didn't even celebrate Christmas until he married Amelia. I used to sit at home with the nanny on her phone the entire day to her family overseas while he went to work.'

She knew she was hearing the truth, there was something in his voice that told her that Christmas had always been hell.

'Not all families are perfect, Holly!'

She could hear the dig and she stared ahead.

'My family's not perfect, Daniel.'

'Well, they come close.' Daniel mimicked her voice when she'd spoken about her birthday. '"My parents always make sure that both are celebrated!"' He reverted to his bitterness. 'Of course they do.'

'Not always.' And she stared ahead at the traffic and she told him a truth, and this time it was Holly who was more speaking to herself. 'They forgot my birthday once.'

CHAPTER TEN

'WHEN YOU SAY "FORGOT…"?'

'They forgot completely,' Holly said.

'Tell me.'

'No.' Holly shook her head. 'You've just admitted that you basically had no Christmas at all growing up, so it seems a bit shallow to be upset about missing out on one birthday.'

'How old were you?' Daniel asked.

'I was six, turning seven.'

So not a whole lot older than Maddie was now, and he could just imagine the hurt it would cause his little sister.

'Tell me,' he said, and his voice was kind and she found that she wanted to.

Silly, that some silly childhood memory could make her eyes burn all these years later.

'Usually we had birthday cake for breakfast on Christmas Day and I opened my presents and then we'd all go through to the lounge and Christmas Day would start. We still do that, though we have champagne now too. It was just one year…' Her voice trailed off as she recalled her confusion when they'd gone straight through to the lounge. And how she'd tried not to cry as she'd opened her presents. 'I kept thinking they were just pretending that they'd forgotten and then I realised they actually had.

Now I look back I can see it had been a difficult year for my mum. My Uncle Harry had been in hospital—he'll be there tomorrow... Drunkle Harry.'

Daniel smiled.

'And Adam, my brother, had been sick with bronchiolitis.'

'When did they remember?'

'When I went to bed. Mum came in to say goodnight.'

'Were you crying?'

'No, I had my nervous smile on!' Holly said, and they both laughed but then both fell silent.

She stared out of the window, recalling that odd day, and she knew that the tears in her eyes had little to do with some long-ago memory.

It was a little like how Daniel made her feel now.

As if something that was so terribly important to her meant very little to him.

If she hadn't pushed that envelope under his nose, if Kay hadn't prompted him, she'd be minus a chocolate stocking now.

Exactly!

And while, yes, he'd come out to make up for their row, if her car hadn't broken down they'd have already gone their separate ways by now.

Soon she would be forgotten.

Finally his chirpy passenger was silent and Daniel got the peace he had craved, except he rather missed her incessant chatter.

The traffic was barely moving and to fill the silence he turned the radio on and listened to the carols.

Another half a mile, another half an hour.

And still Holly said nothing.

She took out some Christmas cards from her bag and

started to write them but after a couple she gave in and put them in the door pocket. She was tired of being peppy and ensuring that everyone was happy.

Blue lights were flashing up the hard shoulder, though it was the police and fire brigade that were passing them, rather than ambulances.

'Have a look on your phone,' Daniel said, 'and see what's happening.'

'A lorry has lost its load,' Holly said.

'We might need to think about getting off at the next exit.'

'We can't,' Holly said as she went through the traffic updates. 'There's flash flooding and the exit is closed.'

And she expected a hiss of frustration from Daniel but instead he gave a soft laugh. 'Of course it is.' He looked ahead. 'We might have to find somewhere to stay the night.'

'I'm really sorry for messing up your Christmas,' Holly said.

'There was no Christmas to mess up.'

'Oh, that's right, it's just another day.'

She simply could not get how she could be so crazy about someone who cared so little about the things that mattered to her and she actually told him so.

'I'm glad that we're not going anywhere,' Holly said.

'It might start moving.'

'I'm not talking about the traffic,' Holly admitted, and raised the awkward subject in the hope of clearing the air. 'I'm talking about my mythical us.'

Daniel smiled.

'You'd buy me shoes or something for Christmas.'

'I would,' Daniel said, and then frowned. 'Don't women like shoes?'

'Not the flat work ones that you'd get for me. No, it

would be a combined Christmas and birthday present that I'd get from you and one of those horrible cheap cards.'

'I don't do cards.'

'Exactly!' Holly said, and then she sighed. 'I'm sorry I didn't stick to my end of the deal. I always knew I'd be lousy at one-night stands. I really need to loosen up.'

'Then do.'

'It's easier said than done.'

'It is easy, though,' Daniel told her. 'Just think of sex as fun.'

He'd used the F-word again but now it made her smile.

'How?'

'You just don't go looking for a deeper meaning in everything, just, as they say, enjoy the ride.'

'Ha-ha.'

'So what did you get me for Christmas?' Daniel asked, because he really was curious to know.

'Didn't you even open it?'

'Nope.'

'Then you can find out tomorrow. What did you get for Maddie?'

'The necklace you didn't like,' Daniel said.

'I didn't know then that she was five! She'll love it!'

'I hope so. And she'll find out tomorrow that she's adopted an elephant.'

'What did you get for your father?'

'A book.'

'Amelia?'

'A diary.'

Holly screwed up her nose.

'We don't get on.'

'Have you ever tried?'

'Once,' Daniel said. 'Not at first, though. My father and I fell out when he started dating Amelia. I didn't ap-

prove of the age difference. I found it embarrassing actually, and it was clear to me she was just there for the money. Still, once Maddie was born I decided to make more effort…'

'Because you realised they were in love?'

'No, Polly,' Daniel said, and turned and smiled. 'Because Amelia is as shallow as my father is distant and I wanted someone to actually be present for the child.'

The traffic was at a complete standstill. She could see the red brake lights snaking for miles into the distance and the car moved forward about a hand space every five minutes or so.

'I worry about Maddie,' he admitted. 'She's being raised by nannies and neither of them could be bothered to show up for her nativity play.' Daniel gripped the wheel. 'He just doesn't get it.'

'Have you spoken to him?'

Daniel said nothing.

Well, he had been about to give a derisive laugh and say something like 'As if that's going to change anything,' but instead he stayed silent as he thought some more about doing just that.

Again.

'I tried to when she was born,' Daniel admitted. 'It probably wasn't the best time. I had just turned down a surgical position in favour of Emergency. He told me that just as I clearly didn't want career advice from him, likewise he didn't need parenting advice.'

'It sounds like he does.'

The Christmas carols were still playing on the radio, all happy and jolly, and it was Holly who turned it off.

'Thanks.'

Daniel actually appreciated it.

'Why are you leaving?' Holly asked. 'It sounds like you want to be there for your sister.'

'I do,' he agreed. 'But I can't be.'

He knew she didn't understand so he decided to explain. After all, there was no chance of her ever meeting Amelia. 'I really tried to put aside my doubts about the marriage. Last year my father was working and I took Maddie and Amelia to a pantomime and I did all the big-brother stuff. Then Amelia said she wanted to decorate Maddie's room as a surprise and could I help pick out some paper…'

'What did you say?' Holly asked, and her antennae were up.

He could almost see them rising out of her fluffy dark hair and homing in, and, Daniel thought, for someone so sweet she was also rather shrewd.

'I said, no, that there were interior designers for all that and I chalked it up as odd but…' He held out his hand and made a wavy sign that said that the jury had remained out about the small incident but it had seemed odd at the time.

Holly nodded to show she agreed with his take on things.

'Then last Christmas I was invited over, as I have been for the past couple of years. I generally go for dinner, and for Maddie's birthdays and things. Her family were there and Amelia was a bit tense and hitting the mulled wine and then brandy, and then…'

'What happened?'

'I fell asleep on the sofa and while I was gone her family went home, Maddie went for a sleep and my father went to his club. I woke up and she was sitting beside where I lay and she said she was miserable and that though the money was lovely and everything he was

old and she wanted young and, well, he'd never have to find out...'

Oh! She wanted to open the car door and get out onto the freezing motorway just to cool her cheeks.

'We didn't do anything.'

'I never asked.'

'Well, just so you know. Anyway, I don't really need you to believe me.' Actually, he did. 'Even if I'd wanted to, which I didn't, there would have been serious technical issues.'

'So, what did you say to her?'

'Not much.' Daniel sat silent for a moment as he recalled it. 'I told her it wouldn't be happening and got my jacket and went home. Since then I do my best to stay away.'

'I see.'

'Until September this year I worked at the same hospital as my father so it was pretty easy to find out what was going on and to only go over if Amelia was away. She goes on a lot of trips,' Daniel explained. 'I actually hadn't seen her since that day until the department store.'

'Okay, you're forgiven for not introducing me.'

He turned and she was wearing a smile, though not a nervous one.

'Embarrassing, isn't it?' he said.

'For her, I guess,' Holly said. 'Did you tell your father?'

'Good God, no!' Daniel sounded shocked at the very thought. 'I think I have to just accept that I'm not very good at family Christmases.'

'Oh, I don't know about that,' Holly said. 'You didn't do anything wrong, your father doesn't know and your little sister's none the wiser. I'd say you handled it all rather well.'

Daniel gave a small laugh.

No one knew, and certainly he hadn't envisaged telling anyone, but now that he had he felt lighter.

Holly, though, was grumbling as she again checked her phone for a traffic report.

'I'm starting to think I wasn't meant to get home for Christmas.'

'So is everyone else who is stuck in the jam,' Daniel said, and then he was practical, 'We can get off the motorway at the next available exit and try and find somewhere to stay the night or we can press on.'

It was long after ten p.m. A three-hour trip had already turned into six.

'I don't want to ruin your Christmas,' Holly started, and then thought about the long drive home he would have tomorrow. 'I've already ruined it.'

'Holly.' Daniel looked over and but Holly didn't look back, she was till reading the road report on her phone as if staring at it might make things change.

Her Christmas earrings had almost stopped flashing. Like the black box missing in a plane they still emitted the occasional hopeful bleep that Christmas cheer could still be found.

And they were right to hope, for Daniel found himself telling her something truly real...

'This is the nicest Christmas I've ever had.'

CHAPTER ELEVEN

'I NEED TO go to the loo.'

He had guessed she might because she'd kept crossing and uncrossing her legs.

'You went at the service station.'

'And then I drank both of the coffees.'

People were actually pulling over to sort out the essentials but there was no way Holly would be joining them.

Tonight, when she looked back on it, would be embarrassing enough as it was, without her pale moon rising.

'I think it's time we gave in,' Daniel conceded.

Another exit was coming up and it was now or never.

As they inched towards the exit Holly started ringing around local motels and bed and breakfasts from the list that came up on her phone.

'No room at the inn.' She sighed, because it would seem half of their fellow commuters had beaten them to it.

'No *rooms*,' Daniel pointed out, because Holly was trying to find two. 'The first one said that they had a double room.' He saw her jaw tense at the prospect of the two of them and one double bed. 'I've been driving for six hours, having worked all day,' Daniel said. 'I'm tired and I'm hungry. I can assure you that you could get up

and pole dance and I wouldn't notice. Still, if you want, you can have the sofa.'

'What if there isn't one?'

'Then you can have the floor.'

'You're such a gentleman.'

'No, Holly, I'm not.'

With little choice Holly rang back and secured the room and a short while later the car pulled into a bed and breakfast. By now she was past caring if the presents got pinched and so thankfully didn't suggest they haul everything inside.

And he was very pleased that the snowman bag remained safely locked in the car.

Daniel did the checking in and Holly dashed to the loo and then returned to his side, pleased to find that the formalities were over. Daniel was talking to a woman whom he introduced as Mrs Barrett.

No, the formalities were not over!

She proceeded to repeat to Holly all the rules she had just told Daniel.

'No noise after midnight.'

'We really just want to crash…' Holly agreed.

'No parties in the room.'

'Honestly,' Holly said.

'Just let her finish,' Daniel broke in, and it became clear he had tried to hurry Mrs Barrett along a few moments before but to no avail.

There were to be no showers after midnight, clothes were to be worn between the bathroom and bedroom, and shoes were to be taken off and carried up the stairs and not left in the hall and…

'You need to sign the register every time you enter and leave,' Mrs Barrett informed Holly as she handed her a pen.

They took off their shoes and were led up some very creaky stairs.

'Breakfast is between seven and nine, no latecomers.'

'We'll be gone by seven,' Daniel said. 'Is there anywhere we can call to get pizza or…?'

'No.' Mrs Barrett shook her head and no helpful suggestions ensued.

'I'm starving,' Daniel mouthed to Holly, and she laughed.

'Here…' Mrs Barrett inserted a key and pushed open a door, and it was like entering a time slip because nothing in this room could have changed in thirty or so years. It was all crinoline and purple and there were little doilies on every available surface.

And there was no sofa!

'How much do I owe you?' Holly asked once they were alone.

'It's my treat,' Daniel said, and smiled a black smile because, really, this was far from the Ritz. 'Holly, I *have* to eat something.'

'I've got some cheeses in the car in a cool bag,' Holly said. 'And some chocolate…'

'We can have a picnic.'

'Oh, and I got my father some Scotch for Christmas, I'm sure he won't mind. I'll go,' Holly said, 'I know where everything is.'

'No, I'll go,' Daniel said, and picked up his keys. There was no way he wanted her going through the bags.

Daniel went back down and spoke with Mrs Barrett and he even managed a wry smile as she asked him to sign out.

He went to the car and found the cool bag and a present that was clearly a bottle of Scotch and then went back up to the room, threw himself on the bed and stretched out.

'Finally.'

Clearly he would not be giving up the bed!

'I had to sign in and out just to go to the car.'

There were two glasses on a little table with a jug of water and Holly poured them both a measure of Scotch and started to plate up the cheese.

Daniel headed off and had a shower and came back wearing only his underwear.

'You're supposed to be dressed when you come out of the bathroom,' Holly reminded him.

'Well, I would have had I had a change of clothes.'

Soon she was sitting on the floor as Daniel hung off the bed and they ate and drank and chatted and laughed.

It was nice.

More than that, it was the nicest Christmas Eve she had ever spent because, cheese and Scotch aside, Daniel was one of her favourite things, especially when he was half-naked.

He asked a bit about her family.

'Do you get on with your brother?' Daniel asked, and Holly nodded. 'Stupid question—you get on with everyone.'

'Not everyone.' And because he'd asked about her family, now she asked about his. 'Do you remember your mum?'

'A bit.' He nodded. 'She was the one who always made the effort at Christmas and things…'

'What was it like after she died?'

'I went to boarding school,' Daniel said. 'And, to be honest, I preferred being there than at home. It was miserable.'

'Maybe he was grieving?'

'Maybe,' Daniel said. He'd never really thought of it like that. 'I went to Rupert's one Christmas.'

'The one you were best man for?' Holly asked, and Daniel nodded.

'He's a good friend. When I was all set to boycott my father's wedding he talked me round. I guess that I went helps keep things, at least outwardly, civilised.'

'What was Christmas like at Rupert's?'

He shrugged. 'They were all really into Christmas, a bit like your family, I guess.'

'Did you enjoy it?'

'Not really,' Daniel admitted. 'I guess it just showed more clearly all that was missing in mine. I think things are very different for Maddie, though. Not perfect, of course, but a lot better.'

And he knew too that things were better still for Maddie when he was around.

'If you want a shower then you'd better go now,' Daniel glanced at the time. 'It's close to midnight.'

Holly headed out to the shower and had a very quick one and then realised she'd forgotten her pyjamas. She got exactly what Daniel meant about putting on old clothes so she wrapped herself in a towel and legged it back to the bedroom, but as she stepped in she saw that it was in darkness except for a candle.

'Happy birthday, Holly.'

'You remembered!'

'I did.'

'I'd actually forgotten that it was my birthday.'

'No, you hadn't.'

'I honestly had,' Holly said. 'Aren't you going to sing?'

'Nope.'

She knelt down and blew out her candle and found out that it was held in a little piece of carrot cake with orange and cream cheese frosting.

'I got it from Mrs Barrett when I went down for the

cheese,' Daniel explained. 'She warned me again that there were to be no parties after midnight.'

'We'll be quiet, then.'

'You can eat the frosting.'

Holly did and Daniel knelt down too and he had the cake, but one wasn't the same without the other and for that reason *only* they shared a little kiss.

They both tasted perfect.

It was just a simple kiss but both fought the urge to rip off each other's towel.

'Thank you,' Holly said, trying to pretend she wasn't turned on, 'for making it such a lovely birthday.'

'I haven't finished yet.' He got up and turned on the bedside light. 'You've got to open your present.'

'Present?'

'Yes.'

Her present was on the bed and wrapped in lilac tissues from a box that, incidentally, had a purple knitted cover over it.

The bedroom really was a treasure trove of nylon and knits.

'Oh, my!' Holly said when she opened it. Her present was a lovely leather wallet. A little used perhaps, but, actually, it was something of his, and while Holly was a little confused, she still said the right thing for appearances' sake.

'I can't take your wallet.'

'It's more what's inside that is yours,' he told her. 'Open it up.'

There was some cash.

'Count it.'

There wasn't very much, a couple of notes and some coins, and he made a little pile on the bedside table.

'Can you get your hair done for that?' Daniel asked.

'Er, no.'

'Your nails?'

'No.' Holly laughed at the very notion. He really didn't have a clue.

'I'm trying to be thoughtful,' Daniel chided her mirth. 'Could you maybe get a nail polish?'

'Indeed I could.' Holly beamed. 'I could get two, in fact.'

'Well, then, you can do your nails on me.'

'Thank you.'

'Keep looking.'

'There's nothing else…' Holly said, and then her voice trailed off when her fingers found something shiny and silver and she went to hand his wallet back to him. 'You didn't empty it out properly.'

'I did.'

'No.' Holly shook her head. 'You didn't.' She took out a condom. 'You're such a slut, Daniel. You forgot to take this out.'

'No, Holly, I didn't.'

Her cheeks were on fire as he continued to speak.

'One night, just for you…'

'That's such a generous present,' Holly said. 'So selfless.'

'I know. I can be nice like that at times.'

'I mean, you'd have sex with me just because it's my birthday…'

'Not just sex,' Daniel said. 'This would be just-for-Holly sex.'

'So you won't enjoy it?'

'That's not you for you to concern yourself with. Your wish, or rather your birthday wish, would be my command.'

'Just some fun?' Holly checked.

'Exactly!'

'I don't think so.' She shook her head. 'I thought you said that even if I was naked and dancing…'

'I meant it when I said it.' Daniel broke in. 'But that got me thinking about just that…'

'No.'

'Well, the offer is there, just tear the edge off that little wrapper and I'll appear!'

He got into bed.

And she put on tartan pyjama bottoms and a little top that were fine for home but not exactly Daniel Chandler worthy and climbed into bed beside him.

She lay on her back more than a little miffed by his gift offer but also intrigued at the concept of her wish being his command. 'You could be skiing down a mountain one minute and then diving head-first between my legs the next…'

'I'm not a genie, Holly.' He pulled her into his lovely, warm body. 'The gift offer expires at seven a.m. *Then* it's Christmas.'

'Why would you rot things up now?' she asked. 'It's taken three weeks to be talking and it would take us straight back to awkward again.'

'But it wouldn't,' Daniel said. 'I'd just be showing you how to loosen up. You say tomato…'

Holly frowned. 'I don't get it.'

'You call it making love, whereas I…'

'I don't call it making love.'

'You think of it as such.'

'Not really,' Holly said. 'Maybe a bit.'

He was right.

Oh, she wished Daniel wasn't. That she could just take out her heart and leave it on charge overnight, just as she had done with her phone. Yes, she wished she could say,

Go for it Daniel, have wicked sex with me all night and I shan't hurt when you leave me in the morning.

But she didn't work like that.

'The offer's there.'

'Noted.'

Because he clearly had no conscience, Daniel was soon asleep, whereas Holly lay there, listening to the sound of rain against the window and his heavy breathing.

His leg came over hers, but he wasn't making a move, it was just that he was tall and the bed was small.

And once she felt him harden and Holly lay there all nervous and tense and awaiting his pounce.

He didn't.

It was already the best birthday she had ever had!

CHAPTER TWELVE

Christmas morning

IT WAS COLD.

Not just cold, it was freezing.

So freezing that in sleep in they had rolled into the dint in the bed and wrapped themselves around each other, and for Daniel, who didn't really do the wrapped around you type of thing, or rather didn't usually, he woke for the second time with her in his arms and facing away from him.

She had on a little strappy top and pyjama bottoms yet his hand had found its way to her stomach and he went to remove it. His intent was to roll on his back so she didn't feel him hard against her, but then his hand chose to linger and then she stirred and it was a little too late for that.

Actually, it wasn't.

He could still roll onto his back now and then roll out of bed.

They could be up and packed and out of here and heading for her home.

Or he could kiss her shoulder as he had wanted to that morning all those weeks ago.

His hand was lightly stroking her stomach and he could feel that she was trying to keep her breathing even.

So too was he.

'Happy birthday, Holly.'

'Thank you.'

He was breathing through his nostrils in that delicious turned-on, decision-making way. Resisting and yet wanting.

She looked at the clock and saw it was just before seven.

And then everything went black because she closed her eyes to the feel of his mouth and the deep kiss that met her shoulder.

It was a slow, sensual kiss and his tongue was warm on her cold, bare skin and his hand slipped up her top and found her breast.

He toyed with her nipple and then rubbed her breast with his palm and his mouth moved up her neck to her ear so she could both hear and feel his ragged breathing.

Holly pressed her bottom back into him, just because she wanted more of the feel of him hard and turned on.

And Daniel too needed more because he slid the top up over her head, discarded it and then went back to her neck. He loved the feel of her now naked back against his chest.

Now his hand slid down further down and he listened to the throaty moans she made as he stroked her clitoris and delivered little volts of pleasure that had her thighs grip his hand.

And it was all about her yet he stopped just long enough that they both kicked off their bottoms halves. His free hand moved under her torso so he could play with her other breast.

He moved his hand down, sliding his fingers inside her. She could feel him nudging between her thighs, wet, warm and hard.

'Oh, God,' he said, but just quietly and not to her, and for a moment she wondered why. Then she understood, for he knew, even before Holly did, that she was about to come.

It was so intense that she brought her knees up.

There, the sensible part of him warned as she came to his hand. *Leave it there. Feel that bliss on your fingers and then smile and say Happy Birthday.*

It wasn't enough, though.

For either of them.

Her lovely birthday 'gift' hadn't left her sated, it had just made her hungry for more. She turned in his arms and they found each other's mouths briefly before he moved down to kiss her breasts, one by delicious one, tasting them for the first time.

Oh, that mouth, Holly thought as her fingers tangled in his hair. She wished he had two of them so he could keep kissing her breasts while also taking her mouth. His head followed the upward guide of her hand and their mouths met again in a kiss unplanned. Deep, slow and sensual, their tongues mingled and then their mouths parted in private focus as he entered her.

She moaned at the bliss of the slow long strokes that had her wrap one leg around him as they moved together.

They were kissing intensely, stopping only to stare into each other's eyes before kissing again. It was so real, so raw.

Daniel got up on his forearms just to watch her and she pressed her palms into his chest.

The tight, slick grip of her had Daniel revelling in the sensations and then the demand of his pace increased.

The shift in him started to tip her. Even when he had

taken her standing, fast and rough, he had been in measured control.

But now neither had hold of themselves, they were lost in each other. His hand came over her mouth and the sound of her affirmations were silenced. He felt the stretch of her smile on his palm as she realised the noises she'd been making. Daniel would usually have revelled in that but there was something about the simple sound of them, slick and in tune, intensely moving together that enraptured him. He forgot to smile, or to do anything other than focus hard…on her.

His breathing was ragged and hard in her ear as he pulled her deeper into oblivion.

Holly dug her fingers into taut buttocks and the fire low in his spine shot forward.

Her reward for silence? The deep moan of his release.

Heat met perfect heat and though she gripped and tightened and drew him in, as he shot into her, she also unfurled, for she opened herself up to him.

Those last thrusts were exquisite, those deep kisses, while still dizzy, were the most intense expression she had ever known. They coiled with each other, caressed each other, and their lips did not know how to part.

Until they did…

CHAPTER THIRTEEN

THEY LAY AFTERWARDS, both a little stunned by what had taken place.

She had never known just how beautiful sex could be and Daniel had done all he could not to find out.

The only sound now was the rain and they lay on their backs, idly holding hands as their breathing slowed down, and Holly knew, with absolute clarity, the moment he regretted it.

His hand let go of hers and raked through his hair. The sound then was one of tense silence.

'We didn't—' he started.

'I *was* there, Daniel,' Holly interrupted. She didn't need to be told that they hadn't used a condom.

He nodded, only it wasn't contraception that was troubling him, it was the closeness, the absolute abandon that he had never felt with another.

He couldn't pretend that they hadn't just crossed the line.

And neither could Holly.

Had he tied a red ribbon around it last night and shouted *Surprise!* well, maybe she could have chalked it down to experience, albeit a new one.

This, though, felt like she had just handed over her soul, only for it to be promptly handed back.

'Are you on the Pill?'

There were many ways this question could be asked, Holly thought. A necessary way, like a doctor. The hopeful way of a lover wanting to pounce.

Or the Daniel way—please, God, tell me you are.

She didn't answer and he got up and sat on the edge of the bed, reaching for his jeans.

'Yes, I'm on the Pill,' she finally said, just to put him out of his obvious misery.

Daniel nodded but said nothing.

And she stopped trying.

It was quite a feat for Holly, but she just stopped trying to pretend that this was okay and didn't even bother to wish him a happy Christmas, she just pulled on her pyjamas and headed out to get ready.

Daniel pulled on his jeans, loathing his own silence.

And just like the last time there were repercussions.

Big ones.

He was staring down the barrel of a future but he couldn't get a clear shot for all the obstacles that were in the way.

Hell, he couldn't even promise to be there for his sister when she needed him to stay.

'I'm ready.'

Holly stood at the door, but of course it wasn't that easy. They'd made quite a mess last night. He threw the remnants of their picnic in the bin and she packed up a few things.

And they were done.

'Do you want this?' He held up the bottle of Scotch and she took it in almost a snatch.

And whereas they should have been lingering in bed and then heading down for breakfast, instead they were signing the guest register to Mrs Barrett's disapprov-

ing eyes when Holly had to put down the bottle to pick up the pen!

They drove in strained silence on a now clear motorway.

Holly's earrings had stopped flashing and, from his reaction to the morning's events, all hope for them was gone.

'It's left here,' Holly said, even though his phone told them to take a right. 'It's just a bit quicker.'

The village looked gorgeous and they passed a pretty old pub and she already missed the lazy weekend afternoons the mythical 'us' could have spent there.

Had the closeness between them not completely gone.

Had he had the guts to follow his heart.

'Do you want to come in for breakfast?' Holly offered, even though she knew the answer.

'No.'

'Why?' Holly asked, because she needed to hear it.

Daniel stared out at the sleety street and there were times when you really did have to be cruel to be kind and so he gave Holly her answer. 'Because it would mean something to you. Because in Holly's world when the guy she's just slept with comes to her parents' it means something more.'

And she could say, no, it's just breakfast and my mother would never expect me to let you drop me off and not invite you to come in.

But that would be a lie.

If Daniel came in then so too would hope.

'You're right.'

'I can't play happy families, Holly.'

'You don't even want to try.'

'No.' Because over and over it had failed to work out.

'I'm going to go,' Daniel said, 'and you're going to go in and have a wonderful Christmas with your family.'

He got out of the car and started to unload her bags.

'You're not going to change your mind, are you?'

'No.'

'Are you going to go to your father's?'

'I'll drop off the presents and then I'm going to go home and catch up on some sleep.'

And it hurt that he'd rather get back on the motorway and spend Christmas alone than come in and spend Christmas with her.

'I don't know what to say,' Holly admitted.

She should leave it there really, given him a wave and show what a good detached lover she could be.

That wasn't her, though, and so, just as he climbed back into his car to leave, Holly spoke.

'I don't get you.'

'Holly, let's not do this.'

'No, let's.' Holly's smile was black. 'You see, Daniel, I don't think you're an utter bastard. A bit of one perhaps but if you really thought I was going to go and get stupid ideas about us from sex, you'd never have got into that crinoline bed last night. I think you'd have slept on the floor, or even in the car, rather than hurt me. And I also believe if a quick shag was what you'd wanted this morning, then for my sake you'd have managed to resist.' And then she said it. 'But it wasn't a quick shag.'

'Oh, that's right, we made love.'

He could be as sarcastic and derisive as he chose to be, but, as she'd said this morning, Holly had been there too.

And she could point that out to him, but the war was won and Daniel was the victor.

'I'm done,' Holly said. 'I really am. I've made enough of a fool of myself over you. And I'm not going to say

thank you for the lift because the truth is I wish you'd never come out to the car park yesterday.'

'I came out because I didn't want us to end on a row.'

'Do you know what?' Holly retorted. 'It would have been far easier on me if it had.'

She staggered off under the weight of presents and this time she didn't turn around.

Her mother must have been peeking out of the window though because the door opened before she had to work out how to knock.

'Hi, darling, where's your friend?'

'He's not coming in.'

'Oh! But surely—'

'Mum!' Holly said. 'Please.'

If it wasn't Christmas Day she would love to run to her old room fling herself on her bed and cry but, of course, she couldn't.

Instead, she took her bags into the lounge and placed them beside the tree.

And she kept on hoping, so much so that she half expected a knock on the door and for Daniel to say he'd changed his mind, and maybe he'd stay for breakfast.

Instead, with all the bags by the tree, she stood and walked to the window, just in time to see him drive off.

And that was it, Holly knew.

She was never going to see him again.

They were done.

There was no time to process it, though.

Breakfast, as was traditional in the Jacobs family, was birthday cake. Holly blew out her candles and opened her birthday present from her parents and it was a gorgeous pair of earrings.

She took out her cheap Christmas ones that had now

completely stopped flashing and replaced them with her lovely new silver ones.

Then it was champagne with orange juice, though Holly just had orange juice because she was working tonight.

It was smiles and happy all round and Holly joined in, even if she felt as if a part of her had died.

Adam loved his necklace and in turn she loved the travel wallet he had bought, and they traded their gifts with a smile.

Then relatives started to descend and there were parsnips to peel and stuffing to make and then Drunkle Harry and co. arrived.

'I'll take up your coats,' Holly said.

She went up to her old bedroom and took a breath.

'Holly?'

She turned around as her mother came in and saw that she was holding a snowman bag.

'Is everything okay?'

'Of course it is.' Holly smiled her brightest smile but at the last moment it wavered and Holly was appalled with herself when a tear slipped out and she quickly wiped it away.

'Holly?'

She shook her head, because she was simply not able to talk about Daniel without breaking down.

'Is it your friend that wouldn't come in?' Esther checked, and Holly nodded.

'I don't want to talk about it now,' Holly said, and her voice was all shaky. 'I don't want to start crying and ruin Christmas.'

'I seem to remember saying that just over a year ago,' Esther said. 'I sat in the doctor's and I wanted one more perfect Christmas…'

'And we did.'

'Holly, it was awful. Your dad kept slipping out to cry, I burnt the turkey. Harry got so drunk…'

Holly started to laugh. 'It was still a good Christmas.'

'It turned out to be,' Esther agreed.

In the end they'd all had loads to drink and watched a sad film, which had been a good excuse to cry and just relax and stop pretending they were brave.

'You know, I remember when I forgot your birthday…' They just sat there on Holly's old bed and chalked up all the Christmas fails.

'You remembered it that evening,' Holly said. 'And I got a puppy out of it.'

'You did,' Esther sighed. 'Please tell me what's going on, Holly'

And Holly was about to point out that they could do this another time, but then her mum's hand came over hers.

'I know I've been difficult lately,' Esther said. 'But I can still be here for you.'

It had indeed been a long year, one where at times Holly had felt like she'd lost her mum, but it would seem that she was back now.

It was the best gift to have a cuddle from her mum instead of the other way around.

'The guy who gave me the lift home,' Holly said. 'Daniel. I like him a lot, well, I more than like him. I think he feels a bit the same yet he says we're going nowhere. In fact, he's heading overseas…' She gave a pale smile. 'He couldn't make it any clearer that's he's not interested in anything long term but…'

'You still want more.'

'Yes,' Holly said. 'I've never really felt this way before about anyone, not even close.' The one time she

had, it hadn't been reciprocated. 'It's probably for the best, we'd never have worked out. I don't think he has a romantic bone in his body and he's not into Christmas. He's hardly even seeing his family, he just wants to go home to bed…' She shook her head as if to clear it. 'I can't believe I've fallen for someone who'd rather sleep his way through Christmas Day than be with his family.' Holly stood, even though her mum still sat there. 'Come on, we'd better go down.'

'You missed a present,' Esther said, and took a box out of the snowman bag.

'From who?' Holly frowned.

'I don't know,' Esther said. 'I was clearing the paper away when I found it. You brought it with you.'

'No.'

It was a silver box covered in fake snow with a silver bow, and it looked terribly like the ones she had seen in the department store. In fact, it looked a lot like the gift she had been considering getting Daniel.

It couldn't be.

Surely?

She looked at the name on the card.

To Holly
 I hope you have the wonderful Christmas that *you deserve.*
 Secret Santa

Holly tried not to get her hopes up but her hands were shaking as she undid the bow.

It *had* to be from him.

She gasped as she saw a glass ball decorated with her name in silver, and delicate outlines of holly in jewelled green.

What captivated her, though, was the tiny silver envelope inside the glass that had her name on.

'Who's it from?' Esther asked.

'Him.'

'I thought you said he wasn't romantic.'

'He's not.'

'And that he wasn't into Christmas.'

'He isn't.'

Except Daniel had given her the most beautiful, romantic, Christmassy gift in the world.

It was actually the perfect gift, Holly thought as she held it up and the ball spun round, catching the light, but right now it was the letter inside that entranced her.

When would he have put it in her bag? Holly wondered. While they were at the bed and breakfast? But, no, he must have had it before that and then she realised it must have been when they had dragged her parcels in from the car.

When he'd thought she would never see him again.

Oh, it was so much better than a chocolate stocking!

And *so-o-o* much more frustrating!

'I don't see the point,' her father said as Holly hung it on the tree. 'Why would you go to the bother of writing a note that the other person isn't going to read?'

'I'm not sure,' Holly admitted.

'It's like those fire alarms,' mused Drunkle Harry. 'In case of emergency, break the glass.'

'There won't be any emergencies, Uncle Harry.' Holly smiled. 'He probably regrets buying it now. He told me he doesn't want me. I shan't be seeing him again.'

CHAPTER FOURTEEN

HE WAS THE FOOL. Daniel knew it.

As he watched Holly walk to her house in his rear-view mirror, that was exactly how he felt. She was buckling under the weight of presents, and then the door opened and her mother dashed out to help.

He could see her mother's bright silk scarf tied around her head and her slender body and guessed, rightly, it would have been one hell of a year for the family.

And he wanted to go in, to the warmth, to the laughter and fun.

He just didn't know how.

Christmas had always been a let-down.

A huge one.

The build-up would start and it had taken years for him to work out that the promise never came true.

And he was right not to go in, he knew, because it wouldn't be a friend dropping in for Christmas.

Holly was the big one.

The one to whom you promised things like for ever. And those were promises he felt in no position to give, so he started the engine and drove away.

The roads felt empty. Probably because most people were already where they wanted to be.

He pulled into the service station, the one opposite

but identical to the one where they had stopped last night and bought cinnamon and nutmeg coffee and went back to the car and drank it.

Really, Holly had ruined coffee for ever because, though it tasted as bad as it had last night, there was a certain warmth to it, this pleasantness.

He opened the glove box and looked at his gift from Holly, and the ridiculous thing was that he half hoped for a Daniel & Holly snowglobe and some crazy declaration of her love.

He read the card.

To Daniel
From Secret Santa

There wasn't even a kiss!

Well, he guessed there would be something more meaningful inside the wrapping. He opened it slowly and then frowned as a tube of lip balm fell into his palm.

A lip balm?

An expensive lip balm perhaps, but even so…

And then he realised it was Holly's attempt at being bland. Holly doing what he had told her to do and not be so serious about things.

Yet suddenly he was.

He watched as an elderly woman got out of a car and walked towards another. And some children got out and ran to her.

It must be their turn to have granny for Christmas.

Perhaps the families weren't speaking, Daniel pondered, because no one in either car waved to the other.

Yet the kids and the granny were all smiling.

They were somehow making it work.

He thought of Holly, sitting crying, contemplating a

taxi, simply desperate to get home. And he thought of his mother and all the Christmases she'd missed out on.

There were families fighting to be together, longing to be with each other, and there he was, running from his.

He was tired of running.

His phone started to ring; it was Maddie, of course, wanting to know how long it would be till he got there.

'About an hour, I think.'

'Have you got me a present?'

'Maybe.' Daniel smiled.

And then it was a case of please, please, please, could he stay for Christmas dinner.

He was about to say no but then he thought of what Holly had said—that it was embarrassing for Amelia, rather than him.

He could do dinner surely?

'Yes,' he said, and was almost deafened by her squeal. 'I'll see you soon, Maddie. Happy Christmas.'

He loathed that he hadn't been able to make it a happy Christmas for the woman who mattered to him the most.

And so, what was the second-best thing he could do?

He pinched one of Holly's cards from the door pocket and wrote one out for Maddie. Then he drove to his rather odd family and took out the bag that held presents and knocked at the door.

'Daniel!' His father greeted him with a handshake.

Despite the hurts of the past and the hurts of this morning, this Christmas *was* still somehow special. Something had changed in Daniel.

'I love it!' Maddie opened the tiny package and took out a silver neck chain with a little elephant charm with crystal eyes and then she read a certificate that said she'd adopted an elephant. 'Look, Daddy!'

Professor Chandler frowned and put on his glasses

to read the certificate. 'She's adopted an elephant?' He frowned. 'For Christmas?'

He had no idea, Daniel thought.

None.

Yet at least he was trying harder than he had when Daniel had been small because when Maddie whispered in her father's ear, he actually listened and then stood. 'We'll be back in a moment.'

That left Daniel and Amelia and she flushed an unflattering shade of puce and attempted to voice what was on her mind. 'About what happened last year...'

'Nothing happened,' Daniel said. 'And nothing ever shall. Let's just leave it there and focus on Maddie.'

Done.

And he turned as the reason he was here walked into the lounge carrying a very large box that was terribly, and therefore beautifully, wrapped by her.

'I chose this,' Maddie said. 'Jessica said you might not want it as you're travelling but we can keep it here for you when you've gone! You're going to love it.'

Intrigued, Daniel peeled back the wrapper on a very large box and then he gave a very delighted smile, especially at the thought of Jessica trying to dissuade Maddie from her purchase. It was a pink plastic popcorn-maker, with a happy picture of mother and daughter and mountains of popcorn on the box.

'I do love it,' Daniel said, and saw that it even came with a little bag of popping corn.

'You really like it?' Maddie checked, and when Daniel nodded she turned to her father. 'See! I told you.'

'You did indeed,' Professor Chandler agreed. 'Maddie, why don't you get Daniel his other present from under the tree?'

It was a wallet.

A very nice leather one and far from bland it made him smile, given where his had disappeared to last night!

'Thank you.'

And so to dinner.

Amelia declined wine, Daniel noted, and so did he, which he was very glad about given that as Christmas pudding was served his phone rang.

'They'll be wanting me to do a shift,' Daniel said when he saw who it was.

'Tell them fat chance,' his father suggested.

Except he said yes, but only because it was a night shift at The Primary and it was where Holly would be.

Perhaps he could make this a happier Christmas after all.

Or completely spoil it for her?

'I'll need to take food in,' Daniel said, because knowing that lot they would turn it into a party.

'You can take the popcorn machine in.' Maddie smiled.

'I'll see if there's anything nice you can take in,' their father said, and stood.

'Popcorn *is* nice!' Maddie insisted.

'Of course it is,' Marcus said, and he smiled at Daniel over her head. 'So nice that there might not be enough to go around.'

He had mellowed, Daniel realised as he followed his father into a very spacious kitchen, lined with all the mod-cons, all sparkling from lack of use.

Maybe he could, as Holly had suggested, try talking to him.

'There's some pâté and potted…' Marcus said, as he rummaged through the large basket of goodies.

'Dad,' Daniel interrupted. 'I went and saw Maddie perform in her nativity play.'

'I heard that you did. There's probably a ham in the fridge...'

'Dad!' Daniel couldn't give a damn about the ham. 'You should have been there.'

'Oh, come on, Daniel, do you really expect me to cancel surgery because—?'

'Yes,' Daniel said, and then he said it again. 'Yes!' he urged. 'When Maddie's a teenager she might want nothing to do with you but right now she does. You need to be there for the things that matter to her.'

Daniel watched as his father stood there, not cross at the discussion, more confused. 'You've got a secretary.' Daniel thought of Iris. 'I actually looked after one of your old ones the other day. Iris Morrison.'

'She was very efficient.'

'And very under-utilised. She would have loved to factor in your home life. Why don't you go through the calendar and mark out some days for the coming year, like Maddie's birthday and things, and have your secretary organise your schedule around that?'

'I could do that.' Marcus nodded.

He simply accepted the advice and it was then that Daniel realised that sometimes people simply needed to be told. Sometimes the cleverest of people needed help with what others considered the simplest of things.

And so, while they were on the subject, Daniel pushed on. 'And instead of three hours at the club this afternoon, why not take her for ten minutes to the park?'

'She likes the club, there's a playroom there.'

'No, Dad.' Daniel shook his head. 'She hates it.'

'Did you?'

And he could score some points here, Daniel knew,

he could stick the boot in and bring up, oh, so many, many things.

But it was Christmas.

And, more than that, this discussion wasn't about him. It was about a wary-looking little girl who now stood at the kitchen door. 'What are you two talking about?'

Daniel looked at his father, who stared back at his son for a moment and then turned to his daughter. 'I was just saying to your brother that we might go for a walk to the park after dinner if he wanted to come.'

'The park?' Maddie checked. 'The one with swings?'

'Yes.'

'And are you coming?' Maddie asked her brother as Amelia came in.

'I can't,' Daniel said. 'I need to go home and get some sleep and Holly will be back from her family soon...' He shamelessly borrowed Holly, but even if not physically present, by God, it had helped to have her sort of by his side today.

'Holly?' Amelia frowned.

'You met her in the department store the other week.'

'Sounds serious,' his father said, because if it was running into weeks for his son, then it must be.

They had worked at the same hospital after all and word got around!

'It's starting to look that way,' Daniel agreed.

It had actually been starting to look that way for quite some time now but he'd been doing his best not to see what had been right there under his nose.

Yes, try as he might not to be, he was still his father's son.

Though that might not be such a bad thing, Daniel realised, because even a rather old leopard could change its spots.

With a hefty nudge, of course.

As he was about to leave he gave Maddie the card he had written for her in the car.

'What does "ten school pick-ups" mean?' she asked.

'That you've got ten treats next year, though not all in a row.'

'But you're going away.'

'No,' Daniel said. 'I'm not. I might go on holiday, of course, but I'm not leaving you for a whole year...'

And maybe it made no sense to some, she was his half-sister after all, but as her little arms wrapped around his neck, staying close made perfect sense to Daniel.

Maddie was his sister and for her he would be here.

It was a good Christmas.

A great one even, for, as he climbed into the car with his pink plastic popcorn-maker, he watched as his father stood outside, with his daughter hanging off his hand, ready to go to the park.

It was the first time that his father had waved him goodbye.

Ever.

And, because it was Christmas, Daniel tooted and waved back as he drove off.

They looked almost like a normal family!

CHAPTER FIFTEEN

THE MOTORWAY BEHAVED and the drive was made so much easier in her mother's car. Holly had said that she would return it in a couple of days but was seeing in the New Year in London.

With friends and bubbles. She was going to keep all her resolutions this year—one being to be more sophisticated in her love life, and so never make such a fool of herself again with men.

Hell, and if she was ever to have a one-night stand again, she would call the shots—she would climb out of bed, get dressed and walk off without a word. The thought made Holy smirk.

Next year, though.

Right now she knew she had to feel this pain. She had Daniel's present swathed in bubble wrap on the passenger seat and she knew that this year Boxing Day would more like Box of Tissues Day!

Holly got to the hospital and parked, then unloaded all the food her mother had prepared for the night staff. There was rather a lot! She staggered again through the car park and was under the bright lights of the ambulance bay when she heard her name being called.

'Holly!'

A gruff voice had her turn around and she saw a little group standing around a wheelchair.

Holly made her way over, and as she did so a delighted smile split her face. There was Albert, sitting in the wheelchair with a drip attached to a pole and wearing a heavy Christmas jumper and a woolly hat.

She hardly recognised him.

'What are you doing, sitting out here with pneumonia?' Holly both scolded and smiled as she spoke.

'The nurses on the ward said the same,' Albert admitted, 'but it's too stuffy up there.'

'He wanted to come out for some air,' the elder woman explained. 'I'm Dianne, his niece.'

'It's lovely to meet you.'

'This is Emily,' Albert proudly introduced his family. 'She's both my great-niece and god-daughter. They brought me in some Christmas dinner and Emily has made me these.' He opened a tin and showed some beautifully decorated mince pies. 'Take one for your break,' Albert offered.

'I think Holly's got enough food to be going on with,' Dianne said when she saw Holly hesitate.

Usually she didn't accept food from patients and Dianne was right, more mince pies were the very last thing she needed. But, Holly guessed, it must be rather nice for Albert who had spent the last years begging to have food to give some.

'I'll have it on my break,' Holly said. 'If you could just…'

Dianne laughed and selected a pie and added it to the mountain of food that Holly carried.

'I'd better get inside,' she said to the little family. 'Happy Christmas!'

'And to you, Holly.'

'You made it.' Kay beamed as Holly came in. 'And you're early!'

'Someone can go home,' Holly offered, because the staff had done the same for her on the Christmas party night.

'Well, I'll send Anna home. Laura isn't getting here till later so I'm hanging around till then. I have to say, though, for Christmas night it's pretty quiet. Maybe, for once, everyone's behaving.'

Holly had worked a couple and maybe there were jinxing themselves by admitting it, but it actually was quiet. Christmas night was often the busiest with feuding families as well as too much food and alcohol combined. Also there was sometimes the very sick who had held on for that special day.

But, yes, tonight was quiet—at least it was in Emergency, though Kay soon told her that it was otherwise elsewhere.

'Theatre is busy and Maternity is steaming.'

'Who's on tonight?' Holly asked, and they glanced up at the doctors' board and saw that Daniel Chandler was down to work in Emergency tonight.

'We've got...' Kay frowned. 'That can't be right, he's left.'

'No,' Anna called out. 'We had to ring everyone but Daniel agreed to work it.'

And Holly blinked.

She couldn't do this.

She could not keep saying goodbye.

Or, worse than that, she could not keep getting her hopes up because that was what she repeatedly did.

Well, not any more, they were done.

No way would Boxing Day be spent in his bed.

Two-Strikes-and-You're-Out Dr Chandler.

He came in then, carrying boxes and food and with a mince pie on top of it all. Unshaven and gorgeous, he gave her a smile.

'Take your stuff around to the staffroom,' Kay told them, though for Holly it was a rather awkward walk.

'I see you have a mince pie.' Holly said, determined to keep this about the patients rather than them. 'Is that one of Albert's?'

'It is,' Daniel said, and told her he'd been outside chatting with them too. 'The family's moving to the country and apparently there's a little cottage on the grounds. Albert and Dianne both happily admit they'd kill each other under the same roof, but if he has the cottage he can have his privacy and they can keep an eye—'

'He's going to live there?'

'Yep,' Daniel said as they arrived at the staffroom and started to unload all the food. 'Great, isn't it?'

It truly was.

'Why have you brought in a popcorn-maker?' Holly asked.

'Don't you like popcorn?'

'I love popcorn.'

'Then I shall make you some later.'

Holly said nothing, she just headed to the changing room and arrived at the nurses' station a few minutes later in her scrubs and wearng her Christmas earrings.

Everyone was gathered, even Daniel.

'Happy birthday, Holly...' the call went up!

Kay went into her bottomless bag and pulled out a parcel. 'That's from all of us. We were going to do you a cake but...'

'I've had a lot of cake today!'

'We'll do cake next year,' Kay said. 'For your thirtieth.'

Holly groaned. 'Please, don't remind me! Anyway, I'm not working next year, I'm putting in my request now.'

'Did your mother tell you to do that?' Kay asked.

'I shan't be at my mother's on my thirtieth.' Holly smiled sweetly. 'I'll be getting drunk and having anonymous sex with a stranger.'

Kay puffed out her cheeks and tutted but everyone else laughed, even Daniel, and she was proud of herself indeed.

She would get over him.

Holly just had to get through tonight.

She opened her present and found it was a gorgeous jumper that she'd seen online a while ago. She had shown it to Anna, but it hadn't been available in her size.

Yes, she had very good friends.

She read her card and even Nora had taken the time to sign it.

'How's Paul?' Holly asked.

'He's fantastic. He even remembered where he'd hidden Nora's present.' Kay beamed. 'It was in with the lentils.'

'Well, thank God he came out of his coma to remember.'

'It's an eternity ring. No doubt she'll be down later to show it off to all the night staff...' And then her voice trailed off and she looked at Daniel. 'Are you wearing lip gloss?' Kay frowned.

'I am.'

'I can't keep up these days, I have to admit. Men wearing make-up...'

'I like it,' Daniel said. 'It keeps my lips soft, supple and kissable.'

There was something different about him that Holly couldn't put her finger on.

He wasn't at all aloof, he was lighter, funnier and now a part of the team, but it was more than that.

It was as if Daniel had become Daniel.

And, even more so, she wanted him.

CHAPTER SIXTEEN

'HAPPY CHRISTMAS, HOLLY.'

With just an hour left of the big day, and only a couple of patients trickling through, he found her standing at the nurses' station, pulling up some antibiotics that weren't even due yet, and he said what he wished he had said this morning.

Holly was very glad that he hadn't wished her a happy Christmas then, only because she'd have flung it back at him and said he'd ruined it.

Twenty-three hours into Christmas Day she was ready to hear it.

'Thank you.' She smiled. 'And to you.'

It *had* been a happy Christmas, Holly thought as she tapped the little air bubbles out of the syringe.

Despite the tears to come and the hurt yet to heal, it had still somehow managed to be the best Christmas and birthday she'd ever known.

'Was Santa good to you?' he asked.

'He was,' Holly said, wishing he would leave her alone, because it was hard to chat and play friends, but she tried. 'And Secret Santa was *very* good to me.' She looked into those absolute navy eyes, and there was still no silver, no little aqua dots, and she knew she loved him. 'Though he went way over budget...'

'Count yourself lucky. I got a lip balm.'

'The crème de la crème of lip balms,' Holly corrected him.

'Was I to think of you when I applied it?' Daniel asked, and it was he now who looked for a deeper meaning.

'No.' She shook her head. 'It was my I-am-so-over-you present. A bit nicer than I'd have got for others but certainly not in the chocolate stocking category.'

'What's wrong with a chocolate stocking?' Kay asked as she bustled in to get her bag and finally go home.

'Nothing,' Holly said.

In fact, a chocolate stocking was a whole lot less confusing than Daniel, and his romantic gifts and come-to-bed eyes, followed by the silent treatment the morning after.

Aaggh!

She wanted to scream but she didn't and no way, *no way* would she ask what was in the letter.

'Did you get any presents, Daniel?' Kay asked.

'I got a wallet from my father and stepmother,' Daniel said, 'and a popcorn-maker from my sister. We had a good day.'

'You stayed for dinner?' Holly frowned.

'I did.'

'Don't you get on?' Kay asked.

'Not really,' Daniel said. 'Though it's my stepmum that's the problem at the moment. Still, I do have a young sister…'

'How old is she?'

'Five,' Daniel said.

'And so how old is your stepmother?' Kay exclaimed in her less-than-tactful way.

'Twenty-seven.'

'Dear God!' Kay was stunned. 'That would be hard.'

'Actually,' Daniel said, picking up a file for the next patient, 'it's not. Much to Amelia's disappointment.'

Holly and Kay looked at each other as Daniel went to walk off. Holly could not believe he was finally being open about it, and as for Kay…

No, she wasn't subtle and she was also very, very shrewd.

'Did she come on to you, Daniel?'

Holly held her breath, wondering what his reaction would be.

'Last year.' Daniel nodded.

'And did you respond in kind?'

'Kay!' Holly admonished. Kay just went too far at times and Daniel clearly agreed because he turned around.

'No, I did not!' Daniel was all snobby and angry but it would seem Kay wasn't being nosey, she was just being very, very honest.

'I did!' She went purple in the face. 'Why do you think I work every Christmas? I'm trying to keep away from Eamon's twin?'

She was Irish, she was funny and it *was* Christmas night.

'One year his fecking mother made the same jumper and gave it to them for Christmas and so they were both wearing it…'

Holly watched a smile inch over Daniel's face as Kay proceeded to tell her story in the way only the Irish could.

'Well, I had everyone at the Christmas table, they were all getting on with their starters, and, given I had to get things ready, I ate mine quickly. I went into the kitchen to sort out the main course. I was taking the foil off the turkey and then Eamon came up behind me and he pinched my bottom and then we had a kiss, as you do…'

'Indeed,' Daniel said.

'It was quite a kiss actually,' Kay elaborated, 'but I told him that I needed to get on with dinner and that I'd deal with him better later and I gave it a little squeeze...'

And Holly laughed as Daniel's eyes popped a little.

'Then I walked through with the turkey and there was Eamon, sitting where I'd left him, and his brother was walking behind me... I knew I'd just got off with my husband's twin.'

They laughed so much!

Just laughed and laughed because somehow all families had their dramas and tales, all families were a little crazy.

Especially at Christmas.

'Did you tell Eamon?' Holly asked, when she had remembered how to breathe.

'Of course not,' Kay said. 'I mean...' She stopped talking in mid-sentence and looked over Holly's shoulder, and Kay's expression was so stunned that both Daniel and Holly turned around to see what had halted Kay in her tracks. 'Louise!'

It was Kay's daughter, accompanied by a very nervous-looking young man whose arm she was clinging onto.

'I was going to call you from Maternity...' Louise started to explain to her mother and then stopped as clearly another contraction hit. 'I don't think I'm going to get there.'

And Kay, the most competent, the most experienced, the utter glue of the department and, Holly guessed, her family too, just stood there not moving, like a tree in the middle of a field.

'Come on, Holly.' It was Daniel who moved.

He went over, shook the man's hand and found out his name—Gilbert—and then he guided Louise into a cu-

bicle and Holly followed them all in. 'Let's help you up onto the trolley...' Daniel started, but Louise held onto the metal edges for dear life and started to bear down.

'Why don't we let the maternity department know?' Daniel suggested.

'I just have,' Kay said. She was present now, though not fully recovered from the shock of her daughter's arrival, but her voice was very deliberately steady and calm. 'They'll send someone just as soon as they're able to.'

Kay had brought in a delivery pack and Holly and Daniel were getting Louise up onto the gurney as she spoke on. 'They're very busy up there and, given we've got a registrar and,' she added, 'I'm also a midwife...'

'We'll be fine,' Daniel said in his composed, deep voice just as he had the night Paul had come in.

And he was calm, though not so aloof now, for he gave Kay's shoulder a little squeeze.

It was everything that was needed now.

CHAPTER SEVENTEEN

'We'll be more than fine,' Kay said as she rallied. 'Now, Louise—' she was as direct as ever '—do you want me to wait outside? Just say if it's awkward for you to have your mother here.'

'*No-o-o-o!*' Louise shouted as another contraction took over and she clutched both her mother and her partner's arms and bore down.

Holly was very quickly opening up the delivery pack. This baby really was in a hurry to be born!

'When did the contractions start?' Holly asked.

'Only an hour or so ago,' Gilbert answered. 'Though she's felt a bit off all day.'

'Why didn't you say when I called?' Kay asked.

'She didn't want you to worry, given how busy it is at Christmas,' Gilbert said, 'and we thought it would take ages.' He was trying to take in the speed of it all.

So was Holly—the head was almost out.

'Louise,' Daniel said. 'A big push, please.'

He was very polite as he made his request and Louise went from red to purple as she complied and then she made a request of her own. 'Can my mum deliver my baby?' she asked.

'I think that would be rather wonderful,' Daniel agreed.

When Kay came round, Holly watched as Daniel gave Kay's shoulder not one squeeze but two.

The first was to say, *I'm here beside you*, because for Kay this was the most important delivery of her life.

The second squeeze told her that she'd got this all under control—a midwife, a mother, a fabulous nurse, Kay was about to deliver her own grandchild.

And she coached her daughter well and soon a little head with dark hair was out and, with this push, the baby would be here.

'Oh...' Kay guided her grandbaby out into the world and delivered the vigorous bundle up onto Louise's stomach.

Daniel was there so he could step in if Kay became overwhelmed but it was simply a very beautiful birth.

'A girl,' Louise cried. 'Gilbert, we've got a little girl!'

He was a very proud father and Daniel handed Gilbert the scissors so he could cut the cord as the tiny little girl started to cry.

Holly was close to tears herself.

All births were beautiful but this one felt especially so. And yet Holly felt sad.

'You have a visitor...' Laura popped her head around the curtain.

Eamon was there to take his wife home and when Louise called for him to come and meet his granddaughter he got the surprise of his life.

Holly knew she couldn't hold it together any more and when the midwife arrived from Maternity she slipped out and went and hid in the dark small theatre to let a few tears trickle out.

She had never felt so happy and sad at the same time.

She not only loved him, she really *liked* Daniel too,

and she didn't want him to be gone. She didn't *want* to have to get over him!

So she sat and decided to have a little Holly pity party and for ten minutes she sat there, but just as she was going to sneak out to sort out her face she heard his voice.

'Holly?'

She was too tired to even jump.

He didn't turn on the lights and she didn't turn her face to where he stood at the door.

'You have a namesake—they're going to call the baby Holly.'

'That's nice.'

'You forgot to do something today and so did I.'

He turned on the big bright lights then and he politely ignored that her mascara was down to her chin as he held up two Advent calendars.

'There's still five minutes left of Christmas.'

Even chocolate couldn't help with the way she felt, but Holly gave a thin smile and took her calendar and went to open the double doors.

'What do you think it might be?' Daniel asked, but Holly didn't answer. It was the last chocolate, the last special day, the last of them.

'A chocolate-covered gold leaf star?' he suggested. 'Or a little white chocolate dove filled...'

Oh, dear, just as he was getting the hang of Christmas the master chocolatier failed him. It was another little ball with red and green sticking out and a dusting of icing sugar.

'I think this must be why they ended up in the discount store,' Holly said.

They had come this far with their Advent calendars and so were sort of duty bound to eat them really. Even as they opened their mouths and dropped the chocolates

in, both hoped they were wrong and that this time it would taste delicious.

It didn't.

'I hate glacé cherries.' Holly pulled a face and swallowed the bitter chocolate.

'And me,' Daniel said as he did the same. 'I think the chocolate's burnt!'

Then they looked at each other and, though she smiled, it was a sad one.

He loathed that he had hurt her.

Really hurt her, he knew, because they *had* made love this morning, and he had been an utter bastard afterwards.

'Don't you want to know what's in the letter?' Daniel asked.

'I'm going to smash it in the morning and find out,' Holly said, and they both smiled at the vision of her angrily taking a hammer to that blasted ball.

But then she started to cry.

'Go away,' she said.

'I can't,' Daniel said. 'Holly, I've been trying to leave for weeks but I can't. You've got me working Christmas, and adopting elephants and lining up in department stores for three hours just to get the perfect gift.'

'Three hours?'

'Which was plenty of time to change my mind, but I didn't,' Daniel said. 'I'm even arguing with elves…'

'Why were you arguing with elves?'

'I don't think my letter was effusive enough for them and, please, when you smash the decoration, bear in mind—'

'We both know I'm not going to smash it.' Holly sighed, but then she frowned. 'Bear in mind what?'

'That it was written before we…' He really struggled with the next two words. 'Made love.'

She smiled at her small victory.

'I shall bear it in mind!' Holly agreed. 'So what does it say?'

'I can't tell you. Elf rules.'

Holly rolled her eyes.

'Actually, if you guess correctly, I'll tell you so.'

'I don't want to guess.'

'What do you *think* the note might say?' Daniel insisted.

And so Holly thought for a moment and she smiled before delivering another little victory. 'I think it says "Are you on the Pill?"'

Daniel also smiled at her vindictive reference to that morning. 'I'm going to love rowing with you.'

And she could have sworn her earrings flashed, or was it hope that darted past her heart as he made reference to a future *us*.

Stop it, she told herself.

'What would you *like* the letter to say?' Daniel pushed.

And she knew what she'd like it to say, but she diluted it down, of course. 'That you like me a lot.'

'Correct,' Daniel said in sarcastic response. 'I got the little elves to write, "Dear Holly, I like you a lot." What would you *really* like it to say?'

'Don't,' Holly said, 'because I'll get all carried away and then…'

'You can get carried away, Holly. What would you like the letter to say?'

And she would be sophisticated next year.

'That you love me?' She said it as a question but it was the truth—it was what she wanted the letter to say.

She had no pride left and the emotional desert that was Daniel would just have to deal with it.

He gave a small snort at her soppy response. 'We've slept together twice, Holly.'

'I know.' She worried her bottom lip. 'It's embarrassing really…'

'What is? Your devotion to me?'

Holly nodded.

'I like it.' He grinned. 'Next guess?'

'No.' She shook her head. 'I don't like this game.'

His mouth gaped open and for the second time in their short history he pointed at her. Caught! 'You wanted it to say "Marry me"!'

'No, I didn't.'

'Holly, I don't hold out much hope for us if we're already reduced to lying. Did you or did you not hope it said that?'

'In very abstract wild dreams, possibly, while knowing of course it didn't say that…'

She had to know what it said.

'I'm going to go out to the car now and smash it!'

She was.

Holly was through being led down some emotional garden path by Daniel.

It was four minutes to midnight and with any luck that stupid ball would be history soon.

'Holly.' Daniel caught her arm as she went to go. 'Perhaps I should tell you that, for an inordinate sum, you can purchase a duplicate letter.'

'Oh.'

He opened his new wallet and instead of a condom nestled in the corner there was another shiny silver package and in the teeniest letters she saw her name.

It was rather tricky to open, but finally Holly got the letter out and she stared at the tiny squiggles.

'I can't read it.'

This was torture!

He went into a drawer and took out the magnifying glasses used for the most delicate suturing and she put them on and the tiny words came into clear view.

Dearest Holly,

I can only say this from a distance and only once I'm safely gone.

Sorry for being so contrary. You truly didn't deserve it. I want you to know that I've been cold and held back because, in truth, if I ever was going to settle down, and if there ever was that one person, then it would be you.

Daniel xxx

'The elf didn't approve,' Daniel said.

'Well, I do.'

As he took the magnifying glasses off her a part of her didn't want him to, she just wanted to stare at his words. But as the world came back to normal size she stared instead at him.

Into those absolute navy eyes that she had fallen in love with on sight.

And now she could admit it, not just to herself but to him.

'I love you.'

She'd never said it before, well, to her family and the dog and things, but not in the way she said it now.

'I know,' Daniel said. 'And I can't believe that I didn't want you to. I can't believe that I kept trying to avoid

hearing those words. But *you're* the reason I couldn't leave and the reason I want to stay...'

Oh, there was work, and there was his sister, but his world had only fallen into place when she had entered it.

Life had started to get better the day Holly had arrived and it had made him not want to leave.

'It's you,' Daniel told her. 'And if you'll have me, and we hurry, you might get that winter wedding.'

'You mean it?'

'I more than mean it,' Daniel said. 'I've even chosen the location. We're getting married in a castle.'

Later he would tell her about a family holiday and happy memories and miniature castles and motorways on Christmas mornings and all of those things, but right now there was but one thing to be said.

'I love you, Holly.'

He said the words that he never had to any other and then he lowered his mouth to hers.

It was a soft and delicious kiss and it tasted of glacé cherries with a faint trace of bitter, burnt chocolate.

And it was wonderful.

* * * * *

A BABY ON HER CHRISTMAS LIST

LOUISA GEORGE

To Iona Jones, Sue MacKay, Barbara DeLeo, Kate David and Nadine Taylor, my gorgeous Blenheim girls—thank you for the great weekend at the cottage and your amazing help to brainstorm this book.

You guys definitely know how to rock a writing retreat. xx

CHAPTER ONE

Nine months ago...

'I'VE FOUND A baby daddy!' Georgie's wide grin shone brighter than the Southern Cross, her dark brown eyes sparkling even in the bar's dim light.

Liam watched, dumbfounded, as excitement rolled off her, so intense it was almost tangible.

'Well, not a daddy as such. I should really stop saying that. But I have found someone who would be perfect to donate his sperm…which I know makes you shudder, so I'm sorry for saying The Word.' She gave Liam a wicked wink that was absolutely at odds with this whole one-sided conversation.

Whoa.

Too gobsmacked to speak, Liam indicated to her to sit. She tossed her silk wrap and bag on the back of a chair, put her drink down on the table and plonked in the seat opposite him at the only free table in Indigo's crowded lounge.

A baby?

He felt the frown forming and couldn't control it—even if he'd wanted to—and finally found his voice. 'Hey, back right up, missy. Am I dreaming here? I thought you just said something about a baby…'

It had been too long since he'd seen her looking so

happy so he was wary about bursting her bubble—but, hell, he was going to burst it anyway. Because that's what real friends did—they talked sense. Just like she'd done the first time they'd met, in the sluice room of the ER; he a lowly med student, losing his cool at the sight of a lifeless newborn, she a student nurse with more calm and control and outright guts than anyone he'd ever met. She'd let him shake, allowed him five minutes to stress out, then had forced him back into the ER to help save the kid's life. And they'd been pretty much glued at the hip ever since.

So he needed to be honest. He raised his voice over the thump-thump-thump of the bar's background bass that usually fuelled their regular Friday night drinking session, but tonight the noise was irritating and obnoxious. 'I go away for three months and come back to sheer madness. What happened to the *Nothing's going to get in the way of those renovations this time*? *I'm on the real estate ladder now and going up.* What the hell, Geo? A baby? Since when was that on your to-do list?'

Stabbing the ice in her long glass with a straw, she looked up at him, eyes darker now, and he caught a yearning he'd seen glimpses of over the last ten years. She thought she hid it well, but sometimes, when she was distracted or excited, she let her tough guard slip. 'You, of all people, know I've always wanted a family, Liam. It may not have been at the top of my list because I always believed it would just happen at some point. But I can't keep putting it off and leaving it to chance, because chance isn't going my way. And I refuse to prioritise decorating over having a baby. That would be stupid.'

In his opinion, having a baby was right up at the top of stupid but he kept that to himself. And, for the record, it wasn't just decorating—her house needed knock-down-and-start-again renovations. 'But what's the hurry? You're

only twenty-eight. It will happen, you've got plenty of time. You just need to find the right guy.' And why that made him shudder more than the *sperm* word, he didn't know.

She let the straw go, then pulled a hair tie from her wrist and curled her long wavy hair into a low ponytail. Her hair was the same colour as caramel, with little streaks of honey and gold. He didn't need to get any closer to know that it smelt like apples or fruit or something vaguely edible. And clearly he'd been away too long if he was starting to notice stuff like that.

Luckily she was oblivious to him staring at her hair and thinking about its colour and smell. 'Oh, yes, and the candidates for husband are queuing up at the door, aren't they? You may have noticed that the pickings for Mr Perfect are slim and slimming further by the day in Auckland. There's a man drought. It's official apparently, New Zealand has a lot fewer men than women my age. Why do you think I've needed you to...*expedite* a few dates for me?' Her shoulders slumped. 'I know we've had fun setting each other up with potentials over the years, but I'm starting to think that—'

'That maybe you're too...picky?' He raised his glass to her. 'Hey, I don't know, but perhaps you could consider only having a one-page check-box list that potentials need to tick, instead of fifteen?'

Her eyes widened as she smiled. 'Get out of here. It is nowhere near fifteen.'

'Not on paper, no. But in your head it is. I've seen you in action, remember. *He's not funny enough. Too intense. Just a joker. Doesn't take me seriously. Just wanted a one-nighter.*' Truth was, Liam had been secretly pretty damned proud she'd spurned most of his mates' advances and that she'd ended most flings before they'd got serious. There was something special about Georgie and she deserved a

special kind of bloke. He hadn't met one yet that would be worthy of her.

'So I have standards. I'd settle for Mr *Almost* Perfect if he existed—which he doesn't. I'm getting too short on time.' Her red, loose-fitting summer dress moved softly as she shrugged delicate shoulders. 'I don't know about you, but I get the feeling that asking a man to father your children on a first date might just scare him off.'

'Well, hell, if I asked a man to father my children on any date it'd either be in a nightmare or because I was hallucinating.'

She rolled her eyes. 'You know very well what I mean. And, yes, you are the straightest guy I've ever met.' Her eyes ran over his chest, lingering a little over his pecs, throat, mouth. Why he noticed he didn't know. And, even stranger, he felt a little hot. When her gaze met his she gave him her usual friendly smile. 'You're looking mighty fit these days, Dr MacAllister. How was Pakistan?'

'Hot, wet and desperate.' As with all his aid missions, he didn't want to relive what he had seen. Enough that he had those images in his own head, without sharing details with others.

'But at least you know you were doing good out there. What were the conditions like? Are you okay? How are you feeling? When do you leave again? Please be happy for me.'

This was always how it was with Georgie: random conversation detours and finishing each other's sentences. But things generally flowed and they knew each other so well that often they didn't have to speak to communicate. So with the sudden baby daddy bombshell he'd never felt so excluded from her life. 'I'm fine. Knackered, but fine, looking forward to a few weeks' locuming at the General's ER. At least there's running water and reliable electric-

ity. And I have a decent bed to sleep in. The next planned rollout for me is in South Sudan in a couple of months.'

'But if they need you earlier…'

He nodded. 'Sure. It's the way it is.'

'I still don't know how you manage all that to-ing and fro-ing. Here a couple of months, then gone again. I like staying in one place.'

And he didn't. The longest he ever stayed anywhere was when he came back here because he needed a semi-permanent job to help fund his aid work. 'But I'm never going away again if it means I come back to crazyville baby talk.'

'It's not crazyville.' Again with the eye roll. He didn't even have to look. This time it was accompanied by an irritated shake of her head. 'I've made a decision to do this now. On my own. I know it'll be tough and it's not the perfect image I've always had in my head about a mum and dad and two point four kids, but that's too far out of reach right now. I've had to curtail my dreaming and get real. Being a solo mum is just fine.'

She stopped talking to take a long drink of what looked a lot like lemonade. On a Friday night? Could be that she was actually serious about this. 'I want to conceive and carry to term, and have a baby…*my* baby…and, if things work out, have another one too. But that's probably greedy and selfish.'

'You deserve to be, Geo, after what you've been through.' *But now? Why now?*

'So, I'm looking forward, and taking an opportunity. Endo is a lot less active during pregnancy so if I could manage two pregnancies in quick succession…if the IUI works, that is… IVF would be a whole different ball game.'

Trying to keep up he lifted his palms towards her. 'IUI? IVF? Slow down a bit. So you're not thinking turkey baster? Or just plain old-fashioned sex? That is a relief.'

'Believe me, I'll do whatever's necessary.'

He didn't doubt it. And finally the reality was sinking in. She was going to do the one thing he'd sworn never to do—and because he was her friend she'd expect him to be supportive. 'So what tipped you over to the dark side?'

And, yes, his reaction would not be what she wanted, but: a) he couldn't help it and; b) he wasn't prepared to lie just to make her feel better. It was precisely because of their friendship that he knew he could be straight up with her.

'You are such a grump. For me there is no dark side. Being abandoned at two days old and having literally no one from then on in has made me want to feel part of something…a family. You know that. I just want what everyone else has, Liam—to feel loved, to be loved. To love. And I have no doubt that there will be some hard times, but I will never leave my baby on a doorstep for someone else to find, and condemn them to a life of foster-homes and social services, like my mum did to me. I will cherish any child I have. I've had my share of dark sides and being pregnant and a mother isn't one of them.'

Her nose wrinkled as she reached across and lightly punched him on the arm. 'So, I was worried things were getting worse endo-wise, so I asked Malcolm to run some more tests at work a few weeks ago.' Her hands palmed across her abdomen—subconsciously? Possibly. Protective? Definitely.

'You've been having more pain? Oh, God, I'm sorry, Georgie. That sucks. Really, I thought you were managing okay.' Liam hated that. Hated that even though he fixed people up every day he didn't have the answers to Georgie's problems and that they were running out of solutions as time ticked on. His heart thumped in sync with the music, hard and loud in his chest. 'What did he say?'

'That the endometriosis is indeed getting worse. That

everything in there's getting blocked up and scarred and it won't be long before I'll need pretty major surgery. That it's only a matter of time before pregnancy is going to be nigh on impossible. At least, without a whole lot of effort and money and no promises at the end.'

Her eyes filled with tears. Which, for Georgie, was such a rarity Liam sat there like a useless lump and watched in horror, unable to move. She was the strongest woman he knew. She'd faced tough battles her whole life and she never tired of fighting. No matter how ridiculous her plan sounded, his heart twisted to see her hurting. 'You know how much I need this, Liam. I thought you'd understand. I thought you'd support me. You know, like good friends do? I've been there for you regardless and I kind of hoped you'd feel the same.' Her hand reached for her gut again. 'This idea? This is a good thing.'

It was the worst thing he'd ever heard. 'And so who is going to provide the...?' He couldn't bring himself to say the word. For an accomplished medic he had trouble imagining what went on behind closed doors at the IVF clinic.

'Sperm? I've decided I'm going to ask Malcolm.'

'What?' Liam almost choked on his beer. 'Your boss?'

'And that's wrong, why? He's smart. Not unattractive. Owns a successful IVF clinic and has helped thousands of women achieve their dreams, so he's compassionate too. Those are all the right kind of genes I'd look for in a father for my child.'

'He's still also your boss.'

She hip-planted both hands. 'And I'm pretty sure he'd want to help. He sees this kind of thing every day, so to him it's not an unusual request. I'll ask him to sign a contract to keep things simple. I have enough money put by to keep me going for a while and the clinic has agreed to reduce my hours after maternity leave.'

Maternity leave. Contracts. That sounded far from sim-

ple. And the money she had put by was supposed to be for renovations to help her become more financially independent. 'Seems like you have it all figured out.'

'He knows how much I want this. How much I need to know DNA and family history. It's been my life's dream. Just a little...*expedited*.' She gave him a smile at their shared joke.

Liam didn't feel much like laughing. Sure, she'd talked about this on and off over the years but now the reality hit him in the gut like a two-ton truck. She wanted a baby. A family. Kids. 'Surely asking your boss is downright unprofessional. Unethical.'

'A friend helping a friend? Since when did that cross any kind of line?'

'Where would you like me to start?' It crossed more lines than Liam cared to think of. It would be like...like if he offered to father her child. Ridiculous. Ludicrous.

Wouldn't it?

The thought flitted across a corner of his mind. He pushed it away. Ludicrous indeed.

'Malcolm saw how upset I was at the results.' As she spoke she seemed to loosen up a little. Determined, but calm. 'I've asked to have a meeting with him next week. If he says no then I'll have a rethink.'

'It sounds messy to me. How about using one of the anonymous donors at the clinic? You get to know about their family history, too. You can choose anyone that ticks your fifteen pages of boxes.' He didn't know why someone anonymous fathering her child seemed like a better option. It just *felt* better. A long way from right, but better. 'And why didn't you ask me?'

What the hell?

He didn't even know where that question had come from. As she stared at him his chest tightened.

'Is that what this is all about? You're upset because I

didn't ask you? Honestly? The man who comes out in hives when he even sees a baby?' As soon as the words left her mouth she closed her eyes and pressed her lips together. Too late. After a beat or two she slowly opened her eyes again and winced. 'Oh, my God, I'm sorry. Really. I'm sorry, Liam. I am. I didn't mean... I'm so sorry. But I just know how you feel about families.'

'Do you?'

She looked surprised at his question. Probably because he'd kept his past to himself and never spoke about what he wanted for the future. But families and babies were something he definitely had an aversion to. No, not an aversion, just a deep desire not to go there. Ever.

Her voice softened. 'Since you always refuse to talk about anything deeper than what you had for lunch, I have to surmise. You have a track record of emotional avoidance. So I've always assumed that big loving, meddling, messy, happy families aren't something on your wish list. In all honesty, you'd be the last person I'd ask. And, judging by your current reaction, I think I'm right.'

Liam's face was all shadows and hollows. His blue eyes had darkened to navy. Only once before had Georgie seen him look so utterly haunted, and that had been the day they'd met and she'd forced him to work on that newborn.

Later that night, when they'd gone for the first of many subsequent beers, the alcohol had made his tongue loose and he'd mentioned a family tragedy involving his sister, Lauren. But then had clammed up so tight Georgie had never been able to open him up to that particular hotspot conversation again. And since then he'd absorbed whatever it was that had thrown him off balance that day. Until now.

His voice was low when he eventually spoke. 'I just think you could have talked to me about it all first. Put more thought into it.'

'I don't think that's possible, it's all I've been thinking about for weeks, turning scenarios over and over in my head.' She watched as anger and hurt twitched through him until he wrestled it under control. Why couldn't he just smile and pat her hand and say what a brilliant idea it was? Her words had obviously been a low blow. She'd always respected that he had his reasons for not wanting a family, even if he'd never really fronted up and explained why.

Some support would have been nice, but hadn't she heard this kind of story so many times at work? Babies, IVF and the sometimes desperate journey towards parenthood made strong couples stronger and weak ones fall apart.

Then thank God she and Liam weren't a couple because, judging by this conversation, they'd fall at the first hurdle.

He was her friend, her closest friend in lots of ways; she always took his advice, always went to him with problems. And now she was all kinds of confused, needing time to think and reaffirm.

She stood to leave. 'Look, this was clearly a mistake. I'm going to go home so we can both take some time out. I'm sorry if I've ruined our Friday night. But, you know, I don't know where we'd go from here. Trying to play your wingman and find a date for you with some poor unsuspecting woman just isn't my idea of fun right now.'

He tipped his glass towards her again, but he didn't get up. Didn't try to make her feel better. And he always tried to make her feel better.

Which was why his opposition was spooking her more than she'd anticipated. Still, she'd made this decision and she was sticking with it.

She had no choice. This was her life. Her chance.

And to hell with him if he wasn't going to be there right

when she needed it most. She threw her wrap round her shoulders. 'I'll…I don't know…see you later?'

He watched her stand. He still didn't move but his voice was more controlled as he gave her a small smile. 'Heaven help us all when you start taking the hormone injections.'

'Oh? Why?'

'Aren't they supposed to make you all antsy and volatile?'

'What?' She couldn't bring herself to tell him she'd been taking them already. And, yes, she was being antsy. But it was his reaction that had made her like that, not the medications. 'Maybe, just maybe you have royally pissed me off. And to add insult to injury, you're now being condescending. Patronising.'

'Just honest. As always.' Yes, she supposed he was. One of things she relied on him for was his frank honesty. 'So when is it all happening? The impregnating thing?'

'So very clinical, Liam.'

'Yes. Isn't it?'

'I was hoping it would be in the next couple of weeks if possible.'

The glass in his hand hit the table with a crash. 'What? So soon? You don't mess around, do you? You don't want to talk a bit more? At least listen to someone else's opinion?'

'And have you try to convince me against it? I don't think so. I don't need your negativity. It's a chance, Liam. I need to take it.'

For a few seconds he looked at her. Just stared at her. She couldn't read him. The man she'd thought she knew pretty much inside and out, and she couldn't even guess what he was thinking.

After a torturous silence that seemed to increase the tension tenfold, he spoke, 'Yes. Yes, you do. Take the chance, Geo.' Now he stood up and walked her to

the door. Once outside he didn't wrap her in his usual goofy bear hug. Didn't graze her cheek with a kiss and a smile. Didn't give her a wink and make her laugh. 'Let me know how you get on.'

'Why? So you can make me doubt myself all over again?'

He took her by the shoulders and his gaze bored into her. 'Because I'm your friend, Georgie.'

And then she ached for him to give her one of his hugs more than anything else in the world. But he turned away. Back towards the bar and the white noise that seemed to be mingling with his words and filling her head with doubts.

What if he was right? What if this was the far side of crazy? What the hell did she know about family anyway? About parenting? It wasn't as if she'd had any experience on either side of that particular fence. What if Malcolm didn't follow through? What if he did?

Worse, what if this rift meant that the friendship she had with Liam would be broken for ever? He was the closest thing she had to any notion of family, and the thought of not having him in her life made her suddenly feel empty and cold.

Torn and confused, she climbed into a waiting cab and watched him retreat to the bar, his dark T-shirt straining across well-defined broad shoulders, and a gait that screamed defiance.

And what the hell was going on with those pecs? The man had suddenly developed muscles of steel. Strange, too, that in the midst of all this turmoil she should even notice. That, and the shape of his lips, the way his mouth curved and softened as he smiled, which had been rare but welcome tonight. Those hormones were clearly playing havoc with her head.

But judging by the sudden strange slick of heat that hit her breasts and abdomen—which surely must be a reaction to the muggy Auckland evening—they were messing with her body too.

CHAPTER TWO

Mum's had a stroke. Had to go back to UK. Don't know for how long. Will keep you in the loop. Sorry. Can we have that meeting when I get back?

SHUTTING THE IVF clinic room door, so she could have a moment to take it all in, Georgie stared at the text, her gut clenching. Bile rose to the back of her throat. She felt dizzy.

And downright selfish.

Inhaling deeply, she pulled herself together. For goodness' sake, it wasn't the end of the world, just the end of an opportunity. That was all. There would be another chance, next month or the month after. Some time. With a different donor.

She should be feeling sorry for her boss, not herself.

No worries, Malcolm. Safe journey. Sending hugs for your mum x

And yet she felt as if her world was closing in on her, that she was fast running out of time and her dream was getting further out of reach. Scrolling through her texts, she found her conversation thread with Liam and started to type. Then stopped. She hadn't heard a thing from him

for four days, and even though she knew he'd be busy, catching up on everything at work, she felt a little lost. Normally he'd text her with funny stories from his shift, jokes, stuff. Just stuff. But ever since Friday she'd been hit by silence. And it hurt a little that he knew what she was going through but didn't want to see how she was doing.

Okay, it hurt a lot.

So maybe that would be the norm from now on. She didn't want to think about that. But for the last few days it hadn't been just his absence that had been on her mind. It had been that crazy tingly feeling that had swept through her body the other night, just looking at him. And then an out-of-proportion feeling of loss that he wasn't being supportive. It was absurd. Seemed those meds made her overreact in lots of different ways.

The clinic room phone interrupted her thoughts and brought her back to reality. 'Georgie speaking.'

It was Helen, the receptionist, and Georgie's good friend. 'I have a patient here, Kate Holland. Says she doesn't feel too great. Can you see her straight away?'

'Kate? Sure, I remember her, she was in just the other day. I'll be right through.' Helen rarely showed any kind of emotion, so the anxiety in her voice made Georgie take notice. Putting her own worries aside, she made sure the clinic couch was ready, opened up Kate's notes on the laptop then collected her patient, who appeared noticeably short of breath, flushed and anxious.

'Kate. What's the problem? Are you okay?'

'No. I feel pretty rubbish, actually. My stomach hurts and I'm so thirsty.' For a toned and fit marathon runner Kate climbed onto the bed with a lot of effort.

Alarm bells began to ring. Georgie settled the young woman against the pillow, silently counting the laboured respiratory rate. 'You've been having the injections, right? Any other problems? Nausea? Vomiting?'

Kate nodded. 'Yes. Twice this morning and I feel really sick now. But so thirsty.'

Georgie took her patient's hand and measured her pulse. Fast and thready. Any number of scenarios raced through her mind. Fertility drugs had a tranche of usually mild and temporary side-effects, but when they were severe they could be life-threatening. 'Peeing okay? If you can do us a sample, that'd be great.'

'Not much at all. But I'll try.'

'Okay, when you next need to go, yell out.' Giving Kate a quick examination and piecing together her patient's history, Georgie reached a preliminary diagnosis. It wasn't what either she or her patient wanted to hear. 'How long have you felt like this?'

'The past couple of days or so. I started feeling really sick yesterday.' Kate gripped Georgie's hand, her flushed face tight and scared. 'But please don't tell me we have to stop the injections. Please say we can do this. It's our last chance.'

Georgie gently encouraged her to lie back down, not wanting to upset her even more but realising that time was of the essence. 'I know, Kate. I know. But don't get ahead of yourself. I'll quickly get the doctor to come check you over, he'll probably suggest you have a short stay in hospital, just a few days or so, to check everything's okay...'

After the doctor had confirmed Kate's diagnosis, Georgie arranged the next few steps. 'Because you're publicly funded, we'll transfer you to the General Hospital gynae ward, that's the closest to your home. They'll look after you. I promise.'

'What about the IVF? Will that happen now?'

Georgie took her hand again. 'Sweetheart, you remember the doctor saying you had something called OHSS? That's our medical shorthand for ovarian hyper-stimulation syndrome. That means your body has reacted very

strongly to the drugs. You have too much fluid in your abdomen, which is why you're out of breath. You're dehydrated, but we need to watch how much fluid you drink because we don't want you overloaded. You have a swollen red calf, which might mean you have a blood clot. We've arranged for some scans and a few more tests at the hospital. You need to rest and let your body heal before you do any more.'

'We can't afford any more. This is it, our last chance. Mark will be so disappointed. He's been really positive this time round, we both have. We talked about a Christmas baby, he got so excited. He wants to be a dad so much.' Fat tears rolled down Kate's red cheeks and Georgie's heart melted.

Some people, such as Kate, were lucky enough to be eligible for publicly funded treatment for a limited number of cycles. Having already waited for months and had one failed attempt, this was indeed Kate's last chance. She and her husband Mark had a low income and there was no way could they afford the high costs and even more time off work for private IVF. Life was so unfair sometimes.

Georgie dealt with these scenarios in her job every day, and she'd always managed to keep a professional emotional distance, but today it felt deeply personal. She knew how desperate it was to have a ticking clock. And a chance that could be blown for any random reason. 'We'll do the best we can for you, Kate.' But she wouldn't make any promises. It wasn't her style to give her patients false hope, no matter how much her heart ached in sync with them. 'In the meantime, you have to get better.'

If anything, it made Georgie more determined to grab her chance as soon as she could. Deciding to go through with it was the first step on what she knew was going to be a long road. She had no illusions as to the prospect of being a single pregnant woman, then a solo mother. It would be

immensely rewarding. It would be hard. And with no one else to help shoulder the burden she knew there would be times she'd find it difficult to cope. But she would. She'd been on her own her whole life. She didn't need anyone else. But needing and wanting were two different things.

On days like these she'd usually ring Liam and have a whinge. Often he'd suggest a drink or a movie or something to cheer her up. But as he'd gone AWOL and she didn't fancy another grim conversation, she'd do things differently tonight. He certainly wasn't the only friend she had in the world.

'Okay, that's me over and out. See you in the morning,' Liam called to his secretary, then grabbed his work bag and made his way through the crowded ER to the exit. It had been one hell of a day, dealing with staff shortages, bus-crash casualties and the usual walk-ins. What he needed now was a sundowner at the local and an early night.

The hospital doors swept open and he took his first breath of fresh air for eleven hours. It was tinged with a familiar fragrance that had him turning his head. She was standing way over to his left, half-hidden by a tall confident-looking man, and Liam would have missed her and walked by if he hadn't caught that sweet, flowery scent.

For some reason, as he saw her deep in conversation with a stranger, his heart hammered. Mainly, he suspected, because he'd bawled her out the other day and hadn't had the chance to make things right. 'Georgie. Hi. What are you doing here?'

She whirled round, her cheeks reddening, her green nursing scrubs making her look younger somehow. Vulnerable, which she'd hate. There was a ripple of tension as her shoulders straightened, but she masked it. 'Oh. Hey. I'm dropping off a patient's bag. She had to be admitted

unexpectedly and left it at the clinic by mistake. This is her husband, Mark.'

'Liam. Hi, I work here.' As he shook hands with the guy the heart-hammering slowed a little. Was it wrong to feel relief that his friend wasn't sick, but that another man's wife was? Damn right it was. But relief shuddered through him anyway. 'Is everything okay?'

'Mark's wife, Kate, has OHSS, so she's feeling a bit fragile. Mark's on his way up to see her on Ward Three.'

'Ah, yes. I remember seeing her name on the admissions board. She'll be okay, mate. She's in good hands.'

The man nodded grimly and headed through the main entrance. Leaving just Liam and Georgie and a weird sense of displacement. Georgie played with the handle of her handbag, looked at her feet. 'I should probably go.'

Not without some kind of resolution, he thought grimly. This was painful. They'd never had this kind of weird, tense scenario play out before. 'Wait. Are you okay?'

What he meant was, *Are we okay?*

'Yes. Thanks. You?' She raised her head and looked at him. She looked tired, drawn. The edges of her eyes were ringed with black. Which was a far cry from the last time he'd seen her when she'd been brimful of excitement, and he'd stomped all over her happy mood. Was the dark look just for him or had something else happened to her?

Okay, stop guessing and cut the crap. 'Look, Geo, I didn't mean to pee all over your parade. I'm sorry about the other night. I was tired and just caught by surprise.'

'Clearly. And you've been too busy to send a text?' But the iron-clad barriers seemed to give just a little with his apology. 'Or did they get lost in cyberspace, along with your good manners?'

'As it happens, things have been manic here. I've done four long days with the last vestiges of jet-lag messing with my brain.' She didn't need to hear all that. 'I did think

about texting you more than a few times. But I wasn't sure whether you'd slap me or eye-stab me with one of those killer looks you save for especially annoying people that drive you mad on purpose. And I wasn't up to taking the risk.'

That, at least, got a smile. 'Aw, Liam, I'd never eye-stab you. How could you say such a thing?'

'I know what you're capable of, my girl. Downright scary at times.' He walked with her towards the car park, feeling a little more relaxed. 'Er…done the deed yet?'

'By which you mean the assisted fertility?' Georgie slowed and gave him what he had come to recognise as one of her false smiles. Her mouth flipped up into the usual grin, but her eyes didn't shine. In fact, nothing about her was shining tonight. Even her *caramel* hair—it was just plain weird that he'd started to notice things that he'd always glossed over—seemed dulled. 'Malcolm's had to go away due to a family crisis, so I've put off asking him.'

'Oh. I see.' And with that news he really should have been cock-a-hoop but he wasn't. Strange emotions rippled through him, mainly disappointment for her. It was what she wanted. She'd been so excited and determined the other day, to the point that he'd been unable to talk any sense into her.

Now she looked like she needed bolstering. 'Okay. So you've got plenty of time. I'm sure you'll be fine waiting just a little while longer. Have you had any thoughts about asking anyone else? What about the donor lists?'

She frowned. 'Yes, well, it's far from ideal. And, like I said, time is something I don't have a lot of.'

'You sound like you're waiting for the guillotine or something. Just a touch dramatic, Geo?'

'You think so?' As they closed in on her car they stopped. She pointed up to the second floor of the hospital with a taut finger that was definitely capable of eye-stabbing if

she so wished. 'That lady in there has been trying to get pregnant for five years. And nothing. Zilch. Nil. She's had one chance at IVF, which came up with disappointment, and now everything's on hold until she gets better from the side effects of trying to stimulate her ovaries. I expect that if she gets the go-ahead again she'll have to pay megabucks...and even then it might not work for her.

'I do not want to be that lady, possibly looking at years of pressure and stress. I've got to start the ball rolling and damn well soon. Otherwise when and if I'm finally in a committed relationship with someone who loves me, it might be too late. I have a window of opportunity in my cycle coming up very soon. And I'm disappointed that I can't take advantage of it. Dramatic? If you say so. But, then, you're not the one staring down the barrel of a ticking time bomb.'

'Wow. See? Scary.' He stepped back. 'I'll just make sure I'm out of eye-stabbing range.'

She stalked off to her car, then stopped abruptly and turned on him, gravel scraping underfoot. Never before had he seen such passion and anger and determination and spirit in anyone. 'For once in your life, Liam, take me seriously.'

'I do. All the time. I was just trying to make you feel better.'

'Well, you didn't. You know what? I bet we could spend the next few weeks going round in circles with this and you'd never understand.'

Oh, he understood all right. He'd been thinking about it for days, ever since she'd brought the subject up. In fact, that ludicrous idea that had flitted through his head had taken seed and would not let go.

But the ramifications were huge.

She glared at him, her eyes fierce, curls springing loose and free around her face. Her mouth taut and determined.

She looked magnificent and terrifying, like the time she'd pushed him into Resus for that baby. And many times since when she'd been hell-bent on partying hard or just grasping life in her hands and making the most of it. She'd been like that since he'd known her—reaching, grasping, dreaming. Making her life full, taking what she wanted. Because she'd had so little for so long she hadn't wanted to waste a moment, and she defied anyone who stood in her way.

She was strong and staunch and loyal and in that second he knew that if *his* back was against the wall, she'd do anything for him. Anything.

And so here they were at an impasse. All he had to do was offer her what she wanted.

Great to help out a friend, but at the same time he was held back by…abject *fear*. Fear, that was it. The increased heart rate, sweaty palms, gut clench. He was scared as hell at the prospect of it all, of letting everyone down. Of not loving enough. Or, worse, loving too much. And he knew damned well how that panned out. He wouldn't be able to function around a child or be part of her cosy family. But if he didn't do it then she'd be forced to choose someone she didn't know or give up altogether—and he knew, too, that that was not part of her dream.

Despite all the late-night musings and the words going round and round in his head, he knew it was the most stupid idea he'd ever had.

But the words lingered. Lingered still as he saw her shrug her shoulders. As she turned her back to him and opened the car door. Lingered as he watched her swipe her hand across her face to stop a rogue tear. She wouldn't even allow herself to show her bitter disappointment. That almost broke him in two.

It would cost him little in time and effort. Not overtly anyway. He'd have to deal with the ramifications later.

But right now his friend was hurting and there was something he could do to help. One singular thing. He could be that guy. The one he wanted to be, the one who took an emotional risk and helped a friend in need, whatever the personal cost.

Before he'd had a chance to second guess himself the words were tumbling out. 'Georgie, wait. I'll do it.'

Her voice was small and he could hear the pain, and yet deep down there was some hope as she turned to face him. 'Do what?'

'I'll be the donor.'

'You? *You?* Why?' Her laugh was bordering on sarcastic.

He took a step forward. 'Because I'm taking you seriously. This is what you want. What you deserve.'

She wagged her finger, fast. 'Oh, no. No. No. No. No. No. No. Not happening.'

'Unless you have a particular aversion to passing along my DNA? If I were to look objectively I'd say I was pretty okay. I'm a doctor, so not dumb. Oh, and my compassion knows no bounds. Apparently you like that in a father figure. I'm funny—always a winner.' He pointed to his abs, which he sucked in for effect. 'And pretty much the most devastatingly good-looking man in town.'

And bingo—his aid work meant he'd be out of the country for most of the rest of his life if he wanted. So he wouldn't be forced into any emotional attachment. This was a purely altruistic act. Which begged the question—what the hell did he want?

This wasn't about him, he reminded himself. It was about Georgie. 'How could you not want to use my *sperm*?' He whispered the last word as reality started to seep through his feel-good fuzzies.

The sarcasm melted away and the laugh was pure Geor-

gie. 'Yeah, right. That's objective? Don't get above your-self. For one, you have a slightly crooked nose.'

He ran his down his ethmoid bone and he gave her his profile view. 'Rugby injury, not genetic. Besides, you can hardly see it.'

She cocked her hip to one side as she perused him. 'You have particularly broad shoulders.'

'Great for tackling and giving great hugs.' And he should know. He'd done it often enough. Usually as he was patting women on the back and wishing them well. *It wasn't them, it was him.*

She frowned. 'But not great for wearing halter-neck tops.'

'Ah shucks, and now you've spoilt my dress plans for tomorrow.' Funny, but it felt strange, being analysed in such a way by a friend.

'On the other hand, you do have…long legs.' Her voice cracked a little as her gaze scanned his trousers. Her pupils did a funny widening thing. A flash of something—and then it was gone. Two red spots appeared on her cheeks. 'Ahem, big feet.'

'And we all know what that means.' He winked. 'Any boy would be happy with the MacAllister brand of DNA. If you bottled it you'd get a fortune.'

'Oh, yeah? No girl wants big feet. Bad for shoe buying.' She gave him a final once-over glance. Then her voice softened. 'Really, it's a lovely offer and I'd be stupid not to take you up on it. But what about you? You don't want this. You really don't want this.'

'But you do, Georgie.' There was a long beat while he tried to put into words the weird feelings he was experi-encing. He could give her the chance she wanted, on one condition. 'But we'll need a contract. I don't want any in-volvement.'

'Oh.' Giving the minutest shake of her head, she held

her palm up. 'You'll be the baby daddy but don't want to be *the* daddy?'

'Yep.'

'Oh. Okay. Then I'm utterly shocked that you've offered. Why would you do that?'

Not wanting to dig up something he'd pushed to the darkest part of his soul, he gave her the scantest of explanations. 'Happy families isn't my style. But a happy Georgie is. I'll do it. Just agree before I change my mind.'

'Oh, this is fast and so out of left field.' She put a hand to his shoulder, ran her fingers down his arm. And in the cool late summer evening goosebumps followed the trail of her warm skin against his. 'Can I think about it? Get used to the idea?'

'Sure.' He needed time too, his chest felt blown wide open.

'It would mean a lot of changes. For us.'

'I know. I realise that.' And if it hadn't been Georgie's dream on the line, no way would he ever contemplate something like this.

She looked hesitant, shocked, but hopeful. 'So...well, we could have a contract similar to the clinic's standard donor document. We can use that as a blueprint. If that's what you really want?'

'That's what I want. No involvement, nothing.'

'I won't ask you for anything else. Ever. Trust me.'

He did. Absolutely. He just wasn't sure how much he could trust himself. 'Yes. Definitely. A contract will be best.'

'And it'll mean tests. Soon. Like this week.'

'Whatever it takes.' Although the altruistic vibe was fast morphing into panic.

'Oh, my God, is this really happening?' She reached round his waist and pulled him into one of her generous

hugs. His nostrils filled with her perfume and he fought a sudden urge not to let go.

Her body felt good close to his. She was soft in his arms and her head against his chest made his heart hurt a little. He'd missed her these last few weeks. Especially these last few days. They never argued.

And this…was just a hug. Nothing strange there. She gave them all the time. And yet… He was aware of the softness of her body, the curve of her waist… He swallowed.

Nah. She felt just the same as always. Just the same old Georgie. She turned her head and looked up at him, her dark eyes dancing with excitement, the evening sun catching her profile. For a second she just looked into his eyes. One. Two. He lost count. She had amazing eyes. Flecked with warm gold and honey that matched her hair. His gaze drifted across the face he knew so well, and a shiver of something he didn't want to recognise tightened through him.

She pulled away quickly and the connection broke.

Thank God, because he was getting carried away in all her emotion. And that was definitely not something he was planning on doing. Emotional distance was the only thing that stopped him wreaking any more damage on those he loved. Hell, he was his father's son after all. Emotional distance was what MacAllister men did better than anyone else. But somehow he didn't think that that admission would go down well on Georgie's tick list.

'Thank you. Thank you so much. It means a lot to me.' She placed a gentle kiss on his cheek. Again with the goosebumps. This time they prickled all the way to his gut and lower. 'I'll mull it over and…um…let you know? Soon as possible?'

'Okay, and I'll get the turkey baster sorted for when you say yes.' Now he needed to ignore the strange feel-

ings and off-load some of this ache in his chest. He saw a damned long run in his immediate future.

Her demeanour changed. She brushed a hand down over her scrub trousers, all business and organisation as she took a shaky little step away from him. 'Like I said, we'll do it the clinic way.'

'For sure. Any other way would be just too—'

Her head tilted a little to the side. 'Ick?'

He grinned. 'Is that a technical term?'

'Absolutely. For that weird feeling you get when you think about sleeping with your best friend? Like sex with your cousin? Right? Weird.' Shuddering, she looked to him for reassurance.

Which he gave unreservedly. 'Right. Yes. Ick's the word.'

The notion of them having sex had rarely arisen. Back in the early days he'd caught himself looking at her and wondering. She'd walked through his dreams many nights. He'd tried to imagine what kissing her would have been like. How she would taste. How she would feel underneath him. Around him. But he'd never put any of that into words for fear she'd run a mile. He'd never asked more from her than what they'd already had and, frankly, he'd believed that any kind of fling would inevitably ruin the great friendship they'd built up.

She was worth more to him than just sex. And seeing as that was the only thing he ever offered to women, he'd never wanted to risk doing something so pointlessly stupid and losing her.

Plus, while Georgie was funny and loyal, she'd never made a move or seemed interested in him in that way. They'd had an implicit agreement that anything of a sexual nature could never happen. So he'd sublimated those imaginings until he'd stopped having them. Had lost himself in other women.

Which made it all the more nonsensical that he'd started noticing things again…like her smell, the colour of her hair, her eyes. Surely it could only mean some sort of nostalgia for the younger Georgie in his past when the present was shifting out of his control?

CHAPTER THREE

Eight months ago...

Hey, stranger. Thought you'd want to know that your genius sperm has done what it was designed to do... I'm pregnant!

Great news. Congratulations.

Finally, an answer. Biggest news she'd ever had and not one exclamation mark. Not one. No cheers or fanfares. No questions. Was he not just a little curious? Pleased for her? Maybe it was the whole emotionless text thing stuffing up the sentiment of his message, but hadn't the man heard about emoticons?

Disappointed, Georgie texted him back.

I'm so excited! :) Catch up soon?

Sure. Things are a bit busy right now. Packing. South Sudan. In two days. I'll try come over to say bye.

Okay, your call.

He was heading off again and he'd try to come and see

her? *Try?* What the hell…? Packing didn't take two whole days. He was the world's lightest traveller.

And, actually, it was her call just as much as his. Worrying about contacting him had never been an issue before and it shouldn't be now just because she was carrying his baby. *No. Her* baby. He'd made that very clear. But surely they could still be friends? She wasn't going to allow this to change what they had. Why should pregnancy make a difference?

But it did, she realised. Not just to her relationship with Liam, but to her. She was going to be a mum. *A mother.* With a family. Something she'd never had before. She was going to be part of something…more.

She put a hand to her very flat, very *un*pregnant-looking stomach and her heart did another flip. It was still so early, too early to grow attached; any number of things could go wrong. But it was already too late. Her stomach tumbled as she closed her eyes, imagining.

Hey, there, little one. Nice to meet you.

And that was about all she dared say. She felt something tug deep inside her. These days she seemed to be so emotional about things. About the baby. About Liam…

Well, if he wasn't going to make an effort then she damn well would. She wanted to celebrate and send him off on his travels with no tension between them. Georgie stabbed his number into the phone and left a message: 'Hey, step away from your backpack. Let's do something. I won't take no for an answer. I get the feeling you're avoiding me. But if you are, please don't admit it. Just say you've been busy. Mission Bay? Six-thirty. I'm hiring bikes. No excuses.'

'Are you bonkers or just straight up certifiable?' Three hours later his voice, behind her, although irritated and loud, made her heart jig in her chest. He'd turned up at

least, and for that she was grateful. 'Cycling? In your condition? Seriously?'

'Oh, for goodness' sake, I'm fine. How many times have we done this?' She turned and pretended to scowl, but her scowl dropped the moment she set eyes on him. He was wearing a scruffy old T-shirt that hugged his toned muscles and was the same vibrant blue as his eyes. Faded jeans graced his long legs, framing his bum…and, no, she'd never really studied it before, but it was deliciously gorgeous. No wonder he had a queue of women trying to encourage him to commit.

Heat hit her cheeks and shimmied down to her belly, where it transformed into *What would he be like in bed?*

And that was just one of too many thoughts about him recently that were way out of line.

To distract herself from staring too long at the man who had suddenly become a whole new fascination for her, she clipped on her helmet and prepared to use up some of this nervous energy. Pregnant, yes. Petrified, indeedy. Strangely excited just to see her long-lost best mate? Very definitely. And that made her legs twitch and her stomach roll.

'I needed some fresh air. It's such a beautiful evening and it's the weekend tomorrow. Freedom! We could get fish and chips and eat them on the beach later.'

He frowned and pointed to her helmet. 'Take it off, Georgie. It's too dangerous. We haven't been cycling for years, you could fall off. Why you suddenly want to do it now I don't know.'

'Because it used to be fun and I don't know why we got out of the habit of doing it. I want the fun back.' She shook her head in defiance. 'And stop being ridiculous. You're a doctor, you know very well that at this stage in pregnancy it's perfectly fine to exercise. Come on, I'll be fine, it's not as if I'm bungee jumping. Although, there is

a free slot at the Skytower at eight. So if we hurry...' She handed him his helmet and stood, arms crossed over her chest, until he'd put it on over that grumpy face. 'Breathe, Liam. Breathe. It was a joke. And do try to keep up!'

The sea air was filled with salt and heat and the smell of a distant barbecue. Overhead, seagulls dived and squawked, making the most of a bright summer evening's scavenging. Mission Bay was, as always, filled with smiling people, cycling, blading or running along the seaside promenade. On the right, beyond small beach inlets and a turquoise sea dotted with anchored yachts, the mighty volcanic Rangitoto Island stood verdant and powerful. On the left they cycled past coastal suburbia, higgledy-piggledy candy-coloured houses clinging to the steep hillside.

Georgie pedalled hard, keeping him in her slipstream, ignoring his concerned cries. She could do this. She needed to do this to show him—and herself—that she was still the same old Georgie. And if she could also purge those weird fluttery feelings that seemed to happen whenever she saw him, that would be even better. Because this new Georgie who kept popping up with hot thoughts about Liam was unsettling in the extreme.

Usually he raced ahead, screaming over his shoulder for her to go faster, but today he seemed happy to pootle behind. She had the distinct feeling that, in his own way, he was keeping watch over her.

After a few kilometres, pedalling towards towering city skyscrapers, she turned and cycled back to the row of Victorian buildings flanking a children's playground and large fountain. Toddlers kicked and splashed in the spraying water, watched over by attentive parents.

Georgie braked, imagining being here some time in the future, showing her little one the exciting new world. Making everything a game, lining up her pram with the others, chatting to parents about nappy changing, bed-

times and the terrible twos. Her heart zinged. It seemed that, despite all her best efforts, she was starting to see everything through a different, pregnancy-coloured lens. With a heavy heart she glanced at the young dads splashing around and on the reserve, throwing balls to their sons, cheering, encouraging and, most of all, laughing.

Liam had been definite in his refusal to be a father. She understood that some people didn't have the need for kids in their lives, but that didn't mean she liked the idea. How could someone not want to know their own flesh and blood? It had been a question burning through her for her whole life. How could you just walk away and not want to be found, not want to make contact? What the hell ever happened to unconditional love?

It went against everything she knew about him. He was gregarious, funny, and cared deeply about the people he helped. But if he really meant he wasn't going to be involved she'd have to be Mum and Dad to her child. After all, in the children's home where she'd eventually settled, one parent was always better than none at all.

As Liam approached she flicked the bike into gear and cycled on to a small caravan advertising fish and chips and ice-cold drinks. 'Usual? Snapper?'

'Of course. And a large portion of chips. Tomato sauce...' He grinned, pointing to a can of cola. 'And all the trimmings.'

'I don't know where you put it all.' His belly was hard and taut. Body lean. Again with the full-on flush as she looked at him, this was becoming an uncomfortable habit. 'If I ate half of what you ate I'd be the side of a house.'

'You can't exactly worry about putting on weight now, can you?' He laughed and gave her a look she couldn't quite decipher.

Having returned their bikes to the hire shop, they walked in step down to the beach and found a spot on the

sand in the warm, soothing last rays of the day. Liam sat beside her and they ate out of the paper in companionable silence, pausing every now and then to comment on the food. The fish was divine, as always, the chips hot and salty, the cola too cold and too fizzy. Everything seemed exactly the same as it always was, except that it wasn't. She didn't know how to begin to have any kind of conversation that referred to being pregnant without causing another rift between them.

In the end she decided that rather than going over and over things in her head she was just going to say what was bothering her. She waited until he met her eyes. 'I wanted to say thank you, thank you, thank you for what you did.'

'It's fine. Honestly. Congratulations. You must be pleased.' He didn't look fine, he looked troubled as he leaned in and kissed her cheek, long eyelashes grazing her skin. 'You're looking good. Feeling okay so far?'

'Feeling a little numb all round, to be honest. It's real and happening and I can't quite believe it. I'm so lucky for it to have worked first time round. But it does happen.' She ran her palm across her tender breasts. 'No morning sickness yet, but my boobs are pretty sore.'

'Yeah. It happens. Wait till the varicose veins and heartburn kick in then you'll really be rocking.' He gave her a small smile, smoothing the tiny lines around his eyes, and for a second she was ten years younger, meeting him for the first time. All über-confident medical student who had been knocked sideways by the tiniest of beings—so small she'd fitted almost into the palm of his hand. Never had Georgie seen anyone look so frightened by something so frail, the cheery self-assurance whipped from him as if he'd been sucker-punched.

He'd been honest and open and warm. And since then she'd stood with pride at his graduation, cheered him on the sidelines at rugby games, dragged him kicking and

screaming to ballet performances and musical theatre, entirely happy with what he'd had to give her. Just a simple, uncomplicated friendship.

But now his eyes roved her face and then his gaze dipped to where her hand was over her breast. Suddenly she felt a little exposed and hot again under his scrutiny. She kept her eyes focused on the top of his head but eventually he looked back at her as if he was going to speak. A flash of something rippled through those ocean-blue eyes. Something that connected with her, something more than warm, which made her belly clutch and her cheeks burn. Heat prickled through her, intense and breath-sapping.

Her fingers ached to just reach out and touch his cheek. Just touch it. To see what his skin felt like. To feel his breath on her face. Her mouth watered just looking at his lips. Open a little. Just a little… Her breath hitched. He was so close. His familiar scent of male and fresh air wrapped around her like a blanket.

Close enough to—

He shook his head as if confused and disorientated. Then he shifted away and focused on the remainder of his food. Meanwhile, she breathed out slowly, trying to steady her ridiculously sputtering heartbeat. Had she imagined that flash of heat? Those feelings?

Yes.

It was all just her stupid clunky imagination.

She would rather die than ask him and be laughed at… or worse. That kind of conversational subject was explicitly off limits and would only cause tension. It was bad enough that she'd created this difficult atmosphere in the first place. But now, to… Oh, my God. The thought flitted into her brain and rooted itself there, so obvious, so immense, so downright out of this world… *No.* Surely not. She didn't. Couldn't.

She fancied him? Fancied the pants off Liam MacAl-

lister? The guy she'd got drunk with, thrown up on, told her deepest dirty secrets to? She wanted to kiss him? Really? Truly? Her heart thudded with a sinking realisation. Things between them were complicated enough, not least because he was going halfway across the world in less than twenty-four hours and she had no idea when she would see him next.

She couldn't want him, and he certainly wouldn't want her, especially with a baby in tow. Not now. Not ever. End of.

Hell, no.

Georgie was wearing a soft white lacy bra.

That was all Liam could think of. Not how amazing it was that she was pregnant. Although that was pretty amazing. Foolish and foolhardy and well beyond his comprehension too. But she did have a kind of warm glow about her, a softness he'd never seen before. He was no longer even registering how far beyond stupid she'd been to race along the pavement on two thin wheels when anything could have happened to her.

No, the only thing that took up room in his thick head was that her small perfect breasts were covered in lace.

As she leaned forward to take another hot chip, her top gaped a little more and he caught a glimpse of dark nipples. Cream skin. He swallowed. Dragged his gaze away and looked out at the boats bobbing on the turquoise water. What the hell was wrong with him?

Why, when he needed to put distance between them, had that whole concept suddenly become too hard to contemplate? He'd gone from not thinking about her in that way to not being able to stop thinking about her in the matter of a few weeks. He'd kept away, making excuses not to see her, just to get his head around everything. And

it had failed spectacularly because the moment she'd told him she was getting on a saddle he'd thundered down here with a distinct determination to convince her not to. He'd always teased her, had fun with her, joked around with her, but never until now had he had this need to protect her. Even if it was from herself.

And he was damned sure it wasn't just because she was pregnant. But he wished to hell it was. Because that was none of his business. Because that he could distance himself from.

Couldn't he?

Man, his life was changing in a direction that was beyond his control and it was taking a lot of getting used to. His life, yes. But another life, a new life, was growing inside her and he was struggling to get past that.

After finishing her dinner and crinkling up the paper into a tight ball, she spoke. 'You didn't have to sneak into the clinic during my lunch hour, you know. I would have given you some space.'

'It just didn't feel right.' He looked everywhere but at her. The finer details of how he'd provided the sperm were definitely not for this conversation. Even more, he'd really not wanted to alert her to the fact he'd been in her workplace, doing the deed in a side room. 'Man, they ask a lot of questions.'

'Tell me about it. They always ask a heap of stuff about your parents too. Any genetic conditions, inherited diseases. Has either parent had cancer, heart problems, high blood pressure? It kills me just a little bit to not know. In some ways it's a whole clean slate and I don't know about any inherited illnesses that may be hanging over my head. But in other ways it's a jigsaw, trying to piece bits together.' She shrugged, trying for nonchalance, but Liam knew just how much she'd ached to know just something

about her mum and dad. 'I don't even know who I got my eye colour from, for God's sake.'

He wanted to say it didn't matter. Because even if you did know who your parents were, it didn't mean a damned thing. It sure as hell didn't mean they loved you. Or maybe that was just his. But, then, how could he blame them? 'Well, at least you know little Nugget there will have big beautiful blue ones, to break the girls' hearts.'

'Or brown. She could have my brown ones.' She glanced over at him with a curious look and he immediately regretted mentioning any kind of pet name. He was not going to get involved. He would not feel anything for this baby. Which was currently only a collection of cells, not a baby at all. Not really.

His chest tightened. Who was he trying to fool? He could barely look at Georgie without imagining what was growing in her belly.

Who. Who was growing in her belly. *His baby.* He was going to be a father. And what had seemed such a simple warm-hearted gesture to help out a friend a few weeks ago had taken on a whole new meaning. This was real. This was happening. She was having his baby.

For a moment he allowed himself the luxury of the thrill of that prospect, let the overpowering innate need to protect overwhelm him.

Then he remembered a very long time ago, as a young boy of eight, the excitement deep in his heart as he'd felt a baby's kick. His hand on a swollen bump. The soft, cooing voice. A new life.

Then it was gone.

Ice-cold dread stole across him like a shadow. It didn't matter how far you ran, your nightmares still caught up with you.

He quickly tried to focus on something else. 'So, plans for the weekend? After the bungee is it whitewater raft-

ing? Paragliding? How about base jumping? All perfectly suitable under the circumstances.'

'First I thought I'd go running with the bulls, then perhaps a little heli-skiing.' She threw the rolled-up paper ball at him. Missed. Completely. 'Idiot!'

He threw it back at her. 'Bingo. On the head. Your aim is appalling.'

'Show-off!' She threw it towards him. Missed by a mile. Went to grab it. He reached it first and held it high above her head. Way out of her reach. She jumped to get it. Failed. Jumped again. Then she playfully poked him in the stomach so he flinched. 'Ouch!'

'Yes! Got it.'

He grabbed her arms and pulled her into a hug. Tickled her ribs until she yelped for mercy. Felt the soft heat of her breath on his skin. The way she moulded into him. Warm. 'Play fair.'

'Says the man with elastic arms. You have a natural advantage.'

'And you...'

Grinning and breathless, she pulled away, but not before he'd got a noseful of her flowery scent. She smelt like everything good. Everything fresh and vibrant and new. Something spiralled through him. A keening need. Rippling to his heart, where it wrapped itself into a ball of content, then lower to his groin, where content rapidly turned into a fiery need.

He let her go as his world shifted slightly. This could not be happening.

She sat back down, pink-cheeked but smiling. 'Actually, I thought I'd rip up the carpet in the spare room and see what's underneath. I'm hoping it's going to be one of those miracle moments—*Ooh, look, the last owner covered a perfectly intact parquet floor*—like on the DIY TV shows. But somehow I doubt it.'

'So do I. You'll be lucky if there's a decent layer of concrete there. Thinking about your dilapidated house makes me laugh. Either that or I'd cry. It needs serious work.' And thinking about something tangible and solid made a lot more sense than thinking about the searing lusty reaction he'd just had that had thrown him way off kilter. 'Don't get your hopes up. I've seen that old scabby carpet. The walls. The roof. My guess is that the previous owners only spent time covering up just how badly falling down the place was.'

'Aw, you know it was all I could afford. And it's a nice neighbourhood, good school zone, so will be worth a lot more by the time I've finished. Worst house on the best street and all that. And the roof is sound, it just needs some TLC.' She pouted a little and his gaze zeroed in on her mouth. Plump lips. Slightly parted. The tiniest glisten of moisture. He leaned over and dabbed a drop of ketchup away from her bottom lip. His thumb brushed against warmth. And his body overreacted again in some kind of total body heat swamp, accompanied by a strange tachycardia that knocked hard against his rib cage. The beach seemed to go fuzzy out of his peripheral vision as she blinked up at him, surprised by the sudden contact. Her lips parted a fraction more and if he leaned in he could have placed his over them.

And now he was seriously losing his mind.

Clearly he needed to get laid and quickly. With someone else.

Georgie moved away, frowning. She might have said his name. He didn't know. He willed his breathing back to normal.

Where were they? Oh, yes. The house. For God's sake, he needed to get up and go. This was crazy. This irrational pointless need thrumming through his veins. Crazy and sudden and he didn't know what the hell he was doing

any more. Or where this had come from. But he wished it would go as suddenly as it arrived. 'It'll be great when you're done. Lots of potential.'

'So you said when I bought it. But now I've got to capitalise on that. I've chosen some paint. I thought a soft cream would be nice and I'll add colour with blinds and cushions, nursery furniture. I saw a great changing table in a second-hand shop down the road from work—all it needs is a lick of paint, I'm not going to be one of those mums who—'

'A bit early for nesting, surely?' He gathered all the wrappers up then stood, offering his hand to pull her up.

She threw him a look filled with hurt, brushed her clothes down and reached for her bag. 'Well, I've got to start somewhere. Nine months flies by, believe me. I see it all the time at work—people often don't even come up with a name in that time.'

Ignoring his hand, she stood without help and looked out at the ocean. Her shoulders taut, back rigid. Her jaw tightened.

He'd meant that she shouldn't be too sure that this early pregnancy would last the course, that she needed to wait before she spent money on things. Invested. But saying that would be crass. Distasteful. Working at the fertility clinic, she was well aware of all the pitfalls and rewards of pregnancy. And judging by the way her eyes glittered with any baby talk, she was very invested already.

When she turned back to him her eyes were blazing. 'You remember that first night in my house, Liam? When we sat on packing crates and talked all night about the plans I had for renovations?'

'Of course I do.'

'I'm still the same person. I still have that dream. It's going to be a fabulous place. Then I will sell it and climb that property ladder, baby in tow. We'll be zillionaires by

the time I've finished. It just needs a bit of imagination, more time and a few willing hands.'

There was a long pause in which he felt sure she was waiting for him to offer to help with the decorating.

He'd returned from Pakistan planning on doing just that. But if he got involved in doing up her house that would mean more time spent with her and that was diametrically opposed to his plan. Which had been to ease himself out of her and her baby's lives. Gently. Without her really noticing. Just longer absences that she could fill with her antenatal classes, nursery shopping, other pregnant friends—because she must have them. Everywhere he looked these days there were blossoming bellies and tiny squawking babies.

But now, seeing her pregnant and the immediate emotions that instilled in him, his plan seemed like a crock full of madness.

So all the more reason for him to get out quickly. He couldn't be ruled by emotions, he never let that happen in his professional or his personal life. It was too dangerous to do otherwise.

'Anyhoo...' Her eyes were clouded now as she blinked away. She rooted in her bag and pulled out a folder of papers, clearly trying to keep her voice steady. Goddamn, everything he did hurt her. She cleared her throat. 'Here's your signed copy of the contract from the clinic. Helen was supposed to mail it to you, but I offered to bring it along here instead. As you saw, it's pretty standard stuff. You get no claims, no guardianship or visitation rights, you're not a legal parent, you have no parental rights...yada-yada. Just what you wanted.'

'Oh. Okay. Great. Thanks.' In black and white it seemed so cold-hearted. And yet it absolved him of everything. No responsibilities. He took it and shoved it in to his back-

pack. He didn't need to reread it. He was signing every right to this child away.

Truth was, his thoughts about this baby were so blurred now. He'd thought it would be easy to walk away. But… well, it wasn't easy at all. He felt like he was giving his child the same fate he'd had—a life with little contact with his father. A life wanting something…guidance, truth, recognition. He couldn't give his child that. He just couldn't. But what could he give? What did he have left?

Georgie peered up at him and everything he knew about her was in that guarded look in her eyes. She understood his pain, but was equally angry. She was putting her needs first. And she needed to, he didn't blame her a jot for that. 'That's what you really want, isn't it, Liam? You don't want to help me get a nursery ready—that is clear. Or choose decor. Or talk about baby things. You don't want me to be pregnant. You don't want any of this…'

'Look, Geo, that's not it. I'm thrilled for you. I am. It's what you want and you look so happy, how could I not be pleased for you? I thought this was what you wanted.'

'Me too. But I don't know how you can do it. The more I think about it, the more I don't understand you. I've known all along that you cut yourself off from any kind of decent meaningful human connection…' She twisted in the sand and stepped towards him. 'So just explain to me one thing: what are you so afraid of?'

'I'm not afraid of anything.' And that was the biggest lie he'd ever told. He was afraid of the responsibility of another baby's life, of not being able to protect it from harm. Of loving too much. Of dealing with the utter heartbreak if something went wrong, because he didn't think he could live through that again. His heart raced as blood drained from his head, from his face. 'Nothing.'

'I watched you, Liam…that day in Resus, when your

whole world crumbled at the sight of a sick baby. I know you are carrying some terrible burden and, through knowing you for ten years, I think it has something to do with your family. Your sister Lauren?'

He railed around, wishing he didn't know her so well, wishing she couldn't see through the barriers he'd erected. 'It has got nothing to do with anyone.'

'If you choose to let whatever happened colour everything you do for the rest of your life then I can't help you. And I want to, I really do. But I can't bear that every time I mention my baby—*our* baby—you flinch. So I'm going to do this my own way. I'm sorry if that doesn't work for you. Just go off to the South Sudan and do your precious job.'

'What?' His heart thumped harder, fast and furious. 'Is this about my job now as well? You don't like it that I'm going to be leaving all the time, is that it?'

'It's about everything, Liam. About your attitude, about your refusal to admit what's bothering you, the damned contract that means you will willingly let our friendship irrevocably change and allow a baby to be fatherless, and, yes, it's about your job. It's dangerous, and scary for those of us left behind.'

He shoved his hands in his pockets. He could barely look at her. By donating his…by delivering the goods, he'd done what he'd thought was the right thing—he *had* done the right thing—but the fallout kept coming. 'That job keeps me sane.'

'And drives me mad with worry. But I don't know why we're even bothering talking about this. You've got your contract, you can go off unhindered by any kind of sense of responsibility.'

Responsibility? That was the one single thing that drove him to do what he did. Every damned day.

She whirled around and stalked away, but paused, momentarily to turn back. Scraping her hair back from her face, she glared at him, her body language so at odds with her words. 'Stay safe.'

CHAPTER FOUR

Four months ago...

'ONCE THE PAIN relief kicks in you can take him to X-Ray. Let's see exactly how far up the little tyke stuffed the ball bearing, shall we? Depending on where it is, he might need a sedative for us to get it out. But we need to know more before we do anything else.' Through the fog of his sleep-deprived brain Liam offered the concerned mum a smile. Just a little shut-eye between his plane hitting the tarmac and coming into work would have been nice. Still, boys would be boys, and stuffing things up nostrils was par for the course for a four-year-old.

Hopeful images of a little boy who looked a lot like him flashed through his head. He batted them away. He'd call Georgie and talk to her *later*, explain his plan, what he wanted...once he'd worked out exactly what it was he was going to say. Theoretically it made sense to have some contact with his baby. He'd be responsible for finances and guidance, provide things. No emotional involvement. No day-to-day stuff—he didn't want to tread on Georgie's toes. But enough that his child would be able to identify him as his father. He was responsible, for God's sake.

All very good in theory, but in practice he had no idea. Maybe this was just another of his ludicrous plans that

would be fraught with endless fallout. But somehow he did not like the idea of being a dad and not having at least some contact with the child.

The little boy's mum laughed, but Liam could see by her lined forehead and forced smile that she was still anxious. It didn't matter what befell a kid, their parent always worried.

'I don't know why he decided it needed to go all the way up his nose. I just wish he hadn't found it at all. I'll kill his dad when we get home. Leaving little things on the floor is so dangerous.'

'I guess having kids means big changes. It takes a bit of getting used to.'

That thought had been running over and over in his head since he'd left. Would he be like that with his child? Worried sick if it stuffed something up its nose? Would he refuse to let them play outside in case they injured themselves? He'd seen extremes in this job. Neglect that almost tore his heart in two, and the worried well who caused a fuss over nothing. Where children were concerned, it was difficult to get the balance right. But generally it didn't matter where he was—flooded Pakistan, drought-ridden Africa—parents were the same the world over. They loved. They gave their children what they could. They worried.

He tried to find the wee lad a smile.

The boy grinned back. With sticky-out ears beneath sand-coloured hair he was pretty cute. And now, with the analgesic kicking in, clearly unbothered by the metal ball in his left nostril. 'I liked it. It was silver. I wanted to smell it.'

'Oh.' Kids said the strangest things. Stupefied by his inadequacy where children were concerned, Liam wondered whether you should talk to them like adults or use special kiddy words. He stuck to plain and simple. 'Metal ball bearings don't have a smell, buddy. Now, don't put

anything else up your nose. Not even your finger. Off you go.' He turned to the mum and relaxed a little. It was far easier to talk to a grown-up. 'See you when you get back from X-Ray.'

The kid laughed at Liam's grumbling stomach, clearly unfazed by whichever way Liam spoke to him. 'What's that funny noise?'

'It's…er…' Not often he was lost for words. 'I'm hungry. My tummy's asking for lunch.'

'Metal balls don't smell and tummies don't talk.'

'No. Well, I don't suppose they do. But they growl, like mine, so go on and get your picture taken so we can see inside you. Skedaddle.'

And lunch was supposed to have been six hours ago. But since then he'd had a steady stream of minor emergencies on top of a few pretty major ones. Now, shift almost over, he could finally go home. Looking forward to getting something into his stomach that wasn't yet another Sudanese stew or tasteless plane mush, he strode across the ER floor, past the whiteboard. And stopped. Turned. Refocused on the names. *What the…?*

White noise filled his ears, his appetite replaced by an empty hole deep in his gut as he hot-footed it back to Minors and threw the cubicle curtain open. Sure enough, she was there, head in her hands, making soft snuffling noises.

'Georgie? What the hell—?' Four months he'd lain sweltering in a too-hot tent and she'd been tattooed onto the back of his eyelids as he'd gone to sleep, their last conversation going over and over in his head. Making things right hadn't seemed possible from the dodgy dirty-walled internet cafés he'd visited sporadically, so his emails had been short and perfunctory.

He'd spent weeks wondering what he'd say when he saw her in person, how he'd feel when he saw her carrying his baby. How he'd feel when he saw her, period.

He hated it that she had put a line under their friendship, ending everything so abruptly. But none of that mattered now, none of it.

He tugged her into his arms, hauled her head against his chest and stroked her back. 'Hey, don't cry. It's okay. It's okay. Whatever's happened we'll fix it. It's okay.'

Firm hands pressed on his chest and gripped his shirt. Her voice was low but not upset. In fact…was she laughing? 'Oh, my God! Liam. You're back! When?'

He'd finally stopped shaking enough to concentrate. Goddamned ER doctor and he'd crumbled the second he'd seen her name. *Georgie. The baby.* He didn't know which thought had come first—one had been so quickly followed by the other. And if that wasn't the most bizarre sequence of mind mess he didn't know what was.

And now she was here, damaged somehow—because this was where damaged people came. And that was just the staff. Worst-case scenarios flitted through his doctor's brain, fuelled by his own awful experiences. 'Early this morning. I was going to call you once I'd had a sleep, but they needed me here urgently. I didn't even get the chance to go home. But what the hell—?'

'Don't get carried away. And, no, I'm not crying.'

'What happened? The baby?' He took a step back and surveyed her belly with quick observations. She had a rounded-out bump now, small and perfect, but the rest of her was thin. Too thin. Grimy, dusty. None of this added up. 'Is the baby okay?'

'Yes, everything's fine. Except…' She finally let him go and moved her hand away from her face. 'I hurt my eye.'

Her right eye was weeping, closed and puffy. Her cheek was swollen. 'Whoa. Great job. What did you do?'

'I smashed a wall through and got dust or shards of chipboard or plaster or something in it. It hurts like hell.' She grimaced, swabbing at her damp face with a dusty fist.

Thank God she was okay. Thank God the baby was okay. Unfamiliar feelings sliced through him, accompanied by a strange lumpy sensation in his throat that made words hard to find. 'You were knocking a wall through? On your own? Are you mad?' He hauled in air. 'Don't answer that. I know the answer. Which one?'

'The kitchen-lounge one. I thought it'd be nice to have one big sunny room all finished in time for Christmas. Imagine what fun it'll be to have dinner in there.'

'The legendary Georgie Taylor Christmas, with enough liquor to sink a ship. And enough food to feed an army. But couldn't it have waited until you got help? Christmas is months away.'

'I've got to be prepared, Liam. This renovating lark takes time and I want Christmas to be perfect this year. I have grand plans.' With her one good eye she glared at him. 'If all you're going to do is tell me off, I'll ask for someone else to deal with my injury.'

'Go right ahead, missy. I think you'll find I'm the most experienced doctor here but, please, feel free to find someone better. I'll take you on a tour if you like. See if any one takes your fancy.' He thumbed the teary trail across her cheek. As he touched her an immediate heat suffused his body. He took his hand away, shaken by such an intense response. 'Oh, sorry, I forgot, you can't see.'

'Excuse my bluntness, Dr Mac, but your bedside manner is slipping. You're supposed to be nice to people when they come and see you with an injury. Basic ER doctoring.' She stuck her tongue out and if she'd felt any electric surge at his touch she didn't show it. He'd thought he'd purged her from his heart, that if he'd worked harder, faster, later then he wouldn't care so much. *Feel* so much. Too bad it hadn't worked. He didn't want to feel anything at all.

'Looks like I suck at interpersonal skills.' He picked up

her chart and feigned calmness. 'That was meant to be an apology, by the way.'

'Must try harder. See me after class.' Her lips pressed together tightly. She took a breath and let it out slowly. She definitely looked thinner than the last time he'd seen her, cheeks a little more hollow. Her hair, T-shirt and jeans were covered in bits of wood chip and plaster, but her eyes…well, her good eye had darkened shadows round it. She gave him a reluctant smile that had him craving more. 'Oh, Liam, I've missed you. Missed this.'

Me too. 'Okay. So sit still and let me have a good look.' He tipped her chin towards him. And, yes, it would break every damned oath he'd ever made but, hell, if those lips weren't made for kissing. Which would be a pretty dumb move all round, because things would never be the same again. 'Trust me, I'm a doctor.'

She laughed. 'The old ones are the best. I bet you use that on all incapacitated women?'

'Only the bloody foolish ones who are hell-bent on being so independent they do themselves a mischief. You tried to knock down a wall on your own?' He focused on her eye, not her lips. Damaged or downright sexy. Either way his heart hurt.

'And who else could help me? I'm hardly going to pay someone.'

'You could have waited for me.'

'We both know that that wasn't an ideal option. I didn't know when you were coming back or if we were still friends. Are we?'

The heart hurt intensified. 'Come on, we'll always be friends, whatever happens. Now, let me look.'

'Okay. Give it your best shot.' She managed to open her eyelid a tad but blinked so rapidly he knew it was painful. It slammed closed again, tears rolling down her cheek.

He grabbed a tissue and wiped them away, unwilling

to risk a skin-on-skin encounter again. 'Hey, it's okay. I forgive you.'

One eye widened in disbelief. 'What? You? Forgive me? But you were the one—'

'Seriously, no need to cry over me.'

Her lips pursed. Pouted. 'I'm not crying over you, matey. I just can't stop it watering.'

He looked away and began writing on her charts, mainly because it was far easier to do that than look at her. At least he didn't want to kiss the charts better. 'Well, whatever you've done, you've made an almighty mess in there. We're going to need to give you an eye bath to get the gunk out and then get an ophthalmic opinion.'

Her shrugging shoulders confirmed her agreement. 'So you'd better get it organised, then. You must be busy with more needy people than me. I don't mind seeing someone else. That would be if I could see at all.'

'Actually, I'm finishing my shift very shortly. I've got one patient to review then I'll sort out your referral while you have an eye bath. As soon as I'm done I'll wait with you.'

She shook her head. 'No need, honestly. If you don't want to.'

'Of course I want to.' He wasn't letting her go that easily. 'I know I made you angry and for that I'm sorry. I know I can be blunt and unthinking at times, but I realise there are two of us in this friendship...'

'Three now,' she hissed at him, rubbing her belly. His heart gave a little jerk. *His baby.* At once he felt proud and anxious. Excited and terrified.

Protective. Should he say something now?

No. She was damaged and he needed to deal with that, get things on a firmer footing. And work out exactly what it was he wanted to say. What kind of involvement he wanted. He rubbed his hand across his forehead. 'Come

out with me for dinner, like old times. We could do fish and chips with extra grease, your favourite. Or curry. Thai, Chinese?'

'Urgh. Please. Don't mention—' She held up her hand then covered her mouth. 'I should have… Oh. No.' She grabbed the back of her chair and stood. Swayed a little.

'Should have what?'

She murmured through her fingers, 'Eaten something. I'm sorry, I have to—'

Then she was ripping back the curtain and staggering across the corridor to the toilet, leaving grubby handprints along the wall. He was beside her in a millisecond. Maybe she'd hit her head too and forgotten to mention it? Concussion? 'What's wrong?'

'Morning sickness? *Morning?* Yeah, right. Liars. All-day sickness, more like. Switches on at the thought of food. Goes away when I eat. In all this excitement I forgot to eat.' She pushed him back away from the bathroom door. 'Wait. Please, wait here. Before I chuck on your shoes.'

And he got a distinct impression that she probably didn't care if she did. 'No, Georgie, you can't see a thing. I will not wait. I will stay here and make sure you're okay.'

'Go do your patient review. You're not the boss of me.'

'How old are you?' He'd spent ten years getting to know that no one could ever be the boss of Georgie. He could hardly leave her and go back to ball-bearing-in-nostril kid when she was like this. 'You infuriating woman—'

But he stopped arguing as she slammed the door open and crouched down while he held her hair back in a thick makeshift ponytail. Her body shook. He held her steady.

This was his fault. He'd allowed this to happen. He'd facilitated this. He ran his hands across her back, felt the knobbly bones of her spine through her loose-fitting T-shirt. Jeans hanging off her hips. She was definitely thinner. This pregnancy was taking a toll on her and she

was so damned proud she would never think of mentioning it. She needed a good meal. To be looked after. Someone to take care of her while she grew her baby, instead of believing she could do it all on her own. 'Does this happen a lot?'

'Enough.' She rocked back on her heels and wiped her mouth with toilet tissue.

Putting his hands under her arms, he hauled her up, made sure she was steady on her feet, watched her wash her hands and splash her face, wincing as cold water hit her eye. 'You're losing weight.'

She looked at him in the bathroom mirror, dried her hands and threw the paper towel in the bin. Peered at her eye in the glass. The swelling had worsened. Her one good eye pierced him. 'So are you.'

'South Sudan can do that to a guy.'

'Don't tell me you gave half your food away again?'

'I can survive. They don't have enough. I had plenty even with half-rations.'

'So how was it?'

'Messy. Murky. Complicated.' Like the rest of his life. 'But I'm back here and I want to know about you. How long have you been vomiting and how many times?'

'Simmer down. A few times a day. Counting wasn't helping. Let's just say, too much. It's perfectly normal. It's supposed to go once I hit the second trimester, so it'll be gone any day now. I'm fine.'

Fine? She was a mess. 'And in between the vomiting you're working full time and then taking out your frustration on your house walls? When do you rest?'

She threw him a smile that stopped way short of her dark eyes. 'Well, you know what they say about giving a job to a busy person. That's me! I like being busy.'

'No, you don't, Georgie. You like getting drunk in grungy bars playing loud eighties rock anthems, you like

blobbing on the couch and watching reruns of your favourite soaps until you can say the dialogue better than the actors, you like strawberry ice cream, but not berry swirl. You like doing nothing at all if you can help it. You do not like to be busy.'

Uh-oh. Hip-planting was occurring. Both hands fisted. Bad sign. 'Well, you can add doing renovations when pregnant to that list. Go figure, you learn something new about people every day.'

'You know what they say about people like you?'

'No.' She turned to him and swayed a little, her cheeks drained of colour. Her eyes fluttered closed as she steadied herself, leaning against the sink, hands flopped to her sides. She looked exhausted. He wanted to swoop her into his arms, wrap her up in bed and look after her. As if she'd ever let him. 'Tell me, Liam, what do they say?'

'That only the pig-headed, wilful, independent and stubborn will not listen to anyone else. To the detriment of their health. You can't get sick, this baby needs you to be well. You need to stop and rest.' And he was not going to stand by and let anything bad happen. Period.

But contrary to everything he expected from her, she didn't rally. Her shoulders sagged as she gripped the sink, her voice so small he had to strain to hear her. 'Okay, okay, I get it. I'm done arguing. Whatever you say, you're the doc.'

Things must be bad. Never in all the years he'd known her had she so much as uttered a single word that would make her appear less than über-confident and capable.

He took her by the shoulders and steered her out into the waiting room. Found her a chair. Sat her in it. Put a finger over her mouth to hush any complaints.

She needed him and he wasn't going to let her get sick on his watch. It wasn't as if she could call a relative to come look after her—she didn't have any. No one to look

out for her, to give her a break when she needed it. To take the baby for a few hours when she needed sleep. To babysit. Did she really have a clue how hard this parenting was going to be? 'You're going to start taking it easy. Doctor's orders.'

CHAPTER FIVE

'LET ME HELP YOU. Be careful, you have a nasty corneal abrasion.'

'So you keep saying. Urgh. So I'll play pirates and keep wearing the eye patch, me hearty.' Georgie had to confess that even though the thick white cotton wool patch didn't help much with healing, and made her look a lot like a numpty, it protected her eye from the glare of her house lights and made her think seriously about wearing safety goggles in the future.

But one thing she'd be reluctant to confess out loud was that the moment Liam had said she needed to take things easy it had felt as if a huge weight had been lifted from her shoulders. Because it was all very well trying to be big and brave and bold but sometimes, just sometimes, she tired of having to rely solely on herself for everything.

A deep breath escaped her lungs as Liam pushed the front door open. She was home. She could relax. At least in theory. It was a little harder in practice, having him in her space, being big and bold for her. Why had he suddenly come over all macho? Why did that make him even more desirable?

For that matter, why hadn't her desire dampened down over the last few months? And why was a man in combat kit and biker boots infinitely more attractive than any-

thing else? She turned on the doorstep. Pregnant and now injured, this was not a good time to be finding her friend attractive. 'Thanks for getting me home. I'll be fine from here. Maybe we could catch up tomorrow when we're both feeling better.'

'Hey, what's the hurry? Are you scared about what I'll do?' He shook his head, eyes glittering with tease as he surveyed her body. If she wasn't mistaken, tension of a very sexual kind rippled between them.

Air whooshed into her lungs as she gave a sharp intake of breath. She wasn't afraid of Liam at all, she was more scared about what *she* might do, suddenly alone with him and very, very hot. 'No...er...I—'

'Don't panic. If it's a total mess I won't get mad. I'm here to help.'

He was talking about the state of her house. Not... *of course not*...anything else. 'I'll be okay. Honestly. Go home, you look beat, Liam. You must be jet-lagged and knackered.'

'Listen to yourself, Geo. You're not letting me help. You don't have to do everything on your own.'

'Of course I do. And I like it. That way I don't have to compromise on anyone else's plans, don't have to work to their timetable, I can just please myself.' She placed her hand against the wall and kept him on the doorstep.

He shook his head. 'Has anyone ever told you that you're the most stubborn person in the world?'

'You? Many times. But you're saying it as if I might care. And I don't.'

'Well, today you're my responsibility and I promised the discharging medical officer I'd take care of you.'

'But you were the discharging medical officer.'

'Go figure. So I'll fix you some dinner, have a look at the damage you've inflicted on your poor house. Make

sure you're OK. Then, once I'm satisfied, I'll leave.' He went to squeeze past her, but she blocked his way.

'Promise?'

He frowned. 'If that's what you want.'

She wanted him to be happy about the baby—the single most important thing, and which he'd hardly mentioned. That was all. Well, and to hold her again. Possibly kiss her. Make out, maybe... But that would be a wish too far. 'What do you want, Liam?'

'To make sure you're safe, crazy lady. That's all.'

As he peered through the dust and grime he scratched his head, fluffing his short dark hair into little tufts. 'Bloody hell, Georgie. It's worse than I imagined.' He stepped in, walked across the floor, leaving large thick footprints in the grey film that coated everything. 'What the hell have you done?'

She hid a smile as she followed him into the house where she'd half knocked through the wall, making her downstairs pretty much open-plan. She had grand plans for this room, plans she'd been aching to share with some-one. Him, mainly.

And even though she'd been beyond angry with him for the last couple of months, it was good to be able to see him—through her one useful eye—and talk to him. Be-cause she'd been honest when she'd said she'd missed him.

She hadn't expected to have those strange feelings rat-tling through her again, though. She'd put it down to a cluster of hormones, but when he'd held her, cradling her head like she was something very precious, her heart had done a little leap. More, her body had started to hum with something dangerous. It was a bad idea, having him in her space. 'Personally, I think it's looking great. That old par-tition wall made everything dark and dingy. Just needs a little bit of cosmetic work and it'll be fine.'

'Plus finishing off. Cornices, a new floor.' He tapped

along what remained of the plasterboard wall. 'You go and sit down in the lounge, if you can find the sofa under all this mess. I'll finish this off, clear up, then sort out something to eat.'

'You're hardly dressed for it.'

He looked down at his ex-army fatigues. 'They're old. I don't care. You just sit tight. That is, Miss Independent, if you know how to let someone else do the work.' He picked up the hammer and his forearms tightened. Capable hands, plus mussed-up hair already, and he hadn't even lifted a finger. How was she going to cope?

For a few minutes she lay back on her couch, closed her eyes and let relaxation take hold. It was lovely to lie there, listening to the crash of the hammer. The crumble of plaster, his deep male grunts as he swung and hit. He worked for a while then there was silence.

It stretched.

Suddenly interested in what was happening—or not— Georgie opened her eye and peered across the settling dust.

Oh, good Lord. Her stomach contracted as she inhaled a mouth full of dust. He'd taken off his shirt and was now measuring across the space with an industrial tape measure. Defined muscles stretched and contracted as he moved. Tight abs ridged down to his trouser waistband, a sexy smattering of dark hair pointed to a promised land. The man had no business looking like that, all sunburnt and muscular and just too damned hot. She swallowed, her mouth suddenly dry. Her throat was tight. Her breathing came quick and fast.

Staring was rude.

She reclosed her eye.

No good.

She wanted to look again. It was like watching bad reality TV: she knew she shouldn't watch, but she couldn't help herself. The man was gorgeous. And, heck, she'd al-

ways known what his body was like. Days spent with him at the beach had had little effect on her in the past. But now... Wow. He'd developed strength and solidity and muscles. Filled out into those broad shoulders. Her body hummed with need.

He turned to face her. 'You okay? You need anything?'

Not the kind of thing he'd want to give her. 'I'm just fine, thanks. But I wanted to let you know I'm sorry that you left and we'd fallen out. I was worried about you, you know, the whole time.'

He winked at her. 'Forgiven. Just about. I hate this arguing. It's not like us. We don't argue.'

So many firsts for them. 'You do realise that not once have you asked me for any details about the baby? About when it's due. Or if I've had any scans. Which I have.'

'I didn't know where to start.' Dropping the hammer to the floor, he looked lost. Shame faced. Terrified. 'This is all so new. It's pretty intense to get my head round.'

He was a long way behind her in this. For the last few months she'd been wondering whether her child having a father around mattered. Whether, in the long term, it would matter to him.

God, there were so many things she hadn't thought of when she'd gone hurtling into this process. Things she should have talked to him about. Things that could make or break their friendship for ever. It was already spinning out of control.

She pulled a scrap of paper from her purse, taking another risk at rejection. If he baulked at this then she'd reconsider. She got up and walked over to him. 'Here, have a look. An early scan. More of a blob really, but there she is.'

'She?' He took the paper in a shaking hand but didn't look at it. His face paled, he swallowed. And again. 'Too early to talk about gender, isn't it?'

She shrugged. 'I just think of her as a girl. Don't know why.' She pushed the paper closer to him. 'Take a look.'

His fingers closed over the top corner of the paper. He took a deep breath and looked down. No sound. No emotion. Nothing flickered across his face. Nothing to register that this was his child. That she was carrying his baby. Then he raised his head and gave her the scan picture back. 'My God.'

His voice was hollow and raw and she wondered what he was thinking. Maybe he was happy that she was happy but didn't know how to show it.

Her throat filled. 'I don't know what to say or do to make this easier...or less complicated. I know this is going to sound very selfish, but I want everything, Liam. I want this baby, but I don't want to lose your friendship.'

'And I...'

She thought he was going to say more but he didn't. His hands dropped to his sides as he shook his head and turned away.

Despite his doubts, he'd given her this gift. How could she have been so angry with him? He looked so empty and confused that she stepped forward and wrapped her arms round him, pulled him to her, and he responded by holding her close.

Her hands ran over muscles, dips and grooves of naked hot skin, slick with a light sheen of sweat. Her heart began to pound as awareness surged through her. His smell of surgical soap, aftershave and pure male heat filled the air. She inhaled it. And again.

His face was inches from hers. His breath feathered her skin. But she daren't move. Something stirred inside her deep and low. Her breasts tingled for his touch. Was he feeling this too? She hoped...but then what? This whole crazy messed-up situation didn't need complicating further. If he knew what was running through her brain right

this second he'd probably walk away and never come back. For all she knew, he was probably planning that anyway.

Keeping her eyes tightly closed, she held her breath, felt him relax against her, felt his grip on her lessen. She didn't want him to let go. She wanted…

'Thanks for that, you old bat,' he whispered, lips pressed against her cheek, his scent intensified along with the tingling through her body, pooling in her groin. She couldn't think of anything but him, being in his arms, how good this felt.

Heat swamped her. There was no point pretending that what she felt for him wasn't real, that this was just a hormonal response. For goodness' sake, she'd been struggling with these weird emotions for months now. And, yes, she wanted to kiss him. She had to know what he tasted like. How he would feel.

With every risk of him leaving—and with no thought for the consequences—she turned her head, met his mouth. Felt his surprise resonate against her lips. Then a groan. A growl. A need.

Liam registered the first touch of Georgie's lips as his heart slammed loud and thunderous in his chest. For one split second a dark corner somewhere in his brain considered that this was the far side of madness—but then that thought was gone and he was left with nothing but heat and need raging through his veins.

Cupping her face in his hands, he opened his mouth to her. Felt her shaking body, heard the guttural moan from her throat, felt her tight fists grip his trouser waistband as he dragged her closer. And each of her responses fed his need. She tasted wet and hot and soft. Of salty tears and fresh pure joy. He closed his eyes at the sweet sensations she instilled in him.

Her hands made a slow trail to his backside as she

clamped her body to his and she moaned again as she felt him harden at the press of her hips. He liked the way she felt against him. Liked the feel of her fingers on his body. The thrill of her touch.

As his hands slid down her back he brushed against her bra strap and the memory of those perfect nipples covered in lace made him ache to touch them. Slipping his hand under her T-shirt, he worked his fingers to her breast, felt the hardening nipples beneath silk. He wanted to feel them against his skin. Naked. Wanted to suck those dark buds into his mouth. To taste her everywhere. Wanted to feel her around him.

'Oh, God, Liam.'

'Georgie…' He opened his eyes, and immediately registered the harsh reality. *Damn.* This was Georgie. She was injured and pregnant and he was supposed to be looking after her.

Not taking advantage of her. This was Georgie. His best friend. The hands-off friend.

Who was pregnant.

With his child.

And, yes—ever since he'd held that picture in his hand and felt the deep singular ache in his heart he'd known that he'd fight heaven and earth for his baby. This was something that was a part of him and he couldn't turn his back on that.

He'd been about to tell her his plan. About the financial help he'd decided he wanted to give. About giving his son or daughter the best. Because they deserved it, Georgie did too. But…when it had come to it, after holding the scan in his hands, he'd panicked. He needed to be sure.

And then…this…had blown his heart wide open.

My God. Kissing Georgie.

In the cold stark light of day that dark corner of doubt started to flourish. Another person he would let down.

His life was littered them. He sure as hell didn't want to include Georgie and the baby in that line-up.

The shock of what they were doing made him break away. He did it with little finesse and immediately saw the embarrassment or disappointment or just plain confusion flash across her gaze.

What the hell just happened? He coughed, cleared his throat, tried to sound a lot less shaken up than he felt. 'Well, that was unexpected. And not at all like kissing my cousin. But, then, Mike never was much good at tongues, apparently. You, however...'

'Always the joker.' She twisted away and stalked back into the lounge area, wringing her hands in front of her, clearly trying to work out how they'd gone from friends to...this. And what the heck they were supposed to do now they'd crossed an unspoken line. 'I'm sorry. I shouldn't have done that.'

'No.' He followed her but couldn't find it in him to sit down. His first and only instinct was to get the hell out. But running out on a woman who was sick and confused would make him a jerk and a coward. Although he couldn't help feeling that he'd already started to put distance there. He wasn't sitting down and talking reasonably, he was edging subconsciously closer to the door. He made himself stand still and focused on her. '*We* shouldn't have done that.'

'No, Liam. *I* kissed you. Embarrassment totally one hundred per cent complete.'

And he'd kissed her back—without any encouragement. What happened to reining in his libido, like any other decent man would? But something a lot like a mind meld had happened, pushing him to continue, and he'd been unable to stop.

Her lips were a little swollen, her good eye misty, hair

messy, as if she'd just scrambled out of bed. She looked sexier than anyone he'd ever seen. Sexy and very off limits.

Actually, sexy, off limits and torn. 'Really, Liam, I think you should go.'

'Yes. I'll come back and finish this off another time.' He went to get his T-shirt, shook off some of the debris stuck to it before pulling it over his head. 'I should order you a pizza or something. You need to eat. Regularly and properly.'

'I can manage a phone quite well.' Waving her hand in front of her, she gave him a brief smile that was laced with hurt. 'Please, just go. You're officially off the hook. Go, and let me die a thousand embarrassed deaths in peace.'

He didn't know what was running through her mind, but he'd take a big guess that it wasn't him actually agreeing with her and leaving. The last thing she needed right now was uncertainty. But everything was messed up and muddied; there he was tangling her pregnancy with his feelings. He was having a hard time separating the baby issue from his attraction to Georgie. If they didn't get everything out in the open, this would be hanging over them for ever. 'But shouldn't we talk about what just happened?'

'No. That's not going to get us anywhere but deeper in trouble. It's pretty clear from your face that you're shocked. Please. Please. Just go.'

'I'll be back tomorrow to help you.'

'Off the hook, I said. I can manage. Please...' She was biting her bottom lip and looking so regretful that he did her bidding. She didn't want him around. And the truth was he didn't much feel like staying when his head and his body were so much at odds and he was at risk of making things worse. Or, even more catastrophic in the long run, helping to make her feel better in the only way he wanted to right now, which would be a one-way ticket to the far side of stupid.

CHAPTER SIX

Mortified. Just downright mortified. Georgie was surprised her cheeks hadn't burnt a hole right through her pillow. Twelve hours later and she was still...utterly mortified. Half peering, half feeling her way around her house, she went downstairs to the kitchen, finished wet dusting all the surfaces, popped the kettle on and contemplated pushing two pieces of wholegrain bread into the toaster. Then gave up on the idea. Ruining friendships had sent her appetite running and hiding along with her pride.

And, okay, so he'd kissed her back, and appeared to have been enjoying it, but the moment he'd cut loose and let her go she'd seen doubt and fear and confusion run across those eyes. Eyes that had turned, once again, a darker shade of navy.

But, man, he'd tasted so good. *Felt* so good. Until the moment he'd jerked away and she'd wished she could have been swallowed up in the house's perennial dust cloud and whirled back to five minutes previously. Before the kiss that had probably, finally, broken their friendship.

And it was all her fault. She'd pushed him in one direction to give her his sperm, acknowledged he didn't want to go there at all but had done it anyway, and then had pulled him to her in a selfish moment of unwarranted and uninhibited need. Putting her head in her hands, she leaned

against the grey kitchen bench, dusty again already, and groaned. Stupid. *Stupid*.

God knew where they'd go from here.

The doorbell rang quick and sharp and then Liam was calling out, and then standing in her lounge, muscled arms filled with brushes and buckets and tools, which he put on the floor in the corner of the room.

'Morning.' He stopped short and frowned, and her stomach contracted. 'Holy cow, you look awful.'

'Thanks a bunch. So do you. Why don't you come right in and make yourself at home?' She tried to make her voice sound nonchalant instead of shaky, but it all just came out weird and high-pitched. She was a little bit relieved to see that he looked like he'd just finished night duty—tired, paler and shadowed with a perfectly stubbled jaw. Which inevitably made her stomach contract again, but this time for a totally different reason.

She peered up at him, trying to measure his mood while at the same time trying to quell the nausea in the pit of her stomach. And she knew it was nothing to do with her morning sickness and everything to do with kissing her oldest mate—and even now, despite the mortification, wanting to do it again. The hot spots on her cheeks reappeared. 'I thought I said you didn't have to come and help. I know you have little time off as it is without bothering about me. I can manage fine.'

'And leave you here knowing what disaster was lurking behind this door? No way. No doubt if I left you in here with a hammer for any length of time you'd be completely blind and crippled within the hour. So basically I'm doing my colleagues at A and E a favour by keeping you out of their hair.' He made no effort to hide his smile. 'I thought we should go out for a while first, take a walk to the French market. Get out of this dust bowl and clear your lungs.' AKA not wanting to be in a confined space

with her. She understood, loud and clear. 'You don't need an asthma attack added to your medical history.'

'My lungs are perfectly clear, thank you.' *Unlike my head*, she thought, which was filled with grimy confusion. 'The dust settles downwards all over the surfaces rather than floating upwards to my bedroom.' And at the mere mention of where she slept, usually near-naked, she had an unwelcome image of him also naked, in her sheets. Okay, so not unwelcome…in fact, very welcome indeed. Just unrealistic. And never going to happen. 'So…er… how are you? Good sleep?'

And maybe it was the mention of her bed that did funny things to him too, because all of a sudden his bravado slipped, he shoved his hands deep in his pockets and his gaze was not at her, but beyond, or around, or anywhere else but meeting her eyes. *Eye.*

An awkward unspoken tension hovered between them as he shifted from one foot to the other. 'I'm fine. How are you feeling? How's the eye? Using the drops as prescribed?'

'Yes, Dr MacAllister.' She patted the new patch gently, knowing that, added to the sleepless eye bags and the uncombed hair, it gave her a pathetically ill look. Still, having managed perfectly well for twenty-eight years pretty much on her own, she was far from fragile, but it did feel nice to have someone ask how she was feeling, even if it was just to avoid talking about the kiss or what the heck they should do now. 'The prickly headache's gone. I feel okay, a little sore, but raring to get going in here.'

'Well, first brioche and espresso are calling. Then you can go and do whatever you want to do for the day and leave me in peace to get this place sorted. I've got more stuff in the car—plaster, rollers, cornices, skirting, protective goggles and face masks. It'll keep me busy for a few…' His fingers speared his hair as he looked at the

room, the magnitude of the utter mess they'd made clearly dawning. *And not just the house*. She'd made a mess of everything. 'Weeks.'

And he was also playing the *let's not talk about it* game. She could do that too. And perhaps, by the time they'd got to the market normality would be restored and her appetite would come out of hiding. 'Okay. Well, I'll just drag a brush through my hair and grab a jumper. Give me a minute or two.'

The sky was a brilliant cloudless cobalt blue as they strode down the hill, past rows of perfectly maintained colonial-style houses, just like hers was going to be…possibly next millennium. Luckily the market wasn't far so they didn't have too many moments of difficult silence to fill before they got there.

They walked through the car park to the stalls dotted around the forecourt of a large open-fronted building selling everything French. Colourful Provençale earthenware sat next to tins of *foie gras* and jars of bright thick jams; soft linens and dainty sprigs of lavender graced traditional wooden dressers; blue and white chequered tablecloths covered a hotchpotch of mismatched tables. People sat around, chatting and eating and laughing.

A stack of antique furniture sat in one corner of the building, rickety tables and chairs, kitchen and bedroom heirloom pieces. Georgie spied a quaint rocking bassinet in need of a little care and attention, adorned with the softest cream-coloured blankets and the cutest coverlets, and her heart did a little jig. It was perfect. But, as with most things here, it was also too far out of her price bracket.

She sighed, dragging herself away from such beautiful things. Buying would have to happen when she could afford it, not when it took her fancy. Liam noticed her gaze drift back to the bassinet but, then, he would. Annoyingly, he knew her through and through. Her heart jig

went into a serious funeral dirge. It seemed everything was an issue between them these days. He nodded at the bassinet. 'Planning ahead?'

'Window shopping. At least that's free. I have to get my priorities straight. Firstly, I have to provide a decent place to sleep. Then I have to provide something to sleep in.'

'Babies cost a lot, eh? So much to think about, it's mind-blowing.' His forehead crinkled as he frowned. He looked as if he was about to say something, then changed his mind and tugged her to the juice bar instead. 'Okay, now you're going to have a fresh juice. Then we'll get a decent coffee and something to eat.'

'But—'

He placed a gentle palm against the small of her back and manoeuvred her towards the juice stall. 'No buts. And we're going to be the same as we always are when we come here. We're going to *ooh* at the cheese and hold our noses at the smell. And buy way too much and not eat it all. And then we'll have to fumigate your kitchen-diner-lounge room thing, whatever you want to call it.'

'I call it my living area, and it's going to be fabulous. But unfortunately I'm not going to eat any unprocessed soft cheese there or anywhere else. Along with alcohol, pâté and most kinds of processed meat that I love, stinky cheese is out for a while. Remember?' She patted her stomach. Damn the man, she was going to mention her pregnancy. It was part of her. Soon it would be most of her, plumping her out like a huge fat cushion. And then there'd be no denying it. Whether he liked it or not.

To her surprise, he grinned.

'Okay, so you're going to look at the cheese section and be downright miserable. Walk straight past the pâté, giving it a cold hard stare. Cast eye-daggers on that devilish salami and *jambon*. And then order a double helping of *pain au chocolat* and a *chocolat chaud* with lashings of

cream, and still wallow in what you can't have instead of what you've got. Which, in my book, is three helpings of chocolate and it's not even ten o'clock.'

He stopped at the juice stall and ordered a freshly squeezed OJ for himself and a 'Brain Booster' for her, like always.

'Which is why you need this vitamin blast to counteract the sugar rush. And now we're going to talk about what happened last night, and when we've stopped cringing we're going to laugh about it. We will laugh. Eventually.'

At her shocked face he smiled again, but this time it was softer and more tender. And she liked it that he was trying to make things normal, that he was making sure she had the right things to eat, and that she was as content as she could be under the circumstances. This was the Liam she'd grown to love. Whoa. *Love?*

Platonically, yes. She loved him as any friend would love a friend. And fancied him, just a little bit. Which was understandable, because a lot of women did. He was just the type that appealed—dashing doctor with a great sense of humour and nice hands. Looking lower, she admired other parts of him too.

Okay, if he kept on staring at her and smiling like that she could definitely fancy him a lot.

'Na-ah.' Georgie shook her head as her cheeks heated again. 'I'm not going to talk about it, I'm just pretending it didn't happen.'

'Well, I'm not. That's not going to work. It's going to be the big elephant in the…market, stomping around with us for ever. So we'll acknowledge that it happened. We'll agree it was—'

'A mistake,' she butted in, before he could say anything else. Because that's what it had been. A huge silly mistake.

'Here you go, you two. Your usual. Beautiful day…' The juice lady passed over large plastic cups of vividly

coloured juice with perfect timing. Georgie took hers and handed Liam his. Then she wandered through the stalls, perusing the locally grown fruit and vegetables, the huge bowls of oily olives and myriad savoury dips, and feigned interest in everything apart from this conversation.

He was by her side in a moment. On any other day she wouldn't have paid much attention but today all her body seemed interested in was getting closer to that smell, in being near him, in having his lips on her skin again. His mouth was dangerously close to her ear. 'I was going to say it was nice. More than nice. In fact, it was a bloody revelation. I didn't think you'd be so…unleashed. But if you want to say it was a mistake, go ahead.'

She twisted to see him, his eyes glinting with tease. And heat. 'It was a mistake. And I'm so-o-o embarrassed.'

His arm snaked across her shoulder and he wrapped her in a sort of guy-style headlock hug thing. Which shouldn't have been remotely sexy but was the biggest turn on since her lips had touched his last night. 'It's okay, Geo. We can move on. It is possible.'

'You think?' Wiggling from his grip, she faced him. 'I kissed you! In fact, I almost attacked you!' The clatter of teacups reverberated around the space, and then ended in an abrupt silence. People stared and then turned away and pretended not to stare, which made everything ten times worse. She lowered her voice and her words came out a lot like a hiss. 'But, then, you kiss so many women you probably didn't even think much about it.'

Hadn't he? Had it been really not special? Had she not turned him on while she'd been burning up? By saying they could move on, was he trying to say that he didn't want her? Which was what she wanted, wasn't it? An end to these weird feelings? So why did she feel as if she'd been stabbed through the gut?

'To be honest, it's all I've been thinking about for the

last twelve hours.' He steered her to a table and sat her down, grinning. He was enjoying this. Well, of course he was, this was Liam, the great non-committer. 'But what I need to know, Geo, is why?'

'Well…' If she knew that, she'd be up for a Nobel prize or something. The secrets of the universe. The chemistry of attraction. The laws of inconvenience and mortification. All started and ended with the *but why?* of that kiss. 'Haven't you ever wondered about…you know…us? What it would be like? What we would be like?'

He shrugged his gorgeous shoulders, but a tiny muscle moved in his jaw. 'I seem to remember you used the descriptor *ick* the last time we talked about this. So, honestly, it wasn't something I imagined could happen. Then, suddenly…*wham*.'

'I attacked you. I did—*do*—think it's an ick idea. But, then, for some reason last night I felt really connected to you. I'm sorry.'

'Stop apologising. Never apologise for kissing like that.' The waitress brought their order and he took a bite from his *croque monsieur*, which oozed melted cheese over the plate and looked almost as delicious as the man sinking his teeth into it. He swallowed and took a sip of espresso. 'Do you think it's because of the baby? Is this all because I'm the father? Because, frankly, you never gave me any reason to think you liked me…in that way. And, yes, we're going to keep talking about it like we talk about everything, so take your hands away from your face.'

'No. Yes. No. I don't know. It's all become too complicated. I felt weird when I saw you that day in the bar after you came back from Pakistan. Something was different. You seemed different, I felt different. Maybe it was the fertility drugs.' But that was a lame excuse. Lots of women took them and didn't go around kissing inappropriately. She finally had the courage to look up at him.

Yes, something was still very definitely different. The feeling hadn't gone, it had got worse. 'Anyhoo, I got it out of my system last night, and we both know that nothing can happen, don't we...?'

'Absolutely. Understood.'

What she wanted him to say she didn't know. Except, possibly, that he wanted to do it again and again. That he fancied her in just the same way. Okay, she wanted the whole dang fairytale—but Liam had never been much of a Prince Charming, and she definitely didn't suit the Cinderella role, apart from the having no money bit. In that part she was absolutely typecast.

Placing his cup slowly into the white bone china saucer, Liam looked like he was carefully choosing the right words. 'We are in no state to start anything. Imagine if we did the sex thing and then fell out. Imagine if we took anything any further. Me the playboy and you pregnant and vulnerable. You need to think of the baby.'

'So I don't get to have a sex life? Women can have sex when they're pregnant. Numpty.' Her eyes almost pinging out of her head, she picked up her fork and pointed it at him. 'And I am not vulnerable. Dare to say that again and I'll fork you to death.'

'No, never. Please. Anything but that.' His voice rose a teasing octave. Then got serious. 'You are one of the strongest people I've met. It was the wrong choice of words. Your situation makes you vulnerable. But you need someone who'll stick around. Someone who—'

'Wants me?' She closed her eyes wishing to hell she hadn't said that. It sounded so needy, and she wasn't. Just uncertain. And frustrated. Because she wanted to kiss him, she wanted to take him to her bed and tangle in the sheets, like she'd imagined. She wanted him...in a way she hadn't known could be possible. But he didn't want her. And he was trying so hard to put it gently and nicely and

in a friendly way. It was humiliating that he even thought she needed the gentle treatment.

A sharp twist of pain radiated through her solar plexus. Even her own mother hadn't wanted her and had left her in a box on steps outside a church hall with nothing except a small cream woollen blanket and the clothes she'd been wearing. No one had ever claimed her. And bureaucracy and mixed-up paperwork had meant she hadn't been put up for adoption until she'd been too old, so she'd never belonged. Period. No one had ever wanted her.

And to a certain extent Liam was right. He didn't stick around anywhere for long, his job took him to some of the most dangerous parts of the world, and for the most part she thought it was exciting, glamorous even. But in reality it was dangerous. He ran a serious risk of being killed, caught or tortured. Did she want that kind of anxiety to infiltrate her life and that of her child's from here on?

His warm hand covered hers. 'You know I wouldn't do anything to hurt you, right? But we can't put our whole friendship under threat because of curiosity. Things would inevitably change. They couldn't not change. Everything would come under the spotlight—past partners, broken promises, how we fill the dishwasher, whose turn it is to empty the bins. And everything we've ever done with other people will come under scrutiny too, what we've said, what we've done. There'll be expectations, and I'm not good with that. You know that. I don't want things to get complicated.'

Too late, mate. 'Like me having your baby?'

'Yeah. That. It's complicated already, without getting things involved sexually too. Not that I don't want to… wouldn't…you know…mind. That kiss wasn't ick. It was good. Very good.' He shook his head. 'God, this is awful. I think I preferred your way of pretending it didn't happen. Let's go back an hour, shall we?'

Or twelve?

He held her gaze for a few seconds and smiled apologetically. Then his smile melted. As if distracted by something over his shoulder, he turned away. When he looked back he didn't give her eye contact at all. Just stared down at his cup. 'And...'

'And?'

His head jerked up, and he looked spooked and shocked. 'Nothing. Forget it. Just that. I can't give you what you need.'

'I don't need anything. It was only a kiss.' But the caution in his eyes told her he had been about to say something else. Had broken off before he'd dared say it. What the hell? Her heart began to rattle against her rib cage. 'Wait a minute. What are you hiding?'

'Nothing. I don't know what you mean.'

'You look edgy and worried and I've seen that look on your face many times. Right before you give your poor sap of a girlfriend the old heave-ho.'

He looked down at his hands and dragged in a breath. 'Georgie, there's something else. Something I've been meaning to say since I got back, but haven't...quite found the right words.'

The chocolate croissant felt like a hard lump in her churning stomach. Things had become really messed up. 'I won't jump you again, if that's what you're worried about.'

'Of course I'm not worried.' No? Well, he just looked it, then. 'I'm going to help you renovate your house, I promised I'd do that. And I will.'

She knew a man was stalling when she saw it. 'And then, when you've done your dutiful bit and fulfilled the promises, you're going to adhere to the baby daddy contract and do a runner.'

'Far from it. In fact, just the opposite.' He stood up, took her by the arm and began to walk back through the

market. 'Not at all. Georgie, I know it's taken me a long time to outright say it, but I wanted to make sure. I was trying not to mess you around.'

'What? What is it?' *You've met someone. Someone important.* Words clogged in her throat, thick and fast. 'Spit it out, man. I'm on tenterhooks here.'

He gave her a sideways smile. 'Thing is, I do want to be the father of this child. I want to provide, I want to take responsibility for my baby.'

'What? *Your* baby? Your baby? Whoa. That's a surprise.'

'Yes. My baby. It's got my DNA. Just like we agreed. Like you wanted.'

'But you said…' All her ideas tumbled around in her head with a sharp mix of frustration.

All she'd known about him for ten years suggested he didn't want a child. He didn't want a family. He'd signed a damned contract, made that the only condition. So instead of being the far side of elated, her gut felt churned up. Would he change his mind again?

And again?

And then there was the small matter of the kiss, which coloured everything.

His involvement was what she'd wanted ever since he'd offered to be the donor, but this was not how she'd imagined it would make her feel.

Irritated, she shook her arm free from his. Shoppers jostled against them as they headed back towards the house. The busy street was so not the place to be having this conversation. 'I know it's what I wanted, but I thought you didn't…weren't…aren't…' She pulled herself together and chose bluntness and honesty. 'Why now? Why this all of a sudden? How can I trust that you'll take this seriously? You're so confusing.'

Unlike her, he seemed far from irritated, his voice

steady and determined. 'It's not confusing at all. This is the most serious and the most single-minded I've ever been about anything.'

'And you decide to tell me now? Here, on Parnell Road?'

'Okay, I have to admit my timing's lousy.'

'You can say that again.' She whirled round to face him, her head woozy at the sudden and fundamental change in her life. She didn't know how she felt about this. He hadn't exactly declared his overwhelming love for the baby, and she didn't know how she *felt* about him—except that he'd just completely blindsided her and everything was getting more complicated by the second.

And more, she had to be sure this wasn't some passing phase he'd move out of next week, next month, next year. 'Is this some kind of misdirected duty thing? Because you don't get to do that. You don't get to mess around with other people's lives just because it makes you feel better. Here one minute, changing your mind the next.'

'I won't change my mind.'

She tried to stay calm. 'A contract has been signed, Liam. You're legally bound, remember? Clause number six? *"You will have no paternal rights whatsoever over the child, and will have no authority of any kind with respect to the child, or any decisions regarding the child."'*

'Whoa. Really? Off by heart?' He stared at her open-mouthed.

'What? I counsel about this exact dilemma every damned day, Liam. So I know the wording. Okay?'

'So you'll remember clause ten, then? You can agree to me having social contact—at your discretion.'

He'd certainly read it. He'd taken the time and effort to read and research. He was serious. 'Yes, I can, if I think contact will be good for the child. But what do you know

about bringing up a child? About being a father? What's changed for you?'

Love, she thought. She hoped.

Because love for her child, even though it was still so small and so precious, had changed her fundamentally.

But Liam's expression turned thunderous. 'This is ridiculous. I don't want to mess anyone around, I want to be involved—the two things are completely different. I knew you were going to react like this. You just don't want anyone butting in on your little family of two.'

'How dare you? I would love my baby to have a father, you know that. You know I want that more than anything.' She shook her head. Amazing that he could think that. 'Is that what you think of me? That I'm selfish? That I want to keep this child purely for myself, like some kind of...toy?'

'Of course not. But surely, as the father, I have a say in things?' He really meant it. He wanted to be part of this. But could she trust him to be wholly there for them?

'No. Actually, you don't. You signed your rights away. All I know is that not many months ago you demanded a contract and now you don't want that. Maybe next month you'll want the contract again.'

He stopped short, breathing hard, dragged a wad of paper out of his jacket pocket. 'Here. Here's the contract.' He held the papers up and tore them in half. Then half again. Then again. Pieces of ripped paper fluttered to her feet like large bits of confetti. Only this was the severing of something, not celebrating the uniting of something. 'I want to be a father. The father of the child you are carrying. My child.'

And the word 'love' is still not there.

She'd listened hard and it was still missing. No matter how much she wanted it to be there, no matter how much she strained to hear it in the cadence of his words, in the silence between them.

He wanted to be a father, but he didn't want to be a daddy. That was the fundamental difference. He wanted the label but not the emotional involvement. That was Liam through and through.

But, on the other hand, if he was truly serious and did want to be involved, she couldn't deny him that, couldn't deny her child the right to know its father.

Why did this have to be so complicated? Why couldn't he have kept to his side of the deal? Why did she have to have developed more than friendly feelings for him? Those emotions were tainting things, making her think in a way she'd never done before. This whole morning wasn't about the kiss at all. It had never been about the kiss.

His hand was on her arm now. 'Georgie, I don't want to have this conversation here on the street and I don't want to argue. This was the furthest thing from my mind. You look upset and that really wasn't my intention. I honestly thought you'd be pleased.'

Pleased? If his intentions were genuine then she'd be delighted. How could she not want him to be a father? He was smart, funny and, if she was honest, would make a great daddy—if he stuck around long enough. And there it was again, her immediate concern: he just wasn't the staying sort of guy. For whatever reason—and she only knew half of his story—he didn't commit.

She picked the pieces of paper up and shoved them at him. Then hesitated on her doorstep. 'Can we talk later? This is pretty big for me, I need some time to think things through.'

'Yes, by all means, think it through.' He followed her up the steps and when it was clear he wasn't giving up, she took her key out of her bag. As he watched her he shook his head. 'But I need to say this now, Geo, and I need you to listen. It's tough work, bringing up a child. I don't want you to go through it on your own and I don't want our child

to miss out on having a father. I know how that feels and I couldn't condemn my own flesh and blood to that kind of life. Don't you want me to be involved?'

'This is my flesh and blood too. My only flesh and blood. So I've got to be careful, make the right decisions.' At least he had a family. He might not want to have them, but he was tied to them. And now she would be tied to him for ever. Oh, why the hell hadn't she thought this through more thoroughly at the beginning? 'What exactly do you mean by "involved"? Cash? Because that's not enough. Is that why you're here? To pay us off or something?'

'It's been in my head for the last few weeks, I just didn't know how to say it. When to say it. What to say, even. But the more I see you, the more I think about it, the more it makes sense.'

'It's not about making sense, it's about how you feel. In here.' She touched her chest. It felt a little cracked open and raw. 'In your heart and your soul. You can't do something because it makes sense, otherwise we'd never do any of the rash, amazing stuff we do. Like this pregnancy thing from the start. None of it made sense, not to you or anyone else. But it did to me.'

'And it does to me now.'

His words hovered in the air as she thrust the key in the lock and threw the door open. She took several long deep breaths and tried to clear her thoughts.

Then tried to explain them to him. 'If I was going to co-parent I would expect a fully one hundred per cent committed father who was around, who wouldn't flinch during the darker times. Because there will be some, I'm sure.' And although she adored Liam, he wasn't reliable. He was away a lot of the time, never knowing when he'd be home. And she couldn't get past the fact that he'd told her that this baby plan was the worst thing he'd ever heard.

'It's got to be for ever, you can't change your mind again. I don't want to open our child up to a whole world of hurt. I saw plenty of kids at the home whose families made promises and broke them, and in the end broke their kids' hearts and crushed their spirits.'

'I know you had a hard time, Georgie. And that's why I'm here now. So our child doesn't have to go through what you went through.'

'You have no idea. You don't know what it means to be alone. To make up a pretend family because you don't have any. To watch others being chosen. To wish that someone, anyone, would choose you. And to try to be, oh, so brave when they didn't, when inside every part of you is crumbling.' She would never crumble again. This child inside her gave her twice the strength and three times the resolve. 'This is your last chance to decide, Liam. I'll hold you to whatever decision you make now. This is it. No going back. No coming to me in three years, six, twelve and saying you made a mistake and you've changed your mind again. You have to be in or out—for ever.'

This was something Liam could answer. Because this was the one thing he knew. He would not let his child down. He'd known that with every damned fibre of his being since the moment he'd seen her carrying his child. Since he'd seen that scan of a real living being. His child. Their child.

Every single mention of a baby, every thought of who was growing inside her, brought back the crushing pain again. And with that hurt still beating against his rib cage he knew he'd make every effort to make his child safe. Because that was his job. A father did that.

But he was also going to keep any emotions out of it. Because, hell, he needed to keep his heart safe, too. He

would provide from a distance. He would have visits but he wouldn't—couldn't—put any of them at risk by allowing himself to care for them. He would treat his child with the same compassion and consideration he treated his patients, no more and certainly no less.

'I know what I said. I didn't think it through. But this is my child and my responsibility and I will never shirk from that. I don't want your experiences for our child, or mine either. This child will know he's always wanted.' This was not how Liam had imagined this scenario playing out, but he had to go with it. He'd already stumbled too far along without saying what he felt. Although he'd been shocked by the ferocity of Georgie's reaction. He'd seriously misjudged her. She was growing braver and stronger and more independent every moment she carried that baby. 'I am in it for ever.'

'How can I be sure?' Her hands were on her hips while her dark eyes blazed.

'So tearing up the contract isn't enough for you?'

'No. Actions speak, Liam. I want actions—and not dramatic hollow ones like those shreds of paper.'

Now this was well and truly out in the open he knew there could never be any more kisses. He needed to keep a good long distance from her, too. Anything else would make things far too complicated. They could both be good parents if they were a team, a *platonic* team. Messing with that, opening a whole potential for destruction, would be a recipe for disaster.

He knew how much pain a child suffered when their parents couldn't bear to look at each other. Knew how destructive it was, watching arguments unfold, always calculating when the bomb was going to drop. Always being on guard. Always feeling, believing, *knowing* that every single ounce of friction was his fault. He couldn't

put his own child through that, so if there was no intimacy there would be no chance of that damaging scenario happening. 'You'll know, Georgie, because I'll damned well prove it to you.'

CHAPTER SEVEN

Three months ago...

'IT'LL KEEP ME *busy for weeks.'*

Ha. He wished.

By Liam's reckoning it should have been finished months ago, but whenever he turned around this tinpot wreck of a house threw another job at him. Georgie had been wrong about the roof. With the winter came high winds that blew off and cracked more than enough tiles for the whole thing to need replacing.

Then there was the floor in the kitchen. Weathered and abused over seventy years, it took four consecutive weekends to sand it down enough that it was even and usable. Then three coats of varnish. A perfect parquet floor it was not, but it was now an acceptably usable one. All done on a tight budget, and fitted in between exhausting twelve-hour shifts at work. It had taken a lot of coercing Georgie to even allow him to do that.

Climbing down the stepladder from where he'd been fixing the new light fitting in the flash living area, he huffed out a long breath. He had to admit she'd had a point about knocking the wall down, the open-plan space was amazing. With the renovated floor and antique white walls it was impressively large and light, with a good flow from

one area to the next. She'd managed to find, on the cheap from a trading website, a set of elegant French doors that opened the kitchen out onto the small deck. Beyond that was a riotous garden, overgrown and dingy. But he had no doubt she had plans for there too. The woman clearly had a gift for renovation.

A loud bang and a very unladylike curse came from above him. Liam was up the stairs and in the bathroom in two seconds flat. 'You okay? What the hell was that?'

'Just a little contretemps with a tin of paint. And… damn, I was so nearly finished.' From her crouched position on the floor she grimaced up at him as a pool of off-white gloop seeped across stained dustsheets. A paintbrush stuck out of her denim dungarees pockets, her face was splattered with paint and she wore a plastic carrier bag tied round her hair. She dabbed at the ever-increasing seepage with a rag, huffing and puffing a little. 'I'm going to have to nip out to the hardware store and get some more paint now. Do we need anything else?'

His eyes flickered from her to the stepladder, back to her. *Unbelievable.* 'You were painting the ceiling?'

'Um…yes?'

'After I specifically told you it was next on my list of jobs?'

'Um…yes.' This time there was no hint of apology. 'It needed doing and it was next on *my* list. I was free to do it, so I made a start.'

'Why can't you accept more than the slightest bit of help without a row? You are slowly driving me crazy. No—make that rapidly driving me crazy.' There was only so much independence a guy could take before it became downright stubbornness, and then it made him really mad. 'You were supposed to be taking a break.'

'Breaks are boring. There's nothing more satisfying than seeing the instant difference a coat of paint can make

to a room. Look, isn't it great?' She gestured at the white over the dirty green and, yes, it looked good. That was not the point.

'And risk a broken collarbone…or worse?' He didn't allow his brain to follow that train of thought. Already she was showing signs of discomfort with her growing bump—all it had needed was one wrong step. 'These ladders are unsteady, and those trainers have a slippery grip. You said so yourself.'

'I was fine.'

'Oh, clearly. So fine that you dropped the paint can?'

'No one likes a smartass.' With an irritated groan she whipped the plastic bag from her head and stuffed it into her pocket, then gripped the side of the bath to assist her to transition from sitting to standing—flatly refusing his outstretched hand. Once up she rubbed her back, which pushed out her stomach, fat and round and very obviously pregnant. Her face had filled out a little too, her long hair, which she'd piled on the top of her head in some sort of fancy clip, was glossy. Man, was it shiny, and it took him all his strength not to pull her close and inhale. Somehow the more annoying she became, the more he wanted her. Seemed he was hard-wired to protect her too.

But he'd never contemplated giving her this job and hadn't thought she'd be so hell-bent on doing what she wanted. How much did he need to do to show her he was invested too? She'd taken him at his word and had never referred to the contract again, but he knew she watched him and wondered. Every day. And every day he tried to prove to her he was up to the father job.

He just hadn't contemplated how hard it would be to keep his emotions out of the agenda.

'How about you sort out the cupboards in the kitchen instead, like we talked about earlier? I'll do this when I've finished the lights downstairs.'

And, yes, it was like this every week. She had a problem or, more usually, the house had a problem and he had an insatiable, irrational need to fix it. Except the biggest problem was that he shouldn't be here at all. The baby wasn't due for months, so in theory he could let her get on with it. But, well, he couldn't.

Her voice had a sudden edge to it. 'You can't bear to be in the same room as me for five minutes, can you?'

'Sorry? What on earth are you on about?'

'It's just that every time I go into a room you leave it. It's been going on for weeks, it's like there's a revolving door. Me. You. Me. You. I'm getting dizzy.'

'Ridiculous.' Truth was, he couldn't bear to *not* be in the same room. Being with her was killing him. A long, drawn-out agonising death of lust. He was doing this for the sake of his child, making sure they had everything they needed. At least, that was what he told himself, and not because he didn't want to wake up every morning and not have the prospect of seeing Georgie's smiling face or inhaling her scent that pervaded everything in the house.

'Is it me? Is it seeing me like this that you don't like?' She paraded in front of him, laughing, sticking her tummy out—there was a bubble where her belly button protruded. 'Because I happen to love it.'

He laughed. 'Or maybe it's a coincidence, ever thought of that? Perhaps I just always happen to be about to leave when you come dashing in. Bad timing, maybe, and you're looking for it so you have confirmation bias?'

'Yeah, right. Never try arguing with a know-it-all doctor. I notice it because it happens, matey. And don't deny it.'

Avoiding the wet paint, he took her hands and faced her, putting a serious tone in his voice, ignoring the immediate sharp jolt of electricity that ran through him as he touched her. 'Okay, yes, Geo, you're right. I'm sorry to

have to break it to you, but you do look terrible, hideous, unsightly. In fact, I was going to ask you to cover up with that dust sheet. But now you've spilled on it I'll just have to put up with you as you are.' He laughed at her tongue sticking out of her mouth. 'Yeah, really, I can't bear being with you, and that's why I spend every spare hour here, doing your bidding.'

If only she knew how partly true those words were. It was seeing her, full stop. Seeing Georgie carrying his child, seeing her turn this dilapidated wreck into a home for her family. His family.

Every time he turned around there was something else: the piles of gifted baby clothes; the stockpile of nappies for newborns. The baby scans on the fridge—the most recent one at twenty weeks, where he could see every finger and toe. Where the ribs encased his baby's fast-beating heart. Its chubby belly. The MacAllister nose.

Liam's heart swelled, then tightened. The memories threatened to swamp him again. He rubbed his chest, but the pain wasn't physical, it was psychological. And every time he saw Georgie it got worse.

And still he kept on coming back. Because he couldn't not. Because he couldn't contemplate an hour of his life when he didn't see her.

She dropped her hand from his grip and began wiping a paintbrush on the rim of the can. 'I am grateful, really. You don't have to give up all your spare time...' Her hand went to her belly and she made a sharp noise. 'Oh!'

He knew that look. He knew most of them now, thank God, because she never complained about any of the changes she was experiencing and he knew a few of them must have taken some getting used to. A rise of eyebrows and a gentle smile meant baby movement. A frown but determined-not-to-show-it stubbornly stiff jaw meant she had backache. A fist against her chest meant heartburn.

He'd never been so aware of anyone in his whole life. 'Kicking again?'

'Yes. It doesn't hurt, it just makes me jump. It's weird. though, I don't know if I'll ever get used to it—it's like a whole crowd of butterflies stretching their wings. He's a little wriggler, this fella. I think he might be a martial arts expert when he grows up.'

He nodded towards her belly, his heart suddenly aching. 'She might be a dancer? Cheerleading? Gymnast? Scottish country dancing? That has kicks, doesn't it?'

Her eyebrows rose. 'The ones I learnt at school had a lot of skipping in circles and peeling off. I don't remember kicking. Apart from hot sharp prods to my nine-year-old partner's ankles. He had no clue what he was doing and was far happier pulling faces at his friends than swinging me in a do-si-do.'

Then clearly the boy had been a prize idiot.

Clearing the paint pot and mess out of the way, Liam stood her in front of him. Goddamn, she was beautiful, all flushed and smiling. He had to admit that being pregnant suited her. She'd never seemed so content. Apart from the odd moment when he'd catch her staring out of the window into the distance, or looking at him with a strange expression on her face. 'Show me?'

'What? Scottish dancing, in a tiny bathroom? Are you nuts? Silly me, of course you are.'

'Probably.' He took her hands in his and twirled her round. 'Like this?'

'Not even remotely.' Her head tipped back as she laughed, and for the first time in for ever things were back to normal between them. There was no baby, no contract, no tension, just two old friends messing about, like they'd done hundreds of times before. He twirled her again, faster, and caught her in his arms and she squealed, 'Stop! I'm covered in paint, my hands—'

'Are fine. Now, show me what to do. Like this?' He made a woeful attempt at a highland jig that had him stumbling over the stepladder. 'Clearly this needs practice.'

'And a lot more space.' She sucked in air, and again, doubling over with laughter. 'You are a lot worse than David Sterling.'

'David?'

'My nine-year-old partner. Broke my poor innocent heart when he kissed Amy Jenkins at the Year Four social, but at least he had rhythm.'

'I have rhythm.' And Georgie's heart was too damned precious to be broken again. Although Liam had a feeling that when all this was done, he'd be no better than David-bloody-Sterling.

'Oh, yeah?' She prodded him in the stomach, and he wondered whether that was a step up or down from being kicked in the ankle. 'I've seen your rhythm, mate, at Indigo, late at night, when you're filled with booze.'

'Bad, huh?'

'Actually, no, not at all. You're a good dancer, probably better than I am if I'm honest. But I'm not exactly going to want to admit that, am I?'

'You, my lady, are such a tease.' Feeling suddenly way out of his depth, he gave her a smile and it was pure stubborn willpower that stopped him from kissing her again.

'Really? You think so? I haven't even started.' She smiled back and the air between them stilled. Her hand slipped into his and squeezed, and she peered up at him through thick dark eyelashes. And he was sure she was just being Georgie, but that kiss hovered between them again, in her words, in the frisson of electricity that shivered through him. In the touch of skin on skin. Her voice was raspy. 'Is it just me or is it very hot in here?'

'Hmm. You want to try peeling off? That might help. I could give you a hand. That is one thing I am very good at.'

He rested his palm on her shoulder, toying with her T-shirt sleeve. Her pupils widened at his touch, heat misted her gaze and he knew then that she was struggling too. That just maybe she wanted the physical contact that he craved.

But, goddamn, he knew that was the most stupid thing to say, especially when they'd agreed to go back to situation normal between them—but it was out there now. He was tired of fighting this…and absolutely sure he shouldn't have said those words.

Time seemed to stretch and he didn't know what to do. Apologise? 'Georgie—'

'Oh. There it is again. It always takes me by surprise.' Shaking her hand free from his, she pressed her hand to her belly again watching his reaction, eyes wary now. She gave her head a little shake as she stepped away. 'And don't look so worried. I won't ask.'

'No.' She wasn't talking about his faux pas. Once she'd asked him if she wanted to feel the baby kick and he'd refused. Point blank. And she'd never asked him again, but sometimes made a point of telling him when it was happening. And, by God, he wanted to, but he knew he couldn't, that with one touch of her, and of their baby, he'd be compelled to want more. And that didn't fit in with the emotionless parenting idea. Or the platonic parenting either.

The atmosphere in this minuscule room was reaching suffocation point, he needed to cut loose. 'Okay, so break time. You go put your feet up and I'll pop out to the hardware store. We need more sandpaper anyway. I'll get more paint, and I've got to get the right bulb for the light fitting—you got screw-in instead of bayonet.'

'Oops. Sorry. And when you come back, do you think we could spend more than two minutes in the same place? You won't run out on me?'

The ten-million-dollar question. 'This house is throw-

ing us so many problems we have to divide and rule if we're going to win. Now, get that kettle on and I'll bring back biscuits for afternoon tea.'

'Are you sure?'

'Buying biscuits isn't exactly a difficult task. Of course I'm sure.' And, yes, he knew that wasn't what she'd meant. Dodging bullets seemed the aim of today. 'Chocolate? I know, white chocolate with raspberry. Two packets.'

She threw him a huge grin. 'Oh, Liam, I do like it when you talk dirty.'

He could have been out for another few months and it wouldn't have been enough to stop the need surging through his veins. In less than an hour he was back, trying to locate her, with his peace offering of her favourite biscuits. She wasn't in the kitchen, and the contents of the cupboards were still in boxes in the same place on the floor.

Wondering if she was actually doing as he'd suggested and taking a nap, or on that damned stepladder again, he mounted the stairs two by two, in total silence, glad that he'd fixed the creaking floorboards. The bathroom was empty.

Intrigued, he walked along to her bedroom, heard the radio, a song he didn't recognise, and she was singing along. It sounded ditsy and bright and he knew he should call out, make her aware of his presence, but something compelled him to be quiet as he approached her room. He told himself that he didn't want to make her jump.

She was standing in front of her closet, holding a black lace dress up against her body and looking in the mirror, turning from side to side, stretching the fabric across her belly. The work dungarees had gone, and now she was wearing flannel shorts and a baggy blue T-shirt. After a few seconds she frowned and threw the dress on the

chair then shook her hair free from the hair slide. It cascaded down her back, a river of lush honey curls. Her breasts strained against the T-shirt. She was dusty and paint-streaked and fertile and ripe. She looked sexier than any skinny model on the front of the magazines, sexier than any woman he'd ever laid his eyes on. His heart stuttered. He took a step forward, paused.

She still hadn't heard him. Her humming continued. Taking a brush from the closet, she gathered a fistful of hair and started to brush rhythmically. And even though he knew he shouldn't be standing here, watching her do this, knew he was breaking a zillion unspoken promises they'd made in the aftermath of the single kiss, he still couldn't bring himself to speak. His throat was scratchy and raw, and his body was on fire. Each swipe through her hair was considered and resolute, her slender arm moving up and down, almost trancelike, what he could see of her face was calm and relaxed.

She was lost in thought, and still singing the upbeat, happy song. The reverence with which she took each brushstroke made his heart contract. The glossy sheen of her hair, the ridges of her back as she moved and shifted from foot to foot. Her body swayed a little, her backside bopping to and fro; and maybe it was the heat from before, the soft light in the room, the smell of her, the intimate nature of watching her, but he struggled with a powerful urge to carry her to her bed and make love to her.

He realised he was hard, that his hands were clenched against his body's strain towards her. That he had to consciously control his feet and make them still.

How could someone doing something as mundane as brushing their hair bring him to the edge of reason?

After a few moments she started to coil her hair back up onto the top of her head again—and that was it—his

control was lost. In a second he was behind her, hands on hers, whispering close to her ear. 'Don't. Leave it down.'

In response to his sudden arrival she turned, shaking. Confusion racing across her face. And heat too. 'Oh, my God, Liam. You made me jump.'

'Sorry. I just...' He curled a lock of her hair around his fingers, pressed it to his mouth.

She placed her hands on his chest, that intimate gesture firing more need through him. 'What?'

'I can't do this any more.'

'Can't do what?'

'I can't keep away from you. Ever since that kiss I've been hiding out.'

She let out a long breath and her face creased into a soft smile. 'I knew it. I knew you were up to something. See. I told you. You are avoiding me. I was right. I'm always right.'

'Intuitive, perhaps. Give a guy a break. I was doing the right thing.' He touched her lips with the pad of his thumb, tracing the soft path, the delicate curve. They were pink and moist and kissable. He remembered how good she had tasted and suddenly he couldn't wait any longer. Finesse lost, he dragged her to him. 'Come here.'

She inhaled a stuttered breath, her lips opening a little, her body trembling. And made a concentrated effort to calm it. She briefly closed her eyes, opened them again. 'But I thought—'

'Shh... Thinking is overrated.' He reached his arms round her thickened waist, pulled her closer, spiked his hands through her hair and nuzzled right into it. Cupping the back of her head, he held her face close against his throat. Just held her against him until the shaking stopped. Until he could look at her again. He wanted to kiss her, but he wouldn't, wouldn't make things difficult. But he

could hold her. Could feel her soft curves and taut belly pressing against him.

Breathe.

He prayed for the awareness and attraction to go, to be left here with just his old friend Georgie and nothing else, nothing complicated, because he knew that by taking those steps across the room he'd made things muddier than ever. But it was so compelling to hold her, to feel part of something so good. To be, for once in his life, actively looking forward, instead of just running from the past. To be accepted for the man he'd grown into.

Only now he knew how it felt, he didn't want to go back. Couldn't go back.

And then…the strangest of sensations. A tiny shiver against his hip, something almost ethereal…then it was gone.

His baby kicking.

Breathe.

But there was no oxygen. His chest hurt as he tried sucking in air, there was no space for anything more, emotion had filled his chest. A hard core of deep affection, a protective need, a desperate ache. And pride. His baby was moving, stirring in her belly. The shaking started again, but this time it was his body that was on the edge of control. 'Was that…?'

'The Scottish country dancer?' She pulled away a little and pressed a palm against his cheek. 'Yes, Liam. It was. There it is again.' She reached for his hand and pressed it against her bump. It was a flutter, not a whack. At least, not against his palm. The whack to his heart was mighty, though. And, God, no, he didn't want to feel this. Not this ache. Not this wanting. He didn't want to feel anything.

'Wow.' It was all he could manage. His throat was thick, his heart rampaging as all the pain came hurtling back.

Pain, and yet something else, something profound that made his soul soar.

He didn't know what to think or what to say as he stepped back. He'd been trying to avoid any kind of physical contact with Georgie but he'd been unable to stay away, had been compelled to hold her. Now his reasoning had been proved right. All his emotions were getting tangled up and he didn't want that. Didn't want any emotions to get in the way of clear thinking.

Obviously sensing him detaching already, she tugged at his hand and pulled him to sit on the bed, her other hand stroking his shoulder. And it was tempting to sit with her and let her stroke the tensions away, but he couldn't sit, so instead he walked to the window and looked out at the encroaching night. Dark shadows filled the garden, like the dark shadows in his heart. He needed to find some place where he could breathe normally again.

Georgie's voice reached to him. 'I know this is hard for you. I just don't know why. I'm trying to understand, I really am, and I'm trying not to push, but I want to know. I might be able to help. Tell me about your sister, about… Lauren.'

'I can't… I don't want to.' Didn't want to spoil this moment, where *this* child was vivid and vibrant and had so much potential.

There was a long silence where the night breathed darkness into the room, and he thought she might have fallen asleep.

When she eventually spoke she sounded disappointed, and that was so not his intention. 'Some time, then. Tell me some time.'

But it was too much to ask of him. He didn't even know what words to use. Lauren…had been there, and then she hadn't been. And a huge hole had blown open in his eight-

year-old heart that had never been filled with anything other than anger. At himself, mainly. At his parents.

And now... 'It'll only spoil everything.' He forced air out and inhaled again, trying to make some space in his chest, but still he felt constricted and tight. 'Let's get the hell out of here. I need to breathe.'

CHAPTER EIGHT

'The Pudding Place?'

'The right choice?'

'Oh, yes. Most definitely. These desserts are to die for. I couldn't think of anywhere more perfect.' Georgie's gaze slid over the rows and rows of chocolate éclairs, mini-Pavlovas and baked cheesecakes in the little dessert-only café, and then landed on Liam. She regarded him with caution. Whatever had been haunting him had passed. The shadows on his face had cleared a little, leaving him pale and reserved and yet trying so hard to act normal. She hadn't realised how emotionally distant he could make himself, even when he was in the same room.

For so many years his background had never mattered to her and she'd respected his need for privacy and put his quirky way with relationships down to immaturity at first, then pickiness, but now she believed it was meshed in fear. Of what, she wasn't sure. But now…now it meant everything. It meant the difference between them surviving this strange set-up they'd created or failing it.

If she could understand why he held back so much, perhaps she could help him surmount it. Because although he'd shown commitment with his time, she still didn't wholly trust that he would be there when it mattered. That

he wouldn't change his mind and run. And she wasn't prepared to take that risk with her heart or her child's.

A waitress arrived and asked for their order. Georgie couldn't decide. 'I think I'll have one of each. To start with.'

'You sure that's enough?' Liam laughed, a little more carefree. 'Or are you just keeping it light until your appetite really gets going?'

'This eating-for-two business is pretty damned good. I'm going to miss it after the baby comes.'

He gave his order then turned the menu over and over in his hands as he spoke. 'In South Sudan it's not uncommon for women to have large families, sometimes up to twelve kids. Imagine the fun you'd have then: eating for two for ever.'

'I'd be the size of an elephant if I did that and be on a perpetual diet for the rest of my life.' The chocolate éclair was divine. Great choice. Thick and rich and moist. It slid very easily down her throat. 'But, listen, you never tell me properly about your trips. It's always *murky* or *dry* or *messy*. But it must be way more than that.'

Leaning back in his chair, he crossed his arms and watched her eat. His gaze wandered over her, causing a riot of goosebumps over her skin, and she stared right back. Splatters of cream paint stuck to his old grey T-shirt. Funny, she remembered buying that for him years ago at a gig she'd been to when he'd been covering the night shift. It had been a little baggy on him back then but now it barely contained his solid biceps and stretched across a chest of muscle. His hair was sticking up in odd places, and he was dusty.

His knuckles were scratched and his skin torn. He looked rugged and edgy and it was such a turn on to watch him move she could barely think straight. This was dangerous territory. Every second spent with him was push-

ing her closer to an edge she knew was going to be at once delicious and yet potentially soul-damagingly painful.

He took a sip of hot black coffee. He'd ordered just that, no food. With wall-to-wall dessert on offer the man was clearly mad. 'So what exactly do you want to know?'

'What kinds of things do you get up to out in the field? The people you meet. I know you usually work at the tent cities, but what are the real cities like?'

His shoulders lifted in a sort of nonchalant shrug. 'The agency gang are pretty solid— people who want to do good, but all fed with a huge dose of reality. We know our limitations, there's never enough of anything—resources, people, help—but there's no point beating yourself up about what you can't achieve, you just get on and do what you can. While we're there the team always develops a huge bond, but such intensity can also drive you completely nuts. We do what we can in desolate and desperate parts of the world. There are, sadly, too many of them. But we do make a difference.'

'Well, there's no shortage of work, judging by the stories in the papers about floods, earthquakes and war zones. There's endless need for you everywhere.' He went to them all without any hesitation and she'd never once heard him utter one word of complaint about the harsh conditions he must have to endure, and the terrible things he must have seen. He kept everything tight inside him, but she didn't doubt he made a difference. He must have saved hundreds of lives and given thousands more help and much-needed hope. 'And the people you help? What are they like?'

'Desperate. Stoic. Honest. Victims. They have nothing apart from the clothes they stand up in. No homes, nowhere to call their own. There's always a threat—if it's not soldiers and fighting, or landmines and rogue devices, it's weather. Too much rain, or not enough. They need so

much more than we can give them. But we fight to save their kids' lives. It's important to have a generation of hope that can break through the cycle of poverty and suffering.'

Pride rippled through her chest, her already tender heart bruising just a little more. Between him and her baby her emotions were being bumped around all over the place. 'But isn't it desperately heartbreaking? I know when I worked on the paeds oncology ward it damn near broke my heart.'

Again with the shrug. 'Of course, but it's uplifting too. You try to keep the emotion out of it, or you'd never survive. You can't carry all that and more around with you all the time, you just get on and do the job. I've learnt to detach.'

Hallelujah. 'Oh, yes. I've seen you detach, my friend. I have personal experience. You're pretty expert at it.'

'Yeah, well. I don't like getting in too deep.' He tried for a smile, which at once made him look boyish and yet very, very sexy. 'It brings me out in hives.'

'That much is obvious. You have form. Lots and lots of form. I'm thinking Sally the medical student, Jenny from Hamilton and Hannah the interior decorator. Poor Hannah, she was nice. You really broke her heart.'

'She was talking babies, mortgages, retirement homes...' He visibly shuddered. 'She had our whole future mapped out on the first date. And she even had a cutesie name for me. Seriously, one evening spent together and suddenly I was Macadoodle-doo. No one does that.'

Georgie couldn't help but smile. 'Oh, yes, they do. It's part of the relationship ritual. It's about creating a whole new world of two, developing a language you wouldn't speak to anyone else. I think it's endearing.'

'It isn't.'

She laughed. 'You know your trouble? You just need to let people in a little.'

'Really? My trouble?' His laugh was brief. 'My relationships have given you lots of entertainment over the years, missy, and vice versa. But I've never thought you had trouble that needed fixing. I just took you the way you are. I still do.'

'Even pregnant? Because that took a bit of getting used to, didn't it?'

His eyebrows rose and he let out a big breath. 'Yes, even pregnant. Look, things have been very weird since this whole pregnancy thing started, but I'm doing my best to deal with it.'

'I know you've been working really hard on the house. And it's been brilliant.' But he still had a damned long way to go—like talking about the baby unhindered, like being in the same room with her, like being able to look at the baby scans with joy instead of concern and fear, as if he expected pain.

Although the last day had proved he could spend some time with her. But with what consequences? She'd almost dragged him to the bed the minute his breath had touched her neck. Holding back was the single most difficult thing she'd ever had to do.

Up until now she'd been the only woman he'd never detached from and it broke her heart to think she could well end up being just another one to add to his list. One kiss and they'd been on shaky ground ever since. Every movement he made, every space he filled, she was aware of him. Too much. Way too much. And that stunt in the bedroom had her flustered all over again. She was fighting the attraction but she didn't know how long she could hold out.

'I'm sorry. You're right. It's just…I can't help noticing that when you're struggling or getting close to someone you always cut loose right at the point when things start getting interesting. Like…' She wasn't sure of the wisdom of bringing this up, but if she didn't then he probably would

anyway, if the conversation at the French market was anything to go by. 'Like earlier. Weird, but I really thought for a minute that you were going to kiss me.'

'Oh. That.' His mouth had been close to hers, his raw masculinity emanating from every pore. She'd wanted him with a fierce and frightening urgency, had wanted him every day while he'd been up that ladder, flexing his arms to the ceiling, carrying timber around the house, hammering nails. Every. Damned. Nail. Each hit with the hammer had made her hot and bothered—and she was sure it wasn't good for her, or the baby, to have such a need that was being unfulfilled.

At what point, she wondered, did desire ever go away? Because for her it seemed to be getting worse by the minute, and just when she thought it was waning, he'd do something as simple as open a damned can of paint and just watching his hands move so confidently made her all hot and bothered again. Worse, the way he looked at her with such heat in his eyes made her believe he felt the same but that he was fighting it every step of the way.

But why?

Friendship. They had a decade of past and a long future hanging on the choices they made now.

There was a beat before he answered, as if he was debating what to say and how to say it, and she wished this situation hadn't made him so guarded. 'Georgie, make no mistake, I do want to kiss you, but I have just about enough self-control to hold myself back. It may not be a good idea to talk about this.'

'You did at the market.'

'That was before it had become a…habit.' He looked at his hands. They were still damned confident, even wrapped around a coffee cup, and she remembered what it had been like to feel so wanted as he'd hugged her.

'One kiss is hardly a habit.'

'Not the kiss. The wanting.'

'Ah.' Words were lost somehow between her throat and her mouth. The café sounds around her dimmed and her senses hyped up to acute overdrive. It was hard to breathe. Hard not to stare at those lips, those eyes, that face. Hard not to imagine what he could do to her and what she could do right back. Hell, he'd just admitted he wanted to do it again, so should she just kiss him anyway?

She felt like she was on a seesaw, her heart pulling one way, her head tugging the other. Up. Down. Up. Down. It was exhausting and exhilarating. With one look she could be flying, one word and she'd be hurtling back down to earth.

She struggled with her composure, but as always was falling deeper and deeper under his spell. And she could have struggled just a little bit harder, walked away, called a halt, but she didn't. Pure and simple. 'And why would you want to be so self-controlled?'

'Because it's too much to ask of us.' His eyes were burning with a sudden heat that felt as if it reached out and stroked her insides.

'We've already been through ten years. We already ask a lot of each other.'

'But now you're asking questions I don't know the answers to. You never did that before. You're trying to fix me and I don't need fixing. I don't want to be fixed. If we continue like this, things will change. Things have changed, and I'm not sure I like it, or want it, or know how to handle it, without letting you down.'

Part of her believed that to be right. He was being chivalrous and living up to his values, being honest about where things could or couldn't go for them. There was surely no future, especially with his emotional barriers. They were utterly and completely incompatible.

The other part of her wished he'd give up on his good

intentions and kiss her anyway. Because she could see neither outcome sat comfortably with him. Perhaps she should just make it easier for him. It wasn't as if she didn't know exactly what she was getting into. And if something didn't happen soon she would finally know what it was like to die from desire. *Fan the flames and let them burn out.*

'I've a feeling it's already a little late to worry about things changing between us. Don't you think? I'm not the only one here wondering what it would be like if we kissed again.' Pricking some vanilla cheesecake onto her fork, she offered it to him across the table. 'Don't you get just a little tired of being so saintly?'

'Yes. Every single moment I'm with you.' He leaned forward again and she was transfixed as he closed his mouth over the morsel of food. Heat shimmied through her as he very slowly chewed then swallowed, the movement of his Adam's apple dipping up and down strangely and compellingly sexy. Her eyes slid from his throat to his mouth, a guarded smile on a face filled with dips and curves she knew so well but had never really explored. How she wanted to trace her finger along those lips, to run her hand across his cheek and feel the rasp of his stubble against her skin. To scale the furrows of his cheekbones.

His voice was an octave dirtier when he spoke. 'My mind is working overtime, thinking of the things we could do together. But I'm sure it's just a passing phase. All interest in the new curves and stuff. I just want to touch you. It's a man thing—feral and protective and instinctive. We can't help it. Nature's a bitch sometimes. If we act on these instincts and then it doesn't work out, that's a lot of friendship down the drain. We need to co-parent on a platonic and sensible basis, not give in to rash lust and then have regret to deal with too.'

'Oh, so you mean the bigger boobs are distracting you? Interesting...' She very slightly arched her back as

he lowered his gaze to her breasts. A powerful need zinged through her. She wanted him and was resorting to seduction of the clumsiest kind. But she couldn't get him out of her head. She needed to know what it would be like to be with him. If only one time. Just to hold each other as lovers, unlike the way they touched each other now, as friends. She wanted to stroke him, kiss every part of him. And if she didn't do it soon she'd go completely mad.

One day they'd look back on this and laugh. If they were still speaking to each other. 'So it's nature that's making you look at me like that?'

'Like what?'

'Sex.'

His pupils flared at the word. 'It'll wear off.'

'I sincerely hope not.' She finished the last bit of dessert in one big, almost but not quite satisfying mouthful. She had a feeling there was only one thing that could satisfy her right now, and it wasn't cheesecake. 'We should give in to our natural urges sometimes, it's bad for us to repress them all the time, apparently.'

'It's even worse to break something that's pretty solid.'

Their friendship. But that was true and lasting and proven. 'Why would it break? It doesn't have to break, not if we don't want it to. We can do whatever we want. It's our choice.' She couldn't resist stretching her fingers across the table towards his. For a few seconds just their fingertips touched. Then, without looking at her, he slid his fingers across hers, intertwined them, stroked his hand across hers. His skin was rough but his touch was soft. His heat spread through her, up her arms, to her back, down to her belly.

After a moment of such an excruciatingly sexy caress he turned her palm over and lifted it to his mouth. His kiss was hot. He licked a wet trail to her forefinger. She snatched her hand away before a moan erupted from her

throat. Even so, her voice was filled with need. 'We should be getting home.'

'We? Is that an invitation?' His face cautious, and turned on at the same time, he scraped his chair back to go.

Finding him her sexiest smile, she whispered back, 'Honestly, Macadoodle-doo, since when have you ever needed an invitation to my house?'

'I think maybe this time I do.'

She hadn't answered him in words, but she'd taken his hand and led him out of the café like a woman on a mission. Thank God she lived only a short drive away because he couldn't have waited many moments longer. Liam didn't know when he'd ever been so burnt up about a woman.

They bypassed the living area and made it to her bedroom without words, without kissing. He went in first, held open the door and she walked straight in and turned to face him, a question on her face. A dare. A promise. There was space between them. It would only need one step.

Just one.

He faltered. For a few moments neither moved as they stared at each other. This was happening. Really happening. The step from friends to...to whatever this was. *Lovers* might have been doubtful, but the trajectory from restaurant to street to bed was unstoppable. The air in the room seemed to still. One second. Two. With every lingering moment heat spread through his body like a raging fire, threatening to engulf him. If he touched her now there would be no going back.

This could have been a time to leave. He almost took a sideways step, his hand lingering on the doorhandle, but faltered again.

As she watched him a slow sexy smile appeared on Georgie's lips, and if he'd had any flicker of doubt that she didn't want this it fled right then. And that was when,

he supposed, he should have drawn that line, the one they shouldn't have stepped over. Or where they should have agreed what this meant. But he was too consumed by her, by this need to utter a word.

In the end he didn't know who made the first move but suddenly she was in front of him, or he was in front of her and his mouth was hard against hers. This time there was no hesitation, no coy shaking. This was pure need and desire. She tasted of chocolate and vanilla and every flavour in between. Her mouth was wet and hungry and it fired a deeper, hotter want within him. Jaws clashed, tongues danced, teeth grazed. There was nothing sophisticated about the kiss, no gentle sucking or tender caress. It was messy. Dirty. Hungry.

His lips were on her throat as he dragged her T-shirt up around her neck, ripping it as it snagged on its journey to the floor. Finding what they wanted his hands cupped her beautiful breasts over her bra, then under her bra to the accompaniment of a deep guttural moan. She pressed against him, writhing against his thigh. 'Liam, oh, my God, I want you now.'

'I want you.' For a brief moment he acknowledged that this could be the singularly most stupid thing he'd ever done. Then that thought was gone, erased with more of her kisses and the press of her fingertips against the top of his jeans. He sucked in air as she played with his zip. And, no, he did not want to hesitate for a second—but his hand covered hers. 'You first.'

Her bra hit the floor and then her shorts, and he was walking her to her bed and laying her down on the flowery duvet he'd seen a hundred times before but never in this light, never at a moment like this. Everything was familiar and yet unfamiliar, like her. His mouth found her dark hard nipple and sucked it in. She was divine, so sexy, her nip-

ples so responsive. *She* was so responsive as she writhed against him, nails digging into his back until he groaned.

As his mouth started its journey south, kissing carefully over the undulation of her belly, her hand stopped his and her voice was, for the first time, wary. 'Is this really stupid?'

'Without a doubt.'

'Yeah, I thought so. Dumb and then some.' Her mouth was swollen and red. He knew it had been a long time since Georgie had been kissed, and kissed like that—because he had been the last one to do it. God only knew when she'd last had sex but unless he was mistaken he could count the time in years, not months. So this was important. She'd chosen him.

He relieved her of her panties, hands skimming a belly that was plump and soft. He followed a trail of dark hair down her midline, watching her squirm as he parted her thighs and found her centre. He slipped a finger in, two, and felt her contract. She moaned, 'Oh, yes.'

'Crazy?'

'Madness.' She arched against him. 'But that feels so good.'

He kissed a slick trail to a nipple and smiled against it as she bucked in pleasure against his hand. Then he found her mouth again, her tongue tangling with his as she unzipped his jeans and took him in her hand. His gut contracted. He was so hard, so hot for her, and, damn, if he didn't have her soon he was going to explode.

She rubbed his erection against her sweet spot and he could feel the wet heat of her. Then she pushed him against the mattress and straddled him. 'I want you inside me, Liam. Now. Please don't do the whole slow build-up thing. That's been happening for days, months if we're honest. I just need to feel you inside me. Otherwise I'm going to just about die.'

'Don't do that. No. We can't have that.' And without any further encouragement he slid deep into her. She was so ready for him, he could feel her orgasm building already, her walls contracting around him as she pulsed with him. She met his rhythm, found his mouth again and he was lost in sensation after sensation of her mouth, her centre, her weight on his thighs. Her scent around him, her heat around him. Deeper. Harder.

He wanted to slow down time, to hold onto this moment but the luscious heat of her, her sexy, knowing smile made him sink deep into her. 'Oh, my God, Georgie, you're going to make me lose it.'

He fisted her hair and dragged her face to him, kissing her long and hard until he was fighting for breath, until the pace increased, faster and faster. Her eyes closed as he felt her contract around him, her body shaking with the strength of her orgasm. *'Liam. Liam.'*

Never had his name sounded so sweet, so wanted, so precious. He was lost in her, in her voice, in her heat, grinding against her, hard and fast and deep, until he felt his own climax rising and then crashing on a wave of chaos and kisses.

For a few seconds she was quiet against him, Liam could feel her heart beating a frantic pulse against his chest. Her hair was over his face. She was covered in a fine sheen of sweat, fists still clinging to his shoulders, pinning him against the sheets. He was already hard again, thinking about a few moments' repose, then maybe a shower—preferably with her in it. It was startling, surprising and felt surreal to be here, with her, doing this.

So he wasn't prepared for her words as she bolted upright and her hand went to her belly. 'Oh, God, Liam. Oh, my God.'

The baby. For those fleeting moments he'd forgotten,

blown away by the sultriness of her ripe body, of being inside her, of losing himself completely in the best sex of his life. He'd wanted Georgie the woman. Not Georgie the mother. Although she came as a package deal, he knew that.

No, he hadn't forgotten but blocked out that thought.

And then things got very murky in his head. 'What is it? Are you okay? What's wrong?'

'No, I'm not okay.' Twisting away from him, she climbed off his thighs, wrapped the top sheet across her front and curled onto the bed in a protective foetal position, her hands in front of her face. 'Oh, God, best-friend sex. Kill me now.'

'Why the hell would I want to do that?' The laugh erupting from his throat was part relief, part concern because she was right; in fact, they'd both been right. This was the most half-cocked stupid thing they'd ever done.

'I can't believe we've just done that when I look like this.' Her cheeks were red and hot. 'I've never cared how I looked to you before. You've seen me in all states of soberness and drunken debauchery, when I was sick, when I was glammed up to the nines. You've seen me lose my bikini completely in an ill-timed dive into the pool, even caught sight of me in my scaggy weekday bra and pants, and none of it mattered. Ever. But now? Now I'm so embarrassed.'

He stroked fingers down her spine, tenderness for her goofy display of embarrassment meshing with something else in his heart. This was not meant to happen. He was supposed to be creating a safe place for his child, proving he could be a good father. Making sound choices. It was okay to give in to a little sexual play with someone who had no strings attached—but they had a ten-year history and an uncertain and very shaky-looking future that involved another life. They shouldn't be playing at all. He

was getting in too deep, getting himself into a situation he didn't know how to get out of. 'And maybe you're just a little bit crazy? Why do you think I care how you look?'

'Because it's suddenly important. Everything is. I didn't think it would be, but it matters.'

'I don't believe this.' Pulling her hands away from her face, he made sure she was looking right at him. Because, yes, this mattered. She mattered. Whatever else happened now—and already a thousand doubts were stampeding into his head—she had to hear what he was saying. Because she still needed to hear the truth, regardless of what he thought or felt about it. 'Is it enough for me to say that you're beautiful?'

'No. Not really. I'm six months pregnant, for goodness' sake. I'm fat. I'm getting stretch marks. My boobs are huge.'

'Really? I hadn't noticed.' He pretended to take a sneaky peek. And then wished that he hadn't. He could make light of this, but the honest fact was she was beautiful. So beautiful it made his heart ache and he wanted to kiss her again, to make her scream with pleasure. To make her realise just how much she was wanted.

'Well, you've been staring at them for long enough.'

'That's because you are amazing. Beautiful. Fertile. Vibrant.' He took her hand, gently kissed her knuckles and brought her fist to his cheek. 'And I don't care how you look, Georgie. Because, honestly, the wrapping's not what I was making love to.'

Honestly? *Honestly?* His heart banged fiercely as if protesting. What the hell were they doing? She was his friend and by doing this he'd let her down. Period. He was supposed to be the strong one, dammit.

'You know, we should really have stopped before we started.' Dragging her hand from his grip, she sat up. 'If that makes sense.'

'Things stopped making sense a while ago.'

'Yes, you can say that again.' She let out a long sigh but snuggled against him, her hair tickling his nose, baby-soft skin touching his, then closed her eyes. 'That was good, though. Damned good, Macadoodle-doo.'

He glanced towards the bedside table and saw a baby name book, a pregnancy book. In the corner of the room there was a bottle steriliser still in its wrapper next to a bundle of baby clothes. On the floor to his left was a magazine open at a page about safety in online dating. She'd gone through the questionnaire and circled a few As, some Cs, a smattering of Bs. Was she thinking about dating again? Before all this she'd have filled in the questionnaire with him and they'd have been in fits of laughter at the results. But this one she'd done on her own. In private.

Despite the post-coital warm fuzzies he realised with a jolt that he might not be a real and integral part of her new life. She was thinking about a future without him in it. That was what he'd wanted, right? That was why he'd signed the contract in the first place. So she could have her dream life—a partner would be the icing on the cake for her. A husband, two kids and a dog. The family she'd missed out on, growing up in that children's home she'd hated. Traceable DNA.

A husband who didn't keep running away. She deserved that. She deserved the very best.

And even though he knew all the reasons he shouldn't be here, he still kept batting them away, trying to find good enough reasons to stay. But he didn't have many, apart from selfish ones that meant he got the best sex with an amazing woman and then broke both their hearts.

He edged his arm out from under her neck, lay for a few minutes and watched her. She looked so relaxed, so peaceful, so hot that he couldn't bear to think of her with another man. But did that mean he had to commit? What

if it fell apart? That would be all kinds of messy. A family didn't need that. He didn't need that, and she certainly didn't. From his own bitter experience he knew damned well what damage a broken family could do to a child.

Better to stay friends for ever than fall apart as lovers.

Snaking away from her, he sat on the edge of the bed and looked around for his jeans. 'I guess I'd better get off home.'

'Oh, no. Don't you dare move, matey.' Her hands were on his shoulders, gripping them with more force than when he'd taken her over the edge, forcing him to sit back down. She picked up one of the books he'd seen and flicked through it, shoving it under his nose. 'So, I was thinking Desdemona for a girl. Albert for a boy? What do you think?'

'What? You're joking.' Not what he'd choose in a million years. What he would choose he didn't know. He hadn't allowed his mind to wander down that route as yet.

'And in the morning we need to go shopping for a breast pump. There's a new babyware shop opened up on High Street. And I know it's early but I want to get some Christmas decorations from that pop-up shop in Regents mall.'

'Christmas? Already? It's September.'

'My first Christmas in my first home. A baby on the way. I want it to be special.' Her voice was wistful. 'No harm in starting early, and they'll sell out of all the good stuff pretty quickly, you'll see.'

'What was Christmas like at the home?' He knew she tried to make a huge effort to celebrate it every year and asked everyone she'd ever met to eat around her large wooden table—waifs and strays, everyone's uncle's cat... she just didn't want to be on her own.

There was a pause as if she didn't want to go back there. He couldn't blame her. The bits she'd mentioned about

growing up had been a far cry from his early experiences. Until his perfect world had imploded.

She put on her *I'm okay* voice. 'Oh, the social workers and carers tried to make it feel special, but we all knew they just wanted to get our celebrations out of the way so they could finish up and get home to their real families. It was depressing, in truth. This year I'm going to go big. I'm going to get the biggest tree and the most decorations anyone has ever had and cover the place—the tree, the walls, the outside. You know, like on Franklin Road, where every house has decorations and lights? It'll be like that, a Christmas to remember. And then next year I'm going to give Desdemona—or Albert—every damned thing they want. Because I couldn't have what I wanted. Ever.'

He imagined her, stuck in the home, wishing her little heart out and always being disappointed. Life sucked sometimes. For Georgie life had sucked a lot. 'What did you want, Geo? What did you wish for?'

'Ah, you know, the usual stuff.'

He propped himself up on his elbow and ran his fingers across her curves, down her shoulder, to the side of her breast, and stopped for a moment as she shivered under his touch. Then continued stroking her hip. 'No. Really, what did you want?'

She laughed, shyly. 'I wanted to start a collection of Beanie Babies—these little stuffed-toy things. Man, they were expensive and all the girls at school had them for birthdays or Christmas. I saved up my allowance every week and eventually bought a second-hand whale. He was my favourite.'

So he wasn't the only one here who was expert at dodging a question. 'No. Really. You're always telling me to stop hedging—but you're champion of it too. What did you deep down want?'

'Oh, God. However I say it, it's going to sound twee

and crass but…well, I really wanted to be part of something. And now I am. So I got it in the end.' She laughed. 'It only took twenty-eight years.'

Did she mean him? Did she mean they were now part of something? Or did she mean the baby? *Family?* His heart started to pound. What had he done? Given her hope that she belonged to him?

Didn't she? No. No one did. No one could.

What the hell had he done? 'Oh. I see.'

'Anyway, before we go shopping I thought perhaps a big brunch in town first. That's what we'll need, right? A good sleep and then some decent food. Or maybe some food now? Are you hungry? Sex makes me hungry.'

'These days everything makes you hungry.' Okay. He got it that it would be rude and insensitive to split right now. He slumped against the pillow, trying to reconcile his head with his heart, but it seemed they were cursed to be at odds with each other for ever. 'Whatever you want.'

'Really?' Her foot dug him in the thigh. 'What I want is for you to stay. Talk to me.'

'God knows how you have the energy to talk after mind-blowing sex.' He ignored her assertion that he stay. For how long? Tonight? Tomorrow? A year? For ever? Reality was blurring dangerously with the ache in his heart.

One eye opened. 'It's not because we've just had sex, it's because *we* talk, Liam, that's what you and I do. We talk endlessly and have done for a decade. About everything. *Mostly.* We've never not known what to talk about before. How about we talk about stuff…about your work, my pregnancy, this child, your family, why you don't contact them ever? What the heck it is that spooks you so much about creating something that everyone else in the world craves. I want to know about you growing up, and I want to know about Lauren.'

The walls were closing in. It was time for evasive ac-

tion, because he did not want to go there. At all. 'You know, suddenly I'm really fascinated about how breast pumps work. Talk me through—'

'No way, José. You don't get out of stuff that easily.'

'Oh, but I do. By fair means or foul…' The sheet covered most of her body, but her right foot was sticking out. He took it, leaned forward and slowly sucked her big toe into his mouth. He felt her soften against the mattress and her moan stoked more heat in him. That shower scenario was looking more and more attractive.

'Yeow. Definitely not fair.' Four vermilion-varnished toes wriggled against his chin. 'Use that mouth for talking, Macadoodle-doo.'

'Why, when it's so much better at doing other things?' His mouth hit her ankle, the back of her knee, her inner thigh, and he licked a wet trail northwards. As she squirmed he gave a wry smile. Any more wriggling was halted by his hands on her thighs. 'See?'

'But I want to— Oh, yes, that feels good. Just a little to the… Oh, yes.' Her hands fisted into his hair. 'Don't stop now, Liam…'

'I have no intention of stopping.'

'We…can…talk…later…'

Like never. 'Hush. Relax. Enjoy.'

And with that her mouth clamped shut and as he grasped her hand, she did exactly what he'd suggested.

CHAPTER NINE

WHEN GEORGIE WOKE the next morning the left side of the bed was cold. He was gone. As she'd thought he would be. It had all been too good to be true. He'd had second thoughts and hot-footed it to Afghanistan or somewhere equally unreachable. Typical Liam. Typical men. She lay back on the pillow and growled.

And then growled again, because since when had her mood been determined by a man?

Since Liam MacAllister had become…whatever he'd become. More than a friend…and with added and rather nice benefits. He certainly was very, very good at the bedroom side of things, even if he was quiet—*mute*—on the history side. But, hey, a forward-thinking man was always better than one looking back, right?

Although his past had shaped who he was, and that intrigued her. It had also created those barriers he was so keen at throwing up between himself and anyone who wanted to get close. The sex had been a really crazy idea. Lovely but crazy, and now she was even more confused than before. Ask him for clarification? Not likely. She imagined how that conversation might go and decided she didn't need to have him actually voice the rejection out loud.

After a few minutes of lying there, debating what to do,

there was a gentle tapping at the door and in he walked, topless, with jeans slouching off his hips, a tray in hand, a pot of coffee and a plate of something that smelled nice but looked a little…suspect. He gave her a smile as he placed the tray on the bed. 'Morning. Here's a sad-looking croissant I found at the back of the freezer, along with a couple of rogue frozen peas and a lot of ice. There was literally nothing else to eat. Nothing. You really do need to go food shopping.'

'The trouble is I eat it as fast as I buy it. I can't keep up.' Without his shirt *he* looked good enough to eat—did she need anything else? And he hadn't run off, he was here, making sure she ate properly. Was this a dream?

She rubbed her eyes, which she really shouldn't have done because the corneal abrasion was still healing, but it was too late and… Yes, he was still here, not an apparition. With food. And coffee. The man was a god.

The god sat on the edge of the bed. 'Well, seeing as we're having a day off renovating today, I'll make sure we fill up the fridge before we're done.' He buttered a piece of croissant, offered it to her, then waited until she'd opened her mouth and popped it in. 'Come on, get your strength up, we're going to need that soon enough.'

'Thanks. Eugh. Not such a great croissant. I can't even remember when I bought— Wait…we're having a day off? Who says?'

'You said you wanted to go shopping. And I'm tired of sanding and painting and you look like you need a decent break. I want to forget about this dust and dirt and do something else. So I've made some calls. I have a plan: your breast pump will have to wait, along with the Christmas decorations. Eat up and then we'll get going.' He got up as if to leave.

'Not so fast.' She caught his hand and he took it, wrapped his fingers around hers and squeezed. In all the

years of knowing him she'd never been aware of this tender side to him. She liked it. Goddamn, she liked it, just when she was trying to think of more reasons not to like him. Not to lose her heart or herself to someone who wouldn't want it. 'To where?'

'It's a surprise. But there'll be proper fresh air. The sea. Decent food. No dust.'

'Is this just another tactic to avoid the issue? You know…talking?'

He gave her a guilty grin. 'I feel restless. I just need to get going. Out. Somewhere.'

This was the guy who spent most of his life travelling and the last few months cooped up in her house. He never stayed anywhere for long, so she could see why he'd need to cut loose sometimes. Plus, a break would be fun. 'Then what are we waiting for?'

'Well…' He pulled the sheet down a little and exposed her breasts. Then he kissed her neck, her throat, her nipples, and she was putting her arms around his neck and drawing him to her. He whispered against her skin, 'I really need a shower before I set foot outside. You?'

'What? Me and you? In that tiny bathroom? You think we'll fit?'

'If it's big enough for a highland jig, it's big enough for a shared shower. We'll squeeze in somehow.' His fingers stroked down her back and she could see the bulge in his jeans. He was hot and hard for her.

Which made her hot in return. She couldn't resist reaching her hand to his chest. Felt his heart beating underneath her fingers. Solid. Steady. *Liam*. This was Liam. This was all kinds of surreal. She remembered his little dance in her tiny bathroom, the way he'd looked at her, the way she'd wanted to touch him then. How touching him now made her feel excited and jittery and turned on. Not solid

or steady at all. 'But it wasn't big enough for a highland jig, remember?'

'We'll fit. Trust me?'

'I don't know.' That was half the problem. And, yes, he'd stuck to his words and been there for her throughout this pregnancy. Not once had he mentioned the contract again. He seemed committed to the baby, even though there were times when she caught his worried face and just knew the spooks were there, haunting him a little. But he'd surprised her with his resolve. And kept on surprising her, but could a man really change? She just didn't know. For a few minutes last night she'd thought he'd been having doubts, had felt his restless legs keen to leave, had known that if she'd let him he'd have gone. Would she always have to keep anchoring him here? Would she never be enough for his first instinct to be to want to stay?

For now, though, he was here and was asking for nothing more than to spend time with her. Time she didn't want to waste analysing things to death. 'Oh, okay. Where's there a will, there's always a way.'

'Always...' His laugh was deep and sexy and there was no way she was going to put up any kind of fight against those fingers, that mouth, those eyes. Had she been thinking about fighting? She couldn't remember. Her whole world narrowed to this single moment when she could forget everything else. 'So what are we waiting for?'

His hands closed around her fingers. 'Absolutely nothing.'

An hour and a half later, which truly could have been only thirty minutes had it not been for a lovely long shower and a very deliciously sexy start to her day, Georgie let out a yelp of excitement as Liam steered his expensive and very un-child-friendly two-seater coupé into a car ferry terminal. 'Waiheke Island? A day trip?'

'If that's okay?' He looked genuinely concerned that she was happy with his choice. 'I thought it'd be nice to do something different.'

'Yes, it's fabulous. It's a lovely idea. I haven't been there since a school trip years ago.'

He stared across at the ferry. 'My grandparents lived there, we used to go over and stay at their house every holiday when I was little. I can't remember the last time I visited.'

And there was something else she hadn't known about him. Maybe that concern on his face was really apprehension? 'Oh, I had no idea. Will it bring back bad memories for you?'

'I'm hoping to cement some new ones. It's a big enough island for me not to even go there.' A stream of vehicles appeared and queued up behind them as a crew member gestured for the cars to embark. Cranking the car into gear, Liam drove up the metal ramp and parked the car on the ferry platform. Once out, and breathing a lungful of fresh sea air, he slipped his hand into hers and whisked her towards the bar area. 'Come on, let's get a coffee and watch the world go by.'

The short journey across the Hauraki Gulf was smooth and pleasant, enhanced greatly by a pod of dolphins that came alongside to play. Diving and chasing and showing off, they added extra magic to this unexpected trip. Standing on deck, watching him walk towards her with two cups of coffee in his hands, grinning and gesticulating to the wildlife, Georgie's stomach gave a little hearty jump at the thought of a stolen day with Liam. Things were definitely changing, moving along in a direction she hadn't ever imagined. She didn't know if the changes were for the good, but she did know she would never be the same after all this.

Waiheke, famed for its vineyards and olive oil, was

showing the tentative beginnings of the new spring season. After a long wet winter the hills were green, the acres of vines stretching on and on to the horizon were budding and leafy, while ewes watched over lambs in the fields adjacent to the roads. Once away from the main township they headed east along a winding road that eventually opened to vistas of clean empty beaches and blue water sparkling in the pale sunshine. Such a difference from her city house, which she adored—but stepping onto green fields would be nice for a change. Liam had been right, time out would do them both some good.

After half an hour or so he pulled left into a white gravel driveway that led towards the sea. On their right was a large whitewashed colonial house with a sign advertising wine sales and tastings. Georgie was surprised he'd pick a place like this. 'Oh? You booked us lunch at a vineyard? I assume you want to sample the wares?'

'I may have a small glass. But it's not so much the vineyard I was planning to see.' He threw the car into park and got out.

She stepped out of the door and sighed at the wisteria just starting to flower and framing the large wooden door. The soft pink against the white was startling and soothing, and like something from a film set. 'Oh? So what is it? What's the big secret?'

'It's not so big really, more a thought than a secret. Wait and see. And apparently they do a very nice lunch platter. It's huge. Which seems to be the only consideration you make these days when choosing meals.' There was a flurry of activity as their hosts found them a table out in the garden, bottled water and much-needed shade.

The garden was private and secluded, but felt somehow open rather than cloistered. Cushioned candy-striped hammocks hung between trees flanking a small neat square of grass. Palms and large ferns gave much-needed shade.

There were fairy lights entwined around the vegetation that she imagined would give a pretty effect in the evenings, along with tealights in coloured glass jars on the ornate ironwork tables. It was tranquil, cool and very calming, and as they sat she felt some of the tensions of the last few months float away.

The menu was limited but sounded delicious. Suddenly she felt famished and so ordered a large mixed platter that promised fish, freshly cooked meats, a selection of local hard cheeses and lots and lots of bread. Most of which, she knew, she could eat and not worry about them having any effect on her baby. The rest she'd leave for Liam.

As they waited for the food he started to chat. 'Chris, the owner of this place, is an old school friend of mine. He inherited the vineyard from his dad and has turned it into a very successful business.'

As she listened to the sound of…nothing, except the fuzzy hum of bees and faint birdcalls, and took in the impossibly breathtaking surroundings, she felt the most peaceful she'd felt in weeks. Either that, or the sex-induced endorphins had made her limbs turn half to rubber. 'It's amazing.'

'Isn't it?'

'So what made you decide to come here of all places?'

'He sent me a link to his new website the other day. I took a look, saw the photos of the deck and the garden.'

They were momentarily interrupted as their drinks arrived, then were left alone again. Liam took a sip of pinot gris, then put his glass down on the table. 'Then, when I was standing on your deck this morning, looking out at the garden, I thought that we really need to sort it out. The wood's rotting in places and there are nails popping up all over. It's a wreck, Georgie, and could be dangerous if we don't do something about it. The inside of your house is almost complete now so I thought we should

finish things off properly. The baby's coming in the summer, and with the usual Auckland humidity you're going to want to sit outside. I thought the hammock idea would be great. And the palms give great shade. A lawn in the middle would be a pretty cool place for a baby to learn to crawl—no risk of injury.'

'Well, wow. That's really thoughtful. And, yes, it's absolutely gorgeous. I can see it working perfectly in the space I have. That's very kind of you, and especially to bring us all the way out here to actually see it.' She felt a little as if the ground was shifting. Half hope, half...what?

He shrugged, looking a little embarrassed at her enthusiasm. 'It's just a day trip, Georgie.'

But it was one of the kindest things anyone had ever done for her. Why did he have to keep getting better and better? Why couldn't he slink off and make her feel unhappy and not pine for more? In cold, harsh reality she was scared that she'd get too attached to a man who would break her heart. Because even if he did want to be involved in her family, how could she be sure he'd be in it for the long term? With her? How could she be sure he'd love *her*?

'But it's—'

'Oh, here's lunch. And here's Chris. Clearly a busy man, he owns the place, makes the wine and so, it seems, serves the food.' He stood and shook the hand of a thickset man who looked older than Liam's thirty-two years. 'Good to see you, mate.'

'You too.' Liam's friend's eyes grazed over Georgie, down to her belly, and he beamed. 'And you must be Georgie. I'd know you anywhere, that social media's a beast, isn't it? You feel like you know people without ever meeting them.'

'Yes. Isn't it? Hello.' She may have been Liam's friend on any number of social network sites, but Georgie wondered how much Chris really knew and what Liam had

said, if anything, about their unusual situation. After all, not many couples got pregnant first and then had sex. Everything was happening the wrong way round. Besides, the word 'couple' hadn't been breathed out of either of their lips.

They hadn't discussed yet what to say, if anything, to anyone who enquired about their situation. But as that seemed to be changing by the day, it was probably better that they hadn't come up with any definite description. Just Liam and Georgie, same as it ever had been.

Still, the winemaker seemed gentleman enough not to pry and diverted his gaze from her bump back to Liam. 'Look, I've got a bit of a rush on, can't stay and chat. Give my regards to your father, Mac. I hear he's retiring up north.'

Liam's eyebrows lifted. 'Oh? Really?'

It was his friend's turn to raise eyebrows. 'You didn't know?'

'I haven't caught up with him for a while.'

'No. He said as much last time he was over. He seemed a bit miffed. But, then, he always did. Are you going to pop over to The Pines?'

Liam shook his head. 'No. He sold it years ago. No point going backwards, is there?'

'I don't suppose so. Look, thanks for coming. Lunch is on the house. Good to see you.' Chris turned to leave then paused. 'Oh, make sure you try the syrah too. Delicious.'

Lunch was lovely, and as filling as Liam had promised, and Georgie ate as much as she could, managing almost the whole meal without mentioning the last conversation. But in the end it got the better of her. Her heart began to race as she brought up the difficult subject, so she tried to keep her voice level. 'So, when did you last talk to your dad?

Liam shrugged. 'I don't know. Two years ago?'

'*Two?*' It seemed nonsensical to have no communication with family members. If she—

'Look…' Pushing aside his empty plate, he let out a long breath. 'Please don't give me a lecture on how lucky I am to have a father and that I need to make the most of him. I know that's how you feel about families. But it isn't how I do.'

'But—'

'It's a lovely day. I really don't want to spoil things.'

'That may be a little late.' Although she knew she shouldn't have pushed it, he'd brought her out of a desire to help her, and to give her a rest. She was the one spoiling things.

For a moment she thought he was going to stamp or growl, but he fought with his emotions and put them back in that place that he never let anyone see. The man must have some ghosts, she thought, if he was so unwilling to talk. But he was tight-lipped about his work too—he kept everything tied in. Some people needed counselling, but he just wore it all in his skin, would never consider any kind of help, not even to get things straight in his head.

He saw that as a strength. 'Let's not do this today, Geo. Let's enjoy ourselves, plan the garden, take a walk, anything but this. Talking about my family tends to put a huge downer on everything.'

'Okay.' But something niggled at her. Ate away at her gut. She was genuinely trying to help. 'Or we could say everything really quickly and get it out in the open.'

He shook his head with irritation, but he smiled. 'Or say nothing at all.'

'Or I could ask Chris.'

'He doesn't know everything.'

Now she knew she could leave it and walk away and pretend this conversation hadn't happened. Or she could take it a step further…hell, he knew everything about her.

Everything. 'And I know nothing. When did you last see your mother? What is The Pines?'

'Okay, so we *are* doing this.'

She took a sharp breath and threw him her most winning smile. 'I see it as my duty as a friend to annoy you until you actually get to the nitty-gritty.'

'You don't have to take that role so much to heart, Georgie. Maybe the nitty-gritty isn't what you think it is.' He placed his napkin on the table and stood, offering her his hand, but he looked impatient rather than annoyed. 'The Pines was my grandad's house and I am resolutely not going there so don't even ask. Just don't. It's a no. There is no point going over stuff, it doesn't help. You can't change the past and some of it is best not remembered. And I last saw my mother on Mother's Day. I took her out for tea. And it was awkward as always.'

'No. You were in Pakistan, or South Sudan—somewhere. Either way, you weren't here. Make it the year before.' They walked out into the vineyard. Rows and rows of vines stretched before them on and on into the distance. They wandered aimlessly down a row, inhaling the smell of freshly mown grass. 'You know, Liam, your parents will be the only grandparents our child has. Seriously, they are the only other people in the whole world with a connection to him…or her. They are flesh and blood. I really wish you could try to make things work between you all. If not for anyone else's sake, for Nugget's.'

He shook his head. 'Sometimes I wish I didn't know you as well as I do, because then I wouldn't have to put up with this. Trouble is, I do know you and I know you won't give up. At all. Digging and digging.'

'It's what makes me such a good nurse, and why you love me.'

'Love?' He stopped short and stared at her. For too long. For so long she wondered what the heck was going on in

his head. She closed her heart to his shocked question…
love? She didn't want to know his answer. Or maybe it
had always been there and she'd been afraid to look. But
in the end he just shook his head. 'My parents divorced
when I was ten, and neither of them have shown any in-
terest in me since well before then. The feeling's mutual.'

'Why?'

'You really do want to do this, don't you?' He ran his
fingers through his hair, opened his mouth, closed it.
Opened it again. 'Because Lauren died. And rightly or
wrongly we all blame me.'

'Why? What on earth happened? What could you have
done that was so bad?' Over the years Georgie had pon-
dered this. She knew his sister had died, knew his parents
were separated. But piecing the bits together had been like
trying to do a jigsaw with no picture as reference.

They walked in silence to the very end of the row and
onwards towards the ocean, found a crop of rocks in the
little bay and sat on them. A breeze had whipped up, but
the sun still cast a warm glow over them. Even so, Geor-
gie shivered at the look haunting Liam's face. The dark
shadows were back. His shoulders hunched a little. He'd
already let go of her hand and even though they were
sitting side by side it seemed almost as if he'd retreated
within himself.

His voice was low when he finally spoke. 'She was a
premmie, born at thirty weeks, and had a struggle, but she
finally got discharged home. She was doing well. She was
amazing. Really amazing. The light of our lives.'

Georgie sensed something terrible was coming. She
laid a hand on his shoulder and waited, holding her breath.
The sound of waves crashing onto the shore was the only
thing that broke another prolonged silence. That, and her
heartbeat pounding in her ears.

'I caught a winter bug. Nothing serious, just a stupid

cough, fever and a snotty nose that laid me low for a few days, one of those that most kids get. Mum banned me from being near her. Very sensible, in hindsight. I just thought she was being mean.'

He looked like he wanted to continue but couldn't find words. When he composed himself enough to speak his voice was cracked and barely more than a whisper, 'But Lauren was so fascinating, such a little puzzle of noises and sounds with an achingly beautiful smile, that, as an eight-year-old big brother with a strong sense of responsibility and a lot of curiosity, I didn't want to keep away. So one morning when she was crying I sneaked into her room and picked her up, soothed her back to sleep. I held her for ages, I don't know how long, but long enough for her to go to sleep and for me to care enough not to wake her, so I held her some more.

'A few days later she came down with the same bad bug, but she couldn't fight it off. She tried, though. Tried damned hard. But she just wasn't strong enough.'

He hauled in air and stood, hands in pockets, looking out to sea. So alone and lost that it almost broke Georgie in two. She imagined what it must have been like for a young boy to go through something like that, and her heart twisted in pain. He'd been doing what he'd thought was the right thing. Not knowing how wrong it could be. But the baby could have caught a bug anywhere—in a shop, at the doctor's surgery, in a playgroup. It had been bad luck she'd caught it from her brother. Bad luck that had kept him in some kind of emotional prison for the rest of his life.

At least, Georgie thought, she hadn't had something and then lost it. She just hadn't had anything at all, and in some ways that seemed almost preferable to suffering the way Liam had. Again she couldn't think of anything helpful to say, and couldn't have managed many words

even if she'd known some formulaic platitudes that might have helped. Her throat was raw and filled with an almost tangible sorrow for him. 'I'm so sorry, Liam.'

'To cut to the chase, my parents were never the same after that. Eventually the grief was too much for their marriage. I got lost in the slipstream of guilt and blame. We've all rarely spoken since, doing only the perfunctory family necessities, if that. I suppose you could say it's pretty damned loveless.'

No. *He* was loveless. Losing his sister and then being neglected by grieving parents must have been almost unbearable, especially countered by a flimsy excuse that it had all somehow been his fault. He'd been a child too, for goodness' sake. How could you lay blame on someone who only wanted to give a baby more love?

Georgie knew Liam well enough to know there was little point in trying to convince him that he was anything other than culpable. If he didn't believe it himself, and if his parents, the people who mattered, had never tried to reassure him, then what would her words mean to him?

But she stepped forward and wrapped her arms around his waist, hoping that somehow the physical sensation of her touch might convey her empathy for him in a way that words never could. 'And that's why you fight so hard year after year to save all those babies in those disaster-stricken countries.'

'They just need a chance. I can't right any wrongs and I can't wave a magic wand but I can give them real help.'

'And that's also why you don't want a family of your own.'

'Yeah, I didn't do so well with mine. Lauren dying was hard going, but you get through it. Somehow. Eventually. But what I needed most was help, support, love. And I got nothing. Families can hurt you so badly. I wouldn't want to do that to any child of mine. Worse, judging by my expe-

riences, I'd probably do more harm than good.' He shook
his head, shook himself free of her grip, and walked back
towards the vines.

'No. You're going to be a great dad.'

He pulled up to a halt. 'Really? You think? After what
I just told you? I don't want to go through anything like
that again. I don't think I'd survive it. I don't want to…'
He started to walk again. Head down. Shoulders hunched.

She kept a few feet behind him, giving him the space
he clearly craved. 'To what?'

'To lose something like that again.'

'You wouldn't.'

He railed round at her. 'How can you be sure? How
can you stand there and make promises no one can keep?'

It was all so clear now. His idea of family was broken.
His image of love was filled with so many negative con-
notations he couldn't dare risk himself again with that
emotion. That was why she'd found him so distraught that
first day she'd met him—caring for a sick baby had di-
minished him, reminded him of what he'd lost. But he'd
taken that loss and turned it into his vocation. Not many
could do that. Not many would face their fears every day.

Although he never let it get personal. He never let any-
thing get to him. Ever. That was what the death of his
sister had taught him, to keep everything and everyone
at a safe distance. So he wouldn't feel responsible, so he
wouldn't have to face the prospect of more pain if things
got sticky. Hell, she'd been watching him do it for years,
and had never felt how much it mattered. But now, *God*,
now it mattered.

And still she was left only with questions. If that was
how he felt, why had he torn up the contract? Was this all
just some duty kick he was getting?

What would become of them all?

Sometimes she wished she had a crystal ball and could

look into her future and see how it all worked out. But this time she was afraid. Afraid that what she'd see wasn't what she wanted.

She left him to meander through the vineyard, stopping to look at the tight fists of bright red buds at the end of each row, gathering strength to grow into flourishing roses, and to watch tiny white butterflies skitter past. And as they walked she noticed his shoulders begin to relax again. The sunshine and quietness chased the shadows away and eventually he came back to her, took her hand in his and walked towards a cluster of old stone buildings.

But before they left the vines Georgie paused and looked at the tiny fruit gripping tightly onto ancient gnarled wood. 'Do you think Chris would mind if we tried one of the grapes?'

He laughed. 'I think he probably would, but they're not remotely ripe anyway. They'll make our stomachs hurt.'

'But they're award winning, it said so on a big certificate on the wall back at the restaurant. Should we try? I've never had anything award winning straight off the vine before. How about you? You should try one.'

'No.' He pulled her hand away from the plant and hauled her against him. His eyes were hungry, his breathing quickened as he looked into her face, at her eyes, at her mouth. He was a complex man filled with conflicting emotions—but that didn't make her want him less. He was real and, yes, he was complicated. He was layered and that was what made him all the more intriguing.

He cupped her face and stared into it, his expression a mix of heat and fun and affection. Then he pressed his mouth to hers and kissed her hard. It was a kiss filled with need, with deep and genuine desire. This was new, this... trust, this depth, sharing his worse times and dark past. It was intense and it was raw but Georgie felt a shift of understanding to a new level. A new need. His grip on her

back was strong as he held her and for a few moments she thought he would never let her go. And, holding him tight against her, she wished that very same thing with every ounce of her soul.

'Can I drive the car? Please?' Georgie grabbed the keys from Liam's hand and he let her take them. Let her run to his pride and joy and take the driver's seat, which he would never ever normally do. But, well hell, just telling her about his old life had set something free from his chest. He felt strangely lighter, freed up a little.

But then, as he climbed in beside her, his gaze flicked to her belly and there was that hitch again, the one that reminded him that happiness was always fleeting. That love could hurt just as much as it could give joy. He'd thought he'd be able to distance himself emotionally from her, and from the baby, but in reality the feelings just kept hurtling at his rib cage, ripping his breaths away, one after the other. Hard and fast until he didn't think he'd ever be able to breathe properly again. He didn't know whether to run away from her or keep a tight grip. But staying close opened them all up to him wreaking havoc again.

'Where are you going to drive to? Palm Beach is nice. There are some good shops in Oneroa. Or we could go for a walk along Rocky Bay.'

She ran her fingers over the leather steering wheel. 'No. I remember from my school history classes that there are tunnels somewhere left over from the Second World War. Do you know anything about them?'

'Stony Batter tunnels? Sure. My grandfather helped build them actually. He was born here, camped in the fields just up past Man O'War Bay through the last years of the war.' Sheesh, he'd opened his mouth and now he

couldn't stop his past pouring out. 'He used to take me up there when I was a kid.'

She flicked the ignition and drove back towards the main road. 'Do you want to take a look?'

Did he? That would mean a drive past The Pines and a whole lot more memories. The weeks they'd spent here as a real family. Complete. God, why had he decided to come here to relive everything again? Why? Because, for some reason, Georgie made him feel as if anything was possible. Even overcoming a dark and murky past. Who knew, maybe he could squeeze his eyes shut as they drove past The Pines and he wouldn't feel the dread already stealing up his spine. 'Okay. If you insist.'

'I do.'

But that was a mistake. Memories joined the swirl of pain in his chest as they closed the kilometres between the vineyard and his old holiday home. Part of him wanted to grab the steering wheel and head straight back to the ferry terminal. But it was too late.

The Pines stood tall and dark and ominous as they drove past, the short driveway leading to the front door, still painted dark blue, ancient pohutakawa trees flanking the lawn, laundry flapping on the line, all gave his gut a strange kick. Memories of happier times filtered into his head—his father swinging him round and round, his mother laughing at their antics and calling them for dinner. The long leisurely Christmas lunches filled with fun and excitement—midnight mass, waiting for Santa, opening presents on Christmas Day morning.

They had been happy, once upon a time. But once that dream had been shattered, it had never been possible to reach that state again.

He let his gaze wander, turning his head slightly as the large rambling house went out of view. Glancing at him,

Georgie jerked the car to a halt. 'That was it, wasn't it? The house?'

There was no point lying. 'Yes. It looks as if someone is renovating it.'

'Do you want to go and take a look?' Her eyes were kind as they settled on him and he knew she was trying to do the right thing by making him confront his demons. But he didn't need to do that here, he confronted them most days as it was. 'I'll come with you, you won't be on your own.'

'Let's keep driving.'

'Actually, no.' She drew up at the side of the road and before he could stop her she'd done a U-turn and they were back at the house.

'Georgie, I know what you're trying to do. It's okay. I'm fine. Things are fine.'

'Sure. If you say that enough times you might just believe it. I, however, take a little more convincing. Come on.' She stepped out, leaned against the car and wrapped her arms around her chest as she stared at the house. 'I can imagine you playing there in the garden. Causing mayhem. It's a real family home. Three generations all together. Nice.'

'It was once.' He wrenched himself out of the car and looked over at the house, fighting the tightness in his throat. 'The last time I was here was for my grandad's funeral.'

She turned to him, hair blowing wildly in the sudden breeze. 'I'm so sorry.'

'He lived here all his life, he loved the place, said he didn't need to go anywhere else.'

'It's nice that you have family history. It must be reassuring to hear about the past, thinking that your grandad walked along these same paths as you. It gives a connection, doesn't it?' Slipping her hand into his, she left it

at that. But her words kept coming back to him as they walked across the road past the house and looked out over the bay towards the tiny islands dotted around the horizon.

Liam remembered his grandad telling him about the antics he and his mates had got up to here on the island—fishing, drinking, farming. How he'd courted Liam's grandmother for two years but had always known he'd marry her. How they'd devoted years of their lives to the community here. Liam had always known his ties to this place but it had been too easy to take them for granted. Then he'd tried to put as much space between him and them as he could.

He looked at Georgie now in profile, those gorgeous lush curls whipping in the wind; she would never know if they came from her mother's side or her father's. Those soft brown eyes—a hint of Maori blood? Italian? Again, she'd never know. That staunch tilt of the jaw—well, that was pure Georgie, from years of forging her independence and stamping her place in this world. How she'd turned her life into such a success from her rocky beginnings, he would always wonder at. She had no memories of any kind of family time, good or bad, no special Christmases, no history to talk of, no stories to tell her baby.

Nugget.

Fear washed through him. Fear and hope mingling into a mish-mash of chaos in his gut. He was going to be a father.

He was going to have to create memories for his child too. A history. And a future.

See, this was why he'd been against families for so long. Because the unbearable weight of responsibility meant you had to stop hiding yourself and be someone good. Deep down good. Unselfishly open and honest. You had to let go of the past and be that person, the one everyone

relied on. The one everyone looked up to. The one who knew there was danger and risk in opening his heart, but did it anyway.

Trouble was, he just didn't know if he could be that man.

CHAPTER TEN

One month ago...

TIME WAS MOVING FAST. Too fast.

The next few weeks were a blur of sensual lovemaking and laughter. It seemed, to Georgie at least, that sex could be a good mix with friendship after all. Liam was still funny and helpful, he still hammered nails and painted walls. He made her laugh and sigh with delight. They chatted and joked about pretty much everything, as ever—and it seemed almost as if something inside him had been set free.

Except…there was that nagging worry that things were rattling towards an abrupt end. And there was still a part of himself that he held back, that she couldn't break through.

Georgie's head was in a state of flux. She didn't know what he wanted, and she wasn't sure what she wanted out of this either. There'd been no discussion of expectations and she was too scared to ask him about…*what next*. All she knew was that having him in her bed and by her side made her feel the very best she'd ever felt. Although she'd never again mentioned his past, she also didn't want to discuss a future.

Because for the immediate future—which in her terms amounted to the next eighteen years—she wanted what

she had never had: a stable, loving environment for her child. She wanted her baby to feel loved and nurtured, as if it were the centre of the universe and not, like her, alone and unwanted. She wanted her child to not have to fight every day to be noticed. She wanted her child to feel completely and utterly confident and…loved. Just loved.

So, in reality, she needed to forget about any kind of intimacy with Liam, shouldn't waste precious time wondering how it was going to work out—because she should be concentrating on getting through the pregnancy and planning to bring up a child as a co-parent with a friend.

Which didn't work so well for her when she was lying next to him in bed, or trying to do the nine-to-five at her day job when her head was full of naked images of him earlier that morning.

'Georgie, did you manage to get the blood-test results for Kate Holland? She's coming in this afternoon and I want to make sure she's all set.' Malcolm had returned from settling his mum into a nursing home in Dorset and had hit the clinic with renewed vigour.

Georgie watched as he bustled around the office, ordered and officious. He was a nice guy, but had some traits that she found just a little irritating. In retrospect it was good that she hadn't asked him to be the donor for her child. What on earth had she been thinking? But, then, on the other hand, Malcolm was nice. Just nice. Not anything else. Not complicated, not sexy as all hell, not a brilliant kisser—okay, so she didn't know that, but he didn't have sexy lips.

'Georgie?'

Malcolm. He was sitting at the desk opposite her now, face masked by a computer screen. 'Oh, sorry. Yes?'

'Blood results for Kate Holland?'

'Yes, I phoned the lab to chase them again an hour ago and they said they'd email them through. They should be

here…' She tapped on her keyboard and brought the work up on screen. 'There you go. I've directed them to her file. All looking good. She'll be pleased.'

'Thanks.' Her boss's head popped up over the monitor. 'Georgie, are you okay?'

'Absolutely fine, thanks.' And so far she hadn't let her thoughts interfere with her job, but they were definitely trying to filter in. Which was annoying in the extreme, because she loved this job, needed the pay, loved helping people reach their dreams, so *focus* was the watchword of the day.

'If you need to talk anything through I'd be more than happy…' Malcolm's face disappeared back behind the computer screen, but after a few moments it reappeared again. 'No pressure, though.'

'Seriously, I'm fine. Tired, but that's to be expected.' And in truth the lack of sleep wasn't all pregnancy related.

Malcolm looked hugely relieved at the prospect of not having a stressing-out employee on his hands. She hadn't mentioned to anyone at work who the father was and wanted to keep things quiet. It was far too complicated to try talking about this kind of thing here. Everyone thought they knew everything, everyone thought they understood and they were all so lovely and well meaning, but how could they understand when she didn't even understand half of it herself?

Malcolm went back to tapping on the keyboard. 'Ah, I see we have Jo Kinney arriving in ten minutes for follicular monitoring.'

'I know, I made the booking, but don't worry—I'll make myself scarce. I understand how frustrating it is to see pregnant tummies in a fertility clinic when you're struggling to get even a fraction of the way.'

Her boss's voice was concerned. 'I'm hoping the counselling sessions are helping her.'

'I think so. The last time she was in she confessed to feelings of uncontrollable jealousy if any of her friends told her they were pregnant. And she's not talking to her sister at the moment because she's carrying twins. It's all so very difficult for her.' Since she'd become pregnant Georgie had been at pains to make sure she'd been extra-compassionate with her patients. She had what many of them only dreamt about and that was something she would never take for granted. 'I do have a feeling that she'll get there in the end, though.'

'We can only hope so. Don't look so worried, I'll give her the best shot we have.' Malcolm stood to leave. 'So do me a favour and take a lunch break for a change. The sun's shining and the yachts are racing out on the gulf. Get some fresh air. And while you're out, buy some tinsel, we need to Christmas this place up a bit, and last year's decorations are looking a bit sad.'

'Now you've definitely asked the right person for that job. I don't need to be asked twice to go Christmas shopping.' Smiling, Georgie stood and took off her name badge. She had plans to meet Liam for lunch, but had kept that information under wraps. Meeting him in secret for snatched lunches added to the excitement. 'Actually, I'm also going to go and take a sneak peek at that new baby shop. They import things from Europe apparently, it sounds wonderful.'

'Don't go buying the whole place up.'

'I won't. I'm just going for ideas. After the renovations I don't have much left over for the frills.' She grabbed her bag and made a quick mental list of things she needed. A pram, a cot, cloth nappies, a stroller. Basically, the essentials. It was only window shopping, but it was lovely to dream.

The light warm breeze was welcome after the cloistered atmosphere in the clinic. Summer was edging in

and starting to make its presence felt; the shoppers and
office workers on High Street had shed their thick wool-
len coats and knee-length boots. The shop displays had
Christmassy reds, greens and silvers instead of wintry
blacks and browns, Georgie noted, and that made her feel
bright. Despite not knowing which way was up with Liam,
there was so much she should be thankful for. She had a
great house, a great job with understanding and support-
ive colleagues. She had a future right here in her belly.
There were many not so fortunate.

She almost broke into song, with the buskers churning
out the old Christmas favourites…and, strangely, hear-
ing 'Away In A Manger' brought a lump to her throat. A
happy lump.

Choosing a colour theme for her tree this year was hard,
but in the end she went with traditional red and gold. A few
new baubles. And a named one for her and one for Liam.
And for Nugget too… Desdemona didn't fit.

The baby shop was exclusive and expensive, she could
see that just from the window displays with beautiful
hand-carved cots and no price tags. When she entered
the well-dressed shop assistants greeted her with expect-
ant smiles.

'Just looking, thanks,' she answered their question-
ing faces, and wondered whether she'd have been better
walking past and on to the more affordable chain stores
further down the road. But, oh, it was such an adorable
place, decorated with luxury Christmas items—'Baby's
First Christmas' bibs, blankets, towels. Miniature stock-
ings hung from a makeshift mantelpiece. She eyed a kit
for a hand-sewn advent calendar and made a mental note
to add it to her ever-growing list. That would all have to
wait until next year. Nugget's real first Christmas, and
she'd make sure everything would be just perfect.

No, this Christmas would be special too. She had the

feeling that waddling around trying to feed an army would be too much for her this year, so it would be just her and Liam, if she could lure him away from that ER…for the first time in her adult life she'd have a quiet one. At the thought of just the two of them spending such a special day together she grew a little hot. She imagined waking up to a special Liam Christmas surprise…and her cheeks flushed.

But where was he?

Clearly, he'd been held up by some emergency or other, but soon she'd need to get back to work, so she headed for the exit.

'Georgie? Hey, is that you, Georgie? Wow! Look at you. I had no idea…' It was Kate and Mark Holland, hand in hand staring into the same shop window.

'Kate?' The woman looked a darned sight healthier than she'd looked before, when she'd been bloated and on bed rest and pretty damned miserable. 'Lovely to see you. How are you doing?'

Kate's eyes twinkled. 'Not as well as you, clearly. My goodness, this is a surprise. When are you due?'

Georgie resisted running her hand over her now huge bump. 'Eight more weeks, end of January. A summer baby. Believe me, I am not looking forward to waddling around in that humidity.'

'Do you know the gender? What about names?'

More things on her list. She'd been putting off talking to Liam about names again, and when she'd jokingly mentioned it he'd ended up…well…it had been very nice indeed. 'No, I don't know the sex, I want it to be a surprise. And names are so hard to choose, don't you think? Picking one's hard enough, but a middle name too? That's all kinds of heavy-duty responsibility. Imagine picking a name and them hating it for the rest of their lives.'

'So you have some planning to do. I like the traditional ones myself. Make a list.' Kate seemed genuinely pleased

for her and wrapped her in a gentle hug. 'Lucky you. I really am pleased.'

Georgie told herself to get a grip as her throat filled with emotion for Kate. Her hormones were all over the place today. 'I saw you'd booked into the clinic this afternoon—what's the plan?'

Her patient gripped her husband's hand as they both smiled. 'My mum's given us some money for one more round, an early and very unexpected Christmas present. I can't tell you how amazing that is. I just can't give up. I just can't.'

'That's great news. Really brilliant. I'll keep everything crossed for you and we'll do everything we can at the clinic.' Georgie knew exactly how Kate felt and wondered just how hard she'd have fought to feel the way she felt right now. Hell, she'd have kept on fighting until she'd had no fight left. And then she'd have fought harder still. Nothing was as precious as this child, getting this child. Having this child. It was the first time that Georgie had ever sensed what it would be like to be part of a family. To belong. To love and be loved, unconditionally. And Liam fitted into that picture too. No matter how much she tried not to, she couldn't help but do some serious Christmas wishing on that account.

'Thanks.' Kate bit her lip and her eyes briefly fluttered closed. 'I'm a bit worried, to be honest. I don't want to have another major disaster like last time.'

'Okay, so the first thing you have to do is stop worrying. That's not going to help at all. We'll start you on a lower dose of stimulation drugs this time and monitor you very closely. There's nothing to say that you'll have the same experience again. Really, try to relax, that's the best thing you can do. I'll see you later and we can talk more then.'

'Okay. See you soon.'

Georgie was about to leave when she felt a prickling

along her neckline. Turning, she saw Liam approaching and felt the immediate rush of bright light whenever she saw him. 'Hey. Did you forget the time?'

'I'm so sorry. Just one thing after another today.' He shook his head and pecked a kiss on her cheek. 'Did I miss the shopping? Come on, let's go. I'm starving.'

'Me too.'

He grinned. 'No surprises there. What's in the bags?'

She hid the bag of named baubles behind her back and grinned right back—he'd probably think she was just a sentimental old sook. 'Not telling.'

'Aw…come on.' As he spoke his mobile phone went off. He shook his head in irritation, dragged his phone out of his pocket and looked at the display. 'Look, I've got to get this.'

'Who is it?'

'Just MAI.'

'The agency? Why? What do they want?' She felt the colour drain from her face. He'd been home so long this time. Long nights she'd kept him to herself like a delicious secret, always knowing that this day might come but pretending that it wouldn't. Convincing herself that it wouldn't matter anyway, that she was on top of her feelings about him. She'd managed to leave herself enough space and hadn't fallen for him so completely that his leaving would damage her.

Besides, he didn't have to go. The baby was due soon. He would turn them down. He would stay. 'What do they want?'

'No idea.' He shrugged. 'Sorry again. I won't be long.'

He turned a little away from her and she stared into the shop window, half looking at the too-expensive wares, half-listening to his side of the conversation. It would be fine. She would be fine. He wouldn't run, she trusted that he wouldn't go now, not when she needed him.

'Hey. No worries. Where…? How long…? Why…? What do you need?' Suddenly his voice went quiet and the bright light inside her went out.

He stayed quiet for a few moments as he listened to the caller. Then he looked over and caught her eye. There was something about his tense expression that made her heart stumble. Guilt? Panic? He tried for a smile, but it was more regretful than reassuring. Then he closed his eyes, turned his back to her, shoulders hitched.

Something was wrong.

She strained to listen, but whether he was hiding the information from her or protecting her she didn't know.

She heard her name.

She heard 'pregnant'.

She heard, 'Yes, I'll do it.'

Then he stood stock-still.

Something was wrong. Numbness crept through her. The only things she could feel were the fast, unsteady beat of her heart and the clench of her fists around the shopping bag handles.

Something was wrong but, unlike her house, or the garden or the zillion things that had broken over the last few years, Liam wasn't going to fix this.

Liam snapped the phone into his pocket and turned to face her, already understanding that she'd heard a little and assumed a lot. Things were careering out of control in every direction he turned. 'I'm sorry. Again.' It was inadequate, he knew, but it was heartfelt.

'So you keep saying. What for? Being late for lunch or agreeing to whatever it was you just agreed to?' Her eyes were dark, her cheeks hollowed. She knew him too well, Liam realised. He couldn't hide things from her. 'What did they want? No…more to the point, when are you leaving? Where are you going?'

'Sudan. Tonight.'

'They need you, right? There's no one else? Absolutely no one else? Tell me they were desperate. You had no choice?'

The pause he gave was too long. Long enough for her to read between the lines. They'd sort of asked and he'd sort of offered. And, yes, there were others who could have gone. He'd just fast-tracked himself to the top of the list.

Things between them had got so complicated so quickly, he was thrashing around trying to make sense of it. But he couldn't.

Yes, he loved waking up with her. Yes, he loved spending time with her. Too much. It was all too much and he was starting to want things, to feel things he shouldn't about the baby and about her. He was supposed to have kept his emotions out of all this and yet here they were washing through him. Guilt. Panic. Adoration. Need. *Fear*.

And taking that risk was a step too far. He needed to get his head straight. To have time to think. Sudan was the perfect place. It wouldn't be for ever, but it might just be enough to get things in order again, so he could be rational and stop these gut-wrenching emotions messing with his head. 'Well…'

He could hardly look at her, but he had to face her anger. Which was swift and fierce and almost tangible. He could see her starting to close down.

She shook her head and strode past him. 'Okay. So you've made your decision. I have to go to work. I'm going to be late.'

Liam followed her down Queen Street towards her clinic, trying to keep up. The way she'd looked at him he could have sworn she'd wanted him to say something more. Something profound. But he wouldn't lie to her, let her think one thing, believe something—*want* something—that he wasn't sure he could give. Hell, she was

hearts and flowers all the way and he was, in comparison, a lost cause. He shouldn't have let things get to this point. 'For a woman who's seven months pregnant you can sure keep a good pace.'

'That's because I'm in a hurry. My clinic's due to start and you're making me late for *my* job. You're not the only one with a strong work ethic.' She was in front of him now, grumping over her shoulder. And watching her stalk ahead, all proud and indignant, made him want her more. Which gave him every reason why he should get that damn flight.

'Georgie, we need to talk about this.'

'Really? You think?' She stopped outside the clinic. 'When you've already made your decision? You jumped at the chance. No hesitation. I didn't see much talking going on between us.'

He followed her up the stairs and into a meeting room. He closed the door and went to sit opposite her across a table. The table was too big, the room too sterile.

Her words echoed off the walls. 'And you don't know for how long. You never do. It could be months.'

'Look, it'll be okay. Everything will be fine. The deck's almost finished, the garden just needs some final touches. Don't do anything until I get back.'

Those lifeless eyes regained a spark that flamed. 'So this is your idea of being in it for ever? A lifetime commitment, and this is what you're promising? You won't be here geographically—and I can probably handle that. A lot of mothers have to deal with that. But…oh, this is unfair. I'm being unfair.' She stood up. 'I knew this all along, but—'

'What? Say it… Say what you're thinking.' He reached across for her hand, but she pulled it away. She was closing down. 'Talk to me, Georgie.'

'What's the point?'

'It's what we do. Talking.'

'Not, it appears, about the important things. Not when it matters. You should have discussed it with me first. *We* should have decided.' She took a deep breath and huffed it out. 'You say you're committed, that you want to work as a team, as a co-parent, but the moment they call, you jump. *You* choose. You can say no. You can stay here. There is a get-out clause. I do know.'

It was important that he remain calm and let her anger bounce off him. 'It's my job, Georgie. I've been home for a long time.' *Home.* That thought made Liam's stomach clench— it was the first time he'd thought of anywhere as home. Georgie's home. His heart swelled in pride at what they'd achieved at her house, but simultaneously he felt as if it was being slashed into pieces. 'This will be the last time. I'll make sure I resign completely after this.'

'I'm sure that's what they all say, and I'm sure they mean it too. Besides, I know why you do it, month after month, serving your penance to Lauren. I get that. I wouldn't ask you to give it up. But now? Right now? When you have a choice and you chose them. You chose them. Unbelievable.' She began to pace the room, glancing every few seconds at the clock. Which ticked away the minutes sonorously, ominously, like a sentinel counting down.

She stopped walking. Her hands gripped the back of a chair. There was a small hole in the dark grey fabric, the edges frayed. She seemed to stare at it as she spoke. 'So you told them? About the baby?'

'Yes.'

'And you might not be here for the birth?'

'They said they'd try to make it happen.' The ache that had started in his throat seeped into his chest, getting more raw and more real.

Distance. That's what they needed, then they'd be able to think and talk and act rationally, without the sideshow of pumping hearts and that long aching need. He needed

to feel about her and the baby the way he felt about everyone else, not infused with some sort of mind-melding, heart-softening drug. That way he would be able to make good decisions, act responsibly.

He walked to the window and looked out at the street below. It had started to rain. Heavy clouds spewed thick drops over the passers-by below.

Finally, she came to him and made eye contact. But it wasn't what he wanted to see. All affection had gone, all excitement and hopefulness.

Somewhere along the way all his emotions had got locked up with her. Every day started and ended with thoughts of Georgie. As he turned to the window he caught sight of a stack of magazines and remembered the online dating article. She was hoping for something more.

She wanted a declaration, he supposed. Something that told her how he felt about her, about this. But he didn't know what to say. Couldn't express the chaos, couldn't see through those clouds, only that his heart felt raw at the prospect of not being here. Of letting her down. But it wasn't fair to make her believe a lie.

Her voice was cold. 'And they're going to try? Is that what we've got to look forward to? You trying?'

'Surely that's better than me not trying? I'll call when I get there. I'll call as often as I can. I'm sorry it's not going to work out exactly to plan.'

'We didn't have a plan, Liam. That's just the problem. We just pretended everything would be fine, and it's not. It won't be.' She shook her head, her ponytail bobbing from side to side. She looked so young. And so cross. So magnificently annoyed. 'I won't hold my breath about the calls. I know what those satellite phones are like. You've never managed it before.'

It had never mattered so much before.

She was distancing herself from him, he could see.

She was systematically putting space from her emotions, he recognised it because he'd done it himself so many times—but she never had.

When she looked back at him her resolve seemed clear. The emotions were settled, she was cold and distant. Things had irrevocably changed—including the emotions whirling in his chest like some sort of dark storm cloud, whipping away the oxygen and leaving nothing in its place. An empty chasm that hurt so hard.

He was going to help those who didn't have the wherewithal to help themselves. But, bone deep, he knew he was going because he couldn't not. Because facing other people's truths was always easier than facing up to his own. 'They need me there.'

'And we need you here.'

He looked over at the shopping bags she'd dropped on the floor. 'You bought decorations?'

'Suddenly I'm not feeling very festive. You're not going to be here.'

'I doubt it.' And that was all his fault. She'd been looking forward to spending Christmas together and he'd ruined it.

He turned to face her as hurt and pain whipped across his heart.

Her arms hugged across her chest. Her eyebrows rose as she infused her voice with a brightness she clearly didn't feel. 'So go. Save some lives. Come back safe and then be a good father to your child.'

'It'll only be for a few weeks. I'll get back for the birth. I'll make it happen.' His child. It was so close now, a few more weeks and he'd be able to hold his child.

Was that why he'd taken this job? Because he was too afraid? Was he too afraid to love his child?

To love Georgie?

That idea shunted him off balance. He didn't want to

look too deeply inside himself, at his motivations, so he was going by gut feeling here, because that was all he had to go on. His head wasn't making any sense. 'And what about us?'

'Oh, Liam, we want different things, I understand that now. I feel that now. I want a big messy family with two parents who love each other, with doting grandparents who want to share the joy, and you don't want any of that.' She touched her heart and a little piece of him shattered because he knew what she was saying. That this was the end. 'We just don't have the same dream.'

No. Now his heart was being ripped away. He didn't want to hear those words, to feel this hurt. But he knew that it was the only way they would ever be able to get by, to see each other and survive. Maybe one day they'd find a place where they could be friends again. 'And when I come back?'

'We'll have rewound in time to before the baby. To before you came back from Pakistan. Back to when we were just friends. When things weren't complicated. You can have your life and I'll have mine and we'll meet somehow in the middle, for this little fella. Co-parents, like we agreed.'

'But—'

'No.' Her hand flicked up to stop him speaking. 'It's what I want, Liam. What I need to get through all this. Things are going to be hard enough as they are without wondering what you want from me too, worrying if you're going to change your mind or choose something else, something more appealing. Because you do that... don't you? So it'll be better if we have no promises. No pretence. No ties between *us*. No *us*. Just this baby.'

'But—' He wanted to fight her, to fight for them, but she was right. It was easier, cleaner if they broke every-

thing off now and got back to being friends again. If that could ever happen. Time apart would help. It had to.

'I'm used to being on my own, Liam. That way there aren't any expectations. I can't spend my life wanting people to love me if they don't. If I'm not enough, that's fine. I'll be enough for this little one.'

You're more than enough for me. For anyone. But love? That was another level he hadn't dared strive for since Lauren. Something he'd closed himself to. Love? Nah, he couldn't trust himself to go there. 'I'll be back as soon as I can. I'm sorry, about everything.'

'No. This is all my fault, Liam. I should have listened to you in the first place. It was a beyond crazy idea. And now our friendship is ruined, we can't talk without shouting. You're leaving and we're arguing. We never did this before, we used to go to the pub and give you a good send off, and off you'd trot, with a damned fine hangover, to save the world. And we cheered from the sidelines, proud and happy that you were doing something most excellent and good.

'But look at me, I'm not cheering now. I resent you for going and that's not how it should be. You'd resent me if I asked you stay. We're caught between our own needs and wants and it's too hard to live like that. Everything's changed between us. You said it would and it has. It's me who should be sorry. I made you do this. I kissed you first. I took you to my bed. I'm sorry for all of it.'

'Never. We've created something. A child. *Our* child. We can't ever be sorry for that.' He tried to pull her into his arms, to kiss her once more. To taste those honeyed lips, to feel her, soft and gorgeously round, in his arms. To feel that sense of belonging that she gave him, that reason to stay. To make him stop running from the past and look ahead to something different, something better, something

not haunted by what happened before. Something more than good. But she stepped away, out of reach.

So far out of reach he didn't know if he'd ever find a way back to her.

'I need you to leave now.' She wanted him to stay. Wanted him to want to stay with her and the baby, and make a family of three. Oh, God, she wanted him. Wanted more. Wanted so much more. Wanted a different way to describe what the two of them had shared. It didn't necessarily need paperwork—she didn't expect marriage, but she did want commitment. Not just to the baby but to her. She wanted to be part of something long term. With him. She wanted her dream.

But he was running away, and he'd given her no choice in the matter.

And, yes, he'd shown commitment to the pregnancy despite her initial doubts. Not once had he wavered when even she'd had the odd wobble about impending parenthood. Hadn't he helped her create a beautiful space for her and their child? Hadn't he designed a garden? Hadn't he made sure she was safe, that she ate the right things, that his child was cocooned in the right environment to grow?

But he had still never said the word 'love' to her. Not about her or his child. Or about anyone or anything, for that matter, ever. He was all locked up in the tragedy of his baby sister and it was desperately sad but she wanted him to love someone.

She wanted him to love her.

And he couldn't. Because if he did he wouldn't be heading off on some mission that he didn't need to go on. He'd be here, holding her hand and planning a happy Christmas, supporting her in her last couple of months of pregnancy.

Was it too much to ask? Was she expecting too much?

No. It was what every couple strove for. She wanted him

to feel the same way about it all as she did. She wanted him to share that excitement she felt whenever she lay in his arms. The way her heart soared when he was inside her. The sensation of utter completeness when he looked at her, when he made her laugh. She wanted him to love her and the baby the way she loved him. Wholly. Totally. Without reservation.

And there it was. The naked, ugly truth. She'd fallen in love with him.

When she should have been putting all her attention into this baby, she'd gone and fallen for its father—the wrong kind of man to love.

No.

She tried not to show her alarm and fixed her face as best as she could into an emotion-free mask as she walked away from him, while he stared at her uncomprehendingly, his hand on the doorhandle.

No. Don't go. She wanted to shout it at him. To hurl herself at him and be a barrier between him and the door. But what would be the point? Letting him go was the right thing to do. What was the point in making someone stay, hoping they would learn to love you? Hoping…

She loved him. Completely. Devastatingly. Instead of protecting herself against more heartache, she'd allowed her life to be bowled over by a man who couldn't and wouldn't ever love her. It was a simple and as difficult as that. How stupid.

And now, even worse, she was tied to him for ever. She'd insisted on that. And he'd agreed. He'd torn up the contract in a dramatic gesture of commitment and determination that had both impressed and scared her. And despite everything she knew about him, she'd believed him and somewhere deep inside a little light had fired into life and it had grown and she'd hoped…

And now the light had blown right out.

Because, after all, she'd been the silly one in all this, she'd allowed herself to dream, had allowed herself to slip under his spell, had willingly given her heart to him. He'd always been upfront. And you couldn't be more upfront than jumping on the first plane out of Dodge.

Liam had been right all along. Love could be damned cruel. She could never let him know. 'I need you to leave. Now. I need you to go, Liam.'

'Georgie—'

'Go. I have to work.' She watched the door close behind him, and almost cried out, almost declared herself, to see if that would make a difference to him going or staying. But she wasn't about to play games, give him tests, make him say something he'd regret. Or that they'd both regret.

But, still, nothing took away from the fact that she loved him. She had probably always loved him—as a friend, as someone who she could confide in and share a joke with. He was, deep down, a good man who was conflicted, who was trying to hide from hurt, and after his experiences who could blame him? His flaws made him even more likable. Falling romantically in love with him had been the icing on the cake and she would be proud for her child to have him as a father. One day she would tell him that. When she could look him in the face again. When her heart had stopped shattering into tiny pieces.

With shaking hands she picked up her shopping bags, took out the tinsel and gaudy baubles and threw them on the table. That would be for later, for a time when she felt like celebrating. Right now Christmas loomed ahead a sad and sorry affair. A Christmas without Liam. She'd wrapped him up in her festive excitement, made him the best present a girl could have, and he'd gone. Left her, just like her mother had.

One day she'd find someone who wanted her enough to stay around.

She took a few deep breaths, swiped a hand across her face and caught a tear. And another one. Then gave up the fight and let them flow.

My God, she thought as she looked in the staff-room mirror, she needed to pull herself together; this clinic could be hard enough without the nurses falling apart too.

'Come on, girl.' Plumped up her cheeks and dried her eyes. 'There are plenty who are much worse off.' Like the people Liam was going out to save. Like the ones she had booked in now, who looked to her for support and advice. Who didn't have a healthy baby in their bellies. Who needed her dedication and attention to get them through. She allowed herself two more tears. Exactly that. One for her, one for her baby, then she took another deep breath, put on her game face and went back out into the world.

CHAPTER ELEVEN

Two weeks ago...

LIAM LURCHED AGAINST the cold hard passenger seat as the Jeep bumped over potholes along the pitted dirt track. 'Man, these roads don't get any better. I'm going to be covered in bruises before we get to the camp.'

'Aren't you pleased to be back?' Pierre Leclerc shouted above the din of the engine, his words tinted with his French-Canadian accent and vestiges of the countless places he'd visited in his long aid career. He cracked a booming laugh and hit Liam on the thigh. 'We missed you.'

'Ah, shucks, mate, I missed you too.' Like hell he'd missed them. He'd struggled every kilometre, every minute of the interminable flight, the uncomfortable transit, the stench. The seven-day layover in Juba, getting supplies, waiting for the right documents, stuck in bureaucratic hell. The long drive out here. Every second wishing he'd had the courage to stay in Auckland with Georgie.

He just couldn't get rid of the memory of her. All grumpy and stroppy, stomping down the crowded street, the swing of her backside, the tense holding of her shoulders, the swish of her ponytail. The closed-off posture. The truth of her words. *Our friendship is ruined.* But it was all too late.

Pierre leaned across. 'I hope you bought us something decent for our Christmas stockings?'

'I have something to help us forget, if that's what you mean.' Patting his duty-free purchases of rum and whisky, he joined in the laughter, trying to be friendly, wishing like mad he was back in New Zealand, far away from this nightmare of dry earth and flies.

I made a mistake, he thought. *I made a million of them.*

They pulled into the camp compound, the dull corrugated roof of the medical building half-hidden by a layer of brown sand whipped up by the morning wind. A thin pale grey sky stretched above them, promising little relief from the scorching sun.

Liam looked around at the thousands of tents and crudely made straw structures lining the gravel and mud path. Sun-bleached rags, tied between sticks and corrugated metal, provided the best shelter they could from relentless heat. A group of women huddled around a water tap. 'It hasn't changed at all.'

'Nothing much changes around here. It's like *Groundhog Day.*' Pierre pulled out a handkerchief and swiped it across his forehead. 'People still arrive every day seeking help, and we still struggle to house them, to feed them, to provide adequate clean water. There aren't enough toilets, the kids are all getting sick. Nothing changes at all.'

Except last time Liam couldn't wait to get here. And this time he couldn't wait to leave. 'So, what's planned for today?'

'Immunisation programme. Training the new assistants so they can go on and run it solo.'

'Okay. Let's do it.' Liam jumped down into the fog of red dust created by the Jeep wheels.

Within seconds, dozens of semi-naked children appeared screaming, laughing and singing, surrounding Liam and Pierre and clinging to their legs. Such joy in

everything, even in the direst circumstances. But that was kids for you: they didn't overthink, they didn't worry or analyse, they just got on with life, running forward to the next great adventure. There was a lesson there.

Pierre steered him into the medical centre. As they squeezed past the long queue of sick people waiting to be treated Liam found himself wondering where to begin, but as always Pierre had the routine down like clockwork. And Liam easily slipped back into it.

'Okay, your turn.' He beckoned to a mother holding a small child in her arms. 'How old?'

The woman looked at him, not understanding. She offered him the child, a boy of about twelve months, scrawny and lethargic with the telltale potbelly signs of malnutrition.

'He's about one year and a half.' The base nurse translated the woman's local dialect, 'His name is Garmai. Just out of the supplementary feeding programme two weeks ago.'

Liam checked him over and measured the child's arm circumference to determine the extent of malnutrition. Garmai would probably spend the best part of his life growing up in a refugee camp, his home town too dangerous to go back to as rebels terrorised the streets and drought stole their crops. So different from the life his own child would lead in New Zealand, where water came through invisible pipes below the ground, machines worked with the swipe of a finger and food was plentiful.

And a father half a world away.

What the hell had he been thinking?

'Eighteen months old? Really?' He spoke to the nurse. 'It looks like he still has signs of mild malnutrition. He needs to go back to the feeding centre, not stay here where he's probably only going to get sick again.'

'There isn't room. They discharged him because there's too many more coming every day.'

'They'll have to make room. This child needs help and I don't want a half-hearted effort.' He turned and smiled at the mother, trying to dredge some hope when there was little. 'I'm going to have a child. To be a father.'

He'd never given any personal information to anyone here before, not even to the staff—but the words just tumbled out. Pride laced his voice as his thoughts returned again to Georgie for the umpteenth time that day, along with the familiar sting of regret and yet startling uplift of his heart. Every thought of her brought a tumbling mish-mash of emotions and a fog of chaos. 'Soon. Very soon.'

The mother gave him a toothy grin and gabbled something to him, but a high-pitched scream grabbed their attention. A heavily pregnant woman half walked, half crawled into the room, clutching her stomach. She was immediately ushered back out and into the emergency area by two nurses.

Georgie? *Georgie.* Of course it wasn't Georgie. He'd left her to face her biggest challenge alone back at home. How would she cope with the pain of childbirth? Did she have a plan? Why the hell hadn't he made sure she had a plan? He'd phone her again, at least try to, tonight, and make sure she was okay. That was, of course, if she ever deigned to speak to him again. Her silence had been deafening.

Unlike the squawk of chattering voices and laughter and screams that filled the room as a huddle of women walked towards the emergency area. He looked up at the nurse for an explanation. 'The pregnant woman's sisters, here to help.'

'Great. She'll need some support.' He looked back at the boy, then jerked his head up again at another straggle of women walking through the room.

'The birthing attendants. The mother's mother. Her aunts.'

'Are they going to have a party or something? There's a lot of them.'

The nurse beamed. 'Of course. Family is very important here.'

As it was to Georgie. And she was going to be alone.

And that was his fault.

Watching those people come together to help their sister, to celebrate family in all its messy glory, made his heart clutch tight and he realised that Georgie had been wrong about one thing: he did want the same dream. He'd spent the last nine months trying to fight it with his head, but his hands had worked on her house, her garden, building a home for them all, a home that he loved. His arms had held the woman he adored, cradled her belly holding the baby he so desperately wanted.

For the first time in years he saw his own needs with startling clarity. He wanted to look forward instead of back. He wanted to be a father his child would be proud of. He wanted a family.

Hell, Georgie had even got him thinking about his own mother and father. And how much, deep down, he wanted to make some kind of contact with them again. He'd make a start tonight. He'd phone them and tell them they were going to be grandparents.

He wanted to be part of something good. He wanted somewhere to call home, a community of friends. Someone to love. And to be loved. The same simple dreams as every single person in this camp. He just hadn't realised it until now.

Most of all he wanted Georgie, with such a passion it stripped the air from his lungs. But he knew her heart came with a proviso. He had to love her. She wouldn't accept any less than that.

He had to love her. *Had to?* Could he do that? He sat for a moment and that thought shook through him like a physical force. He let her image fill his brain, suffuse his body with so many wild emotions. His throat filled with a raw and unfettered need.

Man, how he wanted her. He missed everything about her. He wanted her. Dreamt about her, saw her soft beautiful eyes in everyone's here, her kindness in the gentle touch of strangers, her compassion, her independence that frustrated and endeared her to him. He missed her so intensely it hurt. He needed to touch her, to lie with her, to fight with her. And, of course, to make love to her over and over and over. And such a need and such a want could only amount to one thing.

He did love her.

He'd been fighting so hard to protect himself he hadn't seen the single most important thing that had been happening.

God. He loved her and he'd walked away. No, he'd *run* away, afraid of how much she made him feel things. He'd messed up everything and now was it too late to start again? Would she even let him in the house? Would she let him love her?

Did she love him back?

He needed to know. He needed to make things right. He needed to go home.

A scream and a healthy wail echoed through the flimsy walls. New life. New beginnings. Not just for that family in there. But for him. Being here reminded him how fragile life was, and he needed to spend the rest of it with the woman he loved.

It was time to act. He needed to get back to her. Before Christmas, before the baby came. Before he lost any more time being here instead of there. He stood up and realised that a queue of people had formed, all staring at

him in this tin-roofed lean-to in a place, it seemed, even God had forgotten.

Damn. He'd made too many mistakes and being here was one of them.

But how the hell to get out of this godforsaken dustbowl and bridge the fifteen thousand kilometre gap to be home in time?

Christmas Eve...

'Kate? Is that you? Hey, it's Georgie. From the clinic.' Georgie gripped the phone to her ear and tried to keep her feelings in check. This part was always the most emotional bit of her job but she wished, just this once, that she could see Kate's face when she told her the news. Knowing exactly how her patient would be feeling at this moment, she wanted to wrap her in a hug. In fact, wrapping anyone in a hug would be lovely—it felt so long since she'd done that. One month, two days and about twelve hours, to be exact. Not that she was counting.

And the loneliness was dissipating a bit now, especially when she distracted herself. Which she felt like she had to do most minutes of most hours, because he was always on her mind. Just there. The look on his face as she'd called the whole thing off, haunting her. But it had been the right thing to do. A very right thing.

'Yes?' Kate's voice wavered. The line was crackly. 'Yes?'

'I've got the results from the blood test you came in for earlier today.'

A sharp intake of breath. 'Yes?'

'So...' Georgie read out all the numbers, knowing that this gobbledegook would mean the difference between heartache and ecstasy for this couple. 'So, all that means we have good news. Great news. You have a positive preg-

nancy test. Looks like you're going to have a very happy Christmas. Huge congratulations. I know how much this means to you.'

There was a slight pause then a scream. 'Oh. My God. Really? Really? Are you sure?'

Georgie couldn't help her smile. Her heart felt the fullest it had in a month. Since, exactly, the moment she'd watched Liam disappear from the clinic. 'Yes. It's very early days, obviously, and we still have to take one day at a time. But, yes, you are pregnant.'

'Oh, thank you. Thank you so much. Mark will be so thrilled. I know how much he wanted this. We both do. We can't thank you enough.'

Georgie ignored the twist in her heart at the thought of how gloriously happy this couple would be, together. Expecting a baby, making a family. Of how much Mark would be involved, and how much his love and concern for his wife always shone through his face.

It did not matter, she kept telling herself, that she was facing all this on her own. She would be fine and one day, maybe, she'd find a man who wanted her too. 'Okay, so we need to make another appointment for you for a few days' time to check the HCG levels are rising as well as we want them to, which means you'll have to come in before the New Year,' Georgie explained. 'I also need to book you an ultrasound scan…'

'Not long to go for you now?' Kate asked, after they'd finished the business end of the call. 'How are you feeling? Excited?'

'Very. There's just over a month to go and I don't feel remotely ready. I still have heaps of shopping to do, and I haven't even thought about preparing my delivery bag.'

'Get your man to spoil you rotten over the holidays, then. Make him do the fetching and carrying while you put your feet up.'

Familiar hurt rolled through her. Emails had been spo-radic. Phone calls virtually non-existent. The only news she got was on the TV or radio. But even then she wished she hadn't heard anything. Too many people being killed. It was too unsafe. And all this stress just couldn't be good for the baby, so in the end she'd switched the damned TV off and played Christmas music to calm her down. 'He's overseas at the moment. I'm not sure when he'll be back.'

'That's a shame. What are your plans for Christmas?'

'Oh, just a quiet one at home.' She thought about her Christmas tree with the lavish decorations that she'd even-tually found the motivation to finish last night. The small rolled turkey she'd bought and the DVDs of old Christmas movie favourites stacked up waiting for her to watch in the evenings. It was going to be an old-style Christmas, just her and Nugget. Not what she'd hoped for. And that was fine. It really was.

'Well, have a good one. *Kia kaha.*' *Stay strong.*

'Yes, thanks. Bye.' Georgie smiled as she put the phone in the cradle. Broken heart or not, she fully intended to.

Six hours later she was standing on the deck, adding the final touches to the outside decorations to the jolly and earnest accompaniment of carol singers blasting through her speakers. The deck may not have been quite finished, but the garden looked beautiful, with the candles flicker-ing in the darkness. Liam had been right, the winery gar-den idea had worked well—just a shame that the edges still needed to be finished off.

But tomorrow's forecast was for sunshine and she had no intention of sitting inside when she had such a fairy-tale place to spend the day. The hammock had her name on it, along with a glass of cranberry and raspberry juice, a large helping of Christmas pudding and a damned good romance novel.

There was just one more string of lights to hitch onto a

branch to make everything perfect. Standing on tiptoe, she reached up and tried to throw the lights around the branch.

Missed. *Damn.*

She tried again. Missed again. Stretching forward, she flung the lights towards the branches, the weight of her baby tummy dragging her forward and off balance.

Stepped out into…air.

She felt the scream before she heard it, rattling up through her lungs, into her throat that was filled with panic. The one single word that came to her, the only thing she wanted right now. 'Liam!'

Then she flailed around like a windmill as there was nothing and no one to stop her fall into darkness.

Now…

Pain seared up her leg with even the slightest movement. She was sure she'd broken her ankle—it was twisted at such a strange angle caught in the gap between splintered wood and the garden wall. A bad sprain anyway, too sore for her to put her weight on, and she was too wedged in to be able to lever her big fat belly upwards.

So she was stuck. *Damn.*

And hurting. *Double damn.*

And how long she'd lain here calling for help, she didn't know, but the moon was high in the sky now. Typical that she'd left her phone in the house. Typical that the neighbours had gone to their holiday home by the sea. Typical that it was Christmas and she was on her own. And the music she'd been playing seemed to be on repeat and if someone didn't turn it off soon she'd go down in history for being the first woman to have been turned clinically insane by Rudolph and his damned red nose.

And it hurt. Everything hurt. Including her heart, because she felt stupid and sad, here on Christmas Eve, alone

and stuck. And for some reason her usually capable mind set had got all mushy and she felt a tear threaten. And more than anything she missed Liam.

That was it. She loved him and she missed him with every ounce of her being. And he wasn't here and he never would be. Not in the way she wanted.

She tried again to wriggle free but her ankle gave way and she didn't want to put more pressure on it. Thank God it was summer and the night was warm. At least she could be grateful for that small mercy.

No. She wasn't grateful, she was angry. With herself, with Liam, with everyone and everything. Was she going to be stuck here all damned holiday? 'Hey! Anyone? Lady with a baby here. Stuck. Help?'

Rudolph with your nose so bright...

'Shut up! Please. Someone. Help.'

Once she'd calmed down a little she tried pulling herself up again. This time she managed an inch. Two...but then nothing more. She was about to call out again when a sudden searing pain fisted across her body. And her feet got wet.

Her heart hammered just a little bit more. No. Surely not?

The baby? Now? She pressed a hand to her belly and spoke in the softest voice she could muster. 'No, Nugget! Don't you dare make your appearance here. You've got five more weeks to cook. You stay exactly where you are.'

She waited, biting back the pain from her foot. Trying not to cry. Maybe it had been a Braxton-Hicks contraction? Maybe it was all just practice?

No such luck. More pain rippled across her abdomen, sapping her breath and making her grip tight onto the side of the deck. That one had hurt. A lot. 'You are just like your father, you hear me? You have lousy timing.'

How could she have a baby here, when she couldn't

even lift her leg up half an inch? Never mind that it was five weeks early. What was she going to do? Her lips began to tremble.

No. She wasn't going to cry. She was going to be fine.

More contractions rippled through her. Faster and more regular and every time they hurt just a little bit more. Time ticked on and she wanted so much to move, to free herself. To walk, to bend, to stretch.

And then more contractions came and the night got darker.

To cope with the pain she tried to conjure up an image of Liam, pretending he was here with her. Pretending he was helping her. Pretending he loved her. Because only that would be enough.

Think. Think. What could she do?

She didn't want to think. She wanted someone to do that for her, for a change. She wanted to be tucked up in bed, her head on Liam's shoulder, wrapped safe in his arms. She wanted— 'Owwwww. This is all your fault, Liam MacAllister. I hate you. I hate…*youooooww.*'

'I'm sorry. Is this not a good time?'

And now she was hallucinating, because through all this thick soupy darkness and Rudolph on repeat and searing pain she could have sworn she'd heard his voice.

She decided she was going to go with it. Maybe she was already clinically insane after all. 'Yes. You bet your damned Christmas socks it isn't a good time. I'm caught between a deck and a hard place. My foot's broken and I'm having your baby.'

'Right now?'

'Yes, right now.' She spoke to the Liam-shaped smudge that appeared so real it was uncanny. And to her endless irritation her heart did a little skipping thing. She didn't want it to skip. She wanted it to stay angry because that was the only way she was going to get through this. 'What

the hell are you doing here anyway? Aren't you supposed to be healing the sick? Giving alms to the poor?'

Then he was there, really right there, with his scent and his capable hands, and he wasn't panicking like she was, he was talking to her in a soothing, very understanding voice. 'Let's get you… Oh.' His hands shoved under her armpits and he tugged. 'You're stuck.'

'Give the man a medal. Yes, I'm stuck. I've broken my ankle and Desdemona's about to make her— *Owwwwww.*' Pain ripped through her again. The contractions were coming faster now. More regular and more intense.

But he was here. Like some goddamned guardian angel, he was here. For her. He'd come back. For her?

Or was it just for the baby? She couldn't think about any of that right now. He was here.

His voice soothed over her again. 'You're going to be fine, really, but I think we need the fire brigade or someone else to help lift you out. I don't want to hurt you…'

You already have. 'No way. No way are you getting those good people out of bed on this special night just to come with their special lifting equipment and heft me out of— *Oowwwwww.*'

'Contractions are that regular, eh? We've got to get you out. How about if I…?' He put his foot against the wall and heaved her upwards, and if he hadn't been tugging at her she might have melted into his embrace just for a moment. Just held on tight, just for one solitary moment, to absorb some of his strength and his heat. Just held right on. 'Twist left a bit…wait…slowly…'

'Whoa. Watch it…' Then she was somehow shrugged up and sitting on the deck and her foot was throbbing and her stomach contracting and she gripped onto his old T-shirt while sudden enormous pain rattled through her. 'It hurts, Liam. It all hurts.'

He grimaced a little, she thought. She could just about make him out. The candles had blown out hours ago and she hadn't managed to even plug the fairy-lights in. Some other time she might have thought this was romantic. It wasn't. It hurt.

But then he pushed her hair back from her face and rubbed his thumb over her cheek and she bit her lip to stop herself from crying because he was here and she wanted him so much. But he didn't want her.

He looked right into her eyes. 'I know, darling. I know it hurts. It'll be fine. Honestly. It'll be okay.'

'No, it won't. This baby can't come yet, it doesn't have anywhere to sleep...and I haven't had my baby shower, I want my party. I want to play games—I don't want to do this.'

And I don't want you here to torment me and be the macho hero and loving father when you'll go and break my heart a million times over every time I see your face.

'This. Is. Not. My. Birth. Plan. I want gas and air. Pethidine. *Drugs.*'

'Roll with it, Geo. Looks like you're going to have a special guest of honour at that party. Because this baby is coming, whether you want it to or not. I get the feeling it has your genes when it comes to independence.'

'Oh. Oh. *Owww.*'

'Let's get you inside. It's too dark. I don't know how to help if I can't see.' Half carrying her, half walking her, he managed to get her inside and onto the lounge floor. 'The bedroom's too far. Okay. I'm calling back-up. This baby's in a hurry.'

After stabbing numbers into a phone, he rattled off information and only then did she hear the anxiety in his voice. When he turned back to her she saw him in full light. My God, he was breathtaking. But he looked con-

cerned. No, more than that. He looked haunted. *Lauren.*
'It won't happen again, Liam. It will be fine.'

'I know, I know. Everything's okay.'

'And I think I want to push—'

Everything was not okay.

Liam consciously regulated his breathing, but there
was nothing he could do about his pounding heart rate
and his overwhelming sense of dread. There was every
chance that this could go wrong. This was a prem sce-
nario. The one nightmare he wanted to avoid. It was hap-
pening all over again.

He tried to shake away the image of tubes and an incu-
bator and a tiny pink thing that grew into his crying wail-
ing sister, but had looked so quiet and so sick that it had
almost broken his heart. And of the tiny coffin that had
barely filled the space in the dirt.

So, no, everything was not okay.

He inhaled sharply and took Georgie's hand and waited
until she'd stopped screaming and screwing up her face.
'That's it. It's all good. You're doing well.'

How many babies had he delivered? He'd lost count.
Out in the field where there was little help and lots of dis-
ease, when mum and baby had less than a good chance of
surviving. And he'd never panicked. Not once. But right
now he'd never wanted so much for medical equipment.
For back-up. For the pain in his heart to dislodge so he
could think straight. For the woman and the child he loved
to be okay. 'You're doing good. Now breathe…breathe…'

At what point had he so hopelessly and completely
fallen in love with her? Maybe right then that second as
she stared up at him with such fear and love and relief in
her eyes that it made his heart jolt. Or maybe when she'd
told him to leave and he'd seen the same love shimmer-
ing in her face, even though she had been trying so hard

to hide it from him. Maybe when he'd found her in the ER with a damaged eye. Or when she'd told him she was pregnant.

Or even that very first day in the sluice room ten years ago when she'd taken no nonsense and told him to harden up.

But in the last few days that thought had taken hold of him and he just couldn't shake it off. Damn fine time to realise you loved someone, right when you had a chance of losing them. But whatever happened he had to love her now, from this minute on, and protect her and care for her. And help her. And be brave for her. 'I can see the head, Geo. Breathe for me. Just a second. Breathe.'

'I don't hate you.'

A smile flowered in his heart—enough to take him past the fear and into a place of calm. They'd get through this together. 'I know. I know you don't hate me, Geo. Concentrate on the breathing.'

'Really, I'm sorry. I don't hate you— *Owwwwww.*' Then with an ear-splitting scream a slick baby slithered into his arms. The doorbell rang. Footsteps pounded into the room. Georgie cried. The baby cried. The cord was cut, a murmur of voices. A hearty chorus of congratulations!

And, able to finally breathe again, he was left staring at this miracle. His son. All ten fingers and ten toes and a hefty set of lungs. Who was managing just fine on his own. And suddenly Liam's heart was blown wide open with a different kind of emotion. A searing riotous joy and a feeling that life was just about to get gloriously messy.

Then he looked at his son's mother, who was the most red-faced, tear-stained disaster he'd ever seen. And his heart swelled some more, shifting and finding more space for love for her. And he knew in that moment that nothing would ever be the same because he'd allowed these people into his heart and that was where they were going

to stay. For ever. 'You are amazing, Georgie Taylor. He is amazing.'

'It's a boy? Yes?'

'Yes. He's doing fine. Just fine.' He passed the baby to her to hold, watched as the tiny bundle nuzzled towards her nipple. 'A boy, with great instincts and a particularly well-defined MacAllister package, if I do say so myself.'

'One minute old and you're assessing his genitals?'

'It's a guy thing.' Unable to resist kissing her any longer, he lifted his head and pressed his mouth to hers. 'I love you. I love you, but I need to explain—'

'Whoa? Really? Now?' She nodded towards the team of busy paramedics. 'I've just had a baby and we have an audience, and you want to do this now?'

'Yes. Now, and always. My timing is legendary, didn't you know? I don't care who hears it, I love you, Georgie.'

Her eyes widened but she put a hand between them to create space. 'It's the hormones. You'll grow out of it in a day or two. Then you'll be hot-footing it back to South Sudan at the first opportunity.'

'No. It's taken me a decade to come to my senses, but I love you. I want to be with you. Nowhere else in the world has you, so I want to be here, to make you happy.' His throat caught a little. 'And now we have this one.'

Those wide dark eyes brimmed with tears. 'No. It's because of him that you're here. Not me. You don't love me. You want to. Oh, how you want to. But you don't.'

'Are you for real? I've called in every favour I've ever had and flown halfway across the world. Dashed straight to you. Which part of *I love you* don't you believe?'

She bit her lip and as always her stark honesty was there in her face, in her words. 'I'm scared, Liam. I want to believe it all. Wow, that would be such an awesome dream to have come true, really. I couldn't think of a better thing

I could have. But you don't have to get carried away. I get that you don't like connection.'

She was rejecting him? He hadn't factored that into his plan. 'I have spent every available waking hour for the last eight months here. I have pimped your house, transformed your garden, been at your beck and call. I've been your friend through thick and thin. I am still your friend, Geo. That is the best part about all of this. We are friends first. Doesn't that prove that I love you?'

'I want your heart. Not your duty or your responsibility, or some friendship loyalty thing. I want your true love.' It was there in her face and mirrored in his heart, unfettered, truthful, raw. He needed to make her believe him. She clearly took some persuading. 'I want your true love. For me. I won't take anything less.'

'Wait. Wait right there.' He dashed out to the car, grabbed his things and dashed back. 'The paramedics are waiting outside, they want to take little Nugget—we need a name. Really, we need a name. Just to be checked out at the hospital. And to get your foot sorted. But I want to give you this first.'

He dragged the cot into the lounge and placed it next to the biggest, brightest Christmas tree loaded down with the most garish baubles he'd ever seen. 'Here. I got this.'

Her hand went to her mouth. 'You bought the cot from the French market? And you've painted it? That's very sweet, very kind of you. He'll love it. I love it.'

'And I love you. I bought this for you back then, the day after you fell in love with it. Because you wanted it so much. Because it makes you happy. I just want to do things that make you smile. I love you. Please believe me.'

'Oh, Liam.' Georgie shuffled across the sofa, trying to avoid the pain in her nether regions, her foot, and just about everywhere on her body. But it all faded just a little bit. He loved her? Did he? She'd listened out for it for so

long, but he'd never used the words. She'd wanted to hear it, had waited so patiently for someone somewhere to say those three words to her. She had believed that a declaration of love could only be spoken. The deeds, though—they'd been plentiful. He'd shown her his love instead of declaring it. Every day for ten years.

For some reason she couldn't breathe, her lungs were filled with nothing, her throat choked with a lump of emotion. 'I don't know what to say.'

'Well, don't, then. Don't say a thing. Just listen. I didn't want to fall in love because love can be damned painful. I pushed everyone away to protect myself. I didn't want a family, I didn't want those things you craved. But you've shown me how to make it work, how to take a risk. That fighting for the people you love is the most important thing of all. I love you. Because you are you. You're funny and weird and you laugh at my jokes and your smile warms my heart every time I see it. But best of all we can get through anything—hell, we've stood by each other ten years already. I'm ready for another thirty, forty, eighty... You?'

'Yes. Yes, of course.' She wrapped him into her arms, with a slight protest from the little fella. 'Thank you. Thank you so much. I love you too. Really. Truly.'

'And if you want me to give up the aid work, I will. I'll find something else.'

She shook her head. 'Enough with the crazyville talk. I know how much you need to do that work. Just maybe shorter stints? And we'll definitely discuss it, right? You won't just decide.'

'Of course not. We're in this together.' And the way he was looking at her convinced Georgie that he really did mean it. He planted a kiss on her cheeks, then laughed. 'Hey, it's Christmas Day, you realise? We'll have to think of something festive to call him. I'm sorry, but Nugget doesn't cut it.'

She looked over at the twinkling lights on the tree, at the three baubles centre stage with their names on. At the stack of DVDs and the romance novel. This was not how she'd intended spending Christmas Day, but she couldn't think of a better way. Two guys to look after. Two guys to love her. A family. A proper family—now that had always been at the top of her Christmas wish list. 'There's always Noel or Gabriel…Joseph, maybe? We could call him Joe?'

'Or…Rudolph? Rudi?'

That damned music was still playing in the background. 'Not on your life. Come here and kiss me again.'

His nose nuzzled into her hair. 'I can't think of anything else when I kiss you, my mind goes to mush.'

'That's the plan, I don't want any more suggestions like that. Besides, we've got plenty of time to think of a name, but way too many kisses to catch up on…'

He did as requested. When he pulled away it wasn't as far as he usually went. She liked that. Liked the way he was intent on staying. Liked the way he loved her.

'Happy Christmas, darling.'

'Happy Christmas, Macadoodle-doo.' She gave her man another kiss. Then snuggled into the baby snuffling in her arms. 'Happy first Christmas, Nugget.'

And many, many more to come.

* * * * *

NAVY DOC ON HER CHRISTMAS LIST

AMY RUTTAN

This book is dedicated to some of my best friends. Those who were always there with me during those awkward years when I was like my heroine. I couldn't have made it through high school without my crew.

Love you lots Jenn, Brooke, Wendy, Cara and Sylvia.

CHAPTER ONE

"New York is at a standstill. Bridges and tunnels have been closed. What a great last-minute Christmas gift from old Saint Nick. NYPD are advising if you don't have to go out, don't. New York hasn't seen a blizzard like this since the late seventies..."

Ella shut the radio off. She didn't know who had left it running on an annoying Christmas music channel, but at least the radio host had it right—there hadn't been a blizzard in New York City like this in quite some time.

And she knew that without listening to some awful music station, because her aching feet were a grim reminder of what heavy snowfall did to people. She'd just wrapped up eight hours on the ER floor and since Charles Davenport said that everyone was to stay put because of the blizzard, she was stuck here.

At least the hospital was more prepared for a brownout this time. Well, in theory. Ella would believe it when she saw it. Charles had electricians and system specialists working on the new generators to make sure they didn't fail, like the old ones had.

Still, the storm raging outside was a doozy.

It wasn't like it was anything new, the storm that was, it felt like it had been storming for months on end, but the meteorologists were calling this storm the worst of them

all. Ella was skeptical. How could this storm be worse than the last one? In reality, she thought probably the weatherman was exaggerating and it would be nothing.

But since the new shift couldn't get in, it meant that she was still on duty, even though she had just worked a long one.

Not that Ella minded in the least bit. It meant she could avoid the obligatory family dinner where her mother would lament her lack of having a husband and providing her with grandchildren.

Which was all her parents ever thought she was good for.

"By the time I was your age, Ella, I was married with three children," her mother had droned on. *"If you'd smiled more during your coming out, you would probably have a husband by now."*

Yeah, because smiling more would have helped the men she'd been forced to smile and flirt with change their minds about a short, awkward, ugly duckling in god-awful designer dresses that her mother had picked out for her.

All those society functions had done was reinforce her desire to stay single and become the best damn trauma surgeon on the eastern seaboard.

Which, working under Charles Davenport's tutelage, she was fast becoming. Being snowed in and forced to work while her mother's tedious society Christmas function was taking place was just perfect.

So Ella relished her moment of freedom, far from her mother complaining of her perpetual state of single life, and settled down to enjoy a nice cup of coffee in the empty staff lounge while there was a lull between patients.

Ella sighed as she propped up her aching feet. The lights were off and the heavy snow that was blanketing Manhattan gave a nice calming, glow outside.

And she couldn't remember the last time that Manhat-

tan had been so completely covered in snow. It was nice. She liked the snow. She liked the magic of Christmas on her own. It was her mother who made Christmas painful.

So she didn't mind working an extra shift.

This was heaven to her. She'd catch a few winks of sleep before she headed back down to the emergency room.

"There might be some mistletoe in here!" The lights were flicked on and Ella squinted at the blinding light she was not prepared for.

"What in the heck…?" she asked as she sat up.

Two nurses in Santa caps were standing in the doorway of the staff room, blushing.

"Oh, Dr. Lockwood, we're so sorry, we didn't know that anyone was in here!"

Ella rubbed her eyes and was still seeing two large spots as she sat up. "It's okay. I'm just a surgeon, I don't need my eyes anyway."

Stacey, one of the trauma nurses, chuckled as she began rooting through a box labeled "Christmas Decorations" in the corner. "Again, sorry."

"What're you looking for?" Ella asked, annoyed that her solitude had been broken.

"Mistletoe," said Carol, the other nurse. "We just have some down time and since we're stuck here we thought we would have some kind of Christmas fun."

"Aha!" Stacey shouted, producing a very fake-looking piece of plastic mistletoe. "It's not real, but it should do the job just the same."

Ella just shook her head. "You two have fun with that. Who are you going to kiss anyway?"

Carol and Stacey were always scheming to land themselves rich doctors as a potential mates. They were Manhattan Mercy's version of her mother. They also schemed to set other people up, but mostly themselves. Carol and

Stacey's targets were wealthy doctors, preferably attend-
ings over interns.

"Dr. Zac Davenport!" Carol practically squealed like
a schoolgirl. "He said he's never been kissed under the
mistletoe before."

Ella rolled her eyes and snorted. She could almost guar-
antee that Zac Davenport had been kissed under the mis-
tletoe before. It was probably just a ruse to get a kiss from
a couple of pretty nurses.

Zac Davenport was a playboy, and a handsome one at
that. Sure, he'd aged since he'd come home from his last
tour of duty, but it had made him even sexier. The boyish-
ness had melted away to a hardened man, one who seemed
to hide pain behind those Davenport blue eyes.

Maybe no else saw the pain he was trying to hide, or
how jumpy he was, like when the corks were popped at
the wedding a couple weeks ago, but she saw it. She saw
the change in him, because once upon a time she and Zac
had been close.

Although she thought they'd been closer than maybe
he did.

Still, she was always a sucker for those blue eyes.

Eyes that had at one time caused her to go weak in the
knees and melt. There was a change in his, but Ella seri-
ously doubted there was much of one. Slime was still slime.

You kissed that slime before too.

She'd done more than kiss that slime. She'd given a
piece of herself to him, a piece of her heart, and then he'd
crushed it with his cruelty.

Ella was going to say something else when Zac entered
the staffroom. He didn't see her as she hurriedly stood up,
but her heart skipped a beat at the sight of him. She felt
her knees weaken, her pulse start to race and her palms
grow sweaty. He'd been here a couple of weeks, but she'd

tried to avoid him as much as possible. Not to be on duty when he was.

Apart from the odd blip, it had been working up until now.

Suddenly she felt like that dumpy, awkward girl in the lime-green dress. And she didn't like that much. It was exactly how she'd felt when he'd spoken to her briefly at Charles's wedding.

She'd thought he was off duty. He was supposed to be on the next rotation and part of the staff that couldn't get in. What was he doing here?

"Merry Christmas, Dr. Davenport," Stacey squealed as she ran up to him, holding the ugly fake mistletoe over her head and kissing him on the cheek. Carol snatched it from Stacey's hand.

"Merry Christmas." And Carol kissed him on the other cheek.

"Uh, Merry Christmas…" he said stiffly.

Ella snorted. He didn't know their names. That wasn't surprising. They were only two of the trauma nurses in the department he worked in, why should he know their names? Typical spoiled Zac Davenport. Not a care in the world for anyone but himself.

"Stacey," Stacey said.

"And I'm Carol," Carol said, stepping in front of Stacey. "We're on duty tonight."

Zac looked uncomfortable.

Good.

"Shouldn't you two be out on the floor?" Zac asked, trying to untangle himself from the onslaught of nurses. Ella felt a small amount of pity for them.

"Yes, you two should be out on the floor. There are patients waiting," Ella said stiffly, trying not to make eye contact with Zac.

"Of course, Dr. Lockwood," Carol said. "We'll just take our decorations and go."

Stacey nodded and picked up the dilapidated box where they'd got the fake mistletoe from and left the staffroom.

"Thanks," Zac said. "I wasn't sure how I was going to get out of that."

"No problem," Ella replied, but she didn't look at him. It was better that way.

"Isn't your shift over?" he asked, as he approached the coffee pot where she'd retreated to after he'd walked into the room. In effect, cornering her.

"Yes, but if you haven't heard, most of the next shift is unable to make it in and Manhattan has shut down."

"You worked a full shift, you can just walk home."

"It's not safe," Ella snapped, annoyed that he wanted to get rid of her so badly.

Wouldn't you be pestering him the same way too?

"I'm just worried that you're too tired to work another shift."

She glared at him. "Really? You're concerned about my well-being?"

"You're tired," he said.

"You don't look so hot yourself. You have dark circles under your eyes."

Zac's eyes narrowed and he pursed his lips. "I didn't sleep well."

"Then maybe you should go home and rest."

Zac's eyebrows shot up. "What is wrong with you?"

"What is wrong with me?" Her voice rose an octave and she was annoyed with herself for engaging in conversation with Zac. She'd promised herself when she'd heard that Zac Davenport had been discharged from the navy and was coming to work at Manhattan Mercy that she would keep her distance from him. That she wouldn't let him bait her. She'd worked hard here to build a reputation for her-

self, and just because Zac had come waltzing back to Manhattan and had immediately got an attending position in Trauma because he was a Davenport, it didn't mean that she was going to run away with her tail between her legs.

No way. Not this time.

"You've been acting weird lately. I mean, I tried to speak to you at Charles's wedding and you said nothing to me, and then fighting over that patient? We haven't exactly worked well together."

"Actually, I said hello and goodbye, if I remember correctly, at the wedding. As for the working situation, well, the trauma floor is tense and that was my patient."

Those brilliant blue eyes darkened with annoyance. That mouth, which she was all too familiar with, frowned and he crossed his arms.

"Ella, what is wrong?"

You were my best friend, my first kiss, and then publicly dismissed me in front of our peers. You broke my heart.

"Nothing is wrong." She set down the plastic cup that was half-filled with now-tepid coffee. "You know what? You're right. I'm tired and maybe I should head out in the whiteout conditions and go home."

She turned on her heel and stormed out of the staffroom, clenching her fists to keep herself from shaking.

There was no way she was actually going to head out into that storm. The ER was short-staffed and whiteout conditions didn't make it exactly safe to navigate the streets tonight. It was safer in the hospital.

As long as she could get away from Zac.

She was going to stay, but she just couldn't stay in the same room as Zac Davenport. Not for one more second.

"Ella!"

She heard him shout her name from behind her.

Why is he following me?

"Ella!"

She ignored him and quickened her pace, but she was no match for Zac, who gripped her by the arm and pulled her down a side hallway.

"What?" she demanded as he spun her around to face him.

"Look, I didn't mean it. You can't go out in that storm."

She rolled her eyes. "I wasn't going out in the storm. You really don't think much of me, do you?"

He cursed under his breath, running his hands through his short brown hair in frustration. "What did I do, Ella? Seriously?"

She was going to open her mouth to say something when there was an unmistakable sound of a power surge. An electric hum and suddenly they were cast into darkness.

"What the heck?" she asked. "I thought the new system was supposed to control these brownouts."

There were murmurs and shouts of shock.

"No," Zac whispered. "No."

Ella was surprised by the sound of panic in Zac's voice, the terror etched on his face under the emergency lights. "It's probably just a brownout. Like before. The generator will kick—"

"Son of a…" was shouted as someone further down the darkened hall knocked over a tray of metallic instruments. Followed by the clang of metal echoing and bouncing off the hospital walls.

Zac froze. His eyes were wide with terror as he backed against the wall, trembling. Ella was shocked, because he didn't even seem to know that she was there. His body was rigid in terror. Just like after the corks at the wedding. When the pops had sounded, she'd seen him freeze, then duck under the table. He'd seemed to recover quickly, but afterwards he'd left the room, looking pale. No one had noticed in the confusion of the wedding, but she'd seen it.

"Zac?" she asked softly, reaching out to touch him, but he pushed her hand away, as if her touch would harm him.

A couple of porters who were making their way down the darkened hallway stopped and stared at Zac, who was breathing deeply but clinging to the wall like he was on the edge of a precipice and was about to fall.

And she recognized the classic symptoms of post-traumatic stress disorder. No one had said anything to her about Zac having post-traumatic stress disorder. That would be something they would disclose about a new doctor working at the hospital to the head of that surgeon's respective departments.

I don't think anyone knows.

One thing she did know, she had to get him out of there and calmed down.

"Come on, Zac. Let's go." She took his hand and this time he didn't fight her off. She pulled him into the nearest empty on-call room and shut the door. She led him to the cot and made him sit down. "Breathe, it's okay. It was just a porter knocking over some instruments."

Zac nodded, but didn't look at her. He just took deep, calming breaths.

What had happened to him during his tour of duty?

"I'm okay," he said. "I'm okay."

"You sure?" she asked, not wholly convinced that he was all right.

"I'm fine," he snapped.

Of course, he was back to normal. The ungrateful jerk that he always was. Not even thanking her for taking him somewhere quiet where he could center himself.

"I'm so glad," she retorted. She had to put some distance between her and Zac. "Well, I'm just going to head back to the trauma floor and make sure the patients are okay."

"Sounds good."

Ella pulled on the doorknob and it popped off. She stared at it in horror.

"Did you just pull the handle off?" Zac asked in horror.

"Yes," she said, and then it was her turn to curse. There was no way out of the room. She was stuck there with Zac Davenport until someone came to get them out.

CHAPTER TWO

ZAC COULDN'T BELIEVE he was staring at the doorknob in Ella's hand. He was still a bit in shock. It was bad enough that he'd had that momentary blip of PTSD in front of her. He just needed to put some distance between her and him, but now that really wasn't an option.

It's because you're working too hard.

He shook that thought away. Work was the only thing that helped. It kept the ghosts at bay. Saving lives helped him focus and forget. He was a trauma surgeon, that was his job, and that's all he needed to worry about. Of course it was hard to be a trauma surgeon locked in an on-call room.

"Give me that," he snapped, snatching the doorknob from her and trying to cram it back where it was supposed to be.

"Oh, my God, why didn't I think of that?" She slapped her forehead. "I forgot you had the ability to fuse metal."

Her sarcasm was grating on the last of his nerves.

"Dammit, Ella." He threw the doorknob down and scrubbed his hands over his face. This was not happening.

"It's not my fault."

She was right. It wasn't her fault that the doorknob was defective. She'd made it clear that she wanted to leave the room just as much as he did. And he shouldn't be angry at her, he should be angry at himself.

If he hadn't run after her he wouldn't be in this mess.

If the power hadn't gone out, he wouldn't be in this mess and if that tray of instruments hadn't been knocked over... Just the thought of the metal hitting the polished floor, the clattering against the walls made his pulse kick it up a notch.

Get a hold on yourself.

He didn't want to have another attack here now, locked in a room with her.

Although Ella wasn't stupid. She'd probably figured out that what had happened had been a PTSD attack.

No one in his family knew about it, except Charles, who knew that Zac had been cleared for work. Of course, it rarely made an appearance. He kept it in check.

But even Charles didn't know the exact reasons he'd left the navy and had accepted his honorable discharge. No one needed to know. He'd tried to stay in Annapolis and work there, but working on injured veterans had brought back the horror of his last tour of duty all too well.

And just thinking about it, the screams from last Christmas filled his head.

"I need to sit down." He pushed past Ella in the small on-call room and sat down.

Why did he have to be locked in an on-call room with her right now?

The one woman he'd never really been able to resist. The one woman who his family had been trying to marry him off to since he'd been a young man. He didn't want to ever get married. Adventure had been his goal and family just tied you down, stopped you from living your life. On his own he could do whatever he wanted.

Life was too fragile. Lives could be cut short in the blink of an eye and after what had happened with his parents, with his father cheating on his mother, yeah, mar-

riage was something he'd never wanted. Settling down had never been on his agenda.

Ever.

For so many years he'd tried to keep Ella Lockwood at arm's length, but that summer before they'd both headed off to medical school, they'd connected.

Ella had been so much more than the awkward society princess he'd thought she was. She had been curvy, clumsy and her self-esteem had been shaky, but there had been something about her that had drawn him to her.

And he'd known from past experience he had a hard time resisting her.

Though he'd tried. He'd been going off to Annapolis. He hadn't wanted to be tied down because he'd had these childhood feelings for Ella Lockwood.

Then that Christmas at her parents' home in the Hamptons, right before he was going back, they kissed and he knew he had to walk away from her or there would be no turning back. She fired his blood and it frightened him, the hold she'd had on him. That she still had on him.

After that night he didn't see her again. Not even at the party her parents threw the next day. She just vanished without saying goodbye. It stung, but it was for the best. He couldn't offer her anything, although he never forgot her.

He hadn't seen her in so long.

When he'd learned she was a senior surgeon in the ER at Manhattan Mercy, he'd been shocked. He had been naive to think that the years apart would have calmed his reaction to her. After the horrors of war, he had been certain that she'd have no effect.

He'd been wrong.

So wrong. There was a fire in her, a drive he admired, but she was still off limits. Every woman was. He didn't want a relationship ever. He'd come home to make amends

with his family, but that was it. His stance on marriage hadn't changed.

Zac stood up and pulled off his white lab coat, tossing it on the bed.

"What're you doing?" Ella asked.

"Push-ups," he muttered as he dropped to the floor and began to do push-ups. Exercise and hard work was how he forced his nightmares away. It's also how he dealt with sexual frustration.

Despite the friction between them at work, when he'd seen Ella at Charles's wedding, he'd wanted to kiss her again. To take it further, like he'd wanted to do before he'd left.

But she'd blown him off.

She'd avoided him since he'd arrived and he didn't know why. It had frustrated him. Just like having a breakdown in front of her had.

Most of his family didn't even know about his PTSD, and he certainly didn't want Ella Lockwood to know about it.

He had to put it out of his mind. Talking about what had happened wouldn't do him any good.

"I'll call for a janitor." She pulled out her cellphone.

He stopped his push-ups and sat on the floor. "You have the janitor's number on your cell?"

"There are messes in the ER that sometimes need a janitor's touch stat," she said as she pushed the contact on her phone.

Zac rolled his eyes. "Of course, what was I thinking?"

Ella shook her head. "Hello? It's Dr. Lockwood. Dr. Davenport and I are stuck in an on-call room in the ER. On-call room four at the end of the hall. The doorknob came off. Right. Okay, but...yeah. Okay." She ended the call.

"Well?"

"They're trying to get the power back on. The new generators failed and it's imperative they get the power back on before the battery backups on critical machines fail."

"Of course." He understood, but he really didn't want to start off his shift like this. It was bad enough that he hardly ever slept anyway, but sitting still in a locked room with Ella would exhaust him more.

When he was busy he was able to chase away the demons from his tour of duty and keep the exhaustion at bay. The only thing that calmed him down was saving lives. In the operating room he was in control of everything.

Here he had no control.

Ella sank down on the bed. "At least there are very capable residents on the trauma floor in case something happens. I hate it when the ER is quiet."

Zac nodded. "I'm sure you've trained them well."

"Merry Christmas," she said, then chuckled half-heartedly.

"Yeah, for sure."

"I'm surprised you're on rotation tonight. Doesn't your family go all out for Christmas, like mine?" she asked.

"Yeah, but I haven't been to a Christmas in a long time, and since I'm new to Manhattan Mercy I told Charles that I would work. Pay my dues. I don't want others to think that because I'm a Davenport I get all these perks."

"Really?"

"You seemed surprised by that."

"I am," she said, and sat cross-legged on the bed.

"Why?" he asked. "You know me."

Ella stared at him, but it was hard to read her expression. "I did, but it's been years since I've seen you. You could've changed. I mean, we've all changed."

"Yeah," he said. He'd changed. He was numb and though he survived his last tour of duty he felt like his soul was dead.

He was cold inside. In pain.

"I haven't changed that much, Ella."

Liar.

"Then I'm sorry. It's just…given your name I assumed you got a free ride."

"No, to Charles my name means nothing. I had to interview for a position and he expects me to work hard. I didn't just get this position handed to me. And if I hadn't got a position here I would've gone to another hospital."

"I'm sorry."

"Apology accepted." Zac scrubbed a hand over his face.

"Well, since you've been in the service for so long I thought you'd be with your family instead of working."

"It's more important Charles is off for his boys. I don't have kids or anything to tie me down."

"True," she said.

"How about you? Your parents usually have a big do as well. I know because our mothers competed slightly to get guests to attend."

Ella smiled at him then, a deep dimple on her cheek that just made her smile all that more irresistible, and her blue eyes twinkled in the dim light from the emergency lighting in the room.

"I forgot about that," she said wistfully.

"What? The party or the fact that our mothers compete?"

"Competition obviously. I'm painfully aware of my mother's Christmas party." She shuddered for good measure and he laughed.

He missed these easy talks they'd had. And that thought scared him. How she drew him in. It's what their parents had wanted since they were young. He'd always balked at the idea and resented that Ella had been constantly pushed on him, but there was a part of him that wanted her.

He still wanted her, even after all this time.

When he'd stolen that kiss from her, he'd wanted more. He remembered that kiss clearly, touching her face, the taste of her lips and the sound of the small sigh that had escaped her lips when they'd parted.

Her cheeks had been flushed pink and those blue eyes had dilated with desire.

In that moment he'd wanted more, but her sister had walked in and Ella had run away.

And then he hadn't seen her at the Christmas party, hadn't seen her before he'd left to go back to Annapolis, which he'd thought was for the best. Only he could never get that kiss out of his head. It was the only kiss he'd never forgotten.

Ella was the one who'd got away.

But he couldn't have her. He didn't want to tie her to a broken shell of a man. Didn't want to marry any one ever. He didn't want family. He didn't want to risk his heart to have it destroyed. With love came pain and as he'd served tours of duty he'd seen a lot of pain and suffering. The idea of losing someone he loved that much scared him to his core, because he saw the pain when a parent buried a child.

When a husband buried a wife.

The pain and loss of life.

And he'd experienced it. He'd been too close to it. His heart began to race.

"So, why are you working tonight?" he asked, trying to steer his thoughts away from the painful trajectory they were taking.

"I wasn't supposed to be working tonight. The storm hit and I'm stuck here." There was a hint of happiness in her voice and he couldn't help but laugh at that.

"You sound relieved," he said.

"I am! You know how my mother's parties go. We all dress up in…" Her voice trailed off and she cleared her throat. "They're a dreadful bore."

Zac thought she was going to talk about the terrible dresses that Mrs. Lockwood seemed to like to force her children to wear. The dresses that Ella had worn when she'd been a teenager had never been flattering and he knew that she'd been the butt of many jokes.

She'd been short and had had baby fat. Of course, he'd never noticed the dress. Only the woman. The girl he'd kissed, his best friend.

That baby fat had transformed into luscious curves and as he studied her sitting on the cot he couldn't help but let his mind wander to what was under those dark blue scrubs that she wore.

Oh, God.

"Well, if it's any consolation I think that your mother's parties were a touch more popular than my mother's parties ever were."

She cocked a finely arched blonde brow. "How so?"

"Your mother's parties were never filled with barely controlled hatred between your parents. Passive aggressive digs at infidelity. Pinched and forced smiles. Awkward."

Ella chuckled. "Oh, the polite fight, you mean? And they weren't always. Before…"

"You mean before it came out my father had an affair and a secret love child?"

Ella blushed. "Yes, before that. Before Miranda. Your parents were happy."

Zac sighed. Yeah there had been a time his parents had been happy, but it was hard to remember the way things used to be. And he wouldn't trade Miranda for anything, but trust had been shattered after that and the family dynamic had changed.

And Zac had lost respect for his father and become ever more determined to forge his own way in this world.

"True, before that came to light they were happy."

"My parents aren't perfect. There have been many of those polite fights. 'Henry, dear, perhaps you shouldn't wear that color to the dinner, it clashes with the carpet.' 'Sylvia, dearest, what I'm wearing is fine, it's all that plastic surgery affecting your eyesight.'"

They both laughed at that.

"How are our mothers friends again?" Zac teased.

"It's called frenemies, I believe. They're frenemies."

"That's it." Then he yawned.

"Tired?"

"I didn't sleep well last night," he said.

"You've been working hard since you came on board," she said.

"Look who's talking."

"True, still you really do look beat."

"I'm fine," he said. "Though you just came off a long shift. I really shouldn't be complaining."

Ella scooted over. "Come on, the floor can't be comfortable. At least you can be slightly comfortable as we wait for our rescue."

Ella didn't know what she was doing. She should just leave him on the floor, but he was suffering.

A part of her was glad that he was, but it was small. It was just that vindictive part that she had. The bitter part that still remembered the humiliation he'd doled out to her.

"When are you going to pop the question to Ella Lockwood, Davenport?"

"Pop the question?" Zac asked.

"Yeah, you hang out a lot with her."

"She's going to medical school. We have that in common," Zac said dryly.

"Come on, Davenport, it must be more than that!"

Zac laughed. "I have no interest in ever marrying a pampered society princess."

Ella shook that internal dialogue out of her head. It was dialogue that had always eaten away at her. For years and years. It was her own personal demon she had to fight. Zac had utterly humiliated her in that moment.

After that stolen kiss she'd wanted more from him, but he'd broken her heart. Still, his dismissal of her had caused an awakening.

That night she'd discarded the clothing her mother had picked for her and had done her hair and makeup to her liking and not her mother's. She mostly preferred to go without makeup and forgo the hideous designer dresses. For the first time in her life she'd felt like the person she'd always been hiding.

The person she'd been afraid to show.

His dismissal of her had given her the drive to excel. To prove to him and the rest of the world she was more than a pampered society princess.

To be more than the world her parents moved in, expected of her. She hadn't wanted to be a society wife and mother.

She was going to be the best surgeon she could be. She was going to be respected. Opening yourself up to people just put your emotions, your heart at risk. So she kept herself safe by putting others at a distance.

Under the blonde, curvy, short stature she was a force to be reckoned with when it came to her residents.

When Ella Lockwood told you to move out of the way, you moved out of the way.

Still, another part she'd buried long ago wanted to be a wife and a mother. To have a family, friends. She was lonely, even if she didn't want to admit it. The problem was she just didn't see that happening any time soon.

Now, with Zac's return, there was a shift in her confidence and she didn't like it much. She'd promised herself that she would keep him at a distance. Give him the cold shoulder and let him know that she didn't give a damn about him.

Of course, that was rather hard to do when she'd seen him in an instant so vulnerable and broken.

When she'd seen that weaker side to him. When she'd seen the side of him she'd thought existed all those years ago, until he'd cruelly dismissed her.

They didn't say anything, but she could see the exhaustion etched on his face. And as they sat there in the darkness, with only one dim emergency light in the room, Zac fell asleep. Then he shifted and laid his head in her lap.

Wake him up.

Only she couldn't make herself do it. There had been so many times that summer when they'd connected where they'd been studying and he'd drifted off like this. Where they'd passed out together.

When they had been children, they had been nap buddies. Ella's nanny would place them in the nursery, her in her bed and him on the floor in a trundle bed. In the darkness, while their parents had had parties downstairs, when the raucous laughter of the adults would wake her up and frighten her, Zac would always wake up and climb into her bed.

Suddenly, she was tired.

Her shift had started at five in the evening yesterday and now it was seven in the morning. She should be at home, sleeping, before she was forced to go to her mother's that night.

Of course, the storm had stopped all that.

Since they were stuck, she shifted slightly and curled

up beside Zac. Just like they had done so many times years ago.

It was comforting. She'd forgotten how comforting it was.

This is dangerous.

And that was her last logical thought before she drifted off into her own fitful slumber.

CHAPTER THREE

"GET OUT OF HERE, JERK!"

Zac woke with a start, disoriented, but he was painfully aware there was a soft body pressed against his. And as his eyes adjusted to the light he could see that it was Ella, curled up against him. She was lying half on her side and half on her back. Her wavy blonde hair was spread out on the pillow. Long eyelashes brushed against her pink, round cheeks and those pink lips moved as she murmured utter nonsense in her sleep.

And he couldn't help but smile. He'd forgotten that she tended to be very vocal when she slept.

She'd talked in her sleep a lot. There had been one time, after studying for anatomy, when they had both fallen asleep on the couch and she'd shouted out something about dissecting elves with pizza. He'd cared about her so much back then.

What about now?

"Zac," she whispered, his hands still on her face, their lips mere inches from each other's. Her breathing was heavy, just as his was.

"Shh," he whispered. "Just breathe."

And he brought her lips to his again. It felt so right. It burned his soul and he wanted more.

His blood heated, because he remembered what it was like to kiss her.

Her body shifted and she tossed a leg over him and moaned sweetly in her sleep.

Oh, God.

He closed his eyes and tried to get control.

"You idiot," she murmured.

He laughed quietly to himself and then gently shook her. "Ella, you're dreaming. Wake up."

She curled up closer to him.

He took a deep breath, because her curling up closer to him made his blood heat even more. He had to extract himself from this situation.

"Ella," he whispered, leaning over her.

Her eyes opened. "Zac?"

"Yeah."

She smiled at him dreamily.

Then before he could stop himself he reached out to touch her cheek, her silky cheek. And he kissed her, his lips locking with hers as he pulled her to him, and any kind of control that he had on resisting her crumbled away as he tasted those plump, pink lips again.

It had been so long. He ran his hand down her body, over her curves, recalling how it felt when he took her in his arms and how much he burned for her. How much he wanted her.

Even after all this time, he still wanted her. Any other women he'd known had failed to compare to Ella.

She was in his blood.

Suddenly she pushed him away and her blue eyes were wide. "I don't think this is very smart, do you?"

"Sorry," he said. "Sorry, I... Yeah, there was no excuse for that."

"I'll say! Still, I didn't exactly discourage it. So I'm sorry too."

"No, nothing to be sorry about." He sat up and tried to hide evidence of his arousal by getting off the bed and grabbing his lab coat. "I don't know what I was thinking but that's no excuse. I'm sorry that happened. Exhaustion."

"Or your post-traumatic stress disorder," she said, trying to straighten her hair.

"What?" he snapped, taken off guard. "I don't have post-traumatic stress disorder."

"Oh, come on, Zac. You're not sleeping, you're jumpy…"

"I'm trying to get back into routine." He sighed. "I was cleared by the Annapolis psychiatrists. I disclosed that I'd had PTSD to Charles in my interview, *had* being the operative word."

"Okay," she said, but didn't sound very sure.

"I'm clear, Ella."

Just as she opened her mouth to say something further, the door rattled and then opened. A maintenance man poked his head into the room.

"Sorry, Dr. Lockwood. We got here as fast as we could. We had to get the generators up and running to the essential parts of the hospital."

"It's okay. How long have we been in here?" she asked groggily, not looking at him.

"Only an hour."

"Good." Ella got up and then ran her hands over her scrubs. "I'd better check the trauma floor."

Zac wanted to call after her as she hurried away, but he had to get control of himself.

The maintenance man was ignoring him as he picked up the broken doorknob and scratched his head. "Don't know if I can fix this. It's Christmas Eve and storming— might be hard to get a part in, Dr. Davenport."

"Close down this room, then, Miles," Zac said, reading the man's name tag. "We can't have any more staff locked in here. We're running with a skeleton crew as it is."

"I can take the door off, Dr. Davenport—that way staff can still rest," Miles offered, clearly wanting to hash this out with Zac as he was the only Davenport on shift tonight. "And sorry about the brownout. This new system is having some hiccups tonight, what with the storm and issues with the city's power grid."

"It's okay and the door idea sounds good," Zac said quickly, trying to end the conversation he didn't want to get sucked into. He wasn't Charles or even his father.

He didn't want to make these decisions for the hospital. All he wanted to do was save lives. He would leave the administration stuff to Charles or his father.

Of course, he was the only Davenport on duty and he'd left his brother and father in the lurch for a long time while he'd been on tours of duty. He hadn't come home for many years.

He owed it to them.

Especially to Charles, who'd shouldered so much on his own.

Zac needed to step it up now. He couldn't be so selfish.

"Okay, Dr. Davenport, and about the generators…"

"You do what you think is best, Miles, and I'll approve it, but I have to get back to the trauma floor."

Miles nodded. "Will do, Dr. Davenport."

Zac left the on-call room and searched for any sign of Ella, but she'd vanished.

He wanted to talk to her about what had happened. To apologize again for kissing her. He didn't want to lead her on. He didn't want her to think that there was something there when there couldn't be.

His pager went off.

Incoming trauma.

Right now he didn't really have time to think about Ella or what had happened between them. The storm was start-

ing to take its toll and while the storm raged, they would have a long day ahead of them.

He ran toward the emergency room.

Ella was in the fray, pulling on her disposable yellow trauma gown and gloves. Her blonde hair, which had been loose in the on-call room, was now drawn back in a tight bun. In the emergency room confidence radiated from Ella. In the thick of chaos she commanded respect. Though she was short and might be swallowed whole, she was a giant when it came to her patients.

Dr. Lockwood commanded her trauma team and brooked no fear.

And no one questioned her right to be there.

She barely glanced at him as she tossed him a gown before heading outside to wait in the snow, where a couple of interns were helping the maintenance man clear a path from the freshly plowed drive to the ER doors of the ambulance bay.

In the ambulance bay, it was slightly protected from the elements, but the wind was biting. The snow wasn't as dense, but it still blew in blasts under the protective cement covering.

Ella stood beside him, her teeth chattering as they waited in silence with a couple of residents Then over the howl of the storm and wind they heard the faint siren of the ambulance as it approached.

His pulse began to thunder and even though it was bitterly cold, he could feel the sweat on his brow. The howl of the wind and the screech of the siren melted away and he could hear the sound of missiles. Screams.

He shook those thoughts away. Once he was back in the grind of trauma triaging he'd be okay.

"Zac!" Ella shouted, shaking him. "Look alive!"

"Right."

Ella looked unsure. "Are you sure you're going to be okay?"

"I said I was fine. I'm tired, but I've got this. I can handle this," Zac snapped as the ambulance pulled up, stopping in front of them. He jumped forward and tried to put Ella out of his mind.

Which was easier said than done.

Ella glanced at Zac across the turmoil of the emergency room. He was working on the passenger of the motor vehicle accident, while she was working on the driver. The car had spun out and the car had gone into a cement median, ejecting the passenger through the windshield.

It was a mess.

She'd been worried when Zac, once again, had seemed to zone out when the ambulance had been approaching. Like the noise of the storm, the cold and the ambulance itself had been too much of a sensory overload.

She'd studied post-traumatic stress disorder in medical school. Zac was a textbook case, but he stated he had been cleared.

He'd said he had control of his post-traumatic stress disorder.

She needed to know whether she had to pull him or not. Even though he was a Davenport and his brother Charles was in charge of the emergency room, she was still the most senior attending on duty at the moment.

Right here and now, this was her ER and she couldn't jeopardize her patients or her staff.

Her patient moaned as she palpated his abdomen. He'd said that he was fine and that it was just his arm that was banged up, but the reaction to her palpation had her nervous about something more sinister beneath the surface.

"Mr. Jones, I'm going to just look at your abdomen."

"It's fine," he said through pants and there was some-

thing about him, his movements that threw her off. It reminded her of a person going through drug withdrawal and she couldn't help but wonder if he was an addict. Then she saw his arms. His veins and also his teeth were a mess.

Definitely a user. The labs would confirm it, but she had her suspicions.

I seriously doubt that you're fine.

"I'm going to have a look all the same."

She lifted his shirt and could see the dark discoloration of a bruise across his abdomen. As she palpated again, the belly was not tender but hard. There were no broken bones or bruises on his chest, so she had to assume that the steering wheel had not struck him.

Still, given the fact she suspected that he was a crystal meth user, she had to check to make sure that there was no tear in the aorta, which could result in an aortic dissection. Since he hadn't died at the scene, she had to assume that the aorta was stable, but she was going to check it anyway.

"We need to get him a CT scan, stat, as well as an arteriogram," Ella said to her resident. "Draw the standard labs and get the images done. Page me when you have the images and the lab findings."

"Yes, Dr. Lockwood," Dr. Lynne said, nodding quickly.

Ella headed over to the exam room where the passenger who had been ejected was not doing so well.

Zac had inserted a breathing tube and there was already another tube in her chest to drain away the fluids from a pneumothorax.

Ella stood back to watch. Zac wasn't aware of her presence, but she really had nothing to fear about his momentary blip outside. He was completely in control of his exam room as he worked on the patient.

She moved from the exam room and went to check on some other patients while she waited for the images of the driver.

Those who were still in the emergency room were not many and weren't as urgent as blunt force trauma, but they still needed to be seen. And she seriously doubted that they would be leaving any time soon with this storm.

First she dealt with a patient who was having a severe gall bladder attack. She had the labs drawn to check the liver panels and see if the gall bladder attack warranted emergency surgery or if they could wait.

Then there was a bad sprain and a bump on the head to check out.

Dr. Lynne returned and handed over the tablet with the images. "Here you are, Dr. Lockwood."

The images showed internal bleeding from a ruptured spleen and the lab work revealed that the patient was indeed a crystal meth user. "We need to get him into the OR. I believe that OR One was prepped and ready to go."

Dr. Lynne shook her head. "Dr. Davenport is in there with the passenger. The pneumothorax was extensive and there are no cardiothoracic surgeons at the hospital because of the storm."

Dammit.

"Okay, well, prep OR Two, then. We need to get Mr. Jones in there before he bleeds out. Hang some blood to compensate for the loss while we prep."

"Yes, Dr. Lockwood." Dr. Lynne took back the tablet and left.

Ella felt exhaustion setting in as she glanced around the chaotic ER floor.

Dr. Lynne was her most capable resident and though she'd like to have her in the OR with her, Ella needed her on the ER floor while both the trauma surgeons who were still at Manhattan Mercy worked on patients.

Dr. Lynne would be able to run her ER while she went into surgery.

It was going to be a long day. And the longer this storm

went on, the worse the casualties were going to get. There would be more accidents, more emergencies.

And she was going to be stuck here with Zac, working with him, but all she could think about was the kiss in the on-call room and that was a dangerous path to tread. One she'd promised herself she'd never walk again.

She had to get it together.

She needed more coffee.

A lot more coffee.

CHAPTER FOUR

BY THE TIME Ella finished the splenectomy it felt like she'd run a marathon. Her whole body ached. She was tired, but she had no time to stop as she leaned over the scrub-room sink and rubbed her neck, trying to stretch herself.

Her feet were aching.

She had to stand on a stool to operate. Operating Room Two's table didn't go down low enough for her and Mr. Jones was a tall man. Taller than her. Her feet and her were not friends at the moment. They were screaming at her in protest for still working. When she went off she planned to get a good massage.

"You look tired," Zac said as she leaned against the scrub-room door.

"You're done?" she asked. Then he frowned and her stomach sank and she understood why he was done. "That bad."

He nodded. "Even if a cardiothoracic surgeon had been available, there was just too much damage. She wasn't wearing a seatbelt, the paramedics told me, and her blood was filled with crystal meth. Her tissue was so friable that sutures wouldn't hold."

Ella sighed. "Mr. Jones is stable but in the ICU. Splenectomy, and also his labs showed the drug in his system."

Zac nodded. "I'll give him some time before I tell him about his wife."

Ella's heart hurt. This was the worst part of the job. Especially in light of the holiday. "I'll go with you."

"You don't need to, Ella. You're exhausted." There was concern on his face, as if he really cared about her, but she didn't need his pity.

"I know, but he's my patient and, it's not like I haven't delivered bad news before."

Zac nodded. "A sad reality to our job."

"Have you been down to the emergency room?" she asked as she stretched her back. "Do you know how it is?"

"The same as it was before."

Ella *tsk*ed under her breath. "The calm before the storm."

"Except it's storming now." He gave her a half-hearted smile at his pathetic joke and she couldn't help but chuckle. "At least Charles's new generator system is holding."

"That's something." And she tried not to think of the chaos caused a couple of months ago, the last time the power had gone out.

"Want to go get some coffee before the fray?" Zac asked.

Ella nodded. "Yes."

They walked side by side, not touching and not saying a word as they headed to the staffroom where they'd had their first run-in at the beginning of this crazy shift.

"Look, about that kiss…" He cleared his throat. "I'm sorry. I really didn't mean that to happen. Just exhaustion. As you know, I haven't been really sleeping."

"Traumatic experiences can do that. I'm sorry your last tour was so hard."

"It wasn't," he snapped. "I wish you'd let it go."

"Zac, you had a near meltdown when those lights when out and then at Charles's wedding…"

"What about Charles's wedding?"

"The corks popping? You ducked under the table," she said.

"I dropped my napkin. I don't recall corks popping." He laughed. "It's absurd to think I'd hide from something like that. Really."

"And the lights-going-out thing?"

"A momentary lapse. I have it under control. Just like the kiss. It was a lapse and it won't happen again."

Her cheeks heated in embarrassment. It stung that he was apologizing for something that had been wonderful, even if she hadn't wanted it to happen again.

Liar.

"It's okay. It was my fault. As for that not-sleeping thing, do you want to talk about it?"

"No, there's nothing to discuss," he said matter-of-factly. "I had a bit of insomnia, trying to get into the routine of working at Manhattan Mercy and living in New York again and not on a naval base or on a ship."

"I bet that's quite an adjustment," she said, pushing him, and when he frowned at her, his eyes narrowing, she realized that perhaps she shouldn't push him too far. Although there had been a time when they'd been younger when she and Zac had shared a lot.

This closed-off attitude…this wasn't like Zac.

How do you know? You didn't think Zac could hurt you like he did, but he did. He humiliated you. You don't know him.

"It is."

"Okay, but I'm here if you ever need to talk."

"Thanks." There was no sincerity in that remark. He wasn't grateful, his tone was annoyed. And she knew there would be no discussion. Zac had thrown up a wall.

Even when they'd been young, there had been a wall. He'd hidden his emotions well. He'd played with a poker

face, which was why she'd been duped all those years ago. For a brief moment she'd seen past the rebel and she'd got to see a glimmer of what she thought was the real Zac Davenport, the one she'd known before he'd become a teenager and a man, but after he'd humiliated her, she hadn't known what to believe.

She didn't trust him.

And she was having a hard time trusting him and his surgical abilities right now.

What if something else set him off?

Another loud noise?

He says he's cleared.

Still, she knew what she'd seen at Charles's wedding.

But she really had no proof so she could pull him.

The staffroom was thankfully empty and she poured herself a cup of tepid coffee and dumped a lot of sugar into it. It was probably more than was good for her, but she needed the boost. She sank down in the same chair she had been in earlier.

"Well, at least there's no nurses lying in wait with plastic mistletoe like this morning," he joked.

"They're two emergency room nurses. Do you even remember their names?" she challenged.

"Uh, no..."

She shook her head. "You should get to know your staff better."

He crossed his arms. "Oh, and what're their names, then? Do you remember?"

Damn.

She always referred to them in her head as gold-digger one and two.

"Carol and..."

Zac grinned smugly. "You don't know. Now who's distancing who? You should really know your staff better."

"I don't distance myself from anyone."

"Yeah, right. Those interns are terrified of you. You're so formal. There's a wall up around you, Dr. Lockwood."

You're one to talk about walls.

But she kept that thought to herself.

"I could easily page them and they'd be here in a flash," she teased, changing the subject.

"No, thanks," he said, and he sat down with a sigh, craning his neck to watch the snow still swirling and blowing outside. "Want to make a bet?"

"What?"

"Remember when we were younger we'd make bets? Like how long would it take for Charles to notice how many spitballs I could launch at the back of his head or who could outrun my brother Elijah after we prank-called his girlfriend?"

Ella chuckled. "Right, and we'd wager things like candy and stuff. I don't have any candy."

"How about a dare?"

She cocked her eyebrow. "Seriously? A dare? What're you, like twelve?"

"You're not chicken, are you?" Those blue eyes twinkled.

"No, but I am a professional and I have a reputation to uphold."

Zac snorted. "Oh, yeah, I heard about that reputation. The bulldog, I believe it was referred to as."

"Bulldog?" Her voice rose an octave and then she cleared her throat, annoyed by her nickname. "I'm hardly a bulldog."

"It has nothing to do with appearance. Well, other than your height and the fact that you charge through. Tough."

"Fine. I like that better."

"You do have a lot more gumption than you did when you were younger. It's refreshing." He was giving her a

compliment, but it embarrassed her instead. There was a reason she kept people at a distance and it was Zac's fault.

It was easier than letting people in.

It was because of the way he'd humiliated her, crushed her hopes. The way he'd brushed her aside so easily that had made her work hard to overcome her debilitating shyness and stick up for herself. In a way she should thank him.

Still, the hurt was still raw, because Zac had been the one person she'd thought would never hurt her. She'd thought they were friends. And then more than friends.

"Medical school was tough. You don't become a surgeon by hiding in the corner."

"I never understood why you hid in a corner," he said.

Don't you?

"It's hard to have a voice with a domineering mother." She cleared her throat and changed the subject, didn't want to talk about the way she had been. She was no longer that shy little girl in the frumpy clothes. The girl who was never comfortable in her own skin. The girl who was unpopular and shy. "So what did you want to bet on?"

"Snowfall. How many inches do you think?"

Ella snorted. "That's a pretty pathetic bet."

"What?" he asked, mildly outraged. "Why?"

"If we're going to wager dares then you have to make the bet more interesting."

"Like what?" he asked, leaning forward, those blue eyes and that devious smile making her heart skip a beat.

She drew a total blank. She had to think of something, but a resident knocked on the door.

"Excuse me, Dr. Lockwood?"

"Now's your chance to prove you're not so formal," Zac whispered, but she ignored him.

Ella looked up. "Yes, Dr.— Yes, Ryan?"

The resident looked shocked. "Uh, Dr. Lockwood…"

"You can call me Ella when no one is around."

Ryan the resident didn't look convinced. "I have the liver enzyme panel of the patient complaining about chronic cholecystitis." Dr. Trace handed Ella the tablet.

Zac leaned over her and whispered, "Was that so hard?"

"Shut up," Ella mumbled, as she took the tablet.

"Pardon, Dr.—Ella?" Ryan asked nervously.

"Nothing."

Ella frowned when she saw the high number of enzymes in the blood panel. It meant the liver was working too hard and soon it could cause inflammation to the pancreas known as pancreatitis, which was a worse infection than cholecystitis. And if there was a stone, fragments could break off a gallstone, blocking the bile duct or in very rare cases causing the gall bladder to rupture.

"Take the patient down for a CT scan. I need to know if there are stones blocking the bile duct. If the bile duct is clear, prep the patient for an emergency cholecystectomy by starting them on a course of antibiotics."

"And if there are stones in the bile duct?" Dr. Trace asked.

"I don't suppose Dr. So is in?" Ella asked hopefully.

"No, Dr. So is stuck in Boston."

Dammit.

Ella could perform an emergency cholecystectomy as long as the bile duct was clear. If there were stones in the bile duct, the only way to remove them without doing an open laparotomy was to do an endoscopic retrograde cholangio-pancreatography or ERCP. An ERCP was a delicate procedure only done by trained surgeons, involving cutting into the sphincter of Oodi and sending a small instrument up the bile duct to crush or retrieve the stones.

Even then the ERCP came with complications and they weren't always successful.

"Then we monitor the patient, give them morphine until Dr. So can return."

"If the patient needs an ERCP, I can do one," Zac said suddenly.

Ella was shocked. "You can do an ERCP? That's a highly skilled endoscopic procedure."

Zac nodded. "I know, but I was trained in a lot of different procedures when I was studying at Annapolis. I did a stint on a medical ship and since the particular medical frigate I was on couldn't carry as many staff as a hospital that had specialists, surgeons on these ships were prepared for a lot of things. I can also do a crash C-section if need be."

Ella was impressed and even Dr. Trace was looking at Zac with a gaze of admiration.

"Okay, Ryan, well, you heard Zac. Get the patient started on a round of IV antibiotics and down to CT."

"Yes, Ella." Dr. Trace took back the tablet and left the staff room.

"I'm impressed, Davenport. You really are a jack-of-all-trades."

"Yeah, well, being on duty taught me a lot of things." His expression changed and his brow furrowed, worry lines deepening, and he crushed the empty plastic cup in his hand.

What happened over there?

"I'm going to finish my rounds," he said, standing up. "I know you're here, but I'm officially on duty and I do have some rounds to attend to."

Ella nodded. "Good. Once I hear about the patient I'll have you paged, but if the bile duct is clear I can handle a laparoscopic cholecystectomy on my own."

Zac didn't look her in the eye. "Okay."

That was all he said as he disappeared from the staff-room. The jovial, fun conversation was over and he was

distant again. The wall was up and she wasn't sure she should even bother trying to climb it.

Zac would never change.

And she was foolish to think he ever would.

"That is a nasty third-degree burn you have there. How did you get it?" Zac asked as he examined a patient's forearm.

"Deep-frying the turkey." The man winced. "Only my brother's apartment in SoHo couldn't really handle my deep-frying. We shorted the fuse and then the fat tipped over. I caught the turkey, though."

Zac raised an eyebrow. "Deep-frying a turkey is a thing?"

"Oh, yeah," the patient said. "I always deep-fry the turkey. Granted, my wife makes me do it outside, and we have way more property in Nashville, but my brother and his fiancée insisted we spend Christmas in Manhattan in a cramped apartment that they pay a ridiculous amount for."

"Yes, that is true. Small apartments and large rents." The burn would need to be debrided. There was a plastic surgeon resident at the hospital. The least he could do for this poor man was have his burn properly taken care of. "I'm going to page one of our plastic surgeons on call to help clean up the burn and then wrap it. Do you have a way home in this storm?"

"The cabbie could only get me so far and then I hiked in the rest of the way," the patient said.

Zac nodded. "Well, you can stay here until the storm lets up and they clear the streets. If you're not from New York you could get really turned around in this storm."

"Thanks, Doc. I appreciate it."

Zac turned to one of the nurses who had kissed him under that horrible fake mistletoe, but he couldn't remember her name for the life of him. He'd berated Ella for not knowing or calling the residents by their first names and

now he couldn't remember this nurse's name. So instead he plastered on one of those flirtatious Davenport smiles that he used to be famous for. "Nurse, can you page Dr. Onge to assist this patient?"

The smile worked and the nurse didn't seem upset that he didn't know her name.

"Of course, Dr. Davenport."

"Thanks."

He left the exam room as quickly as he could. He knew that women like that nurse were only interested in him because of his money, his name and his outward appearance. If they knew what a mess he was inside, they probably wouldn't touch him with a thirty-foot pole.

Yes, they would. You said it yourself: money and prestige.

Prestige and the name. That's all people saw in him, which was why he had been so adamant to head to Annapolis and get his medical training there, instead of at an Ivy league college. He had seen what marrying for money and prestige did to people in his parents' circle.

His parents had seemed so happy, but obviously that wasn't true. Even though he and his father hadn't seen eye to eye on many things, it had shattered his whole world when it had come out that Hugo had had an affair. He couldn't take it and instead of staying around for any of the fallout, the navy had been an escape for him. The navy had been his salvation, until that changed, and all he'd wanted was to be back in the safety of his family. Even though he hadn't thought he deserved it.

Zac loved his family, which was why he'd come back to the fold. After moving through natural disasters and war zones, he'd understood the fragility of life all too well. How precious life was, but he still hadn't wanted to have anything to do with any woman.

Except Ella.

Ella had been the only woman who had got to him, but she deserved so much better than he could give. He had nothing to give.

You're afraid, that's why.

He wanted her more than anything and that kiss in the on-call room had reminded him just how powerful her hold was on him, but he couldn't have that.

There were no more emotions left in him.

Only nightmares. He felt numb.

And as he stood at the unit desk in the ER, charting, reality melted away and all he could see was the edge of a jungle, the explosions from an air raid, screams and crumbling buildings.

And then the child.

The child was cradled in his arms while the mother screamed out her grief. She was a local who was a nurse and had come to help. The child was well loved around the base. His name had been Rojas.

The child was dead. And the horror of it all...

He'd tried to save that little boy, but had failed. There was nothing he could've done. Logically he knew that, but in his mind he relieved that moment again and again.

Heard Consuela's screams.

His own body was racked with grief as he held a child, broken, lifeless, who he had spent off time with, playing soccer and helping to do schoolwork.

Gone.

A life cut too short.

"Stay with me, Zac. I'm scared."

"I'm here, buddy."

Get a grip on yourself. You're not there.

Zac knew he had to get better control of this. He couldn't let anyone see him struggling. He'd told Charles he was fine. He'd convinced the Annapolis counsellors

that he was fine. The post-traumatic stress disorder didn't control him. He was still a surgeon above all else.

Maybe it was stupid, but he could work through this himself.

Sure you can. Which is why you hardly sleep.

Zac hurried through his charting and then headed down an empty hallway, where he began to jog the length of it.

The one advantage to the snowstorm was that there was hardly any staff around. No one would question him. No one would notice him down this hallway, running back and forth through a glass walkway where outside the storm still howled, dumping snow on Manhattan.

Even if the storm stopped right at that moment it could take days to shovel out.

He wasn't sure that he could handle being holed up here for days with no escape. He needed some air. It had become harder to breathe. Zac paused and leaned against the glass, watching the snow swirling. There were times the wind kicked up and he couldn't even see the buildings that surrounded Manhattan Mercy.

It was like he was alone here.

Trapped.

Of course, that's the way he always felt. Trapped in his own nightmares. The guilt from not saving Rojas's life, for leaving his family behind and broken, ate away at him.

The sound of a door at the other end of the hallway snapped him out of his reverie and he glanced up to see Ella's possible cholecystectomy patient being wheeled up from CT by Dr. Trace.

"Well, Ryan, what's the verdict?" Zac asked as they came closer. The patient was still out of it. The pain meds they'd given her were doing their job.

"There is a stone in the common bile duct," Dr. Trace said. "The gall bladder is quite enlarged and the patient is running a fever."

Dammit. The patient was on the verge of a burst gall bladder or maybe a burst bile duct. It wasn't good.

"Inform Ella that I will be preforming an ERCP. Have the patient prepped for an endoscopic procedure in the endoscopy suite. Hopefully, all day surgery in the endoscopy suite has been cancelled today due to the weather and we can get our patient in."

"With Dr. So out of town there were no endoscopies scheduled for today. The endoscopy suite is probably not staffed."

Zac cursed under his breath. "Tell Ella that I will need her and you to assist me. Also an anesthesiologist to sedate the patient."

"Yes, Dr. Davenport." Dr. Trace continued to wheel the patient away.

"Don't call me Dr. Davenport—that's my father, my brother and one of my sisters."

Dr. Trace laughed. "Okay, Zac."

Zac scrubbed his hands over his face.

You can do this.

Although Charles wouldn't be happy that Zac was encroaching on Dr. So's department, but really what choice did they have? This was a dire situation.

This patient was getting worse. The bile duct had to be cleared and the gall bladder had to come out.

There was no choice.

He could save this life. He wouldn't let another person die if he could help it. He knew the ERCP was a dangerous procedure, but he knew how to do it.

Control it.

Zac closed his eyes and breathed deeply. That's when he saw Ella's face. She was smiling at him, in his thoughts. In his dreams. He'd missed her too during those years away. He'd missed her even if she hadn't missed him.

You are a good surgeon.
You've got this. You can save this life.
He had no choice.

CHAPTER FIVE

ELLA WASN'T BEST pleased that Zac was going to do an ERCP. The only surgeons who did ERCPs were ones who did them frequently and who were highly skilled.

Zac was a trauma surgeon.

He wasn't a specialist in endoscopic procedures. Only there wasn't a choice.

She bit her lip as she watched them prep her patient for an ERCP. The patient had still been out of it from the painkillers, but the patient's husband had been in the waiting room. She hadn't come alone to the emergency room when her gall bladder had flared up, so they had been able to obtain consent to do this procedure.

And Zac had been right in his instructions to Dr. Trace. When she'd seen the computer tomography scan she could see that they were running out of time. The gall bladder was engorged, full of stones and the patient was on the verge of pancreatitis.

Even if the ERCP was successful, the patient was still at a high risk for pancreatitis.

They had prepped the endoscopy suite to also do the laparoscopic cholecystectomy after the bile duct was clear.

Ella was just hoping that it could be done laparoscopically and that she wouldn't have to do a full laparotomy. Especially if the ERCP failed.

Zac said he could do it. Zac said he'd done it before. Trust him.

Only she couldn't convince herself at this moment to trust him. How could she trust him? The last time she had it had been disastrous.

For your heart. This is different, though. This is your medical reputation.

This was life or death.

Zac glanced up at her over his mask and he narrowed his eyes, glaring at her.

"Why are you staring at me, Dr. Lockwood?"

"I'm not staring," she said.

"I've got this," he said in a fierce voice that was cold, angry. He was warning her to lay off.

"Okay. You've got this." Only she made sure her tone conveyed the severity of the situation, and he picked up on it.

"Yes. I do," he said firmly. "You need to back away."

Dr. Lynne's eyes widened above her surgical mask and Ella's cheeks flamed. It had been a long time since anyone had spoken to her like that. If it had been any other person, if it had been a different situation, she would lay into the person for speaking to her like that.

Especially a new surgeon to the hospital. Davenport or not, she wasn't going to let him walk all over her and do whatever he wanted. On the other hand, sometimes her need to maintain her reputation meant she didn't always have the best rapport with other surgeons. Perhaps, in this case, it was best to just let it go. So she bit back her retort. She needed Zac to stay calm. She needed this to go off without a hitch.

If Zac was confident this could work, that he could do this, she had to let him try.

"Fine." She moved to the opposite side of the endos-

copy suite, waiting until she could get in there and repair the damage of a botched ERCP.

Have some more faith.

Only she was having a hard time trying to have faith in a man she no longer knew. A man who had never kept the faith with her.

She just held her breath as he guided the endoscope down the patient's throat. Ella kept her gaze fastened to the monitor, watching in a bit of disbelief and apprehension as Zac skillfully did what she'd seen Dr. So do countless times.

With precision he made a small incision inside the duodenum and then guided the cannula up the small bile duct, using contrast material to identify the stones.

"There they are," Zac said, talking only to himself. He fed down a small balloon that could be inflated above the stone and help brush it down into the widened opening. "Looks like only one stone, the rest of the duct is clear. Once we get this stone out, it should be a simple laparoscopic procedure to remove the gall bladder. There should be no risk of the clips popping off the bile duct."

Ella didn't respond. She held her breath and watched. Hopefully the stone would move. She didn't have to hold her breath for long as Zac inflated the balloon, brushing the stone down from where it was lodged, cleaning the bile duct of its fragments and clearing it.

She let out the breath she'd been holding.

'Dr. Davenport, the patient is turning yellow."

Ella's head snapped up and indeed the patient was jaundiced.

"Dammit," Ella cursed, stepping forward. "You might've nicked the common bile duct."

"I didn't nick the bile duct." Zac removed the endoscope after retracting the cannula. "The gall bladder could've ruptured."

"We need to get in there while the patient is under." Ella helped Dr. Lynne turn the patient to a supine position, while the anesthesiologist started prepping the patient for a general anesthetic over the deep sedation that was used for the ERCP procedure.

She really didn't want to do surgery in the endoscopy suite, but it was ready. The laparoscopic equipment was here. The staff and anesthesiology was here.

They were short-staffed as it was.

"The ERCP went off without a hitch," Zac snapped. "You know these complications happen with inflamed gall bladders and stones. Why are you so angry?"

"Now is not the time and place, Dr. Davenport." Ella pushed past him as her scrub nurse readied the instruments. "If you could head back out on the trauma floor and monitor the emergency room, that would be great."

Zac glared at her. "Fine."

He didn't say anything else to her as he left the endoscopy suite.

Maybe she was a little too harsh with him, but he was being too secretive. Too evasive about what was really going on with him. Trust worked both ways. She was trying to give him the benefit of the doubt, but when he'd snapped at her in front of one of her interns, humiliating her and destroying the reputation she'd worked so hard to build up in this hospital, that had been the last straw.

She just needed some distance between the two of them.

They didn't both need to be in the endoscopy suite to do a laparoscopic cholecystectomy. Someone needed to be out on the emergency room floor.

As far as she knew, the storm outside was still raging. And even if it was over, they would be flooded soon with casualties in the aftermath, but at least the next shift could get in and she could go home.

Home to what?

And that thought made her cringe inwardly a little.

Her mother lamenting her single state, as she did every year. Complaining about the lack of grandchildren that Ella had provided. That was what hurt her most, because Ella wanted children.

She did, but she just didn't see that happening any time in her future, and her mother's constant reminder of the one thing she secretly longed for was just another slap in her face.

Ella should be used to disappointment by now. She should be used to hurt and pain. Especially at this time of year.

And for the first time since this storm had started, she hoped it would continue for just a bit longer so she could miss out on the traditional Lockwood Christmas and all the disappointments that it brought her.

Here in the operating room she was happiest.

Here she could hide away from the world and all the bitter disappointments.

Here she was herself. Even if that meant she was alone and lonely.

At least she was herself. The real her.

Why was she watching me? Why didn't she back off?

Zac stormed down the hallway, putting the endoscopy suite far behind him. Ella had absolutely no faith in his abilities. He'd told her that he had experience and he did. He had been trained in several skilled procedures at Annapolis. So why didn't she trust him?

He closed his eyes. And became overwhelmed with the sights and sounds of that tragedy.

"Get out of the way!" Zac shouted as he carried the boy in his arms.

Shellfire echoed across the town. Buildings crumbled and people screamed around him.

First a natural disaster and now a rebellion.

Zac dodged debris as he worked side by side with sur-geons from the army on the beach, which was now soaked with blood from the wounded.

Consuela was screaming behind him, weeping as Zac carried her son from where he'd found him, buried under a wall at the mission. A boy who was shy but so curious. He'd clung to Zac.

Now he was lifeless in his arms, but he had to try.

He had to try.

Then pain hit him in the back and he dropped to his knees.

He'd been shot.

"Dr. Davenport?"

Zac startled when a porter called his name. "What?"

The porter looked at him with concern. "Are you okay?"

Zac plastered a fake smile on his face, the one he was so used to using. "Fine. What can I help you with?"

The smile worked. Like it usually did.

Except it doesn't work on Ella.

He shook that thought away.

"Dr. Davenport is on the phone. He wants to speak with you."

Zac cocked an eyebrow. "Which Davenport?"

The porter laughed. "Charles."

"Thanks. What line?"

"Five. You can use the phone in the empty office there." The porter continued on his way down one of the darkened halls. The office was in one of the wards they had shut down to conserve power from their generators while the maintenance crew continued to restore full power to the hospital.

Zac slipped into the empty office.

"Charles," he said, having connected the call.

"Zac, I was wondering how things were going there?"

"The power went out."

"Again?" Charles sighed. "Not surprising, though."

"Why?"

"Most of the Upper West Side is without power."

"What about the new system?" Zac asked. "It's supposed to work when the grid fails."

"They're still working on it, but honestly it's out of their hands."

"Why?"

"The storm is not helping with installation and testing. It's too new, but I didn't have a choice. I didn't want to wait until the new year to install it and I'm glad. Even if it's glitchy, it's working better than before, yes?"

"Yes, the generators cut out for a while, but the maintenance crew have them back up and running. We're conserving power to make sure all essential services are taken care of."

"Zac, I'm not your commanding officer," Charles teased gently.

"You sort of are. You're the head of the ER."

"Yes, but I'm not there and neither is Elijah so Ella Lockwood is in charge." There was an awkward silence between the two of them. "How are things going with that?"

"Fine," Zac said stiffly. "Why wouldn't it be?"

"I noticed tension between you two—"

"It's fine." Zac cut him off. "She's in charge. I get it. It's fine."

"So where is she?"

"She's still working."

"I'm not surprised. She's not one to sit around when we're short-staffed, even if she's supposed to be off duty."

"She's in surgery now," Zac said, avoiding the subject of working with Ella.

"For what?" Charles asked.

"Ruptured gall bladder. I performed an ERCP—"

"You what?" Charles demanded. "That's a highly skilled procedure."

"I know, Charles. And I was trained at Annapolis. The gall bladder didn't rupture because I executed a perfect ERCP. It was badly inflamed."

"Well, I'm sure you and Ella did what was best for the patient."

"Yes."

"I have complete faith in you. I'm very glad you've returned to the fold."

Zac rolled his eyes, but couldn't help but smile at his brother's warm welcome. "Is that all?"

"The storm is still raging. No one is to leave the hospital. New York City has come to a standstill. It's going to get worse before it gets better."

Zac's stomach twisted at that thought. This storm was worse than the one before.

You've got this.

"No one is to leave. Got it."

"Okay," Charles said, and then his voice softened. "Take care."

"I've got this."

"I know. I'll check in again."

"Yes. Give the boys my love. Bye." Zac hung up the receiver.

You've got this.

When he looked up, he felt like someone was staring at him. It was Ella. She'd obviously finished the surgery.

She was watching him with a strange look on her face. She looked away, rubbing the back of her neck, and she slowly walked away from the emergency department toward the staffroom.

His pulse raced as he thought about her. Thought about their first kiss, that stolen moment and her kisses, the soft-

ness of her skin. How he'd wanted more. How he regretted not taking the chance with her.

He could've gone looking for her, but he'd chickened out, thinking it was better, but Ella haunted him. Every Christmas he thought of their kiss, reveled in it, and he beat himself up for not taking the chance to find out if there could've been more than just a kiss that night.

When he'd had to have the obligatory psychiatric review on his return home from his mission, the psychiatrist had told him to focus on one thing in his life. One thing where he'd felt completely at peace. One thing that mattered.

One thing that had brought him joy.

And that had been his time with Ella. If only he'd wanted to settle down and get married, follow in his parents' footsteps, then Ella would've been the woman for him. But he hadn't back then. He hadn't wanted any part of a society life, just adventure and a naval career, even if it meant walking away from Ella Lockwood.

Which he'd thought would be a lot harder than it had been back then, but Ella had obviously wanted nothing to do with him after their kiss, because he hadn't seen her again. He'd been expecting to see her at that Christmas Eve function, but she'd never shown up. So he hadn't been able to say his proper goodbye to her.

And even though he knew that he shouldn't, he followed her now.

Zac found her in the staffroom. She was standing at the large window, her back to the door, her head turning only slightly when he shut the door behind him.

The tension was almost palpable.

"How did the surgery go?" he asked.

"Textbook. The patient is in Recovery. She'll be on antibiotics for several days. Not the best Christmas present."

"No, but at least she's alive."

Every life mattered. And he tried not to let his mind

wander back to all the lives that had been lost. He closed his eyes and tried to drown out the sounds of wounded navy men and women crying out for their loved ones, their families who were thousands of miles away.

"She's alive," he whispered again, shaking those thoughts away.

Ella nodded and turned to look back out the window.

"Is there something you want to say to me?" Zac asked.

She spun around then. "Excuse me?"

"An apology for doubting me."

"No, I'm not apologizing for that, but you should apologize to me!"

He was taken aback by that. "For?"

"For humiliating me in front of my interns and residents. When Charles or Elijah aren't here, I'm in charge. Davenport or not. I'm in charge. I've worked too hard to repair the damage an act of dismissal caused to my self-esteem for you to come waltzing back in and destroy it all over again."

CHAPTER SIX

ELLA'S PULSE WAS pounding in her ears. She really couldn't believe that she'd blurted it out, but she was sleep deprived, edgy and completely emotional.

Zac had humiliated her. Twice now in her life.

And on Christmas Eve.

She didn't really want to lash out at him, not when he seemed to be suffering from post-traumatic stress disorder, but there was only so much a person could take.

"What're you talking about? What do you mean, again?"

And then she balked. Was he really that self-centered? *Are you shocked?*

"You don't really remember, then, do you?"

"Remember what?" he asked in exasperation.

"Your conversation with... I don't even remember who now, but I remember what you said."

"You need to help me here, Ella. I haven't seen you since that Christmas Eve party right before I went to..." Then he trailed off, his eyes widening. She knew then that he remembered it. "Oh, God."

She fought tears that were threatening to spill. She wouldn't give him the satisfaction of seeing her tears, but it gave her some satisfaction that he remembered exactly

what had happened. It had been trivial enough for him to push it from his mind, but those words had hurt her.

Deeply.

They also had been words that had made her stronger. Made her fight harder to get where she was today.

"Right," she said, and then cleared her throat. "I've worked really hard here at Manhattan Mercy. I know you're a Davenport…"

Zac crossed the room and gripped her by the shoulders. "I'm sorry, Ella. For those things I said. I didn't mean them. Those idiots… You know I never wanted to get married and they wouldn't leave me alone."

She opened her mouth to say something, but he just shook his head to silence her.

"I know that's no excuse for what I said. I'm sorry that you had to hear that. And I'm sorry for getting testy before the ERCP procedure. I am finding my ground here. Just because I'm a Davenport it doesn't mean that I have an easy ride here. I've been away. I have to prove myself too and I overstepped my bounds." He let go of her then, but still stood close to her in the dim light of the staffroom.

Her heart was hammering. His nearness and the rush of emotions flowing through her caught her off guard.

Ella was in shock. She hadn't expected an apology. She had expected him to make excuses, but he'd apologized for the excuses. He had apologized for it all, but still something inside her couldn't trust him, because she didn't buy that he was just finding his ground here.

There was more and he was hiding it from her. And she couldn't trust him. Not after the way he'd hurt her. She had trusted him back then too, but look how that had turned out. She didn't want to be made a fool of again. His performance was not her concern.

She was trying to believe him. To see the good.

He was cleared for work with what appeared to be post-

traumatic stress disorder. That's all that mattered and she couldn't emotionally invest in him. Not again.

Still, he was apologizing to her.

And that was something she hadn't expected from him. *Maybe Zac had changed?*

"Ella," he whispered. "Please trust me when I say I didn't mean what I said to those idiots."

"Fine." And she gave him her best fake smile. The one she was so good at putting on. One she was used to doing when she was around her family and their friends.

"Smile or you'll never get a husband," her mother had said to her over and over again.

"You're not fine," Zac said. "I know that smile."

She frowned. "And you're fine, aren't you? Do you want to talk about your post-traumatic disorder attack when the power went out? You say you were cleared, but if things like that set you off…"

Zac shrugged. "What's there to explain? I was cleared. There's nothing more to discuss."

Oh, he was good.

He had the ability to twist words around. Such a smooth operator.

Ella threw up her hands. She was tired of arguing with him about this. "Okay, a panic attack. You're right. I have to let it go."

"Thanks."

She shrugged. "Sure."

"I'm going to get some lunch. It's one. I heard that the cafeteria is still running to feed all of us who are stuck. Want to grab some lunch?"

She should say no. She wanted to stay away from him. Zac was infuriating. One minute she was feeling things for him and things she had thought were long since buried, and then the next moment she was ready to wring his neck.

Of course, it had always been like this between them.

Especially in their preteens. She'd just forgotten.

And she was done arguing. Let Charles deal with whatever it was Zac was hiding. She was done meddling with Zac beyond working together.

He'd apologized. She'd finally got what she'd wanted.

No, you didn't.

Ella shook that thought from her head. "Sure."

They left the staffroom together in complete silence.

"You know I taught you that fake smile, don't you?" Zac said out of the blue.

"Uh, no, you didn't. I taught you."

He raised an eyebrow. "What're you talking about?"

"You're the only one of your siblings who can pull off that smile and that's thanks to me. I've worked with Charles long enough to know he can't do it. He tries, but it just looks ridiculous." Then she mimicked Charles and they both broke out in laughter.

It was a lot funnier than it should be, but she always got a bit giddy when she was tired.

"So what about my other siblings?" Zac asked when they finally stopped laughing.

"I don't know," Ella admitted. "I haven't spent much time with your brothers. I know Miranda can't, but I've never really seen her try. We're not usually on the same shift anyway. Besides, she's been a bit busy lately, hasn't she?"

"Yeah, I don't even want to talk about my siblings' romantic lives, thank you very much," Zac said. He opened the door of the cafeteria, which was fairly busy, but with staff stuck and no relief in sight and most of the hospital shut down except for essential departments, there really weren't many places to go.

Ella's stomach growled. She was starving. "Oh, they have a traditional turkey dinner on special right now."

Zac's brow furrowed. "I haven't really tested this cafe-

teria's food in a long time. I remember not being all that pleased when I was a kid."

"It's changed since then." She picked up a tray and moved down the line. "I'd like a turkey special, please."

The cafeteria worker nodded and prepared a plate with a piece of turkey, stuffing, mashed potatoes, sprouts, bun and cranberry sauce.

"What, no gravy?" Zac asked.

The cafeteria worker shot him a look and Ella chuckled as she thanked the server and continued down the line to grab a slice of fruit cake and a bottle of water.

The cafeteria was not charging today, by Dr. Davenport's orders. A Christmas treat for all those who were stranded by the storm.

She found a table off to the side in a quiet part of the cafeteria. Usually it was louder in here when the hospital was at full tilt. Still, she wanted quiet. Working in the emergency room and on trauma was loud and intense at the best of times, so when she had a moment to herself, she liked to calm her sensory overload in a peaceful corner.

Zac slid into the seat across from her, setting down his turkey dinner and looking at it dubiously. He had opted for an energy drink and pudding instead of fruit cake.

"It's good," Ella said, and she took a bite of her turkey. "It's really good."

"There's Brussels sprouts." He made a face.

"What's wrong with them? They're good with butter and salt."

"When I was a kid my dog wouldn't even eat these."

Ella chuckled. "I thought you guys in the armed forces ate whatever was set in front of you."

"Yeah, but they never served sprouts in the officers' mess hall."

She smiled and popped a sprout into her mouth. "Mmm, so good."

He wrinkled his nose and then saw the fruit cake. "Ugh, I forgot what a weirdo you are."

"What?"

"You eat fruit cake! Who eats fruit cake?" Zac shook his head.

"I do. I've always eaten it."

"I know, hence the 'I forgot what a weirdo you are'."

"What's wrong with fruit cake?" she asked. "I never did ask about your aversion to it. And I suppose they didn't serve this in the officers' mess either."

Zac chuckled as he cut up his turkey. "Yeah, I think I saw an obligatory one floating around at Christmas a few times. Usually, it was soaked in rum, though."

"I do like rum-soaked ones. Once, to get away from my mother's Christmas, I escaped with some girlfriends to Jamaica and had some rum cake down there. So good with the dark rum in it."

"I still didn't touch the cake. The rum, on the other hand..." he teased, winking.

"Why do you hate fruit cake? It's traditional."

"It has hard hunks of fruit. Mystery fruit," he whispered, making a face. "It's weird."

"It's not mystery fruit. It's dried and candied fruit like cherries, pineapple..."

"Okay, but what's the green one? Plus, I hate nuts in anything baked."

Ella wrinkled her nose. "I forgot what a picky eater you are."

"Yeah, well, family dinners were always a wee bit tense around my house in my later years. It didn't give me much of an appetite." He was frowning as he said that and she understood. There had been a lot of tension at the Davenport house when that scandal had broken out and Miranda had been brought into the fold.

When they'd been younger, though, they'd always had

each other. Even if she'd been decked out in some ugly frock or jumper her mother had felt it was appropriate she wore, Zac had always been there.

He'd been her prince in shining armor. Until he hadn't been any more.

Suddenly the turkey dinner tasted like sawdust in her mouth.

"So what is the green fruit?" Zac asked, breaking the uneasy silence between them.

Ella frowned. "You know, I don't actually know."

"I mean what kind of fruit is actually that green?"

She couldn't help but laugh. It was so easy to laugh with him. She'd forgotten that. There was a lot of things she'd forgotten about. Feelings she'd thought were long gone, but were obviously just buried, because they were bubbling to the surface.

"I have the worst feeling I'm not going to get into medical school and then I'll just be this huge disappointment to my parents. Well, not to my mother, who will continue to pamper me like some kind of demented poodle."

"Hey, you've got this," Zac said as he pulled her into an embrace, calming her down from her rant. *"I'll be here for you."*

"No, you won't, you'll be at Annapolis," she mumbled.

He tipped her chin to look down at her, those brilliant blue eyes and boyish good looks transfixing her like they always did. "Ella, I'm always here for you."

And before she knew what was happening he was leaning down and kissing her.

Something she'd fantasized about for so long, but had never thought would happen. And she melted into his kiss.

A kiss she didn't want to end.

"I'm sorry, Ella. I don't know what came over me." He was confused, but she could see a yearning in his eyes. She knew what it was because she felt that way too. About him.

It thrilled her, but she didn't want to get her hopes up.

She shook her head. "Don't be sorry. It doesn't have to mean anything more than that, though I would like it if you kissed me again."

"Are you sure?"

She nodded and felt a flush of warmth run through her.

"Oh, yes."

"Hey, Ella are you okay?" Zac was waving a hand in front of her face.

"What?" she asked, rocked from the memory, which was affecting her now, because her palms were sweaty and her body was very aware that the man who had elicited those feelings in her years ago was sitting across from her.

"You zoned out," he said.

"Tired." She cleared her throat and then picked up her tray. "I should get back down to the emergency room."

Zac nodded and picked up his own tray. They cleared them and threw out their trash. The easy teasing that had gone on before she'd drifted into that memory was gone. He was so charming, he got under her skin so quickly. She had to be careful around him.

Or she was liable to get hurt again.

And that was something she couldn't and wouldn't let happen.

CHAPTER SEVEN

ZAC HAD WORKED ON the opposite side of the emergency room from Ella since they'd returned from lunch. Something had changed up there. And he didn't know what. She was uneasy around him again, almost like she didn't want to let her guard down around him.

Though he didn't blame her.

When he'd realized that she'd heard those awful things he'd said about her, it had made him feel ashamed. He had just been trying to stop a couple of idiots from pestering him. He'd never intended to hurt Ella. He'd never intended Ella to overhear that.

Not at all.

If he'd thought for a moment that she would overhear that, he wouldn't have said those things.

Yes, you would have. You didn't want a relationship and you hated the way people tried to pair you off with her.

Guilt gnawed at him for hurting her.

Even if her mother had dressed her like she was some kind of porcelain doll, all frills and ruffles. She'd drowned in yards of fabric back then. Unflattering and dreadful colored fabric.

It didn't matter.

He saw her for who she really was underneath.

And now she exuded confidence he'd never seen in her before. It made him want her all the more.

When they had been standing alone together in the staffroom, he'd wanted to kiss her again. As he worked on minor injuries it was all he could do to not think about that moment in the on-call room when she'd woken up to see him and had smiled.

Memories of her kiss had got him through so many rough times. And as he worked in the emergency room tonight on Christmas Eve, a hard night for him, he was relying on those memories all too much.

Her sighs, her silky hair and the way she'd felt in his arms.

It had always felt so right. And it scared him just a bit.

It was distracting because it was taking all his strength not to cross the trauma floor and take her in his arms and kiss her again. To continue the kiss from the on-call room.

Don't think about it.

The problem with that logic was then he thought back to Christmas last year. And when he thought back to Christmas last year, all he could hear was the screech of missiles, gunfire and screaming.

"My son. Oh, God. Have mercy on my son." Consuela's voice echoed in his head.

Zac scrubbed a hand over his face, forcing those memories away because he had to regain control. He couldn't let those thoughts in because when he let those thoughts in, he lost control.

"Dr. Lockwood," Dr. Lynne called, running. He watched as Dr. Lynne spoke hurriedly to Ella, concern etched on her face.

"What's wrong?" Zac asked, as he instinctively fell into step beside them.

"It's our accident patient. He's crashed twice and they've revived him. I think he's bleeding internally again."

They didn't say anything as they headed to the ICU, where Dr. Trace was working on bringing the patient back.

Ella began rapid-fire orders to hang blood and get an OR prepped. Zac couldn't help but watch her in admiration.

This was a far cry from the girl who had panicked because she didn't know if she'd be accepted into medical school. The woman who had hidden in the shadows behind everyone.

Now she was a force to be reckoned with, showing the strength that he'd always knew was there but which she'd never revealed. It was a shame that she'd hidden this person for so long, because this woman thrilled him.

As they were wheeling the patient down to the OR another intern came running up.

"The police are here. They wanted to talk to the patient about the accident," the intern said.

"The patient is crashing. They're going to have to wait," Zac snapped, maybe a bit too harshly but a man's life was at stake. They couldn't lose another patient tonight. Not on Christmas Eve.

"My son. Oh, God. My son!"

Get a grip on yourself.

He took a calming breath.

"Tell them one of us will be there as soon as we can," he said to the intern. "Explain to them what has happened."

The intern nodded and ran back to the emergency room.

Dr. Trace and Dr. Lynne took the patient in while Ella and Zac scrubbed. She was mouthing things to herself, her blue eyes wild as she tucked her long, wavy blonde hair under her scrub cap. He knew that look. She was going over what she'd done wrong. Just like he'd done countless times. Like any surgeon when a patient took a turn for the worse after being stable.

"Hey, this isn't your fault. I'm sure the splenectomy

was fine. He was involved in an accident. Missing bleeders happen," he said.

"Or sutures done by a tired surgeon don't hold," she muttered. Then she shook her head. "No, it's not that."

"Exactly. Let's go find out what it is and fix it. Let's give this guy another Christmas, shall we?"

Ella nodded. "Exactly."

They headed into the operating room while the scrub nurse got them geared up. The anesthesiologist had the patient ready and it only took a moment to prep the abdomen. Ella rolled her shoulders as she climbed up on her stool.

"Scalpel."

The scrub nurse handed her the scalpel handle first. Zac stood across from her, ready to assist. He'd done this before, in worse conditions. He could help her find the bleeders, stop further damage to the patient's body.

"The splenectomy looks stable," Ella said on examination, "but where is this bleeding coming from?"

Zac began to suction it away, peering in to have a look, pulling the retractor. "Kidney. Look, the left kidney."

"That's it. Dammit. It was fine when I removed the spleen. It was bruised, but he was still producing good urine output."

The left kidney was not salvageable. Hopefully it was just the left kidney. The brunt of the impact had been on the left side where the car had apparently wrapped around the pole. This patient had been wearing his seatbelt, whereas his passenger, who had passed away, had not.

"My son. My God. My son!"

Zac rolled his shoulders.

Steady. Calm and steady.

"Think of that one perfect moment in your life. The time you felt the most joy," his psychiatrist had said. *"Whenever the stress gets to you, think of that moment."*

The problem was he couldn't think of that moment. Not now. Not with Ella working so hard to save a man's life.

Sweat began to bead on his brow.

Focus.

He couldn't slip back into the nightmare. Not now. He wouldn't lose this life. No more death tonight.

At least Ella didn't notice. She was focused on the patient. Zac reined it in and throughout the surgery he managed to hold it together and that's because he focused on Ella. On that moment he chose, their first kiss and the voices, the horrors passed.

Only focusing on Ella with her right in front of him distracted him in a different way.

And all he could think about was how he'd hurt her.

The kiss he treasured had been tainted by the way he'd hurt her and how he'd been so obtuse and not even known it.

"There," Ella said with relief. "That should hold."

"Good job," Zac said. "Do you need help closing?"

"No, I'm good. I'll finish up here and then I'm going to take a nap if you don't mind. I've been on duty now for over twenty-four hours."

"I'll manage the emergency room." Zac removed the retractor and a nurse took over his spot to assist Ella with the closing. "I'll go talk to the police officers as well."

"That sounds great," Ella said, not looking up at him.

Zac got out of the operating room as fast as he could without trying to draw attention to himself. His body was shaking and he needed to put some distance between him and her.

After he scrubbed out he grabbed the chart for the patient who did not survive the accident and found the police officers were waiting in a small meeting room near the emergency department.

"I'm sorry to have kept you waiting. I'm Dr. Davenport." He shook the police officers' hands.

"Not a problem, Dr. Davenport," the lieutenant said. "I'm sorry it took so long to get to the hospital, but the roads are wicked out there."

"So I've heard. I arrived here before the storm shut the city down." Zac sat down with the police officers. "How can I help you, officers?"

"The patients that were involved in the motor vehicle collision. We have identified them and sent notices to their next of kin."

Zac nodded. "You were told that the female passenger succumbed to her injuries, yes? I was the surgeon who worked on her when she came into the emergency room."

The lieutenant nodded. "Yes. Can you tell us why?"

Zac opened the hard copy of the chart. "She was the unrestrained passenger. The cause was blunt force trauma after being ejected from the vehicle. There were also large quantities of methamphetamine in her bloodstream when the labs came back. We will not do an autopsy until we get permission from the next of kin."

The lieutenant nodded. "They were known drug users, both of them, and they were evading arrest when their vehicle collided with a median and then the lamppost. What is the status of the driver?"

"He's currently in surgery. Sadly one of the side effects of methamphetamine use is the breakdown of tissues and blood vessels. We had to remove his spleen due to a rupture and now his left kidney has been removed because the blood vessels are breaking down. The last I heard he was stable, but he won't be available for questioning for some time."

The lieutenant nodded. "We'll stay at the hospital if you don't mind, Dr. Davenport. Your patient is a wanted felon."

"Of course, Lieutenant. Currently, the cafeteria is offer-

ing free food and drinks for everyone stranded here. Please make yourselves at home and as soon as he's in Recovery we'll page you. In the state he's in, he won't be going far."

"Thank you, Dr. Davenport."

Zac left the meeting room and returned the chart to the unit desk. The emergency room was eerily quiet. And as he walked to the ambulance bay door the snow was still falling heavily. A couple of interns wearing Manhattan Mercy jackets were outside, shoveling away mounds of snow from outside the doors.

It was dusk and even though you couldn't see the sun behind the thick clouds, the small amount of light was dissipating and the street-lamps gave off a warm glow through the thick swirling snow. It was almost magical.

It was peaceful and calm.

Zac closed his eyes and did his deep breathing, trying to calm the erratic beat of his heart. Only it wasn't working. He headed toward the on-call rooms. He had to find Ella, had to talk to her.

And he was angry that he was so dependent on her. He didn't deserve her. He didn't deserve her kindness or her pity. Not after what he'd done to her when he'd been a brash, foolish idiot. As he walked, the power flickered again.

A brownout.

Charles had said the Upper West Side was without power. The generator system was new. Still, that didn't calm the erratic beating of his heart.

The hall that he was walking down was flooded in darkness.

Dammit.

He found the wall. The wall was his anchor and his blood thundered in his ears. He closed his eyes to the darkness, his ears completely sensitive to the sounds around

him, even though the hallway was quiet and no one was around.

Instead he focused on the distinctive hum of silence and the hospital coming back to life again after the generators kicked in.

When light pricked his eyelids, he opened them and took another deep breath. He'd thought he had this licked. He'd thought he could control it, but he'd been so wrong.

And he was terrified over the way it was controlling him.

The way it had a hold on his life.

He was angry, because he didn't want to let it defeat him. So, instead of heading to the on-call room, he started to run, to jog along the empty hospital hallways, letting the endorphins from exercise flood his body with much-needed dopamine.

He could conquer this. He *would* conquer this.

Ella only managed to sleep for an hour before she was paged to the emergency room. She was surprised to learn that Zac hadn't responded to his page.

It was exactly what she'd been afraid of. He'd had a spell and was incapacitated somewhere.

"How long have you tried paging him, Jen?" Ella asked as she took another sip of coffee.

"Just twenty minutes," Dr. Lynne said. "There was an influx of patients that needed some further assessment."

Ella was going to say something else when Zac came up to the unit desk. He looked out of breath, his face flushed.

"Sorry, I was changing the battery in my pager," he said breathlessly. "I got here as quickly as I could."

"The battery?" Ella asked.

"It died when I checked to see if there were any pages. I had to get a new battery pack," Zac answered, not looking at her as he took a chart from Dr. Lynne. "Thanks, Jen."

"Make sure you get someone from Tech to check that out," she said. "It shouldn't have died."

Dr. Lynne backed away and Zac just scrolled through the notes on the tablet, without looking at her.

"Zac, they woke me up because they couldn't find you."

"I know. I'm sorry. I will get it checked out. It's working again and I'm here now so you can go back to sleep." He pushed past her, not looking her in the eye.

She suspected something else.

"Zac, did you have a PTSD episode?"

"No, I was unreachable for fifteen minutes while I changed the battery. I'm sorry they woke you."

"You're pushing me away again. Why don't you admit that you had a PTSD attack?"

Zac's spine stiffened and he fixed her with an icy glare. "I didn't have a PTSD attack. I was cleared for duty. Let it go."

"If you were cleared for duty, why did you leave the navy? You loved the navy."

"I was honorably discharged, Ella. I served my tours of duty and I wanted to return home. Now, if you don't mind, I have patients to see."

She stepped in front of him and whispered under her breath, "Are you capable of caring for those patients? I seriously question it."

"Why?"

"Because you won't talk about it."

"Ella, you're treading on dangerous ground," he said in a low voice.

All she wanted him to do was admit that he'd had a PTSD attack so that she could help him. "I just want to help you."

"I don't need help." Zac walked away from her and she cursed under her breath. How could she have been so daft as to think he would want help. That he'd changed.

He was a Davenport through and through.

That's not fair. You respect his siblings.

It was only Zac who completely infuriated her. They had been best friends once, before they'd hit puberty, then things had changed.

She had become a bit of a hot mess that her mother had dressed atrociously while he'd flourished and run with the popular crowd.

She took a seat behind the unit desk and manned the phones, since she wasn't on duty and she should actually be resting, but right now she had enough adrenaline and caffeine pumping through her that she couldn't sleep if she wanted to.

The phone connecting to emergency services rang and she picked it up. "Manhattan Mercy."

"We have incoming trauma. Multi-vehicle crash. The hospital near the crash site is overflowing. We're bringing them in via helicopter."

"What's the ETA?" Ella asked.

"Five minutes out."

"We'll be ready." Ella hung up the phone and then motioned to Dr. Trace, who was lingering.

"Yes, Dr. Lockwood?" Ryan asked.

"Grab an intern and let's get to the roof. There's a chopper landing."

Dr. Trace's eyebrows shot up. "In this weather? I thought there was a no-fly order."

"It's been lifted for now. Which is good because there's a multi-vehicle crash on the bridge and the closest hospital is overflowing. They have to fly the injured to Manhattan."

"Right away, Dr. Lockwood."

Ella's stomach twisted and she wondered if it was going to be Penny Davenport flying the helicopter again. She'd gotten in so much trouble from Charles the last time she'd flown in a storm.

She grabbed a jacket from the closet and Dr. Trace came over to her, carrying a stretcher with an intern. They took the patient transport elevator up to the roof. The whole time Ella prayed that the power wouldn't go out.

As far as she knew, the tech specialists were still working on it. Even though there were fluctuations in the city's power grid, the new generator was handling the storm better than last time.

The doors opened and the air was bitterly cold, whipping at her face. Because of the high winds, the helipad was clear of snow.

This was dangerous, but the patients had to get in.

Ella prayed the snow would die down and the helicopter could see the flashing lights and land safely. The wind did die down and she was able to hear the whirr of the helicopter as it hovered above Manhattan Mercy. She watched with bated breath as it landed with a tiny bump on the helipad.

The blades stopped, the door opened and Dr. Gabriel Jackson jumped out.

Ella motioned to Dr. Trace, while the intern remained behind in the elevator. They wheeled the stretcher over and Ella saw Penny in the pilot's seat as Gabriel helped them load the patient onto the stretcher.

"I thought Charles gave her heck for flying before?"

"He did," Gabriel shouted over the wind. "But she's the best at these crazy landings so she was given the all-clear. This patient was a pedestrian walking when he was struck by a car and fell in the Hudson River. Very lucky to retrieve him. Suffering from hyperthermia and blunt force trauma. Was resuscitated on scene and intubated."

Ella nodded. "Thanks. Be safe!"

Gabriel nodded while Ella and Dr. Trace pushed the stretcher to the safety of the elevator. Once the helicopter took off and was safely in the air again, the elevator door

shut. The patient's vitals were slipping again as Ella assessed him.

They had to keep him warm, but she had to elevate the patient and check what damage had been done by the blunt force trauma.

Once the elevator stopped at the emergency room floor, Zac was waiting for her.

"Don't tell me it was my sister who was flying the helicopter," he said.

"I won't, then," Ella responded stonily.

Dr. Trace jumped into action, grabbing as many blankets from the blanket warmer as he could.

Zac, Ella and the intern lifted the patient from the stretcher to the exam table.

"His temperature is dangerously low," Zac remarked as he grabbed the warming blankets from Dr. Trace and worked to remove the cold wet clothing and blankets from the patient and then wrap the trunk of the patient's body in the warm blankets.

"He has hypothermia." Ella assessed his ABCs. Already she knew that the patient's airway was compromised as there was a tube down his throat. As she listened to his chest, she could hear fluid. "Suspected pneumothorax. I need to insert a chest tube."

As Zac and Dr. Trace worked on wrapping the patient up the best they could, Ella inserted a chest tube, allowing the free fluid to drain out.

Once the chest tube was secured, they wrapped more warm blankets around him. His temperature began to rise slowly and his readings stabilized.

"We have to get him down to CT and see what damage was done," Ella said.

"I'll take him, Dr. Lockwood," Dr. Trace said.

"Thank you, Ryan." Ella stepped back and let Dr. Trace take point. "Make sure the patient's temperature doesn't

rise too fast, we don't want the body to go into shock especially if there's internal bleeding."

"Yes, Dr. Lockwood." Ella and Zac stepped back to let Dr. Trace and the interns take over while they waited until the results of the CT came up.

"Did you talk to Penny?" Zac asked, breaking the silence that fell between them as Ella charted in the patient's information.

"No, she didn't get out of the cockpit."

Zac nodded and she couldn't help but think about Penny's pregnancy announcement after Charles's wedding. How Penny and Gabriel would make great parents. In fact, she was a bit envious.

It's not that she never wanted to get married, she just didn't want to feel pressured to get married. Her mother's constant lamenting of her single state was annoying, but seeing the other Davenports settling down, her peers having it all, made her think about what she'd always secretly wanted with Zac, before he'd broken her heart.

"She likes to live dangerously," Zac said.

"There was a break in the storm so it was safe to fly."

Zac grinned. "I don't mean flying. I mean her impending motherhood. She's brave."

"You don't want kids?" she asked.

His expression hardened. "No."

"I thought you liked kids. You seem to dote on your nephews."

"I like kids, I just don't want them for myself."

Her heart sank and she was angry at herself.

What did you expect? It's Zac.

"I thought you liked to take risks? A family of your own might be a risk worth taking, but if you're not up to it…"

Zac frowned. "That's a dig at me, isn't it? Not wanting kids has nothing to do with my PTSD. It's personal choice."

"Why don't you just admit that the post-traumatic stress is bothering you? You might still need treatment."

"Why are you so adamant about this?" Zac growled. "It hasn't affected my performance today. I have worked efficiently alongside you. No harm has come to any patient under my care. I was fifteen minutes late to the emergency room. Lay off."

He was right.

Ella sighed. "I'm sorry for getting on your case."

"Thank you."

"I run a tight ship when Charles or Elijah isn't here, Zac, and you have to forgive me but I'm not sure that I fully trust you yet. Though you're right, your performance has been exemplary."

"I'm not fresh out of medical school," Zac said. "I have worked in pressured situations all over the world. I am perfectly capable of dealing with stress."

"Stress?" she asked skeptically.

"We're running short-staffed in a hospital that is experiencing occasional brownouts in the middle of a snowstorm at Christmas. Aren't you the least bit stressed?"

Yes, but not for those reasons.

But she didn't say that out loud.

"Yes. I just manage it differently. Look, I don't know how much longer we have left stuck in this emergency room together, but I promise to lay off. I just want you to promise me that if the stress gets to you, you tell me. If you can't handle—"

"I can handle it," Zac said fiercely.

"Okay." Ella walked away from him. She wished she could believe him.

Are you sure you're not letting your past dictate the uncertainty now?

Before he'd hurt her, she would've trusted him with her

life. Zac had been her best friend and she'd shared everything with him.

She'd dated other men since he'd broken her heart, but never for long. No one held a candle to the memory she carried in her heart and she hated herself a bit for that, because it was clear that Zac hadn't changed. That he was as stubborn as always.

Maybe she was overanalyzing it. Ella pinched the bridge of her nose as a wave of exhaustion washed over her.

These little power naps she'd managed to take since her shift had ended helped, but what she really wanted was an eight-hour stretch of uninterrupted sleep. And she wasn't sure when she was going to get that.

Zac followed her. "Why don't you go back to the on-call room?"

"It's that obvious?" she muttered.

"Yeah. I'm sorry about not responding to the page and for having them page you. Go rest. I promise I won't leave this emergency room until you get at least two hours." He smiled at her, the tenderness etched across his face making her heart skip a beat. It was like the old Zac she'd known before he'd hurt her was shining through.

The Zac she had known once before. The Zac she'd trusted and loved.

Ella sighed and smiled, nodding. "If the storm ends and Charles clears us to leave, you need to wake me so I can go home."

"Do you think you can dig your car out of the parking lot?"

"I don't have a car. This is Manhattan. Besides, I don't live far from here. My grandmother's old apartment at Central Park West is where I live now. She left it to me."

"That is an easy walk. I can see why you don't drive."

"Call me if you need me, Zac." She sighed again. "I'm sorry for questioning you."

"And I'm sorry for snapping at you. I wouldn't be here if I didn't think I can handle it, if the psychiatrists didn't think I could. I will never put a life in jeopardy because of pride."

She was the one being prideful and stubborn right now, and she was holding a grudge. She wanted to trust him. He was trying and she had to give him a chance.

He'd proved himself time and time again.

"Okay, page me if you need me."

She turned to leave when the ambulance bay doors open and a man helping a very pregnant woman came stumbling into the ER.

"Someone, help! My wife's water broke and the contractions are two minutes apart!"

So much for sleep.

CHAPTER EIGHT

ELLA AND ZAC helped the woman into the privacy of an exam room.

"Someone page Obstetrics and Pediatrics," Ella shouted over her shoulder, but as soon as the words came out the power flickered again.

And all they had was emergency lighting in the emergency room.

This is not happening. This is not happening.

If the power was out then the elevators weren't working and Pediatrics and Obstetrics were up seven flights. Which meant that she was going to be helping this mother deliver this baby right here in the emergency room. She just hoped that nothing went wrong.

It was Christmas—wasn't it time for miracles and joy? Not chaos and brownouts. What else was going to happen tonight?

Ella jammed a head lamp on her head, the kind that was used in surgery, and did an examination of the mother. Instead of seeing how dilated the mother was, she could see the head.

So, fully dilated. Okay.

"It looks like this baby isn't going to wait until Obstetrics gets here," Ella said to Zac.

"What?" the father of the baby asked as his wife

moaned. "She went into labor, it just took us forever to walk here in the snowstorm, our phones were down and I dropped the cell phone in the snow…"

The man was babbling. And she couldn't blame him.

"Your first?" Zac asked gently.

"Yes," the man said, and Zac grinned at her. It explained the babbling.

"The baby's head is crowning," Ella said. "What's your wife's name?"

"Barbara," he sputtered.

"Barbara, you're doing great," Ella said. "You need to push when you feel the next contraction, okay?"

"Okay," Barbara panted.

"I thought we had more time!" the father shouted.

"No, your baby is coming. It's going to be okay, I swear." Ella smiled at the anxious couple, trying to calm them both down.

"Yes?" he asked uncertainly.

"It's okay, Dr. Lockwood can handle this," Zac said, stepping in. "Focus on your wife."

Ella placed her hand on the woman's belly and felt the uterus tense with a contraction. "Now, Barbara. Push. Now."

Ella watched as Barbara's husband took his place behind her, holding her shoulders. Barbara glanced up at her husband for reassurance and even though no words were spoken, there was a look that passed between them.

And Ella was envious of the shared moment of tenderness, the connection they had, and for the first time in a long time Ella felt her loneliness keenly.

"Another contraction is coming, Barbara. You need to push," Ella said, focusing on her patient and helping her guide a new life into this world.

Ella had delivered babies before in emergency situations, but not for a long time. The power flicked on, but

even if Obstetrics were to come right now, it was too late as Barbara gave one last push.

Ella had forgotten what it was like to be there when a new life was born. She was so used to injuries, sickness and even death. This was something different. It was amazing. And as she looked down at that tiny helpless baby in her arms, she felt a sharp pang of longing.

The baby cried, clearing her lungs, and Ella smiled, trying not to cry with joy.

"Good job," Ella said, as she lifted the infant and placed it on Barbara's chest. "It's a girl."

Zac leaned in and began to rub the baby with a warm towel, and she let out a small yelp and then another loud cry. And watching Zac bent over the baby, those strong hands rubbing the baby's back so gently, it made Ella's heart skip a beat and wish for something more. It made her wish for what could've been.

Don't let him in.

Except right now, seeing Zac with the baby and basking in the love that was in that room, it was easier said than done.

She looked away, waiting for the delivery of the placenta and trying not to let those thoughts into her mind because it was just a wish. One that didn't come true and would never come true. Zac had made it clear he didn't want kids.

And even though Ella didn't have anyone to share her life with right now, she did want kids eventually.

So she focused on Barbara's continued contractions.

Ella didn't cut the cord right away, because she'd learned a trick from a midwife once to allow the baby to get extra nourishment from the placenta as long as possible.

So instead she waited until that part was delivered, while Zac used a bulb aspirator to clear the baby's mouth out.

Ella couldn't help but smile at the new parents who

were fawning over their baby. She envied them and the joy they had. She couldn't help but wonder if her own parents had ever felt that kind of joy over her, but she seriously doubted it.

Reaching back into her earliest memories, she couldn't even recall her mother being much of a presence in her early life. Just a nanny.

And Zac.

He'd been her family for so long. They'd been inseparable until that Christmas when he'd said those hurtful things.

Up until that point Zac had been her reason for living. No other man had ever compared to her memory of him. It was unfair, but she couldn't help it.

I missed him.

And she was sad for all their wasted years apart.

She glanced up at him and he was smiling.

"Can I see her for a minute, Barbara?" Zac asked, but there was a hint of uncertainty in his voice. "Just need to assess her."

Ella's heart skipped a beat as she watched him lift the tiny infant in those strong hands and cradle it, but also he appeared a bit terrified.

"You okay?" Ella asked. "Do you want me to take over?"

"I've got it. Just not used to holding babies. It's been a while." A sad expression passed across his face and she wondered what had happened to him.

Whatever it was soon passed and Zac became more confident tending to the baby. He smiled and she could see a piece of his hardened wall crumble away as he looked down at the new little girl.

A piece of her melted.

Her pulse thundered in her ears as she watched him smile and dote on the baby with such tenderness.

And all those secret thoughts she'd had when she hadn't known Zac didn't feel that way about her, when she'd thought they'd had a chance, came flooding back. She pictured Zac cradling their child. Her stomach fluttered, watching him be so gentle with something so fragile.

Zac smiled at her again, turning her insides into a puddle of mush.

He winked at her and then walked away as Ella finished up. The cord was cut just as Dr. Trejos, the pediatrician, and Dr. Raj, the obstetrician, came into the exam room.

Ella handed her charges over to the experienced staff and congratulated the new parents. She cleaned up and then found a lounge chair in one of the exam rooms that was used to take blood samples.

She sank down in it and sighed, trying to get her senses under control after watching Zac with that newborn baby. It made her feel all sorts of warm and fuzzy thoughts again. Thoughts she'd thought were long gone, locked away in the remnants of her broken heart.

"You did good there," Zac said, leaning against the open door.

"I didn't do anything. The mother did all the work. I was just there to catch."

Zac was going to say something more when there was a hum and full power was restored. The dim emergency lighting flicked back on and everything lit back up. In the hall there was a collective cheer that the lights were back on.

"That's good. I wonder if the storm is letting up?" Zac walked to the window and pulled on the blind. The snow was still swirling in the darkness, but between gusts Ella could make out a few twinkling lights through the city.

It was peaceful, even amidst the chaos of the storm and the emergency room.

"If the snow stops, maybe they could plow the streets," Ella mumbled.

"I'm sure they're out there plowing now. It's going to take some time. One of the interns said they were listening to the weather forecast and the storm cloud is just hovering over New York City. It's stuck. It won't budge."

"Hopefully Santa can make it into town," Ella teased. "Your nephews would be disappointed."

Zac chuckled softly. "I have a feeling that Santa will make it to Charles's house just fine."

"Do you remember that night we snuck downstairs to see if we could wait for him?"

"I do," Zac said. "And we didn't even make it to midnight."

"When I woke up I was in bed and you were gone."

"Yes, I woke up in my own bed too. Our parents' party ended and I suppose someone scooped us up and tucked us in."

"I was actually more of a Rudolph fan than Santa. Especially as Santa was so discriminatory to Rudolph after all and that elf that wanted to be a dentist."

Zac rolled his eyes. "I forgot how much you loved that Claymation special. I still can't figure out why that one doll was on the Island of Misfit toys. There was nothing wrong with her. I mean, I get the cowboy riding the ostrich, because that's messed up, but the doll looked normal."

Ella started laughing. "I'm too tired to have this conversation with you."

"It's because you're swamped. Crazy swamped," Zac said, mimicking another character from a different Christmas special, and Ella just lost it.

They were laughing together when Ryan Trace walked in the room. He looked confused.

"Is everything okay?" Ryan asked.

"Yes. Perfectly," Zac said, clearing his throat. "The hypothermia patient?"

"No active bleeds," Ryan said, handing Zac the chart. "A few broken ribs, the chest tube is holding. The trachea is crushed, though. He's going to require surgery. I'm surprised the paramedics were able to get a tube down his throat."

"That's not so promising," Ella said sadly.

"If he's stable we'll get him into surgery and fix the trachea." Zac handed the chart back to Dr. Trace. "Prep him for surgery, Ryan. I'll be there as soon as possible."

"The ear, nose and throat surgeon is still here," Ryan said. "He can do the surgery."

"Great. Page him and get the patient ready for surgery," Zac said. "Thanks for the update."

Ryan nodded and backed out of the room.

"I'm so used to being a jack-of-all-trades of surgery when I'm on duty." Zac rubbed his face. "Now you can rest and I don't have to have you man the emergency room."

"Suits me fine." She was exhausted. It felt like she was running a marathon, not because of the double shift but dealing with Zac and all the old emotions he brought out in her.

"You going to go to an on-call room?"

"No, this chair is comfortable and I'm nearby if needed. I'll just crash here for a while."

Zac nodded and flicked out the light. "Have a good rest."

"Thanks."

When Zac left she watched the snow falling outside the window. Except she wasn't thinking about the calming effect that snow usually had on her. All she could see was Zac holding that baby. Unsurely at first, like he'd been terrified, but then it had become easier and she could tell

he'd relaxed, and she couldn't help but wonder if he truly didn't want kids or if it was something more.

And she saw him so clearly, holding a baby with blonde hair and blue eyes. Davenport blue eyes. Their baby. One she had pictured countless times before. It was calming and her last thought before she drifted off to sleep was about the baby, and she couldn't help but wonder what they were going to name her.

As Christmas Eve wore on the emergency room was eerily quiet again. The snow still fell and Zac could feel his own exhaustion kicking in. He hadn't been lying when he'd told Ella he had trouble sleeping. It was true. He struggled with it.

At night he lost control and then nightmares came.

He heard the new baby wail as they wheeled Barbara's gurney out of the exam room.

Zac looked back and couldn't help but smile.

So fragile. So new.

It had been hard at first, holding that new baby. All he'd been able to think about at first was Rojas slipping away from him, but looking down at that new life he'd realized this baby was alive.

He had been holding life in his hands and all those horrors had slipped out of his mind.

And he'd seen the way Ella had watched him with the baby, the twinkle in her eye, and he had been thinking the same thing. Thinking about what if they had gotten married, like their parents had wanted.

Only would they even still be together? He couldn't help but think about his parents. He'd been young when his father's betrayal had come out, but not too young that he hadn't understood the implications.

Maybe he'd never really forgiven his father for hurting his mother. It had disillusioned him. Hardened him. Yet he hadn't stayed around. The navy had been his escape.

It had given him a sense of duty that his father seriously lacked as far as Zac was concerned.

Yet when Rojas had died, all he'd wanted was to have his family back. The stability and safety net his large family provided. He didn't want children of his own, because he couldn't bear it if he lost a child.

Still, there was a part of him that had wanted a family. He wanted kids, deep down. It was just too much to bear and he wasn't sure if he was strong enough for it.

Had being the operative word. Until he'd seen what the loss of a child did. He finished his coffee and thought about charting to take his mind off everything.

The emergency room was in good hands.

Residents were monitoring patients that weren't emergent but who couldn't get into an urgent care clinic.

Colds and sprains.

All of which was easy for Zac to sign off onto interns.

He downed another cup of coffee, trying to fight the exhaustion, because he didn't want to fall asleep. He didn't want to give the nightmares a chance to return. Not when he had been cleared. He wasn't losing this fight. He wouldn't let the post-traumatic stress disorder take over again.

And he was angry at himself for thinking that it could come back. Angry at himself for making Ella doubt herself, for making her feel guilty when he should be the one who was ashamed of what he'd done.

No one has been hurt. You've been in control. You were cleared.

Zac went to check on Ella. He stood in the doorway, watching her sleep curled up in the lounge chair. She looked so peaceful.

She'd changed so much in some respects, but in others she was still the same. He'd forgotten how much she drove

him crazy in one moment and then in the next they were laughing over something only they understood.

He'd missed that.

There was a part of him that had hoped that she would keep in touch when he left for Annapolis, but when he'd never heard from her, he'd brushed it off. He'd known that she'd be busy as well. There had been times when they'd been growing up when they hadn't seen each other for long stretches and when they saw each other again they would pick right back up.

He'd been a fool to think that.

Of course this time had been different and he knew why.

Even though he'd apologized he got the sense that it wasn't enough. And he knew her well enough that once her trust was broken, that was it. It was one of the things he admired about her. He was so glad to see that strong-willed woman come out of her.

Even if that same woman and that same strong will drove him completely around the bend.

And he smiled as he watched her.

That can't be comfortable, sleeping like that.

Zac stepped into the room as quietly as he could and lifted her up in his arms. She moaned slightly and then murmured.

"What's happening? Is the storm over?" she asked.

"No," he whispered. "Just taking you someplace more comfortable."

"I'm fine."

"Santa won't come if you wait up for him," he teased gently.

She sighed and smiled, half-asleep, "You're an idiot, Davenport."

He chuckled softly as he carried her into a nearby on-call room and laid her gently in the bed. She curled up on

her side and opened her eyes. Her blue eyes twinkled in the dark under those thick lashes.

"Thanks," she said. "You were right. That was uncomfortable."

"Just rest."

"What time is it?" she asked, yawning, and he had to fight back his own urge to yawn.

"Seven in the evening."

"The storm still going strong?" she murmured as she closed her eyes.

"Yeah." Then he reached out, touched her silky blonde hair. "Yeah, it's still going strong."

He pulled his hand away as she fell back asleep. He wanted to stay here. He wanted to take her in his arms and never let her go, but he wasn't the same Zac Davenport.

That Zac Davenport, the one she had known when they'd been inseparable, before he'd hurt her, that man was gone.

That man had died on the beach the day Rojas had died.

Yet when he'd watched her help bring new life into the world, something had come alive within him. Something that was unwelcome, something he'd thought was locked away deeply.

He'd seen the way she'd looked longingly at that baby. He'd seen that expression on his siblings' face before. He knew that she wanted children but he just couldn't give his heart over to a child.

And as much he wanted things to be different, she deserved so much more than the shell of a man he'd become.

Zac got up and put distance between himself and Ella.

He had to get out of there, before he stayed forever.

CHAPTER NINE

ELLA WOKE WITH a start and then glanced at her watch. It was ten. She got up and pulled the blind in the on-call room. And still saw snow. Not as much, but there was still snow. As she peered out into the night, she could see in the city lights the drifts of snow that covered the streets.

And as she was watching the snowflakes swirl across the road, she saw the flashing blue light of a plow up another side street.

Good.

This was turning out to be the longest shift ever, but it was still better than going to her mother's and listening to how much her parents were disappointed in her just because she didn't have a man or kids.

Her thoughts turned to Zac. And she couldn't help but think of him, his strong arms around her. He'd changed, but working with him tonight had been like old times. And even though he'd hurt her, she felt like that girl again, she had her best friend back and it was making the longer shift easier.

She almost didn't want it to end. And for one brief moment she thought maybe there could be more.

He doesn't want kids. Remember?

And there was no one else in her life presently that she would think about having a family with. Which made her think of her mother again, harping on her lack of a partner.

It annoyed her that her mother valued life's accomplishments like that. What if she never was able to have kids?

What if she decided to adopt?

Would her mother value her then? *No, because you've always been a disappointment to your mother.*

Ella had never been tall or graceful like her sisters. She was short and curvy. She didn't have the so-called "it" appeal her sisters had.

She'd needed braces and had preferred to have her hands in the mud with Zac than have tea parties and wear dresses. She'd loved medicine and science.

She had been a tomboy and her mother's biggest disappointment.

Not even graduating top of her class at Harvard or being a top trauma surgeon was enough for her mother because Ella was single.

In her mother's skewed view, she had failed.

It made her feel frustrated and angry. Still, there was no point in getting worked up about it now. She'd had a rest and she was going to offer one to Zac now that she was rested. It was nice that he'd come to check on her and then carried her to bed.

The chair had been more uncomfortable than she'd thought, but she'd been so exhausted she couldn't move. She'd never expected in a million years that Zac would pick her up and carry her to bed, like he used to do when she'd flaked out somewhere when they'd been studying and she'd woken up tucked in bed.

Only usually he had been on the floor, sleeping, but he wasn't on the floor in the on-call room. This was a completely different situation and they were completely different people.

Are you?

She tied her hair back in a ponytail and then left the on-call room to check on the emergency room. When she

got down there it was eerily quiet. Which meant it would soon get really busy. She knew it.

This was how it usually went. They would be calm, just like the calm before a storm. She had no doubt that they would soon be flooded with an influx of emergency patients, especially since the storm seemed to be clearing and the roads were being plowed.

Zac was sitting behind the unit desk by the dispatch phone. He was leaning back in the chair, with his feet resting on the desk. She couldn't help but smile, her pulse racing as she thought of his strong arms around her.

And a memory of lying beside him in the grass at her parents' summer home in the Hamptons, staring up through the leaves of the large oak tree they used to climb together. She'd watched him then, thinking about how to steal a kiss, thinking about how much she wanted him, but had been too afraid to take the chance.

Just like now.

He sat up then and started charting. The relaxed stance gone, he was focused on his work. Just like she should be, instead of mooning over him. She was not that girl any more.

Aren't you?

She leaned over the desk. "Well, did I miss the rush or...?"

"You haven't missed the rush," he said before taking a sip of his coffee, not looking at her as he charted.

"The storm seems to be dissipating. I can see the lights out in the city and I saw some plows."

"The governor declared a state of emergency for New York City, Long Island and surrounding areas. I guess you won't be getting out to see your parents in the next couple of days. They've shut the highways down to the island. The priority is to get the city cleared first."

"Oh, dear." She laughed. "I was so looking forward to going to my parents' place on Christmas Day."

Zac snorted. "Your disappointment is obvious."

"Hey, this is a great Christmas so far."

They shared a secret smile.

Zac stretched. "Did you have a good rest?"

"Yes. Thanks for moving me." Warmth flooded her cheeks as she thought about being in his arms. She'd forgotten how safe she felt in his arms.

"It was no problem. You looked so uncomfortable."

"I was, but I was too tired to move."

There was a rumble and they both glanced out the ambulance bay doors to see a small plow go past the doors.

"That's a good sign," she said.

"Yeah, a good sign we're about to be bombarded. I hope you're ready, Dr. Lockwood."

"Don't jinx it."

Zac was going to say something else when the phone rang. All the lines started to light up. "Here we go."

"See, you jinxed it."

"Ha-ha. You man the phone and I'll get the troops ready."

"Aye-aye." She gave a salute and he rolled his eyes, chuckling as he answered the phone.

Zac dealt with Dispatch while Ella had the nurse Carol start to page all available residents and interns to the emergency room. Ella started assigning stations and final-year residents in charge of the interns. The last thing she needed was interns underfoot while they dealt with the influx of patients that was being brought in.

She watched the board as Zac finished with Dispatch, so they were prepared for the worst. There were heart attacks, accidents, broken bones and a wide variety of other patients.

All non-urgent patients were being diverted to an urgent

care clinic that was three blocks away and which had extended its hours to try and give some relief to the hospitals.

Ella pulled on a yellow trauma gown and stood at the door with Ryan and Jen. Usually they said nothing to her, but then she realized she'd never thought of them as Ryan and Jen before.

Now they were more at ease around her and she liked that.

She'd been so busy building walls to protect herself that she'd shut out everyone and completely isolated herself. No wonder she was lonely.

Jen gave her a smile and Ella smiled back with shared camaraderie.

Zac joined them waiting at the ambulance bay door.

"I have bad news," Zac said.

"What?"

"One of the calls was a weather report. This is just the eye of the storm. It's going to get bad again before it gets better."

"Ugh, I thought it was over."

Zac shook his head. "The calm before the real onslaught, apparently. They are also forecasting a storm surge."

"A storm surge?" Ella asked. "That bad?"

"Hospitals near the river could get flooded and according to emergency plans in place since Hurricane Sandy we're one of the hospitals they evacuate to. We are on higher ground, we're at the risk for surges, but only the basement level would be affected."

Dammit.

Ella pinched the bridge of her nose. "It is what it is. Hopefully the surge doesn't happen like it did when Hurricane Sandy hit, but if it comes to that, we'll make do. We don't have a choice."

"I came home from active duty because it was supposed to be simpler."

Ella snorted. "Really?"

"I know, I was slightly delusional." He winked.

Then the whine of sirens could be heard in the distance and as the ambulances pulled up in the large ambulance bay Ella and Zac jumped into action.

They were the front line, assessing the severity of patients as paramedics passed on the information to Ella and Zac.

Broken femur. Ella passed that off to Jen, who'd experience of that before and had an interest in orthopedics.

The head injury from a motor vehicle appeared superficial. The patient was conscious and bleeding profusely with a high GCS score, and that went to Ryan.

"Gunshot victim. Mr. Chow, aged fifty-four," the paramedic said grimly. "Attempted robbery. A family member tried to rob his store."

Ella cocked an eyebrow, but kept her opinion to herself. It was not her place to judge. All she was there to do was heal.

To save lives.

"Gunshots to abdomen, chest, thigh and shoulder," the paramedic continued. "It took us two hours to get to him through the storm. His condition was stable, but it's deteriorating."

Ella glanced down at the man, who had an oxygen mask on. He was conscious, but from the pallor of his face she could tell that he was losing blood. Fast.

"Mr. Chow, I'm Dr. Lockwood and I'm going to take care of you." The wind picked up again, showing they were through the eye of the storm. They were sideswiped by a gust of snow that blinded them. Ella tried to cover her patient as best as she could as ice and snow pelted her back.

The wind blew snow that had already fallen into drifts

around them. It was hard to push the gurney, but Zac stepped up and steered it through the drifts, like it was nothing. All that training in the navy had paid off.

Mr. Chow barely acknowledged her. He was fading fast. "Just hold on, Mr. Chow."

Zac was beside her, helping her push the stretcher across the ambulance bay and into the warmth of the hospital.

"He needs to go to the operating room now," Ella said. "He's been shot four times."

"Four times?" Zac asked. "Yeah, I'll get some O-negative ready and meet you up there."

Zac was incredibly calm under the pressure. Everything was swirling and chaotic and he was thinking ten steps ahead.

Which she appreciated.

Ella wheeled the gurney toward the elevators. She pressed the button, but the moment the button lit up there was another pop and the hospital was cast into darkness again. The generators didn't kick in.

Generators are fixed, my ass.

The monitors that were hooked up to Mr. Chow began to sound alarms. Ella cursed as she jumped into action to insert a chest tube and provide manual ventilation.

Zac found her in the darkness and chaos. Only he was calm and collected, unlike before when the dark and the noise had bothered him. Except that time they had been in the hall by themselves. Perhaps the chaos calmed him?

Whatever it was, she was glad of his focus and his help at this moment. With the new generator system flickering, the storm and being exhausted, she was grateful for his calm presence and help.

"He's crashing. I need to get that bullet out of his chest!" She worked fast to get her patient intubated so that she could manually ventilate him. "I can't wait for the elevator to be up and running again."

"Let's get him into an exam room." Zac steered the stretcher while Ella manually pumped the Ambu bag, allowing Mr. Chow to breathe. "We can operate there if needed. It's not ideal, but it can be done."

They got him into the room and Zac began to take over. They were going to open Mr. Chow's chest and retrieve the bullet. Ella handed over the manual ventilation to a nurse as she helped prep the area. With her headlamp she could see the bullet's entry point, but there was no exit point so it was lodged somewhere in his chest, and given the fact he wasn't breathing, she was hoping that it was in his lungs and not in his heart.

"Hemopneumothorax," Zac said as he listened to the patient's chest. "I've seen this before countless times in gunshot wounds to the chest, especially if it was an RIP bullet."

"A what?" Ella asked, but given the name of it she didn't like the sound of it.

"An RIP, a radically invasive projectile. It explodes when it hits. Whoever shot this gun at him, they were trying to kill him." Zac shook his head. "The ways people think about killing each other, inventing things like this. It just makes me sick!"

Oh, dear God.

Zac examined the entry wound. "I've seen this before. I need to get in there and try to remove the fragments."

"What about the heart?"

"It was on the right side so I would be more worried about the liver. It could be lacerated, but right now we have to get him breathing again and drain the blood out of his chest cavity. Watch for tension pneumothorax."

"How about the exit wounds of the other shots?" she asked. "They don't appear to be RIP bullets. They're through-and-through." She examined the gunshot wound on the thigh. "Didn't touch the femoral artery."

"Good. Pack it." Zac was preparing the tray for a tubal thoracotomy.

She packed it and then checked the shoulder exit wound. which was also a through and through, as was the arm. It was just the chest that wasn't.

It was just that one bullet that had been the deadly one. The one meant to kill.

"Why would the assailant just use one RIP bullet?" Ella wondered.

"Probably could only get their hands on one," Zac remarked. "Probably couldn't afford it."

"Why is this ammunition even sold?"

Zac shook his head. "I don't know. The assailant could've had a cheap knock-off. Perhaps that's why Mr. Chow is still with us."

Ella held the patient steady so that he didn't move around too much as Zac made his incision and inserted a large drain, suturing around it so that it would stay put. Once it was done Ella hung a bag of blood. They would have to monitor the output of Mr. Chow's blood loss and hang blood accordingly.

"What a freaking night," Zac murmured.

The power came back on and as it did the cardiothoracic surgeon who was supposed to be on duty on Christmas Day came rushing into the exam room. Dr. Bentley looked tired and like he had been woken up from a long Christmas nap. He was devilishly handsome and always flirted with Ella shamelessly, though she thought nothing of it.

"I was paged that there was a gunshot wound to the chest? I got here as soon as my street was cleared and then I got trapped in the elevator."

"This the patient, David," Ella said, handing Dr. Bentley the chart. "Through-and-throughs to the leg, shoulder and arm. The bullet in the patient's chest did not have an exit wound and was a radically invasive projectile."

Dr. Bentley swore under his breath. "Has a tubal thoracotomy been done?"

"Yes," Zac replied. "Blood has been hung and the patient intubated. Vitals are currently stable."

"I expect no less from a naval man." Dr. Bentley smiled and nodded. "Well, I'll take over from here, Doctors. I need to get this man up to an operating room. Dr. Davenport, will you assist me?"

"Of course." Zac began to secure the saline bags and lines as they got Mr. Chow ready to go up to the operating-room floor.

Ella stepped back and let them by.

She just prayed that there wouldn't be another power outage.

"Dr. Lockwood," Stacey shouted from Dispatch.

"Yes?" Ella said, turning around.

"Incoming!"

Zac glanced back at her, his expression tense.

"I've got this," she said. "Take care of the patient."

"I'll be back as soon as I can," Zac said.

"I know."

She changed her gown and gloves, disposing of them, and put on a fresh trauma gown, stepping out into the cold, whirling storm and listening for the faint wail of ambulance sirens. As she did so, she was suddenly up to her ankles in pooling water, which was rapidly running across the ground.

A storm surge.

Just what they needed in the middle of the night.

She just hoped the generators would hold. Now more than ever, because if the storm surge was ankle-deep and reaching them, the lower Manhattan hospitals would soon be implementing their emergency evacuation plans and they would be swamped with patients.

* * *

A cardiothoracic fellow managed to stumble in thirty minutes into Mr. Chow's surgery, so Zac was able to scrub out and make his way back down to the emergency room.

He'd heard there were storm surges coming in.

The cardiothoracic fellow had mentioned he'd waded in ankle-deep water to get to the hospital.

Thankfully, the emergency generators were not in the bowels of the hospital. Charles had moved them to higher ground when they'd revamped the backup system as they were safe from the water that might short them out. Still, they hadn't been the most reliable tonight.

And he'd heard from Dr. Bennet that there was still the risk of the grid shutting down.

What they'd experienced on Christmas Eve had been nothing compared to the strength of the storm that was pelting New York right at this moment. He had to get back down to the emergency room floor. They were probably overwhelmed, but more staff had managed to get in when there had been a break in the storm.

He pushed the down button and the doors snapped shut.

Zac wasn't thinking of anything in particular when there was a grind and a flicker of power. He didn't want to be trapped in an elevator, especially as he was a bit claustrophobic. This was the last thing he needed.

He needed to be out there, doing his job. Ella needed him. It was nice to work with her. Instead of fighting over patients, they were working together like a team. Just like before. He hadn't realized he'd missed it so much.

There was a jolt and a squeal of metal.

Dammit. No.

The elevator ground to a halt. And he was trapped in darkness, inside a metal box. His pulse raced and his body trembled. He was trapped. There was no way out. He pushed the call button.

"Maintenance," the voice said on the other end.

"It's Dr. Davenport, Zac. I'm trapped in the south tower elevator somewhere between the operating floor and the emergency department."

"Sorry, Dr. Davenport. We're working on getting the generators up and running. One blew out. It should only be a few moments."

Zac didn't respond, although he wanted to tell them to hurry, but he didn't want his voice to give him away. To let them know just how absolutely terrified to the core he was at this moment, trapped between floors.

Deep breaths.

Right now he had to focus. He had to remember what he'd learned in that mandatory counselling session.

He had to focus on that one perfect moment in his life.

And that was Ella.

He closed his eyes and thought about her and their kiss.

"Ella," he whispered, breaking off the kiss. "If you keep kissing me like that..."

"What then?" she whispered, her hands on his face.

"I don't know." And then he kissed her again. "I don't want to hurt you."

"You won't. We're both leaving for medical school after Christmas. It doesn't have to be anything but this moment."

"I'd never hurt you, Ella."

Tears slipped down her cheeks and she smiled. "I know you wouldn't. You're my dragon slayer."

Zac shook that thought away, because what he'd thought was a joyful moment, a perfect moment, had been marred by him.

He'd told her that he'd never hurt her and yet he had. Those unkind words he'd said had been to stop those other guys from gossiping, from talking about him and Ella getting married, something he'd been tired of hearing about because he'd never wanted to get married. He hadn't

wanted anything to do with his parents' world. Which was why the navy had been perfect.

It had just been talk.

And the wrong thing to say.

He thought of her at the wedding not that long ago. How different she'd looked, but also the same when he'd seen her. How it had torn him up inside that she'd looked right through him like he'd been a ghost.

Of course, now he knew why.

Then her kiss when they'd been lying in the darkness of the on-call room. The way she'd felt in his arms as he'd carried her from the uncomfortable chair to a cot, where they had joked about Santa.

The way she had a larger-than-life presence in the operating room. The way she commanded respect from a plethora of eager residents and interns, all of whom wanted to learn from her, but were also in awe of her. No one wanted to make a fool of themselves in front of Ella. They all sought her approval, but she didn't see it.

She was stronger than she believed.

And he admired her.

He wanted her.

She needed someone better than him and she had been here first. Perhaps he should resign from Manhattan Mercy and let her stay here. He didn't want to hold Ella back.

He didn't deserve her after what he'd done to her. Their chance had been squandered.

Yet another part of him wanted to take the chance, to right the wrong he'd done so long ago.

Perhaps just being with her once would bury the ghosts once and for all?

Perhaps you could find happiness instead?

"Zac?" The voice on the intercom was Ella's.

"Ella?"

"I heard that you were stuck."

"I am. How is it going in the emergency room?"

"Another couple of trauma surgeons made it in, but it's quiet for the moment again. There are storm surges and the snow is blocking storm sewers. The streets in lower Manhattan are flooded."

"That's not helping," he said dryly.

"Sorry, you asked."

"I hate being stuck in here." And he hated himself for saying those words to her at that moment. He hated showing a vulnerable side, but he had no choice. He felt as if he was on the edge of a deep chasm of darkness.

Talking to her kept the hellish memories away.

It helped him keep his mind off the fact he was suspended between floors. In the dark. Alone.

He hated the dark.

"You okay?" she asked. "You've gone quiet."

"I'm thinking."

"I assumed so, there's not much to do stuck between floors," she teased.

A smile crept across his face and he chuckled. "Thanks."

"You're welcome."

"Tell me a joke," he said.

"A joke?" she asked, shocked. "I don't know any jokes."

"Come on, of course you do."

"No, I don't."

"Tell me a surgeon joke."

"Ugh, okay. A man wakes up in a hospital bed and screams, 'Doctor, I can't feel my legs!' And the surgeon replies, 'Of course you can't, I cut off both your arms.'"

Zac rolled his eyes and shook his head. "That's a terrible joke. Who told you that joke?"

"Charles," she said, and then they laughed at the absurdity of it.

"I should've known."

"It'll be okay," she said. "Remember that time you got

stuck in the broom cupboard when we were eleven? We were in there for a while."

"Yeah, but that was different," Zac said.

"Why?"

"You were with me."

There was no response on the other end.

"Ella?" he asked cautiously.

"I'm here," she said. "I'm still here."

"Thanks for being here." He sighed. "I didn't really want to be alone in here."

"No doubt. I know you have issues with small spaces."

"It's why I didn't work on a submarine," he teased. "Still, there were times…"

"Times what?" she gently asked.

"Situations that still haunt me."

"I'm sorry," she whispered. "It must've been tough."

"Yeah, but you always got me through it."

There was another pause. "What do you mean, I got you through it? I wasn't there."

"You were," he said, his pulse thundering, and he wished he could reach through the intercom and touch her. "You were there in my mind. All the times we were together."

He wanted to tell her about how he wished there had been more between them but couldn't form the words.

"You were there, Ella. Always."

The lights came on and the elevator started to move. When he got off on the emergency-room floor, Ella was there waiting for him.

Just like she'd always been there, her eyes wide and breathing fast. And all he could think about was righting the wrong and taking her in his arms.

"You okay?" she asked.

"I'm fine," he said huskily. Every fiber in his being was

telling him to take her, but his conscience was screaming at him that he didn't deserve her.

"Why are you looking at me like that?" she asked, pink blooming in her cheeks.

"That was a terrible joke."

"I told you I don't know jokes."

He took a step closer. He could smell her hair. Roses. Just like he remembered. He reached out and touched her soft cheek. "No, you don't know jokes."

She closed her eyes and touched his hand. "Did you mean what you said?"

"About you being there when I was overseas? Yeah, I did."

She looked up at him and he could feel her pulse racing under his hands. "I'm glad I was there."

"I'm glad you're here too."

And before she said anything Zac took her in his arms, cupping her face and capturing her lips with his.

Even though he knew that he shouldn't, that he was going to leave because it was better for her, he just couldn't help himself.

All he wanted was one more taste of her sweet lips.

To hold her in his arms one more time. To take the chance he squandered and have more of her. All of her. Even for just a night.

"Zac," Ella whispered in shock. "What?"

"I'm sorry, Ella. I couldn't help myself. I've..." And he couldn't find the words and kissed her again, urgently this time because he needed to have her. To possess her. To get lost in her arms. He wanted to know what it was like to be with her instead of just dreaming about it.

"I need you, Ella," he whispered against her lips, drinking in her scent, her taste.

"Zac, I want you too," she said breathlessly. "I've wanted you for so long." He scooped her up in his arms

and carried her to the nearest empty on-call room, shutting the door behind him with a swift kick. He set her down and kissed her again.

"I just want to be with you, Ella. I know I don't deserve it. Please be with me. Just for tonight." He wanted to make up for the past mistake and he hoped she did too.

Her answer was to kiss him again, reaching behind him to turn the lock on the on-call room door. He reached up to undo the messy bun of her cornsilk-blonde hair. He was going to enjoy this moment. This one moment.

Just one last time.

Even if it shattered his soul completely.

CHAPTER TEN

WHAT'RE YOU DOING? What're you doing?

That was the argument from the rational side of her brain, which told her to protect her guard. The other side was urging her to give in and enjoy this moment that she'd been dreaming about for so long.

She wanted to see if her fantasies matched reality. She'd had other boyfriends, but they hadn't been memorable and they had been fleeting because deep down all she'd ever wanted was Zac.

She'd been numb for so long, she just wanted the release of heady pleasure.

That voice of reason was drowning in a sea of need and desire as his lips crushed hers with kisses, his hands in her hair, as she pulled him tight against her body so they were flush. As she felt his hard body pressed against hers, any reservations she had melted away in a rush of lust.

This wasn't love.

And that's what she had to keep reminding herself. Zac Davenport was incapable of love. She'd learned that lesson a long time ago. Only now, at the end, she wouldn't be devastated. She could just enjoy this moment and take it for what it was.

It was just sex.

Plain and simple.

Really?

Maybe it wouldn't be just sex. A part of her hoped that it wouldn't be just that. Deep down, she was secretly hoping for more, but steeling herself for the disappointment because all she knew right now was that she wanted him.

Only him.

What he'd said in the elevator had broken through the guards around her heart. It had melted her resolve completely. She was lost and she didn't care.

All she wanted to do was feel.

The kiss ended, and her breath hitched in her throat as she helped him out of his scrub top and ran her hands over the hardened muscles that hadn't been there before. She let her fingers travel over scars that marred his flesh, scars that hadn't been there before, and she couldn't help but wonder how they had got there.

"Bullet," he whispered against her neck. "It was nothing."

"Do you want me to stop touching you there?" she asked. She was upset that he'd been shot, but he had been in the armed forces so that was always a possibility.

"No, I like it. I like you touching me there." He kissed her neck, right against her pulse point. "Your heart is racing. I can feel it."

And then she placed a hand on his chest. "Yours as well."

He helped her pull off her scrub top and toss it away. Zac ran his hands down her back, causing a shiver of delight to pass through her.

"Your skin is so soft. I'd forgotten how soft it was." His brilliant blue eyes twinkled in the darkness. It was his eyes that always made her go weak in the knees and now was no exception. It was just the two of them here in the wee hours of Christmas Day, surrounded by a storm that had shut down the entire city.

And she wanted to tell him about all the things she'd forgotten about him. How he made her feel. How safe he made her feel.

How vulnerable she was when she was with him.

"God, Ella. I've missed you."

She didn't respond. Instead, she just undid the knot on his scrub pants and caressed him. He sucked in a breath at her touch. She wanted to tell him that she'd missed him too, but that was giving him too much power at this moment. And right now she wanted all the power.

She couldn't let him have too much of her. Even though she wanted him to have all of her right now, and that thought scared her. That he had such a hold on her even after all this time.

Zac's hand drifted to her bottom, his face buried in her neck. His hands on her made her melt with anticipation. Her body craved the connection again. Ella arched her back, wanting to be closer to him. She didn't want any space between the two of them. She wanted to be possessed by him.

Zac scooped her up and pressed her against the cot and she opened her legs, his weight settling between her thighs.

His kisses teased her as he slipped her bra off. She hadn't even realized he'd undone it when he was stroking her back. She had been too caught up in the sensation of his strong hands on her body again.

Zac pressed kisses down her neck, along her collarbone, lower and lower until she felt searing heat from his tongue on her sensitive nipple. First one and then the other.

She cried out. It was an overload to the senses.

Zac touched her everywhere and she caressed him, reaching down to touch him. He let out a growl and pinned her wrists over her head.

"Don't," he bit out.

"Don't what?" she whispered, smiling because she knew exactly what she was doing.

"I want you so badly, Ella. I don't want this to end just yet."

"Neither do I, but I love the feeling of you. I love teasing you."

"Ella," he moaned.

"I want you, Zac." And she did. Her legs wrapped around his waist, pulling him closer as she clung to him. She was begging him to take her. To possess her like she'd wanted so long ago.

She wanted this moment with him. It had always been Zac and it scared her, the hold that he had on her, but at this moment she didn't care.

All she wanted to do was feel.

Zac moved away, only for a moment to get protection, but he was back in a moment. He removed her underwear and now there was nothing between them. They were skin to skin, heartbeat to heartbeat. He was touching her, caressing her between her legs and making her purr with desire. He was driving her wild with need.

"Please," Ella whispered against his ear as she nibbled on his ear lobe, which drove him crazy. "Please."

He didn't respond with words, just kissed her, his tongue pushing past her lips. It was an urgent kiss. A possessive, hungry kiss.

He broke the kiss and touched her face gently. Their gazes locked as he entered her, slowly stretching her and filling her completely.

Her blood heated, like fire through her veins. They were one in this moment. And it felt like he belonged. Like he should always be there.

"Ella," he whispered gently as he kissed her cheeks, her lips, her eyelids. Light kisses. "Ella."

And before she could control them, tears slipped down her cheeks and he kissed those away too.

"I'm sorry," she said, her voice hitching and her smile wobbly.

"There's nothing to be sorry about." He kissed her as he began to thrust slowly. And soon the tears were forgotten and she was swept up in the sensations of their lovemaking. She moved with him, meeting his thrusts. They were one and it was like they had never been apart. Like he'd never hurt her.

Like he'd never left.

Ella came to the startling realization at that moment that she still loved him. She'd never stopped loving him. She'd thought she'd got over him but she hadn't. She'd just learned to exist and it wasn't much of an existence. Her life was numb and lonely.

Her heart ached for him.

She climaxed then, crying out as she clung to him, her nails digging into the flesh on his back. She wanted more and she knew there would be no more after this moment, so she was trying desperately hard to hold onto this moment. To what she had.

Loving him was dangerous for her heart, but she couldn't help it. She loved him. She had never stopped loving him, even when he'd hurt her so, but for her own sanity she had to hide her heart from him. She couldn't open up her soul or heart to him again. It was too much of a risk.

And even though this wasn't the same immature man who'd broken her heart, she just couldn't risk it. She couldn't risk having her world come crashing down again.

She'd worked too hard to repair herself after he'd hurt her.

It was safer behind her walls. Walls she'd built to keep him out.

Walls that you built to keep everyone out.

All they could have was this stolen time in the on-call room. Just like their stolen moment years ago in her parents' library, when they had been alone and talking about heading off to medical school and he'd kissed her. He'd stolen her heart then.

This was all it could ever be between them. There couldn't be any more. At least this time she had come to that realization before she had tried to give him her heart, only for him to break it. She was wiser.

Are you? Maybe you should just tell him.

She ignored that voice. She couldn't tell him. Had to protect herself.

Her life and well-being depended on it.

Ella was still wrapped up in his arms. And he was angry at himself for being so selfish and not thinking about her at all. All he'd been thinking about had been himself when he'd seen her standing there, waiting for him to get off the elevator.

His body reacted and he'd sought the thing that calmed him down.

He'd sought out the only thing that he was addicted to. And that was Ella.

How could I use her again?

"You tensed up," Ella said, propping herself up on one elbow. "What's wrong?"

"Nothing. I..." He sat up, leaving the warm comfort of her arms. "I don't want to hurt you again. I should've—"

"Hey," Ella said, and then he felt her hand on his shoulder. "I wanted it too. I know that there were no strings attached."

"I hurt you so badly all those years ago."

She shrugged. "And you've apologized. It is what it is. I don't have those same feelings that I did back then. I know what this was and I'm okay with it."

Zac was taken back by the way she so easily brushed it off.

Isn't this what you wanted?

No. It wasn't, but it was for the best. He knew what he wanted. He wanted Ella, but she was off limits. She'd always been off limits.

Love and marriage, a family wasn't for him.

So you think.

"Right. Of course."

Ella sat up and began to pull her clothes back on. "Can I ask a question?"

"Sure," he said, worried that she was going to try to delve too deep. And he didn't want her to.

"Why did…? I mean, why did you think of me back then?"

Zac ran his knuckles down her cheeks, reveling in the softness of her skin. He wanted to tell her about needing her, how she was his port in a storm, only he couldn't.

"I just needed you," he said. "The elevator and being stuck… I needed you. I needed to focus on things that made me happy."

Ella didn't say anything at first and he couldn't help but wonder if she believed what he'd said or saw right through him.

Of course she sees right through you.

"And I made you happy?" she asked in shock.

"Of course. Our childhood was happy." He wanted to tell her that it wasn't just childhood memories that had sustained him through the horrors of what he'd gone through, the horrors he tried to forget. It was the memory of their shared kiss, so long ago, and his longing for more.

For all of her.

She seemed disappointed and he was angry at himself for hurting her. Again.

"You can talk to me about what happened over there," she said gently.

Ella was always so giving and it made him feel worse.

"No. I can't."

"Okay, but if you need anything, I'm here."

Zac wanted to thank her, to pull her close, only he didn't. There had to be a separation now. He couldn't drag this on.

"I'd better get down to the emergency-room floor." He hated himself for being so cold yet again and brushing her aside, but it was for the best.

Keep telling yourself that.

He left the on-call room first and made his way to the emergency room. The first thing he saw outside the ambulance bay doors were sandbags. It surprised him. He couldn't believe a storm surge had come this far or that the winter storm raging outside was strong enough to send a storm surge to the Upper West side.

Lower Manhattan, sure, but the Upper West side?

Ella came up behind him, tying her hair back as she stared at the sandbags that were being pelted with wet, slushy snow. If the temperature dropped, they could have a flash freeze, which was worse than snow. Snow was bad enough, but black ice was treacherous.

"Flooding?" he asked Ella.

"Yes," she said quickly, barely looking at him. There was an almost palpable tension between them. She'd brushed him off and he'd done the same when she had offered to listen to him.

It was for the best.

Are you sure?

"Are there evacuation orders?" he asked, trying to change the subject.

"Yes." She continued with her work, not looking at him,

and he was annoyed that she was back to this cool behavior, like when he had first arrived at Manhattan Mercy.

He deserved it this time.

"Well?"

"I have to prepare the team. The evacuation plans are at the unit desk," she said in exasperation.

"I can help prepare the team."

"I don't need help," she snapped. "I've been in this situation before."

"So have I, Ella."

Her expression softened slightly. "Man the phones at the unit desk. Someone needs to."

"Okay, I can do that." He was glad to put distance between them. It was bad enough that he was working Christmas Eve again during another natural disaster.

Lower Manhattan was completely flooded and evacuation plans were in place for Manhattan Mercy to receive any pediatric patients. The pediatric department and the NICU had enough staff and were on standby. The loading dock entrance was not flooded like the ambulance bay doors, so all ambulances for patient transport were being diverted to the loading docks.

"And what about emergency patients?" he asked, before he went to take over the phones.

"If they can get in on foot, we'll take them, but because the ambulance bay has about a foot of water in it we have to divert to Sinai," she said as she began to distribute supplies to the different beds in the triage area.

Last Christmas he'd been on the island of Iphita in the Caribbean, working to help stave off a natural disaster, and then war had broken out. So many lives had been lost and not from the landslide but from the fact that the natural disaster had caused a complete collapse of government.

All the violence and bloodshed.

The government was hardly about to collapse here, but

the thought of having to go through a simulation and then actually go through the execution of a plan for a natural disaster that was about to happen made him feel sick to his stomach.

What he needed now was Ella again, but he wouldn't hurt her. Still, he couldn't help but think back to what had happened. What they'd just shared.

Ella made him forget what had happened during that horrible Christmas last year. She gave him hope. Something he hadn't felt in so long.

Zac turned to head to the unit desk when he heard a cry. A painful, soul-crushing sob. He turned to see a woman stumble in through the emergency-room doors.

The woman was drenched and not appropriately dressed for winter. Her dark eyes were wild and her long black hair clung to her face. The look of absolute horror and terror on her face reminded him of Consuela. And just like that he was thrust back in time to that moment.

"My son! My God! My son!"

Zac shook the thought away. He wasn't going to let this happen again. Not another life lost. Not this Christmas.

"Please! Someone help me!" she cried out.

"Ma'am, how can we help?" Ella asked, rushing to her side.

"My son. Oh, my God. My son!"

CHAPTER ELEVEN

"MY INFANT WAS being transported at the loading dock. We were evacuated from Lower Manhattan Hospital. I had my four-year-old with me, because his father is working tonight. He's a firefighter and is trying to help with the flooding. My son was standing beside me one moment and when I turned around he was gone."

The panicked woman ran her hands through her wet, stringy hair.

"He doesn't usually wander off like this. Especially in a storm. He was frightened. They were so busy at the loading docks, trying to get the patients out of the storm, I followed footprints as far as I could and ended up here. I was hit by a storm surge, though, and… Oh, God. I can't bear to think of something happening to him."

No, this was different. This is your chance. You can save this life.

Zac's stomach twisted. This was all too familiar. He took a deep breath. He had this. He wasn't alone this time. He had Ella.

Do you?

They would find this boy. He and Ella would find him and he could lay his ghosts to rest. He could move on maybe.

He needed to find this child. He couldn't be haunted any more.

He needed his life back.

"Okay, we'll look for him," Ella said calmly. "We'll get you settled first and then I will look for him."

"There's no time for that," Zac snapped, as he grabbed a Manhattan Mercy coat from where they were hanging by the ambulance bay doors.

"Time for what?" Ella asked in confusion as she left the frantic mother with the nurses.

"To get her settled. We have to find that boy." Zac zipped up his coat and then headed out into the storm. He heard Ella calling him, but time was of the essence. The mother was fine, albeit wet.

The boy was not. He was in danger, Zac knew it.

And he needed to save this boy. This couldn't happen again. Another child couldn't die. Not again. If he made this right, maybe everything could work out.

Who are you kidding?

"Zac!" Ella called out, over the roar and rush of the storm. "Wait!"

He glanced over his shoulder to see Ella bundled in a Manhattan Mercy coat, wading through a foot of water left over from the last storm surge and it made him quake in fear. An image of her being swept away hit him hard.

It was a visceral reaction, one he wasn't prepared for. He could see Rojas's face rising from the shadows and the swirling snow like a ghost.

"Go back!" he shouted. He didn't want Ella risking her life. This was his fight. He couldn't bear it if she were hurt.

"You can't do this alone!"

"I can! Why don't you believe I can?" he shouted. "You need to go back."

"I'm not going anywhere!" she shouted back at him, her

eyes narrowed and that fiery temper shining through the snow. "If we split up we can find him faster in this mess."

He scrubbed his hand over his face, the blowing snow and ice biting at his skin. He didn't want to let Ella out of his sight, but she was right. If they split up they would be able to cover more ground.

Still, the idea of something happening to her, of her being swept away or hit by a plow, or even slipping and hitting her head on the ice was too much to bear. The thought of losing her scared him.

If she was out of his sight, this barely contained anxiety would be uncontrolled. He needed her and he knew that the longer they stood there and argued over it, the longer the child was in danger.

"My son! My God! My son!" Consuela's voice screamed.

No, it wasn't Consuela's voice. It was this new mother's. And his own mother's voice crying out when he'd been recovering from his injuries in Annapolis.

"No, we need to stick together. This storm is getting worse. He couldn't have gotten far. Even if he was hit by the storm surge, it's shallow and he wouldn't have been swept out into the river."

"Okay," Ella said breathlessly over the storm. "Where do we start?"

Zac closed his eyes and tried to calm the erratic beating of his heart, which was drowning out all his training, everything he knew about tracking and survival. All he could hear was the howling of the wind and Consuela's wails over her lost child.

That beautiful, happy boy who hadn't needed to die. And this boy wouldn't die. He wouldn't let that happen.

"She was at the loading dock with the child, right?" he asked.

"Yes, that's what she said," Ella shouted over the wind, holding onto her hood so it didn't blow off. "The loading

dock is that way. If we follow that road we can search as we go."

He held out his hand and she took it. He held tight to her. The thought of losing her scared him and the fact that he was so terrified of losing her scared him all the more.

He couldn't be falling in love with Ella.

He didn't deserve love. He didn't deserve happiness and Ella deserved more than him.

"Do you know the boy's name?" Zac asked.

"Josh," she responded.

"Josh?" Zac shouted into the wind.

"Josh?" Ella called. "He's not going to hear us over this wind."

"You're right, but we have to try."

Zac scanned the ground. The snow was drifting, but the water was washing away parts of it. Other parts had been scoured down to the pavement because of the wind. The streetlights were flickering on and off. And overhead the power lines whipped in the wind.

There was a spark of electricity and a zap. Zac froze and looked up to see a transformer box on top of a power line short-circuit.

The power line snapped and a live wire headed toward them. Zac grabbed Ella and forced her to the ground, pushing her into the snow out of the way and covering her body.

"Oh, my God," she screamed. "What the heck just happened? I didn't see."

"A transformer blew in this wind." He glanced over his shoulder and could see the live wire thrashing around in the snow on the other side of the street. And as he watched the wire moving, he saw the child, unconscious and lying in a bus shelter, but between Zac and the boy was the live wire.

He could see there was blood under the boy in the white snow. The boy wasn't in a winter coat, just a sleeper.

And as he looked further up the street he could see the creeping of another storm surge coming their way.

"I found him," Zac shouted.

"Where?" Ella asked.

"The bus shelter. He's injured and probably hypothermic."

If he's still alive.

But he kept that thought to himself. He couldn't let that negative thought into his head.

The live wire had stopped moving. It just sat there, only moving slightly in the wind. When the water hit it, it would be a major conductor and kill the boy for sure. Zac had to get to Josh before the water hit the live wire and he had to give the wire enough of a wide berth so that he wouldn't get hit.

Of course, there was a high voltage and he didn't know if there was differential voltage in the ground. If he put down one foot in the wrong spot and his other foot on another spot he'd be electrocuted.

"How are we going to get to him?" Ella asked.

"We're not," Zac snapped. "I am."

"You'll be electrocuted!"

"Not if I keep my feet together and give it enough of a berth. Just keep to the high ground. There's a surge coming and if you're near the water with electricity running into the ground…"

The implications of the horror that would happen was too much for him to bear. He needed to stop thinking about Ella being in danger if he planned to get through this and save the boy.

He had to forget that Ella was there.

"Okay," she said, and even though she was trying to put on a brave face, he could see that she was terrified as she scrambled to higher ground. "Be careful."

Zac nodded and then took a deep breath. He kept his

feet together and hopped around the live wire, giving it an ample distance but not risking himself to differential voltage that might be flowing through the ground.

He also tried to keep his balance in the blowing wind and to keep his eyes focused on the unconscious boy lying injured in the bus shelter through the snow and the brief moments that it became just a wall of white.

You've got this.

He hopped again and up off the street onto the sidewalk where the bus shelter was. Here he knew he would be safe from the differential voltage that could be pulsing through the ground. As he walked into the bus shelter he lost his footing, smashing his shoulder into the cold, rock-hard metal.

Blinding pain coursed through him and he knew that his shoulder was dislocated.

"Zac!" Ella shouted.

Dammit.

He fell to his knees next to the boy and could see that he was still breathing, but barely. Only he was useless with his shoulder dislocated and the water was trickling in. Using his one good arm and powering through the pain, he managed to lift the boy as the water washed over them. It was cold, like knives against his flesh, plastering his scrubs to his skin.

"Come on, buddy," Zac whispered. "Hang in there. We're here."

And as he looked down into that innocent face he saw Consuela's son Rojas, whom he'd been unable to save. Rojas, who'd liked to play soccer with the navy officers. Rojas, who had always had a funny joke and who'd wanted to learn medicine one day so that he could come back to his village and help the people.

Rojas, who'd died way too young because of unnecessary violence.

And as he held onto the boy, the bitterly cold water swirling around them, he began to weep for the loss. For the boy he hadn't mourned because he had been in shock, seeing a child broken in the middle of a revolution. A boy he'd known and cared for.

The water continued to rise and Zac shuffled to shelter the boy but was limited to what he could do with his shoulder dislocated.

However, the water had caused an electrical surge, burning out the transformer, and the whole block was cast into darkness. Which meant it was safe for Ella to cross.

"Ella!" Zac shouted into the howling wind.

A headlight came on from where he'd last seen her. "I'm here!"

"My shoulder is dislocated. I…" And though it was hard for him to say, he swallowed his pride. "I need your help. The power is out so it's safe for you to cross."

"I'm coming!"

He could hear splashing as she crossed the surge, but the snowstorm intensified and he couldn't see her any more, just the faint light of her surgical headlamp, and he thanked his lucky stars that she'd brought it.

Zac managed to free one arm from his jacket.

Ella appeared in the shelter. "Let's get you guys back to the hospital."

"Get my other arm out of the jacket. We need to wrap this guy up."

"You'll freeze."

"He's been out here longer. I can make it back." He gritted his teeth and she helped free him out of the jacket. He shifted his weight to keep the boy's head elevated out of the water. Once the jacket was off, his teeth began to chatter, which meant he wasn't at that stage of hypothermia that was deadly, but as the boy wasn't trembling, he

was in danger. There was only so long a body could survive in the cold, especially when wet.

Ella lifted the boy up and wrapped him up in Zac's jacket.

"Can you carry him?" he asked through the pain.

"Yes, because you can't. I've got him, Zac."

Zac used his good arm to get on his knees and carefully back to his feet. And then he gripped the back of Ella's jacket so she could guide them back to the ambulance bay doors.

The snow stung his face and he was exhausted. His body felt like it was weighed down and his feet were numb, but it was worth it because the child was alive.

For now.

The power might've gone out on the city block, but the hospital lights were still on. The generators were holding their own.

And that meant warmth.

It felt like an eternity before they were sloshing though the water and snow over the sandbags and into the ambulance bay.

Ryan and Jen were waiting.

Ella handed the boy to Ryan. "Unconscious, exposure, head laceration, but still breathing. You know what to do. Page Pediatrics."

Ryan nodded and carried the boy into an exam room, shouting for warm blankets as he went.

The mother, with a blanket wrapped around her, came running over. Fear was etched into the very pores of her face.

Zac nodded.

She let out a cry.

"He's in there." Ella pointed.

"Thank you!" The mother ran into the exam room, fall-

ing to her knees and crying while they worked on her other child.

Zac felt the room begin to tilt.

"Ella…" he whispered.

"Yeah?" She turned and then her eyes widened as he collapsed to the floor, the world fading out as her arms reached for him.

Ella caught Zac's head before it slammed onto the hospital floor. Her heart had nearly stopped when she'd seen him go pale and collapse. Not that she blamed him. He was probably in agony from his shoulder, in shock and pre-hypothermic.

"Dr. Lynne!" Ella shouted. She needed help. Right now, with Zac injured, she needed to lean on someone else. She wasn't the tough Dr. Lockwood, she was vulnerable, just like that girl from long ago who had been so afraid to say anything to anyone. She needed help.

Jen, who had gone to exam room one with Ryan, came rushing over. Her mouth dropped open, but only for a moment, before she shouted over the commotion, "I need a gurney, stat!"

"Your voice is rivalling mine, Jen," Ella complimented through chattering teeth.

Jen smiled briefly at Ella. "I learned from the best, Dr. Lockwood."

An intern and a nurse came rushing over and all of them lifted Zac onto the gurney. He moaned as he came to. He was still shivering, which was a good sign, but they needed to get him out of his wet scrubs and get some blankets on him. First, though, they had to put his shoulder back into place.

Ella helped with getting his scrub top off. She threw it to the floor while Jen started an IV with fluid to help stave off hypothermia and pain medication for the dislocated

shoulder. The nurse brought in the portable X-ray they used for pediatric emergency patients and Ella prepped him for an X-ray. She couldn't try and put the joint back into place unless she knew that he hadn't fractured a rib and that she wouldn't be breaking something.

"It's fine," Zac slurred through his pain meds. "Just pop it back in."

"You're delusional," she said. "Now hold still."

Everyone left the exam room as she took the X-ray. It flashed up on the computer screen and Zac had been right. It was a simple dislocation.

"Dr. Lockwood, perhaps you want to change out of your wet scrubs," Jen said.

"It's okay, I need to put his arm back into place."

"Now, Dr. Lockwood," Jen said firmly, crossing her arms, the student becoming the master. "You're wet, cold and sleep deprived. Go and get changed. I've handled dislocations before. I've got this."

Zac, under the influence of his pain medications, raised his eyebrows comically and a smile twitched on Ella's face. She leaned over Zac, staring down into those now befuddled Davenport blue eyes that she loved so much.

"I'll be back."

He nodded. "It's fine. I'll be fine. Make sure the kid's okay. That's the most important thing. He can't die."

Ella looked at him strangely. "He's fine, he won't die."

"He's broken." Zac's eyes rolled into the back of his head and she didn't know what he'd meant by *he's broken*. Was he himself broken? Or the boy? The boy was injured and hypothermic, but not broken. Not completely.

She slipped out of the exam room and into the residents' locker room, where she found a spare set of scrubs. She quickly changed and as she tied up her damp hair she heard screams of pain coming from Zac's exam room.

Her heart skipped a beat and she started running.

When he'd disappeared across the road through the swirling snow, she'd heard him cry out as he'd fallen. Had heard the scream of pain, and it had taken every ounce of her being not to run across the road to help him, but there had been a live wire between them.

Watching him hop across the road to avoid being shocked had been bad enough.

And all she'd been able to think of at that moment had been losing him.

He'd hurt her so badly all those years ago, but she still loved him. Try as she may, she just couldn't get Zac Davenport from under her skin. She needed him.

It had killed her to watch him risk his life like that. She'd felt so helpless. She hated that feeling.

It had felt like she was seventeen again and not having a voice as her mother had dressed her in hideous clothing and paraded her around with her two sisters. And her mother had beamed with pride about Ella's older sisters and complained about her.

When she'd had no sense of self-worth.

Her only ray of sunshine had been Zac. He'd given her a voice. He'd given her strength.

He'd been her rock, her reason for striving for more, even though he'd hurt her.

Zac might be used to putting his life in danger, but she wasn't used to seeing his life in danger, and she hadn't liked it one bit.

He'd looked so broken, so defeated, holding that boy the best he could in the bus shelter. Zac had needed her and she'd wanted to be there for him.

She was so afraid. So afraid of being hurt.

So afraid of losing him again.

This had been one heck of a Christmas Eve and the

storm wasn't over yet. She could still hear it rattling the windows of the locker room as she changed.

She just wanted it to end.

All of it. She was tired, but it wasn't so much exhaustion from lack of sleep that was doing it to her. It was emotional exhaustion. She was tired of trying to hide her feelings from Zac. She was tired of denying her feelings to herself.

He screamed again and her stomach flip-flopped.

She ran into the exam room where he was. He was unconscious and his arm was in a sling. Jen Lynne was wrapping him in warm blankets.

"It was textbook," Jen said. "He'll be fine, but his shift for this storm is over."

Ella smiled weakly at her protégé while the nurse cleaned up the wet scrubs and bagged Zac's shoes for him. Ella just stood in the doorway, watching him.

There was a five-o'clock shadow on the strong jaw. It didn't make him look so young any more. His face had matured since medical school, but the bit of scruff made him look a bit dashing. She ran her hand through his dark brown hair and noticed some grey in it.

Stress from serving, but it suited him.

She'd almost lost him tonight. She'd thought he'd been crazy, heading out into that storm by himself. When the woman had come running in, screaming about her son, she'd seen the change in him. The way he'd gone pale, like he'd been staring at a ghost.

Something more had happened while he'd served in the navy, something to do with a child, and that might explain why he'd said he didn't want kids.

She couldn't begin to fathom what he'd gone through, but if it had involved a child… She didn't even want to think about it.

Her heart ached for him. All the pain he must carry inside him.

It explained why he'd acted completely irrationally, just grabbing a coat and running out like that. It had been all she could do to grab a coat and remember to take a headlamp. She was going to give him serious heck for that but, still, the boy had been found and she had no doubt that the pediatric staff and Ryan Trace could take care of the boy.

Right now her main priority was Zac and this emergency room.

"How are the evacuation plans coming, Jen?" she asked Dr. Lynne.

"They've put a stop to them. The whiteout conditions are bad, but they managed to get all the critical patients out of the affected hospitals and into the overflows. Hopefully our generators will hold until this storm ends. It has to end sometime."

She nodded. "Did you have any big Christmas plans?"

Jen shrugged. "Just dinner at my grandmother's house, where she'd lament the status of me not settling down with a man and popping out kids. What about you?"

Ella smiled. "The same, only my mother and not my grandmother."

Jen laughed. "I prefer an extra-long shift in the emergency room any day."

Ella smiled wistfully. "Me too."

And as much as she didn't want to get married and make her parents happy, she understood the appeal at this moment. Sure, she'd been working, but she hadn't been alone this Christmas, like she'd usually been.

Being with Zac again had been wonderful. And for the first time in a long time she hadn't been lonely, feeling like the sunshine in her life was back. She hadn't realized how long she'd been living in the dark.

It had been nice.

She'd forgotten what it was like.

Still, he could leave again and that sobered her. She had to be careful. She made a promise to herself, to her heart.

Never would she go through that pain again. Even if it meant a thousand lonely Christmases. The pain wasn't worth it.

Yes. It is.

CHAPTER TWELVE

Zac woke with a start and it took him a moment to re-
alize where he was in the dim light. He was in an exam
room. He didn't know if it was daylight or still the middle
of the night.

The boy!

He tried to sit up, but his shoulder ached and he was
attached to an IV.

"You dislocated your shoulder," Ella said sleepily, sit-
ting up from where she'd been dozing in a chair that looked
an awful lot like the one she'd been sleeping in earlier. One
that didn't belong in an exam room.

"What about the boy?" he asked.

"He's fine. He's up on the pediatric floor. They put his
little sister's incubator in the same room as him and their
mother is with them. He was hypothermic and needed
stitches, but he's going to be okay."

Zac should have relaxed, hearing that, but he couldn't.
He was still on edge. He could still hear Consuela scream-
ing in his head.

He couldn't control the emotions that were swirling
around inside him. The pain, the anger, the fear.

Nothing.

"Zac? What's wrong? You're trembling. Are you cold?"
Ella got up.

"No," he said through gritted teeth. "It's my post-traumatic stress disorder getting the better of me. Just a panic attack. It will pass."

"I believe you," Ella said softly. "It's been a hard night for you."

He took a deep breath. "Yeah, it's been a hard night for a lot of people."

"The boy is okay."

"I'm glad." He relaxed then. The boy was fine.

Ella touched his head, gently brushing his hair back. "Why are you trying to fight it so much? It's eating you alive. I can see it. I'm here."

Yes. She was here. He needed her.

He closed his eyes and tried to think about her, when they'd been together, but all he could see were the terrible images that had terrified him when she'd come running out into that storm. The thought of her being washed away or injured. Or even lost in the blizzard and succumbing to the elements. They had been paralyzing.

"Why did you have to follow me out into the storm?" he shouted at her. Angry.

"You needed help, Zac. You and the boy would've died if I hadn't come."

Zac took another deep breath. She was right and then he would've been at fault for killing another child.

You didn't kill Rojas. Mortar did. Not you.

"A child…" It was hard to get the words out, but he just couldn't hold it in. He couldn't shake the ghosts away and he just couldn't hold it in any more. She knew he was suffering, she wanted to help, but he was terrified to take her hand. Terrified to take the help she was offering.

"A child died on my last mission." Tears stung his eyes. "I couldn't save him and with that boy tonight…"

Ella grabbed his good hand. "You saved Josh tonight. He's alive. Dr. Bennet from Pediatrics said that if it had

been twenty minutes later, the boy would've died from exposure. You saved him."

"But I couldn't save Rojas," he snapped, then he was angry at himself for snapping at her when she was just trying to help him.

Her expression was empathetic, as if she already knew what was tormenting him. "Tell me about it. Tell me what happened."

Zac rubbed his eyes. He wasn't sure that he could tell her. He'd been hiding it for so long because he didn't want to relive the horror again. Only he was, piece by piece, as it slipped through the cracks in his mind, not all at once.

"There was a natural disaster on the island of Iphita in the Caribbean. The medical frigate I was on was deployed to help. Many locals who were also trained in first aid and medicine assisted us. One nurse named Consuela had a little boy about six years old named Rojas. Rojas went everywhere with her. His father had died a few years back from an infection that would have been preventable had there been clean water."

Ella nodded. "I heard about the cholera outbreak a few years ago."

"Rojas took to me. He liked to run errands for me while his mother and I worked, treating the injured. Then a revolution erupted. A guerrilla faction came out of the rainforest. They were armed to the teeth and were coming to drive Americans off their soil. There was so much bloodshed. Rojas was crushed under rubble when a mortar exploded. He died in my arms and there was nothing I could do. That's where I got this bullet wound. I was shot from behind, a through and through as I was carrying Rojas's body away from the rubble. When I woke up I was back on the medical frigate. Iphita was on the horizon. About three weeks after we arrived back in Annapolis I heard that Consuela had died from an infected wound."

He took a breath. There was a rush of emotion going through him but he couldn't cry. The tears would not come.

"I'm so sorry to hear that," Ella said softly. "That you had to go through that."

"Well, it's part of serving your country." He couldn't look at her. And he hated that he was stuck in this hospital bed with a dislocated shoulder.

"The lost boy, Josh, must've brought it all back."

"It did, and Josh's mother had similar features to Rojas's mother—the hair, the eyes—but after the fact I saw they didn't look alike at all. She just triggered the memory. Her panic triggered it."

"I think a lot of things trigger the memories and you've been fighting long and hard to keep them locked away."

"What is the use of remembering them?" he snapped.

"To accept that what happened was beyond your control and move on."

"That's so easy for you to say, but it's another thing to actually do it. I had to get out of Annapolis. I had to come home and the only way to do that was to bury those nightmares so they would clear me to return to work as a surgeon."

"Zac, I get your motive, but you need to deal with this."

"I'm a Davenport. I was taught to hide my emotions. They make you weak. Look what your emotions did to you. You were stung by words, by a lie."

The moment the hateful words slipped out of his mouth he regretted them. He was a complete monster. He kept hurting Ella.

"You're wrong," she said calmly. "I learned from the pain of that moment when you broke my heart. I learned to hold my head up higher, to take what I wanted and to be one of the best trauma surgeons on the eastern seaboard. I never did properly thank you for that."

It was a slap to him now and he deserved it. He admired

her gumption and so he smiled at her. "You're stronger than I am, then."

"You're stronger than you think," she said softly.

It was kind of her to say that after he'd been so cruel again, but he didn't want her to pity him. He didn't want her to get too close. In order for her to stay strong and successful, she had to steer clear of him.

There was too much wrong emotionally.

He had no really good examples to look up to. His parents were bitter toward each other. His father had cheated on his mother.

What about your brothers and sisters? Haven't they found love?

That may be the case, but he was too broken. Sure, his siblings had had their own trials and tribulations, but none of them had been through what he had. None of them had been in a war zone. None of them understood what he was going through.

It was better that he be alone.

It was better for Ella this way.

"How long am I going to be laid up in here?" he asked, not acknowledging her compliment.

"Dr. Lynne is the one who treated you. You'll have to ask her, but, given that the storm is still raging and you've been on painkillers, probably not until closer to noon. It's five in the morning. The sun will rise in a while, if we see it through all this snow."

"It's been a wild night. I hope Santa made it for all the kiddos."

"Of course he did," Ella teased, winking. "He always finds a way, especially with Rudolph guiding the sleigh."

"Unless you're a misfit toy." Zac smiled at her. Then he sighed sadly and closed his eyes, his emotions raw, but for the first time in a long time he felt like a weight had been lifted off his shoulders.

"You saved Josh's life tonight," she whispered. "Josh will have many more Christmases because of you, you know."

"We saved his life. Together." With his good hand he touched her face. There was much more he wanted to say to her, but he wasn't sure if he could. He drew his hand back and looked away, wincing. "I think the painkillers are wearing off."

She sighed, sounding exhausted, and he felt bad for being laid up and for her having to take the brunt of the work. "I'll let Jen decide if your IV can come out."

He nodded. "I want to help in some way Even if I'm laid up."

"Well, right now you just need to stay put."

Jen Lynne came back into the room. Her lips were pursued and she was visibly stressed. Zac's heart lurched. He was worried that it was the child.

Jen whispered something to Ella and she frowned, nodding quickly.

"What?" Zac asked.

"I have to go and treat the motor vehicle accident patient." And as if she knew that he was worried about the child she said, "It's not the boy. He's stable."

"I need to help you."

"You need to stay put," she said.

"You're not my doctor."

"I know." A strange expression passed over her face, like sadness, and he worried now that she pitied him. He didn't want her to pity him.

Ella rushed out of the room. He wanted to believe her, but he had to see the child with his own eyes before he really, truly let it sink in.

"Jen, is there any way that you can remove my IV and I can get out of this bed?"

"You should really rest, Zac," she said.

"I'm fine. Give me a sling and let me at least manage Dispatch while the rest of you work. I can answer the phone with one arm."

"Okay, but I want you to take it easy."

Zac lay back on the gurney while Jen worked on discharging him.

Ella ran into the intensive care unit while the team was working to revive the patient. The police officers stood outside the ICU door. Ella tried to ignore their presence as she went about assessing her patient.

First he'd gone through his splenectomy. Then his kidney had had to be removed because the blood vessels around it had been breaking down. She could only guess that this time the patient's heart was causing some concerns.

Crystal meth had done a number on this guy. He may have survived the accident because he'd been wearing a seatbelt, but the damage done from the drug was making it impossible to treat him. But treat him she would.

She would keep fighting for his life until the bitter end.

"I need to get another arteriogram done on this patient." She'd done one earlier when he had first come in, as well as a CT scan. On the first there had been no tear in his aorta, but as there was blood in his drainage tube, he was hemorrhaging somewhere. She was going to repeat the X-ray right here, with a portable X-ray machine.

His veins were friable, paper-thin and a complete mess.

Ella moved quickly. The dye was injected so she could see if there was a tear. She took an X-ray of the patient's mediastinum. She waited with bated breath as the images came up on the screen.

Don't be full thickness. Don't be full thickness.

Of course, if it was full thickness he would be dead right

now. When the full thickness of the aorta tore open, all the patient's blood spilled into the chest cavity, killing him.

As the images came up on the monitor, she could see there was a tear. A small one, but there was a tear nonetheless.

They would have to go back in. Given the nature of the patient's vessels and tissue, that small tear could turn into a full-thickness one quite quickly. They had to get in there and repair it.

"Prep an OR and page Dr. Bentley from Cardiothoracic."

"Dr. Bentley is already in the OR with another patient," a nurse said. "He's the only cardiothoracic surgeon who made it in, besides his fellow who is in the surgery with him."

"Okay, well, I can repair it. Prep an OR and let's get this patient down to the operating room stat." Ella left the room to get ready to scrub in.

"Excuse me, Doctor?" the police lieutenant said, stepping forward. "What is going on?"

"The patient needs another surgery or he'll die," Ella said. "I know you have questions to ask him, but—"

"That's okay, Doctor. We understand. We'll go get a cup of coffee. He's still sedated and unconscious so we're not too worried about him leaving. Please keep us updated."

"I will."

The police walked away from the ICU room and she knew from the way they casually walked away that they didn't think the patient would live. And for a moment she had her doubts. The percentages were stacked high against this patient, but she was going to try her hardest and make sure that didn't happen if possible.

She went into the scrub room and began to scrub, while she watched them prep the patient in the operating room.

In her head she was working out how to approach this and as she was doing so she couldn't help but think about Zac.

How when he'd been working on Iphita after a natural disaster, his conditions must've been worse.

There would be no negative pressure rooms. Operating in a tent would be hard, especially if a patient was lying open. The chances of infection would be high and she admired him for that. Just like she admired him for finally opening up to her and admitting to her that he had post-traumatic stress disorder, but she had no idea how horrible it was.

How that must've affected him.

She couldn't even begin to imagine a horror like that.

A child dying in your arms because of a revolution breaking out. She'd had patients die before, but she didn't deal with a lot of children because she worked in the hospital and the pediatric surgeons dealt with child trauma.

And she just couldn't imagine the horror of losing a child and having to live with that. Zac had no closure either, because he had been wounded and shipped out, only learning the fate of people he'd worked with on the island after the fact.

It explained so much. It explained why he was shutting people out of his life and why he felt the need to leave. Why he felt the need to shut her out of his life.

And why he'd been driven to risk his life like that to save that boy during the snowstorm.

It was too much of a burden for him to carry and she wished he would let her in to help him. She wanted to help him.

She finished scrubbing in and then entered the operating room, where the charge nurse assisted her into her gown and gloves, then fastened a surgical headlamp onto her head.

The patient had been given medication to stop his blood

pressure from rising. The bypass machine was ready to go and blood was on standby.

You can do this. You've done surgeries like this before. You can tie off an artery. You can repair a small tear in the aorta.

The mediastinum was washed with betadine and she prepped the surgical field, climbing up on her stool.

The door to the scrub room opened and Zac entered. He had on a mask, scrub cap and fresh scrubs, as well as a sling to hold his shoulder in place.

"Dr. Davenport? What're you doing here? You can't assist me in this."

"No, but I've done this more times than I care to count in conditions a lot less favorable, with good outcomes. I can guide you. I heard that Dr. Bentley was in surgery."

Ella let out a sigh of relief behind her surgical mask. "That would be helpful. Are you sure you're up to this?"

He nodded. "I'm going crazy down there."

"Okay, stand behind me and I'm open to your suggestions."

Zac took his place behind her and Ella made her first incision, opening the mediastinum in preparation to open the chest cavity. It went fairly easily and she injected the patient's heart with cardioplegic solution, which would slow it down while they put him on bypass.

Once the heart slowed down enough she was able get a good look at the small tear. The tissue around the aorta was weak and sewing it up was not an option. Once the patient was off bypass and the heart was beating again then it would just tear through the repair.

"Dacron graft," Zac said from behind her.

"His tissue is so fragile from the meth use. I'm wondering if it will hold." She began to suture off the layers of the aortic tissue. "It just won't hold like this."

"It will hold. Patients who have high blood pressure

and heart problems are able to receive the Dacron graft. It's your only option."

The scrub nurse passed her the graft material and she began to place it over the tear that she had just sutured up. It was a larger patch over the aortic arch and she sutured it over the tear. Her legs were aching and so was her back from standing there so long and operating on this patient again.

For the third time since he'd come in Christmas Eve morning.

The scrub-room doors opened again and Dr. Bentley came in. "I hear that Dr. Lockwood is repairing an aortic arch dissection?"

"I am finishing a repair on an aortic arch dissection, Dr. Bentley. Would you care to see?"

Dr. Bentley was gowned and gloved first before he approached the operating table. "The tissue is very weak."

"The patient is addicted to meth. He was involved in a motor vehicle accident and had blunt trauma to the chest. There was no heart bruise or lung bruise when the patient presented," Ella said as she continued to work.

"Was an arteriogram performed when the patient was first admitted?" Dr. Bentley asked.

"Yes, and there was no tear. I removed his spleen. A couple of hours later he crashed and the artery to his kidney and kidney began to break down. I removed the kidney. Now he has a tear in his aorta. Or did. Thankfully it was not full thickness."

Dr. Bentley peered over and looked at her work. He was close to her and she felt slightly uncomfortable, but shrugged it off "You're doing a fine job, Dr. Lockwood. Nicely done on the Dacron graft. You have fine, delicate suturing skills. Do you mind if I assist?"

"Please do," Ella said, and she was relieved that she had someone helping her with this procedure, especially

someone who was used to doing it. They finished repairing the damage and checking the arteries.

The cardioplegic solution was stopped and Dr. Bentley started the heart again with defibrillators as it wouldn't start on its own after the cardioplegic solution was stopped. It didn't surprise her, given the nature of this patient's health.

The heart did start after one shock and the long slender paddles were removed. Now they would know whether her graft work would hold and if there was any other damage.

"Let's take the patient off bypass," she said, hoping that her voice didn't squeak with apprehension as she said it.

Please. Please.

The bypass machine was shut off and the clips removed to allow the patient's blood to flow back through the heart.

Ella held her breath and both she and Dr. Bentley watched as the heart began to work, pumping the blood through.

And then, like something out of her worst nightmares, the aorta dissected from just above the graft, not on the arch, and the patient's blood began to rush out of the tear.

Dr. Bentley swore. "His tissue's friable. Put him back on bypass now."

The monitors began to alarm and the patient began to crash.

Ella felt like crying, but she knew this was a long shot given the state this patient's body was in. She injected more cardioplegic solution into the patient's heart. She jumped down off her stool as Dr. Bentley came over to her side. He needed to be where she was standing so that he could repair the damage. He'd dealt with this before. She hadn't.

Her stool was moved to the opposite side so that she could assist him in any way she could. As she moved to the opposite side of the table she noticed that Zac was no longer in the operating room.

And she couldn't help but wonder where he'd gone. She wanted to be with him. She needed him now and he'd left, but she had to focus.

Right now she had to try and help save a life.

CHAPTER THIRTEEN

ZAC WALKED AIMLESSLY through the hospital corridors. When he looked out of a window, it was lighter and he could see that the storm was dissipating, but not quite yet. It would take days to dig out the snow and he needed to get out of the hospital.

Only he was trapped.

I shouldn't have gone into that operating room.

He ran his hand through his hair and tried to calm the anxiety that was rising in him. He'd known what could happen during an aortic dissection. He'd seen them and he'd had grafts fail in the field.

It was just seeing Ella working so well with Dr. Bentley. She was at ease with him and he knew that David liked Ella. The thought of Ella with another man enraged him. He'd noticed the surgeon's interest before when he'd come in during Mr. Chow's triage before surgery. From the way David watched Ella and spoke to her, it was obvious to everyone that Dr. Bentley was attracted to Ella.

Except Ella. She appeared oblivious to it.

Still, he didn't want to think about another man's lips on hers. It made him feel sick and angry.

When Zac had been in the operating room, with David working on Mr. Chow earlier in the evening, before David's cardiothoracic fellow had come in, David had

asked Zac if Ella was seeing someone. Or if Ella would be interested in him.

Zac had tried to change the subject and focus on Mr. Chow's surgery. He hadn't been interested in chatting with David about how David had the hots for Ella. His Ella.

She's not your Ella, though.

She could be, but he'd messed up so many times with her. She needed someone more stable than him.

Yet the thought of Dr. Bentley, who was an attractive, successful, intelligent, young cardiothoracic surgeon, taking Ella in his arms and kissing her made him feel so angry, made him feel possessive of her.

Why? You don't want her. She deserves to be happy.

Only he did, but how could he have her?

Zac cursed under his breath and continued to wander until he found himself in the pediatric department, which was jam-packed not only with Manhattan Mercy pediatric patients but the evacuated patients.

The NICU was overflowing into several empty rooms and as he made his way down the hall, there was one last room with an incubator in it and a little boy with a bandaged head in the bed. The mother was curled up in a chair under a blanket.

She startled and looked at him.

"You're the doctor who saved Josh's life."

"Yes. I'm Dr. Davenport, but please call me Zac."

"Dr. Davenport… I mean Zac. I can't thank you enough," she said, and then she smiled. It was a genuine, grateful one and she pushed back the blanket to get up.

"No, don't get up," Zac said quietly, coming into the room. "I'm sorry I wasn't able to come sooner."

Her gaze fell on his arm bound tightly in the sling. "You were injured as well?"

"Just a minor shoulder dislocation. I've had worse injuries." He was trying to brush it off, but she wasn't buying it.

"An arm is important to a surgeon."

"I'll be fine. I didn't need surgery to put it back into place. Surgery would've been worse." He glanced down at Josh and now he really looked at him he didn't see Rojas's face as clearly now. "Your son is very lucky."

"Because of you," Josh's mother said vehemently. "I was so tired with visiting the NICU to help with my premature baby and with the storm. I just turned my back for one moment and then he was gone."

"Rojas is gone!" Consuela shouted in a panicked tone.

"Calm down. Tell me where you last saw him," Zac shouted above the din of gunfire.

"The river, near the mission. He was heading down there."

"Okay, I will find him, Consuela!"

"Promise me, Dr. Davenport. Promise me you'll find him. He's my only child."

"I promise."

He ran off toward the mission. He took a weapon and a pack filled with first-aid materials. He prayed that he wouldn't have to use them. The day was blisteringly hot on top of the gunfire that was breaking out in the village. The once peaceful paradise was no more.

Zac tried to drown out the screams. The pain as he ran. He didn't even dare call out Rojas's name for fear that the rebels would find him and kill him.

As he approached the mission he heard the high-pitched wail of a missile. He could see Rojas standing outside the church, alone and afraid.

"Rojas!" Zac called out. He was twenty feet from him. Rojas turned, tears streaking down his face. "Zac!"

Then the screech of a projectile screamed over their heads, striking the old mission.

"Get out of the way, Rojas!" Zac started running to-

ward the boy, but the wall of the old mission crumbled and Rojas disappeared in a cloud of dust.

When the dust settled, there was just rubble and one little arm sticking out from under it. He tried not to scream at the horror of it. Instead, he ran to the mess and began using his bare hands to dig Rojas out.

Rojas was broken. Even from just a quick assessment of him he knew that the blunt force trauma to the child had caused an aortic dissection. Full thickness.

"I'm scared, Zac." Rojas closed his eyes as Zac held him.

"It's okay to be scared. I'm scared too."

"Stay with me, Zac. Stay with me."

Zac's heart was shattering in two. "I'm here, buddy. I'm here."

Rojas died in his arms. There was nothing he could do for him. They didn't have a bypass machine at the old mission. There were no paramedics and the navy medical staff was informed they would have to leave Iphita as the SEALs would come in soon and try to help quash the violent rebellion.

Zac gingerly picked up Rojas's body. He couldn't leave him here, at the edge of the jungle by a crumbling old mission on Christmas Eve.

It was Christmas Eve. He'd forgotten that it was, but it didn't matter.

He had to return Rojas's body to Consuela.

As he walked back to the village, Consuela began to scream.

"My son! My God! My son."

Zac tried to keep it together as he carried the shattered remains of a little boy who had meant so much to everyone at the mobile medical unit. He felt like a failure for not reaching Rojas in time. It was his fault that Rojas had died.

Before he could say anything to a grieving Consuela,

gunfire broke out and searing pain hit him in the back, burning through him.

He cried out and fell to his knees. Hit again.

The world went black.

"It can happen so easily," Zac said quietly, shaking the memory away.

"I know. I'm never taking my eyes off him again." Josh's mother said. "I'm so very lucky."

"You are. I'm glad you're all doing well."

"Thanks to you, Dr. Davenport." She reached out her hand and took Zac's good one, squeezing it.

"Jean!" A man shouted down the hall.

"Mick!" This time Josh's mother jumped up and threw herself into the arms of a very exhausted-looking fire-fighter.

"Oh, my God, I just got word what happened during the evacuation. Is Josh okay?"

"Yes. Thanks to Dr. Davenport."

Mick Viera looked at Zac. "Thanks, Dr. Davenport."

"It was no problem," Zac said.

Mick rushed to Josh's bedside and touched his forehead. Josh woke and smiled.

"Daddy," Josh said hoarsely.

"Yeah, buddy. I'm here." Mick kissed his son's hand as Josh drifted back to sleep. "What happened? I mean, I know what happened but… Dr. Davenport, can you fill in the blanks?"

"I found him in a bus shelter. He was bleeding from his head, but it was superficial. I'm glad I got to him before the storm surge that was coming."

Zac didn't say anything about the live wire. They didn't need to know that.

The family was reunited.

Josh really was okay.

"Thank you, Dr. Davenport. I don't know what I would do if I lost my family," Mick said, his voice breaking.

"It was no problem." Zac left the room, letting Mick reunite with his young family. It truly was a Christmas miracle. It was magical and for the first time in a long time Zac was glad it was Christmas and that there was a happy ending for someone.

And as he walked down the hall tears stung his eyes. He wiped them away quickly. He didn't want anyone to see them.

They were his tears.

Rojas was gone. There was nothing he could've done. The aorta had dissected because a wall had fallen on Rojas and crushed him. There was nothing Zac could've done. He'd got there as fast as he could.

He couldn't have stopped that wall from falling on Rojas.

You're not to blame. It's not your fault.

And for the first time in a year Zac didn't blame himself. What Ella had said was right. He'd done everything he could for Rojas, but he hadn't caused that wall to fall. The sense of guilt lifted. He needed to talk to Ella. He didn't know what it meant, but he had to talk about it with her. He needed her. Needed to tell her she was right.

After cleaning himself up, he headed down to the operating-room floor.

Ella was sitting on the floor, her head buried in her knees, and his heart sank. He knew then they hadn't saved the patient.

Before he could say her name, to call out to her and offer her comfort, Dr. Bentley came out of the scrub room. He knelt down next to Ella and rubbed her back. They were talking intimately to each other.

They looked so good together.

Ella smiled up at Dr. Bentley and he stood, holding out

his hand. She took it and he helped her to her feet. Once she was on her feet they walked in the opposite direction and Dr. Bentley slipped his arm around Ella, like David was claiming her, and she didn't push him away.

It was like a sucker punch it stung so badly.

What did you expect? You hurt her so badly. She doesn't want you. She'll never want you.

Zac had seen enough.

Disgusted, he walked away.

Ella was beyond exhausted at this moment.

She'd tried so hard to save that patient. Her very first patient of her double shift. The first patient of the storm to come through the emergency department at Manhattan Mercy. If he'd been healthy and not into drugs. If the drugs hadn't destroyed his body so badly, he might've got away with just a spleen injury.

And he would've lived.

Of course, he would've had to wake up and learn that his partner had died because she hadn't been wearing a seatbelt, but she had been an addict too. Perhaps if she hadn't been an addict she would've done up her seatbelt and would've only had minor injuries.

What a different story that would've been. If only.

Ella found the police officers sitting in the cafeteria, nursing another cup of coffee. When they saw her they stood and followed her into a small meeting room.

"He didn't make it, did he?" the lieutenant asked.

"No," she sighed. "No, I repaired the tear, but once we took him off bypass and started his heart again it tore in another spot on his aorta. Instead of a small, manageable one it became a full-thickness tear and he bled to death. His tissue had broken down from the drug use."

The lieutenant shook his head sadly. "It's a shame, but not surprising. Meth is a terrible drug."

"I'm sorry you had to spend your Christmas Eve and now the early morning of your Christmas Day waiting."

"It's okay, Dr. Lockwood, we're used to this. We'll try to contact the next of kin to get a proper identification."

Ella nodded. "And the storm hopefully will let up soon."

"Let's hope so. Merry Christmas, Dr. Lockwood, and thanks for your help." The lieutenant and his partner returned to the cafeteria.

Ella didn't move from where she was sitting in the small meeting room. She leaned back in her chair and closed her eyes. She was beyond exhausted and not even the strongest energy drink could get her to open her eyes.

"Ella, can I have a word with you?"

Ella opened her eyes to see Zac standing in the door. He had a funny expression on his face and he wasn't looking her in the eye.

"Yeah, sure. Are you okay?"

"Fine," he said stiffly as he came into the room and shut the door. "I'm sorry I left the operating room."

"It's okay. Not much you can do with a dislocated shoulder."

Zac nodded. "Right."

"I wasn't there, though," she said gently.

"Weren't where?" he asked gruffly.

"In Iphita. I wasn't there."

"I know. What does that have to do with anything? I left the room because I couldn't operate. I didn't want to get in the way."

"You weren't in the way."

"You lost your patient, didn't you?" he asked, changing the subject from why he'd left the operating room.

"Yes. There was too much damage to his body."

"I'm sorry about that."

"Where did you end up going?" she asked.

"To the pediatric ward. I had to see Josh for myself and… I wasn't responsible for Rojas's death last year."

Ella nodded. "That's good. I'm glad to hear that."

"I have a long way to go." He didn't look at her. "I think I need to leave Manhattan for a while and get some perspective."

She wasn't shocked. He'd run away before by joining the navy. Somehow, deep down she'd known he would want to leave again, even though she'd been hoping he wouldn't. "You're going to leave Manhattan? I think you need the support of your family."

"Ella, they're all busy with their own lives. They all have families."

"You could too, you know." Her cheeks heated with a blush as she realized the words that were tumbling out of her mouth.

"With who? You?"

It was just like it was all those years ago. Another slap to the face. "What is wrong with you?"

"Ella, I see the way you are with Dr. Bentley and I get it. He's handsome, charming and a brilliant surgeon and he likes you a lot. You deserve someone like him. He's everything I'm not, a family man. I'm not a family man."

She was confused now. "What're you talking about?"

"I was there when you were comforted by him. When he put his arm around you. You two looked good."

"Why are you acting jealous?" she asked.

"I'm not jealous."

"Zac, we're just friends. David and I are just friends."

"Ella, you deserve to be happy. He can give you everything you want."

"Everything I want?" She pinched the bridge of her nose and then let out a calming breath.

"A family. You want a family, Ella. I don't."

"You can't leave, Zac."

"Why not?"

She couldn't believe she was going to say this, but she was tired of running from Zac. He couldn't leave Manhattan. He needed to be around people who cared about him. People who loved him.

Like her.

And she felt like that young woman from all those years ago. When she had carefully picked out an outfit that hadn't been something her mother had bought her. She'd done her makeup and her hair. For the first time in her life she'd felt confident and had wanted to tell Zac how she felt.

Only she'd never got the chance to do that because he'd broken her heart.

The problem was, she never had got over him.

Even though she'd been telling herself for years that she had, she really hadn't.

She was still in love with him.

And even though it might kick her in the butt again, even though it might hurt her, she was tired of the walls she built around her heart. She wanted to let Zac in. She had to let him in.

"Zac, I know that I deserve to be happy but I'm not interested in Dr. Bentley."

He frowned, but didn't say anything.

"I'm in love with you, Zac. I always have been. I tried to deny it, but the moment you walked back into Manhattan Mercy I haven't been able to get you out of my head. You drive me crazy a lot of the time, but when we were together again…it felt right. You can't leave Manhattan. You need to stay here with your family. With people who love you. I can help you, Zac. Just give me a chance."

A tear slipped down her cheek and she wiped it away. The rush of emotion was getting to her as she waited for him to say something.

Only he didn't. He just stood there, eyes downcast and not responding to her.

And she got the hint in crystal clarity.

Once again her heart shattered. It was all she could do to keep her composure as she brushed past him, opening the door and heading out into the hallway.

Zac didn't follow her. And why would he? He didn't care for her the same way. He'd been jealous, but he only needed her and wanted her when it was convenient for him.

She couldn't live like that.

Ella wiped more tears from her eyes. She was angry at herself for letting him into her heart again, only to have it crushed once more.

"Dr. Lockwood!" She glanced back to see Jen running toward her.

Great. Get hold of yourself.

Ella plastered a wobbly smile on her face, but it wasn't enough to fool Jen.

"Dr. Lockwood, Ella, are you okay?"

"Fine. I'm just absolutely exhausted."

Jen smiled. "Well, you should go home."

"Home?"

"Yes, the storm is over!" Jen was ecstatic. "Dr. Charles Davenport just called in to release all staff who were stuck here during the storm. Once their replacements arrive, they're free to leave. A new shift of emergency room doctors just came in. You can go home."

Oh, thank God.

"Thank you, Jen. I think I will do just that!"

Jen nodded and turned back toward the emergency department.

Just as Ella started to make her final rounds so that she could leave the hospital, Dr. Bentley called out to her.

"I heard that the all-clear was given and that you might be leaving," Dr. Bentley said.

"Yes. I'm so glad the storm is over and we can leave." Boy, was she ever relieved that she could finally leave. "I just have to do final rounds on my patients and then I can go home and salvage what's left of Christmas."

"I still have a couple hours left on duty before I can leave. I was hoping that later tonight I can swing by your place and we can have dinner."

Ella shook her head in disbelief. "Dinner?"

"Yes." Dr. Bentley flashed her a smile that would probably have melted any other woman's heart, but there was only one man that she wanted. It was just a shame that he didn't want her back but she wasn't ready to date anyone else.

There was nothing wrong with Dr. Bentley, but she was hurting too much.

"If it's all the same to you, could I get a rain check? I plan to sleep for the next twenty-four hours."

Dr. Bentley took the gentle hint and nodded. "Of course. The offer will stay on the table. You're an intelligent, attractive woman, Ella. I would like to get to know you better. I'll see you later."

"Yes. Have a good night." She sighed as Dr. Bentley walked away. If Zac hadn't been in the picture she would've taken him up on his offer, but the problem was that Zac *was* in the picture. He'd come back, and that had been her problem her whole life with trying to date other men. None of them were Zac.

She only wanted Zac, which was the crux of the problem. She wanted someone who didn't want her back.

Ella had to get out of Manhattan Mercy. She had to put some distance between herself and Zac. Permanently. But that could come after she got some sleep.

After she tried to pull together the pieces of her broken heart.

CHAPTER FOURTEEN

ZAC WANTED TO go after her, but he was frozen in shock. He couldn't believe what Ella was saying to him. How could she love him? He'd hurt her so badly. He didn't deserve her love. So he said nothing and he could tell that he'd broken her heart again.

He just stood there, mulling everything over, the ramifications of it all, but he didn't know how to process it.

What was wrong with him?

He knew that it was for the best not to answer her. Not to tell her that he was completely in love with her and had been for some time.

He was just afraid.

He didn't ever want to hurt her. He needed to heal before he could have her, before he could think about having a home, a wife, kids. He wanted kids and he wanted them with Ella, but he wasn't sure that he was whole enough for her.

Maybe you need her to heal?

Zac shook that thought away.

The last thing he wanted to do was hurt Ella and that's exactly what he'd done. He loved her. When he'd seen her and Dr. Bentley and thought about another man moving in on her, it had driven him mad. How could he let Ella go?

You're an idiot.

He was so afraid of all the what-ifs that he wasn't willing to take a chance on anything. He wasn't willing to take a chance on them.

Why couldn't he have some happiness?

You can.

Except maybe now it was too late. He'd hurt her twice. Twice. Though he hadn't known about the first time, but still it was no excuse. Why would she ever want him now?

You have to try. You have to make this right.

"What happened to you?" Charles asked as he came into the staffroom, where Zac had been lying on the couch.

"Long story," Zac said. "What're you doing here? Has the travel ban been lifted?"

"Yes, and I've come to relieve staff so they can go home and enjoy what precious little is left of their Christmas. I've told all the staff that they can take cabs to get home safely. The subway is still shut down because of flooding, but most of the streets are cleared now."

"That's great. That was one hell of a storm."

"It was. So, are you going to tell me about that arm or not?"

"I told you it was a long story that involved electrical wires and ice."

"I heard that you saved a boy from a storm surge, is this from that?" Charles asked, sitting across from him.

"Yeah." Zac sat up slowly. "Charles, I have to tell you something and I don't think that you're going to like it much."

Charles frowned. "What?"

"I was cleared to work in Annapolis, but I don't think I should've gone back to work. I'm suffering from post-traumatic stress disorder. I need to get some proper help."

Charles didn't look surprised. "I knew that you had PTSD, but I thought you were managing it well."

"Ella didn't think so and she was right."

Charles cocked an eyebrow. "Is that so?"

"Why are you saying 'Is that so?' like that?"

"Zac, you're too obtuse to see it, but that girl has been in love with you your whole life. The two of you were like peas in a pod. You're meant for each other."

Zac was surprised to hear his brother talking like this. "What's changed your tune?"

Charles grinned. "Love."

"I don't deserve it."

"Who says?"

"I hurt her, Charles." Zac cursed under his breath. "I don't even know if I know how to love. Look at Mom and Dad!"

"What about them? People make mistakes. Love isn't perfect. You have to work at it. If you're worthy of it. All of us have worked hard for our happiness, Zac. It's not perfect, but I know I would be lost without it."

"I don't think she'll forgive me. I hurt her when we were young. Said some terrible things she overheard. I was so tired of everyone pushing me to marry her when all I wanted was a career in the navy. I didn't want to be controlled by Dad. I didn't want his life. And then tonight… I hurt her again."

Charles narrowed his eyes. "You make that right! She's one of my best surgeons and a good friend. You're a fool to hurt her. You love her, you know you do. I don't know what's holding you back, but you need to fix it because if you let that girl walk out of your life you're making the biggest mistake of your life!"

Zac was taken aback by his brother's outburst, but Charles was absolutely right and he knew what he had to do. Ella had been right, he couldn't get better on his own and he needed the support of those who loved him. He needed Ella.

Only Ella.

She had been the vision of perfection. The happiest memories that calmed him down, and she was the only one who could lead him back through the dark. With her, he could get better.

"I need something from you, Charles."

"What?"

"The Davenport ring. I need to make things right."

Charles grinned. "It's in my safe at home. Ask Grace to open it for you. I'm not going to say that I told you so when I tried to give you the ring at Thanksgiving and you didn't want it."

"Charles, what would I have done with the Davenport ring back then? It was a reminder of things I was too afraid of. It was better I turned it down."

"Well, as I told you back then, you know where to find it when you're ready for it."

"Thanks."

"I would give you the keys to my car, but you're incapacitated. Take a cab, please. I don't want you slipping and dislocating your other arm."

"Thanks, Charles." Zac paused in the doorway. "Uh, one more thing."

"What?"

"Where is Ella's apartment?"

"She lives in the same building as you, you dolt, at Central Park West. You don't know it, but she's right below you."

"What? That's a family property, why didn't you tell me that when I moved in there?"

Charles nodded. "Why do you think I did that?"

"I'll thank you later if this works."

Zac rushed out of the hospital as fast as he could, though, because of his arm, it slowed him down a bit when changing into his street clothes out of the scrubs.

He had to grab the Davenport ring at Charles's place

and get to Ella's apartment before she did. But—a miracle unto itself—he found out she was making one final check on her patients before she left the hospital so he had to time to get to Charles's and get back to the apartment.

He was going to make things right.

He was terrified that she was going to say no and she had every right, but if that happened it would be a cross that he would have to bear. He would spend the rest of his days on this earth trying to make it up to her. And if she never forgave him, he'd understand, but there would only be one woman for him.

And that was Ella.

The thought of a family scared him, but if he was going to traverse this scary road of the unknown, he wanted his equal at his side.

He only wanted Ella. For now and forever.

It took Ella two hours to finish her last rounds on her patients. She changed into her street clothes, glad to be out of the scrubs, and pulled on her boots and winter clothes. Her body felt like it was weighed down with cement.

And when she walked outside she braced herself for wind, blowing snow and cold water, but it was calm. The city was once again alive. The sun was glinting brightly off the snow. It was so bright it hurt her eyes. It had been a long time since she'd seen the sun.

It was lunchtime on Christmas Day and people were starting to come out of their homes after the storm had raged over the city for over twenty-four hours. It was like waking up to a new world as she walked home through a city that was usually loud, bustling and overcrowded.

Right now it was just calm. It was waking up. It was a city that wasn't defeated.

Having been so isolated in the hospital, Ella drank in the

fresh air, but she couldn't really relish the winter wonderland or even feel the Christmas spirit as her heart ached.

She was still angry at herself for letting herself be vulnerable to Zac again. You'd think she'd have learned her lesson all those years ago.

You're a fool who's in love.

Maybe that's why she had never gotten over Zac, because all those years ago she had never been able to ask him. She'd never got the chance to tell him how she felt. Now she had and she had closure.

Maybe now she could move on.

Though it would take some time.

It was like losing her best friend.

Because it is.

A tear slipped down her cheek and she wiped it away with a mittened hand. She had to get used to being lonely again. Zac would leave and it would just be her. Life would return to the way it had been before, even though she didn't want that. He had brought her to life again and she didn't want to be lonely any more. She'd opened herself and her heart to him twice and had been rejected, like he couldn't even think of her beyond someone he'd had sex with. Just a one-night stand.

After all they had been through.

It had crushed her, but at least she felt something. Even if it was painful.

What was it that was said in that old Christmas movie about the knight on the white horse?

She couldn't think of it, but she remembered them saying something about it being dangerous for that knight way up there—that putting a knight up there may cause him to fall. Was that ever right!

The only difference was that this was real life and not a Christmas movie.

Her knight wasn't doing something genuinely nice. He

wasn't going to try and win her back. There would be no happy ending for her, but at least she had her closure now. At least now she could mend her heart and move on. She just didn't know how long that was going to take.

The doorman opened the door for her.

"Good afternoon, Dr. Lockwood. Glad to see you weathered the storm."

"Thank you, Mark." Ella gave him a half-hearted smile. She waited for the elevator. When the door opened a happy family came out and wished her a merry Christmas, and she returned the greeting. She watched them leave the apartment. A mom, dad and two kids. All of them happy.

The love they shared was almost palpable.

Just like the love that was between the Vieras and their two children.

And Ella was envious of that.

She wanted that.

And for the first time in a long time Christmas felt like it was a lonely prospect and she contemplated going to her mother's house, if the roads to Long Island weren't closed.

Ella didn't want to be alone.

She got on the elevator and rode it up. She was going to go straight to bed. She needed a good cry and a long sleep. Then she could go from there.

She unlocked her door and hit the alarm code, before shutting the door behind her. When she turned around she glanced at her small Christmas tree and saw something under the tree. Something that hadn't been there before.

She approached it cautiously and couldn't figure out where a stuffed Rudolph the Red-Nosed Reindeer had come from. She didn't own one and she was a little old for Santa.

She reached out and cautiously picked it up. It was soft and when she squeezed it, its nose lit up. Behind the Rudolph was a small version of the snowman and the elf

who wanted to be a dentist. They were all there, including the little doll with polka dots on her dress. The hideous polka-dot dress that made the doll a misfit toy.

One that was unwanted and unloved. One that was made fun of.

"What in the world…?"

"Think of it as my apology."

She tried not to scream as she spun around to see Zac standing behind her in his street clothes.

"How did you get in here?"

"I was trained member of the armed forces."

"You were a navy doctor."

"As I said before, I learned about combat."

Ella pinched the bridge of her nose. "You need to leave."

"You need to hear me out."

"Why should I hear you out?" she yelled at him. "You have nothing to say to me that I want to hear."

"Not even I love you?"

Ella blinked twice. "What?"

"I said, I love you." Zac took a step closer.

Ella took a step back, tears stinging her eyes. "How can you love me? I told you how I felt and you…you just stood there!"

"Because I was afraid to love you."

"Why? Because of the way my mother dressed me? Because I wasn't tall and graceful, like the other girls? Because I was a wallflower, because I was smart?"

"Ella, I didn't know how you felt back then. I told you, I was getting those idiots off my back. What I said was immature and untrue. I love you. I've always loved you. I was scared to fall in love. I never wanted to get married after witnessing so much death and pain overseas. I didn't ever want that. The problem was I was so afraid of what might happen if a piece of me was missing. A piece of my

heart. Life is fragile, but it's not worth living if you don't take chances."

A tear crept down her cheek. "You love me?"

He smiled at her, that smile she loved so much. "I do, Ella. I always have. I was just stupid and blind and too scared to reach out and take it. When I saw you with Dr. Bentley I was so jealous, but I was still too stubborn to realize that you and I should be together. Forever, because you're my best friend, Ella Lockwood, and I would be lost without you. I need you."

"You were going to leave. To heal."

"I can't heal without you. I need you, Ella. I won't ever be whole without you. I'm never going to leave you behind again. I love you."

"I love you too," she said, her voice hitching in her throat. "The thought of you leaving again, the loneliness was too much to bear. I worked so hard protecting myself from pain that I isolated myself from everyone. I shut out everyone trying to protect my heart."

"I'm sorry for that."

"No, it's not your fault." She smiled. "It was mine. I was too stubborn."

Zac grinned. "You are stubborn."

"I love you, Zac. Wherever you go, I'll go too. I don't want to be alone. I need you to make me whole too."

"I'm going to make this Christmas right. For both of us. It's time for our magic now. Our happiness." He got down on one knee slowly and then pulled out a box. "This was set aside for me, long before I realized that our parents were right and that we were meant to be together." He opened the box with one hand and against the blue crushed velvet was the Davenport ring with the pink emerald-cut diamond.

"Ella, will you marry me?"

Ella began to cry and she nodded. "Yes!"

Zac stood up and then pulled her close with his one good arm and kissed her. She held him tightly. Her heart was bursting with happiness she hadn't known was possible. For so long she'd dreamt about this moment. She couldn't believe that it was here. That it was happening.

And on Christmas. She had never been a huge fan of Christmas. For years it had meant torture with her family, but this…this was like resetting everything. It would be something she could look back on and cherish forever.

A wrong being set right. Her real family being formed and the missing piece of her heart being patched back together.

"I'm so in love with you," he whispered against her ear. "I'm sorry for everything I did. I promise I'll never hurt you again. I can't lose you."

She nodded. "I love you."

He slipped the ring on her finger and then smiled down at her hand in his. "It's like it was made for you."

"Yeah, it does appear that way." She stood on tiptoe and kissed him again. "I love you."

"I know," he teased. "How would you like to spend Christmas Day?"

"In bed," she said wearily.

His eyebrows shot up. "Well, I'll see what I can do with one arm."

Ella laughed. "As much as I would like that, I would rather sleep. I'm exhausted. It feels like I've worked for a year. Maybe we can watch some Christmas movies later and order in, if there's a place open, and just lounge around in bed."

"Sleep sounds great," he said with relief in his voice. He took her hand and they headed to her bedroom.

"By the way, how did you know where I lived?" she asked. "I don't remember ever telling you where my grandmother's apartment was."

"Easy. I live upstairs."

She gasped. "You're the neighbor who is loud in the middle of the night, dropping weights?"

"Guilty." He winked. "You know, I could buy the apartment above from Charles and we could put in a staircase. Spread out a bit in case we have a family."

That caused her eyes to fill with happy tears. The thought of a baby, of a family was almost too be good to be true. She held him close.

"I would say let's get a start on that, but I really am tired."

He chuckled. "We have all the time in the world."

"Not really," Ella said. "Once my mother finds out she's going to want us married as soon as possible."

"Why?" Zac asked.

"She's been planning this wedding for years, Zac. She's not going to wait any longer."

Zac chuckled. "Very true."

They went hand in hand to bed. They fell asleep in each other's arms, sleeping together like they had for years long ago.

It was home.

And for the first Christmas in a long time she wasn't lonely any more.

She was whole.

Finally.

EPILOGUE

One year later, Christmas Eve

"THIS TIME LAST year New York City was caught in a blizzard like no other! Do you remember that, Chuck?"

"I do, Frank. Although there will be snow in the forecast tonight, Old Saint Nick isn't going to give us a wintry blast like last year. Thank goodness. Now, here's a great old song to put you in the Christmas spirit."

"Mom, turn that off!" Ella shouted over her shoulder as she set down her wedding dress on her bed. She couldn't believe that someone had left on a radio tuned to that Christmas music station again! Frank and Chuck drove her squirrelly at this time of year. Just like they had last year when she'd been coming off her shift at Manhattan Mercy and had learned that she was going to have to stay at the hospital because the city had shut down.

That storm had been monumental for the city. And for her, because during that storm she had been forced to work with Zac and that's when they had come together.

Although the storm had done so much damage, for her it was a fond memory. Her first magical Christmas and hopefully not her last.

For her, it was the storm that had washed away the remnants of her old life, making her ready for her new

one. And after tonight she was going to officially be a Davenport.

Although she planned on keeping her last name, much to her mother's chagrin. There were enough Dr. Davenports at Manhattan Mercy to contend with, whereas there was only one Dr. Lockwood.

It would make things so much easier.

Her mother had been horrified when she'd told her that.

"Ella, that's just not done. You need to take your husband's name."

"Mom, it will be so much easier on the staff at the hospital if I keep Lockwood."

"Easier on the staff? Who cares about the staff?"

"I do! So it's settled. I'm still Ella Lockwood, but I'm legally married to a Davenport. You can still tell all your friends that your daughter married a Davenport."

"I didn't turn it on, Ella," her mother said. "I think it was the construction workers. Honestly, you should've got ready for the wedding in Long Island, not in the middle of renovations," her mother complained as she looked at a ladder leaning against the wall.

"The renovations aren't that bad, Mom. They're almost done. We just can't use the stairs to Zac's apartment until the safety inspector comes after Christmas. Besides, I'm marrying Zac on top of Manhattan Mercy so Long Island wouldn't make any sense. What if the storm picked up and I was stranded at your place? The Davenports might think I jilted their son."

Her mother's eyes narrowed and her lips pursed. "That's not funny, Ella."

"Mom, you need to lighten up. Seriously." In the past Ella would have been annoyed that she was with her mother in a confined space and arguing with her, but since Zac had come back into her life she'd learned to lighten up as well.

Dr. Lockwood was still a force to be reckoned with at

Manhattan Mercy, but she wasn't as scary as she had been before. She wasn't as serious.

In the past that would've made her nervous, but now with Zac by her side she was a different force to be reckoned with and she couldn't remember a time in her life when she had been this happy.

"I don't understand why we're not getting ready at the hospital, then," her mother complained. "Not that a hospital is a suitable place."

"Mom, Zac and I wanted it at the hospital. And Zac didn't want me to get ready at the hospital because he said he had a surprise for me."

Her mother rolled her eyes. "I should've taken care of this wedding with Zac's Mom Vanessa. We could've come up with something elegant. Something that would be the talk of the town."

"Zac and I didn't want that. We wanted something different."

Her mother shook her head. "I know, but on the roof of the hospital on Christmas Eve?"

Ella smiled. "It's perfect."

Her mother just threw up her hands and left the bedroom, probably inwardly cursing the folly of her daughter's decision.

And Ella couldn't blame her. She knew that her mother had been scheming for this marriage for a long time and probably had it built up in her head about how it would go. Whereas she and Zac had their own ideas about how their wedding was going to go and she was excited.

She'd made her peace with her mother. And her mother had apologized. Their relationship wasn't perfect, but it was getting a bit better all the time.

Even Zac had mended bridges with his father. Things were looking up.

And one of the best parts of this wedding was that Ella

had picked out the wedding gown herself. She wouldn't let her mother even see it. It was a secret. Even though that had driven her mother batty, she'd wanted to choose her wedding dress herself.

Her mother was done picking out dresses for her.

Ella got dressed in the beautiful lace, three-quarter sleeve gown, the dress that she had picked out. Her mother had wanted something that would make her look like a giant meringue.

And the shoes had almost made her mother have a heart attack when Ella had chosen red high heels with crystals up the back. A nice, bright Christmas red to contrast with the white.

When she was all dressed and came out of her bedroom, her mother was scowling, but then her expression softened and the pride, the approval that her mother had always felt she had to hide from her daughters was there.

Sylvia Lockwood couldn't hold it in any more.

"Oh, Ella, you look so lovely. That's a beautiful dress! Henry, come and look at your daughter."

Ella twirled around as her father, who had been hiding in Zac's study, came out.

"You look beautiful!"

"I'm going to freeze." Ella smiled. "But I love this dress."

"It's perfect. I was wrong and you were right."

"Even about the shoes?" Ella teased as she lifted the hem of her skirt and wiggled her red high-heeled shoe at her mother.

Her father was chuckling as he walked away.

"Even the shoes," her mother admitted. "It will go well with your bouquet of red roses."

There was a buzz and her father answered, "Yes?"

"The transportation has arrived for Dr. Lockwood," the doorman said.

"We'll be down momentarily." Her father turned around, scratching his head. "That was an odd thing to say."

"What?" Ella asked.

"He said transportation. Not limousine or hired car or even taxi."

Ella shrugged. "Oh, well, we'd better get to the hospital. It's getting dark."

Sylvia and Henry grabbed their coats and her father helped Ella put on her white-trimmed wrap. They took the elevator down and the doorman was smiling as he opened the door for her. Ella gasped when she saw a horse-drawn carriage was waiting for her. It looked a bit like a princess's carriage, like Cinderella's carriage, except it was open.

It was a bit gaudy and had her mother's approval written all over it. Ella couldn't help but laugh, but she loved the gesture all the same.

"Oh, how lovely!" Her mother gasped. "But I thought carriages weren't allowed out of Central Park?"

"Special permit," the carriage driver said. "Good thing there's no snow on the streets or we'd have a hard time doing this."

"See, Sylvia I told you it would be a perfectly acceptable wedding," her father said. "Come on, Ella, let's get you up there."

Her father and the footman helped Ella into the carriage. And then her mother was seated across from her before her father climbed in. A blanket was put over them so it would protect her dress. Snow was falling lightly as the lights in Central Park started to come on.

The city was coming alive with Christmas magic.

Unlike last year, when the city had been shutting down because of a snowstorm of epic proportions. The night was calm. And as the carriage navigated the streets of Manhattan Ella got to enjoy the magic of a wintry wonderland and the lights, the rush of people and the gently falling snow.

All too soon they were pulling up in front of the hospital, much to the shock and delight of patients and staff who were coming and going.

There was shouts of "Merry Christmas!" and good wishes as she climbed down from the carriage. Her mother holding her train as they climbed up the steps and entered the hospital's main entrance.

"Perhaps we should've gone in through the ambulance bay?" her father said.

"No, it's bad luck, Dad. No emergency room doctor worth their salt enters the hospital at the start of their shift through the emergency room doors."

"We can't have bad luck, Henry!" her mother said, then she grinned. "This is perfectly fine."

"Yes, of course, Sylvia and Ella."

There was a regular elevator waiting for her and Gabriel Jackson was grinning as he stood in front of the elevator, looking devastatingly handsome in a tuxedo.

"Zac wanted to make sure you got up there safely." Gabriel grinned and shook her father's hand as they all climbed inside. "Penny is very excited to see your dress."

Ella smiled. "I'm sorry to be ruining your first Christmas as parents, Gabriel."

"Penny wouldn't miss her brother's wedding for anything and it was a perfect excuse to buy a gorgeous dress for our little girl."

Ella sighed happily as the elevator went up to the roof. There was a small room where the Davenports and her siblings were waiting. Zac and Charles weren't there. They were outside. She could see them through the windows. Zac had his back to the windows as the snow fell over a beautiful wintry wonderland.

White Christmas lights twinkled over an archway that had been constructed with evergreen boughs and a Christmas tree was off to the side, covered in more white lights.

Around them was the backdrop of New York City, the tall buildings overshadowing them, but as the sun set the city lights made the snow look warm, with a glow.

Everyone else was waiting in the warmth for the bride to arrive. And when she got off the elevator she heard Penny gasp in joy. She was holding her little girl, who was seven months old and looked absolutely precious in a red Christmas dress.

Grace was grinning, standing with Charles's twin boys, who were wearing tuxedoes similar to their father's.

Beside Grace were Hugo and Vanessa Davenport, Zac's parents. They came forward, and even though there was tension between the two of them, they wished her well and then moved on to greet her parents. And Ella hoped one day that Hugo and Vanessa could overcome their differences, but today was not that day.

"Congratulations," Helena said, giving her a quick hug. Helena was another ER doctor and married to Zac's brother Elijah.

"How are you feeling?" Ella asked, because Helena had just given birth to their baby a couple of weeks ago. All of Zac's siblings and respective spouses, soon to be her family too were at the wedding. Elijah and Jude were chatting with Gabriel and Mateo, gently swinging a baby carrier. The baby was sleeping soundly in a warm little bag that was made for cold weather.

"Tired. Have you told anyone…?"

Ella held up her finger. "No. Not yet."

Miranda, Zac's sister and Sarah who was married to Zac's brother Jude came over, having overheard. "Well, you need to tell people soon so that I can tell people my news."

The four of them laughed together at the shared secret. Ella and Miranda were both pregnant. This time next year

there would be a lot of children at the Davenport Christmas function.

Helena winked and went to join Gabriel and Penny.

"Are we ready?" Charles asked, coming inside and brushing the snow off his shoulder.

"I believe so, young man," Henry said.

Charles grinned and then went back outside. Their guests filtered outside to the chairs, braving the cold but still bundled up. The reception was taking place at the Ritz-Carlton, where a lot more of the staff could attend, but for the wedding ceremony it was just the Davenports and the Lockwoods. Charles had become licensed to officiate over the ceremony, since he was the one who had talked some sense into Zac and had been responsible for making sure that Zac got the Davenport ring, which twinkled on Ella's finger in the dim light.

Her eldest sister, Francis was her maid of honor and Ella's older brother, John escorted her mother down the aisle, with her middle sister following a few moments later.

"You ready?" her father asked.

"Oh, yes. More than ready."

Henry nodded and squeezed her arm tightly. The doors were opened and a string quartet she hadn't noticed right away began to play Canon in D by Pachelbel.

It was then that Zac turned around to see her. He smiled that charming smile that she'd fallen in love with, his dark hair covered with thick white snowflakes.

Ella had to choke back the emotions that were rushing through her as she walked toward her future.

Her destiny.

Finally, the worst mistake of her life had been healed. Her heart was whole again.

"Who gives this woman to this man?" Charles asked.

"Her mother and I do," her father said, bending over

and kissing her on the cheek as he handed her over to Zac and took his place next to her mother.

Hugo and Vanessa were smiling, their pride for their son evident on their face.

Ella didn't really hear the words that Charles was saying, she was lost in looking up at Zac. He was grinning at her and she was trying very hard not to cry.

She was also trying hard not to shiver in the cold.

"Do you, Ella Jane Lockwood, take Zachary Xavier Davenport to be your lawfully wedded husband?" Charles asked.

"I do," she said.

"And do you, Zachary Xavier Davenport, take Ella Jane Lockwood to be your lawfully wedded wife?"

Zac grinned and then winked. "I do."

They exchanged rings.

"Then, by the power vested in me by the State of New York, I now pronounce you husband and wife. And about time too."

Zac leaned forward and kissed her, instantly chasing away the cold that she had been feeling as she stood in a snowstorm on the rooftop of Manhattan Mercy. There was an eruption of applause as the kiss ended.

"I love you, Ella," Zac whispered.

"I love you too."

They held hands and ran back down the aisle. Their families were happy for them, but also doubtless happy to get out of the cold.

Once they were inside Zac summoned the elevator and they got on.

"Aren't we going to wait for everyone?"

Zac shook his head. "We'll see them at the Ritz-Carlton. We're going to have a carriage ride together."

"That was wonderful!" Ella said. "Thank you."

Zac kissed her again. The elevator let them off in the emergency room, which was quiet for the moment.

Dr. Jen Lynne and Dr. Ryan Trace, who were now no longer residents but now attendings, wished them well as they left through the ambulance-bay doors, where the carriage was waiting for them. As they stepped outside, a small honor guard from Zac's old unit were standing in their naval uniforms, waiting. They raised their swords over Zac and Ella's heads and they walked underneath them.

"What in the world...?" Zac said as he saw them.

"They were my doing," Ella whispered. "I contacted your commanding officer in Annapolis and he felt it was only right to send off their former captain and naval surgeon right. They'll be at the reception too."

Zac kissed her hand as they walked under the swords at the ambulance bay. "Thank you."

"I love you and you're not the only one full of surprises, Dr. Davenport."

She had a very big surprise she'd tell him about when the moment was right.

Zac helped her up into the carriage and once they were both seated it took off for Central Park again.

"How long will this carriage ride last?" Ella asked as she snuggled down next to Zac's overcoat to keep warm.

"As long as we want. We have to let the others have time to get to the Ritz-Carlton. I thought we could go past Rockefeller Center and see the tree all lit up."

"That sounds nice. You're a bit of a Christmas convert, aren't you?"

Zac grinned. "Look who's talking. Are you cold? Do you want to just skip the lights and head to the reception?"

"We could skip the reception altogether," Ella suggested. "We could stay here."

He grinned and kissed her. "I think your mother and

my mother would lose their minds if we did that. The reception is the only part of the wedding they've been able to control."

Ella sighed. "You're right. We'd better go."

"Would you like a glass of champagne?" Zac asked as he began to root under the blankets.

"No," she said.

He was surprised. "No? I got your favorite bottle of champagne too."

"I appreciate that, but I can't."

"Why?" And then it dawned on him. "Are you serious?"

"How do you feel about that?"

Zac answered her with a kiss. "How do you think I feel about that? I'm so happy."

"Are you? I know with everything that happened last year…"

He kissed her again. "I know and the thought terrifies me to my very core, but if there's one thing I've learned over this past year and dealing with my post-traumatic stress disorder it's that life is too short. You have to keep on living, because there might not be a tomorrow and I don't want to look back and regret not living the life I wanted because I was too afraid about what might happen. I'm truly happy. When are you due?"

"July. Summer in the Hamptons is out, I guess." She grinned wickedly, because she'd loathed summers at her parents' place in the Hamptons. She'd rather go somewhere else for her summer vacations.

Now she could spend the summer in the city, because she had an excuse.

Zac laughed. "Well, it looks like we're staying close to Manhattan Mercy next summer."

"It would appear so."

They didn't say anything else. They just held each other and enjoyed the sight of the snow falling against the

brightly lit city of New York. They enjoyed the Christmas lights and the calm of Central Park, while the rest of the city rushed past them. A busy city on Christmas Eve.

And they dreamed of their future together and all the magical Christmases to come.

* * * * *

LET'S TALK
Romance

For exclusive extracts, competitions
and special offers, find us online:

- facebook.com/millsandboon
- @MillsandBoon
- @MillsandBoonUK

Get in touch on 01413 063232

For all the latest titles coming soon, visit
millsandboon.co.uk/nextmonth

MILLS & BOON

THE HEART OF ROMANCE

A ROMANCE FOR EVERY KIND OF READER

MODERN

Prepare to be swept off your feet by sophisticated, sexy and seductive heroes, in some of the world's most glamorous and romantic locations, where power and passion collide.
8 stories per month.

HISTORICAL

Escape with historical heroes from time gone by. Whether your passion is for wicked Regency Rakes, muscled Vikings or rugged Highlanders, awaken the romance of the past.
6 stories per month.

MEDICAL

Set your pulse racing with dedicated, delectable doctors in the high-pressure world of medicine, where emotions run high and passion, comfort and love are the best medicine.
6 stories per month.

True Love

Celebrate true love with tender stories of heartfelt romance, from the rush of falling in love to the joy a new baby can bring, and a focus on the emotional heart of a relationship.
8 stories per month.

Desire

Indulge in secrets and scandal, intense drama and plenty of sizzling hot action with powerful and passionate heroes who have it all: wealth, status, good looks…everything but the right woman.
6 stories per month.

EROES

Experience all the excitement of a gripping thriller, with an intense romance at its heart. Resourceful, true-to-life women and strong, fearless men face danger and desire - a killer combination!
8 stories per month.

DARE

Sensual love stories featuring smart, sassy heroines you'd want as a best friend, and compelling intense heroes who are worthy of them.
4 stories per month.

To see which titles are coming soon, please visit

millsandboon.co.uk/nextmonth

MILLS & BOON
True Love

Romance from the Heart

Celebrate true love with tender stories of heartfelt romance, from the rush of falling in love to the joy a new baby can bring, and a focus on the emotional heart of a relationship.